Wallace Family Affairs
Volume II Part 2
Love Is Just Enough

Carey Anderson

DEDICATION

This book is dedicated to my family and close friends.
Thank you for your constant support and encouragement,
without you I would be nothing

ACKNOWLEDGMENTS

I would like to thank my baby-girl who is my life's ultimate expression of a dream realized. Thank you for sacrificing mommy time so that I could have the time to work some things out on paper.

I would like to thank my Soul Sistah #1 who has been my captivated audience since middle school. Without your love, support, encouragement, and FIRE I never would've completed Volume I or II, etc. Thank you for bringing me laughter when I couldn't get outside of my head.

I would like to thank my Sister-In-Law for taking time out of your busy family life to humor me with a read through of my latest thoughts and expressions. (SS1 & SIL THANK YOU for the trip to St. Helena where we spent the day lost in my imagination. I will never forget it, and it was exactly what I needed. THANK YOU!)

I would like to thank my dear cousin for reassuring me that my little hobby was relatable and entertaining. You are definitely a speed-reader, thank you for taking time out of your busy life to be entertained by my imagination.

I would like to thank last but not least Mrs. Laverne Dyes! Mrs. Dyes, the day that you read my short story to my class changed my life. Thank you for giving me a positive outlet for all the angst going on in my life. You have forever changed my life, I am so thankful to have ever known you

The saga continues…

Chapter 33

"Plead guilty!!! Don't leave the jail!!!" I said

"Amber, I didn't do it!"

"David please! Please hear me. Plead guilty!"

"I can't do that! I didn't do it. Besides my public defender is getting these anonymous tips that are helping my case."

I got a lump in my throat. How could I make him understand? "I really need you to think about it."

Then I heard the front door slam shut. "AMBER!" My Daddy's voice came booming from the front door.

I hung up the phone. "Yes Daddy?" My heart was fluttering.

I walked in the living room Daddy was livid. "WHAT IS THIS I'M HEARING???"

"Daddy it wasn't like that!" I said putting my hands up.

Andrew came running from the backyard; he heard noise but didn't know what was going on. "Grand Poppa? What's wrong?" Andrew said breathing hard.

Malcolm walked in the door. Daddy looked at me, "I'm so disappointed in you." I felt like Daddy just punched me. I sat down in the chair. "Come here son!" Daddy said to Andrew. Andrew walked over to Daddy. "You're ten years old now. I need you to understand the world we live in." Daddy sat down, and then he motioned to Andrew to come and sit next to him. "Poppa is the Boss, kind of like the King. I'm the son of the Boss, kind of like a Prince. That makes your Momma a Princess. If your Momma is a Princess what does that make you?"

"A Prince" Andrew said

"I've been working very hard so you don't have to hold things down like Poppa, I, or even your Dad has done. You are going to college just like everyone else. You will be a legitimate success! You follow me?"

"Yes" Andrew said

"But at the same time there's going to be people who challenge our throne. When that happens, they have to be put down. Do you remember when you guys went to all those amusement parks?" Andrew said yes. "Our throne was under attack. We had to keep our queens and our next princes safe. You understand?" Andrew nodded. "People had to die in order for that to happen. We don't go hurting people unless they mess with us. Sometimes it makes us sad when certain people have to die, but as a man you have to do what comes next." Daddy took a deep breath.

"Your mother should've never let David raise an eyebrow to her. From the moment he raised his hand to her he started dying." Daddy looked at me, "why did you let this happen? Where would you ever get the impression that this sort of behavior was ok? And your boys know about it." Daddy's eyes were angry.

"Daddy, I was in a bad place. I don't think you'll understand me if I tried to explain it." I pleaded

"Try me!" He said

"Andrew, show Malcolm your basketball skills." I said

"I know you care for this guy, but nobody messes with the bosses' woman! That's right up there with the primal rules! You understand? You have to accept that he's gonna die. You don't cry for him! You understand?" Daddy said to Andrew.

"Yes sir!" Andrew said with a stone face. Then Andrew stood up. "Malcolm!" He said as he led him to the backyard.

Daddy told me to come and sit next to him. I moved next to Daddy on the couch. I told him everything and I do mean everything, from the beginning to the end. Daddy sat there absorbing everything. Daddy said from the moment I chose to go the opposite way of the way he was showing me, my life was leading to this. Malcolm was a good man, but he has his own demons to deal with. None of this minimized my part in any of it. He said I should've broken up with David as soon as I knew it couldn't move forward. Getting pregnant confused everything. Then he asked who I was talking to when he walked in the door. I told him it was David; I was trying to get him to plead guilty. Daddy asked me why I keep trying to save him? I told him David has no idea what he's gotten himself into; I don't want him to die. Daddy said I was fighting a losing battle David was going to die. I needed to let go cause it was gonna happen.

Darryl came downstairs; he got real excited when he saw his grand poppa. He came and gave him a big hug. Daddy asked Darryl where he was coming from. He told him he was strolling around upstairs getting ready for the day. That tickled Daddy so much. He thanked Darryl for that laugh.

Then Sophia called and asked what our plans were for the day? That was code for she needed our help if we weren't too busy. She opened her restaurant a couple of months ago, while I opened my school a few weeks later. Ms. Dubois sent a couple teachers and students my way. She even taught the Saturday modern dance class. I partnered with The Center as sort of a sister company to theirs in the Oakland area. Poppa and Nana volunteered to be silent investors when needed. Uncle Frank as promised funded the purchase of my studio instead of leasing the space. My head hadn't been exactly in the game with losing Momma and then this nightmare with David. Gwen stepped up and helped me get my vision off the ground for my school. In addition to overseeing the design and layout of my school, she was an advertising wizard. Her degree in marketing really paid off. My school, "The North Star Dance Company," and Sophia's restaurant were major achievements for her independent consultation services that she wanted to eventually turn into a marketing firm.

Daddy said he would gladly keep Darryl with him while I took Andrew and Derrick with me to the restaurant. I went to the back and Andrew and Malcolm were playing basketball real hard. Hubby, Dude, and Derrick stood to the side watching the two of them go at it. Malcolm had on street clothes but it didn't seem to matter. Andrew was visibly upset and putting it all on the court. Malcolm was playing on Andrew's emotional state. He kept blocking Andrew's lay up, fouling him just to upset him more; Andrew would get right back out there and keep going. He was determined to score on Malcolm at some point. I stood there watching for a minute; I wanted to tell Malcolm to stop because I could see what he was doing but I didn't feel like being accused of babying Andrew, and he seemed to be handling it. When Andrew finally scored, I told him and Derrick to go wash up because we were going to Sophia's. I asked Hubby and Dude if they wanted to come cause we could use the help. They said yes and ran home to ask their mother. Dude came back and said she told them yes. So they were going to wash up and come right back. I packed up Darryl and he left with Daddy. Malcolm was still lingering. I kept rolling my eyes at him whenever our eyes met, and his face stayed serious.

"I wish I could say this was business and that it wasn't personal. But that would be a lie." Malcolm said matter of factly.

"You look for any and every avenue to hurt me. When will you leave me alone?" I said

"How you figure?"

"I gave you everything! Everything! And what thanks do I get? Yvette and your laundry list of hoes! The first and only time I try to have something real for me; you squash my dream. I've always told you I wanted a family. You never wanted any liabilities, but when I find someone who wants with me, what you never wanted, you won't allow it. It's like I'm forever being punished for ever caring for you."

"I know I don't handle things right all the time, but you don't either. You can blame me for ruining your life, I'll take that, but you will not blame me for him hitting you! Even if I would've never said anything and you did marry him, eventually he would've been kicking your butt up and down the street. That's what you're missing, one way or another he was gonna die. I just can't believe someone like that is who you want to replace me with."

"Why do you keep making this about you Malcolm? I loved David because he wasn't you."

"Right, cause he was timid and sweet. When exactly did he start going upside your head? He was a broke, pitiful excuse for a man, and I know he wasn't satisfying you." I couldn't believe he went there. "Did you notice you still curved to me? Keep fighting it if you want to, but you are my queen."

I had no desire to pursue this conversation anymore. He was trying to get my body to react to him, and I refuse! I turned on my heels and went upstairs. The boys were getting their things together to take their showers. I went in my closet to decide which black slacks and which white button up I was gonna wear. When I heard my door open and close, I knew it was Malcolm. I wasn't in the mood; I didn't feel like playing this game. "What do you want?"

"Lets have this out; I don't want it dragging out for the next however long." He said sitting on my bed.

"I don't feel like doing this right now Malcolm."

"Since we've already established its happening, how long you gonna stay mad at me?"

"Hhhhmmmm, lets see you're gonna kill the father of my kids and you wanna know how long I'm gonna be mad? Oh I don't know; would eternity satisfy?" I came out of the closet with my pants and shirt. I laid them on the bed, and then I rolled my eyes at him. "Can you step out, I need to change."

He leaned back on the bed. "Go ahead."

I gagged and rolled my eyes again. I took my clothes in my bathroom. I was not about to let him watch me dress. "Amber, we have to get past this."

"Really? You took away the one person who wanted me despite you. Then you go home to Yvette and your many hoes. I can't have anybody, but you can have whomever you want. I have always hated your double standard! I even chose you over David. And what do you do. You move your hoes into your shop; kick me out without even discussing it with me. I hate you so much Malcolm! I can't believe I ever allowed you so many chances and each time you break my heart. You don't realize it but you're no better than David. Both of you have humiliated me, and made me regret ever feeling anything for you."

When I came out the bathroom Malcolm's face was angry, but he didn't say anything. My words had wounded him; he sat there unresponsive for a few minutes like he was thinking about my words. He looked like he was searching for words. Then he said, "Momma would say we started this whole thing too young. We created too many wounds before we knew how we would've wanted this whole thing to go." I stood there looking at him. "I'm not ready to be a faithful husband, I'm not gonna sit here and lie about that but I've taken care of you this whole time even while you were with David. I even gave you space to have your relationship. I know removing David means I'll have to step up more around here. I need us to be ok. I'm not trying to hurt you. I love you!"

"No you don't!"

"Yes I do!"

"Then leave David alone."

"Amber! I can't do that!" I could hear his resolve weakening.

"Would it help if I told you that I don't want to be with him? I'll prove it anyway you want, I just don't want him to die."

"Kiss me" Malcolm said. The sight of seeing Malcolm weaken before me definitely turned me on. He's always so big and strong, powerful. I know the thought of Momma had something to do with it, but I would take whatever I could. I kissed him with everything in my body. He started leaning back. Then he pulled away.

"Amber, I can't!"

"Yes you can Malcolm. I broke up with him before this happened. I don't want to be with him."

"So why would you kiss me to save him?"

"Cause you won't listen to reason. I'm just asking you not to kill him."

"Amber, he's an entitled idiot. He's gonna come after you."

"No he won't. He knows I don't want to be with him."

Malcolm grabbed my butt with his big strong hands. "This is a mistake, I can feel it."

"My butt feels like a mistake?" I smiled.

Andrew knocked at the door saying they were ready to go. I told Andrew and Derrick to go downstairs and that I would be right down. Malcolm frowned at me, I told him to stay put, and that I'd be right back. Malcolm said a defeated ok. When I bounced down the stairs, Andrew had an evil look on his face. I gave my car keys to Derrick, I told him to get in the car with Hubby and Dude.

"What's wrong Andrew?" I asked

"Why is Malcolm in your room?"

"I'm trying to get him to change his mind about David."

"You heard what Grand Poppa said." Andrew said

"I did, but Malcolm can talk to Grand Poppa."

"Why does he have to be in your room?"

"Andrew! Stop asking me questions! David and I are not together, I can have whomever I want in my room." Andrew huffed. "Go get in the car boy, and worry about being a child."

When we got to Sophia's the place was hopping. LJ and JoJo were there already bussing tables, but they needed help, so Sophia put Derrick, Hubby, and Dude on bussing detail. She asked Andrew to help Sasha with hosting. I told her I had to go do something but I would be back. She looked at me and asked what I had to do; I told her I had to finish my conversation with Malcolm. She raised an eyebrow and said "conversation"? I kissed her cheek and I bounced out of the restaurant. My mind and my body kept debating with each other. My mind was begging for a moment to think it through. Meanwhile my body was beyond excited about what was about to happen to it. Over these past few years, I've been going through the motions. Every time David brought sex up my body froze over. I didn't want his hands on my body, but I didn't want Malcolm at that point either. It has felt like the dumbest thing to take the pill all these years for nothing. But at this moment I was happy I had been. When I walked in the door, Malcolm was sitting on the couch flipping the channels. His face was serious but not mad. I walked towards the kitchen, and he called out that he already made sure it was locked. How did he know I was going to secure the door? He glanced at me and then he put his eyes back on the TV. I put my jacket and purse down on the chair. Then I sat next to him on the couch, I kissed his neck. He inhaled then exhaled very big. "Stop!" I looked at him with the biggest question mark. "You didn't want me touching you before. Now to save this nigga you're open? All of a sudden the Yvette's and Camille's of my life don't matter?" Then he looked at me. "How much have you changed?" "What does that mean?" I said frowning.

"I don't want to touch you to save someone that I want dead. I've only ever touched you because I loved you and I needed you. If we go through with this, I may never look at you the same. Is that what you want?"

"What does that mean?"

"I've never treated you like I've treated them. You've always been my Queen, but this doesn't feel right. You're willing to have sex with me to save someone we all know is gonna die, playing on my weakness for you. You say you don't wanna be with him, but why would you go through all this for someone you aren't planning to be with?"

"If I'm completely honest with you, can we have this conversation? This is just me and you?"

He turned off the TV with the remote. "When have I ever given you the impression it was ok to lie to me?" His face was completely serious.

I took off my shoes, pulled my feet up on the couch, and faced him. He faced me and looked me directly in my eyes. At first, my eyes fell to the floor, but then I gave him eye contact back. He relaxed a little. "David was the sweetest guy initially. Before we officially got together, he was worried about how he and I being together would affect Andrew. Even when he was whooped from working hard all day, Andrew would meet him at the door and talk his ear off. He wouldn't end the conversation or hurry Andrew a long, he'd let him talk, and he made him feel heard. I pretended like I didn't notice things like that, but they touched my heart. I fell hard for him. I couldn't think of how to break the news to him that I couldn't marry him. So I took another route, I took responsibility for the pain and confusion that I was causing him. The nasty side of him didn't start coming out until after Derrick was born and he started drinking. I knew it was my fault that he was acting that way. He didn't start off that way, and I honestly believe it's all my fault that he's where he is right now. I never told him what you said, you did. Once he knew he calmed down a lot, we kind of reconnected. Once the boys started coming he never treated Andrew any different. I love him for everything he did for Andrew and for what he's meant to me. He made sure I never felt the rejection of another woman, but there's the flip side, I could go down a whole list for you if you want but in the end, he's not you. It is very depressing and confusing to me to hear you say how much you love me, but you have to have other women. Every time I wanna succumb to my feelings for you, the memories of why we aren't together slap me in the face. You are the man about everything else, but when it comes to giving me you, you fail me. Today you were giving in to me, and that ignited something in me I hadn't felt in a long time. I felt like you were giving me something difficult to give away, so I wanted to give you something I haven't given anyone in years."

He squinted, "years?"

"Not since before I realized I was pregnant."

He whistled. "Vulnerability turns you on?"

"It did today. But now I feel rejected so we're back to square one." I sighed.

"Amber, mark my words. He's gonna come after you. He's not gonna leave you to be with me happily ever after."

"Maybe we need to see it to believe. I don't think he'll forget that I broke up with him."

"This is a mistake."

I stood up and slipped my feet in my shoes. "Maybe you're right. I don't know people like you do, or Momma did. But it's not like you will be far away if he does come after me."

Malcolm sighed shaking his head. I grabbed my stuff and we walked out together. He put his arms around me and kissed me deep and strong, my body started mildly shaking just from his kiss. "I can't touch you right now. You have too much faith in him. I'll come for you when it's time."

"In that case you need to be unattached then as well."

He looked at me, like it was not up for negotiation.

****

"Hello, can I speak to Andrew?" These little girls call at all hours.

"Who's this?" I asked

"Toya." The girl said

"Toya do you see what time it is?" I said irritated.

"I'm sorry." She said

"Don't call here after nine, you hear me!"

"Yes ma'am."

I hung up. Andrew peeked around the corner from the kitchen. "Get in here!" He had a slight grin on his face. "If one more girl calls here after nine, you won't be able to tie up my line for a whole week. Do you understand me?"

"Yes" Andrew said with a grin.

"Why does it have to be so many?" I asked

Still grinning, "I don't know." Then he looked around. "Who was it?"

I sucked my teeth. "I'll tell you in the morning. Go finish the dishes."

Andrew took off running. I knew that just meant he was going to be back once he was done. The phone rang again and I sighed real loud. "Andrew's answering service. It is now after ten o'clock, he cannot receive calls after nine."

The caller started laughing. I sat up; I knew that laugh. "So the girls are calling nonstop huh?"

"Yes! When did you get out?" Andrew's head popped around the corner

"Today, I'm at a friend's tonight. Can I come see you guys tomorrow?"

"Aw, there's gonna be a recital at my school tomorrow night. My students have been working really hard. Give me the number to where you're staying; I'll call Saturday after we get off work."

"Your school is open on Saturdays?"

"Yes, but we help out at Sophia's on the weekends. Andrew created a seating process that has just about put Sophia's at the top of Piedmont's list of places to go and eat. They get you in quickly, feed you good, and get you on your way. The boys have been instrumental in the success of Sophia's, plus they earn their pocket change working there."

He laughed, "Darryl works there too?"

"Yes he does."

David laughed, "What does he do?"

"He helps buss the tables, he sweeps, and he collects the tips and put them in the proper cubbies. He's really good too."

"What about Derrick? What does he do?"

"He's good with numbers, he keeps time; he's a lot like Andrew. He's a jack-of-all-trades. Andrew still brings home straight A's, and Derrick does too. Andrew reads books whenever he can steal a moment away and as soon as he's done with a book, Derrick is into it. They want to move Derrick ahead a grade cause they say he's not being challenged enough. I'm still thinking about it, but it looks like I'm going to have to, he's getting really bored in class."

"How old is he now?"

"You don't know how old your own son is?"

He laughed. "He's... Seven right?"

"Ding! Ding! You're right. Tell 'em what he's won Chuck!" I laughed, "He's in the second grade, but his demeanor makes him seem so much older. Nothing seems to faze him."

"That's because he's always following behind Andrew." David said

"If you say so."

"How have you been?"

"I'm fine." I said not liking the turn of the conversation. Andrew walked into the room.

"I miss you!"

"David, please don't."

"I've thought about that morning. I think..."

"David, hold on." I took the phone off my ear.

Andrew's eyes were big, I handed him the phone. "Hello?" He smiled, but his smile wasn't a complete smile. "Good! Good!" Then Andrew looked at me. "Yea, she's good... How are you...? She went upstairs... Yeah... Yeah... I'll tell her... Ok... No.... You know what, I gotta go. Alright... Ok.... She's still upstairs; I think I hear the shower... I'll tell her... Bye... bye" then he hung up the phone and looked at me. "I hate it when Malcolm's right!" Then he walked back in the kitchen.

****

"Thank you everyone for coming out tonight. The students have worked very hard. We hope you enjoy!" I said at the end of my introductory speech. The night went smoothly, and the audience was packed in my theater. Malcolm stood on the sideline with me, helping me with everything, and putting his arms around me in between rest. Affectionate embraces had become our thing. That and talking, sometimes we'd sit and talk for hours. Every once in a while we'd kiss, but mainly we hugged and held each other.

Of course, my boys, and the girls were the stars of the night. Andrew and LJ choreographed a routine for the nine of them. Dude wasn't much of a dancer, but I always gave him an A for effort. Sasha and Tanisha started the routine. Derrick, Hubby, JoJo, and Dude kicked it up a notch. Andrew and LJ brought it in, and Darryl was the finale. The crowd who was already into their routine went absolutely wild when little Darryl came in perfectly. My babies knew how to work the crowd. I didn't try to scan the crowd, but my gut told me David was out there. My family was all through the crowd, I never asked Malcolm if he told everyone to back off, but since David was alive last night, I assume he has sent word. I told Malcolm right away that David called; he didn't seem surprised or concerned. At the end of the night as I thanked everyone for coming out, Malcolm walked out with a large bouquet of long stem red roses. He kissed my cheek and the crowd cheered. Completely embarrassed I dismissed everyone. Nana and Poppa came and congratulated everyone on a job well done. We all went to Sophia's for cake and coffee afterwards. Malcolm sat next to me and he kept telling me how well tonight went. I could feel eyes on me but I couldn't tell where they were coming from. Saturday morning we got up as usual, and we headed out to Sophia's. My stomach felt weird about the day, but I told myself it was residual butterflies from the night before. When we got to the restaurant everything was business as usual, the place was packed. Andrew's seating system kept new customer wait down to fifteen minutes maximum. Customers would get a kick out of how young the boys and Sasha were. Sophia would come out and greet customers personally whenever she could pull away from the kitchen. A lot of the time customers would be so surprised that someone so young would be so successful in the restaurant business especially in our current nineteen eighties economy. As I took the order at one of my tables, I noticed a little girl kind of hanging out by the hostess station. She wasn't obvious but she definitely had Andrew's attention. When Andrew saw me looking he blushed, the girl looked at me with a question mark. I put my order in then I walked towards the front. I could see Andrew giving himself a pep talk as I approached. My eyes bounced between the girl and him. Andrew tried to keep his eyes and body from reacting, but I could see him internally dreading this moment. When I got to the station, I looked at Andrew. He turned red, "momma this is my friend Toya." The girl did a double take when she saw me. "That's your momma? Wow!" She said looking at me.

"What does that mean little girl?" I said not liking the sound of it. She tried to figure out how to fix it, but she couldn't so she just smiled an embarrassed smile. "Andrew you've got work to do, send this little girl away!" Then I gave him one more look and I walked away. I could hear Andrew telling her she had to go or he'd hate to be her when I came back. I saw my face in the window as I walked away; I swore I saw Momma that made me laugh to myself. Around four, Darryl was starting to burn out so I told Sophia it was time for me to go. Hubby and Dude wanted to stay, they called their momma, and she said it was ok. As I was telling Andrew that little girl better not come back, Malcolm and Tanisha walked in. Tanisha was coming to help out, and Malcolm was coming to check things out like he normally does. I told him I was taking Darryl home. He said he'd bring the boys home in a little bit. Darryl and I stopped by Bob's for a scoop of ice cream on our way home. When I pulled into my driveway, I noticed a car I didn't recognize sitting in front of the house. The windows were tinted so I couldn't see if anyone was inside. I took Darryl inside and I made sure I locked the door behind me. Every so often, I would look out the window to see if the car was still there. When Malcolm brought the boys home, I watched him approach the car and then shake hands with the person in the car. I exhaled a big sigh of relief. The night seemed more normal; Derrick and Andrew made dinner, Darryl made the salad. Malcolm and I sat all hugged up in front of the TV. When dinner was ready, we sat at the table like a family. I asked Andrew who that little girl was. Andrew blushed again; he said she was just a girl from school. I asked if she was his girlfriend and he got all blushy. I rolled my eyes, I told him not to have her coming down to the restaurant. Then he asked if she could come and take classes at the center. I told him that was fine but she had to pay for her classes, and he had better not pay for them for her. Andrew spent the rest of the evening on the phone. Derrick sat in the chair with a book, and Malcolm played checkers with Darryl. Darryl was really good, but you had to watch him because he'd sneak a move past you if you let him. Malcolm's walkie-talkie was going off a little more than usual. Andrew got off the phone so he could call Juan. I put Darryl to bed, and Derrick followed suit. Andrew said goodnight and he went upstairs. Malcolm said his man out front had to go handle some business so he was going to stay. I playfully asked him where he was gonna sleep, Malcolm told me not to play with him. He was exercising control but he wasn't above climbing in my bed. Juan called the house after midnight; I could see the hesitation on Malcolm's face. I told him to use his key when he came back. I gave him a key over a year ago just in case of emergency. He never needed to use it, because we were normally home. At the door, he kissed me long and deep, he told me he was coming up to my room when he came back. I smiled and said ok. At that particular moment, I didn't care about Yvette or any of the others. I had been dying to feel him again, but I kept it to myself as much as I could. I took a quick shower and I put on a pretty long silk nightgown I bought for just in case. When my head hit the pillow, I fell asleep. I woke up to the sound of the refrigerator door closing. I figured one of the boys got hungry or Malcolm. I wanted to see Malcolm's reaction to seeing me in my nightgown. I put on the matching robe and I went downstairs. The light was on in the kitchen, when I walked in the kitchen, I caught myself from screaming. It was David he was drunk and it looked like he was trying to heat up some food. He smiled at me. "You look beautiful!"

My heart started beating. "Thank you. How did you get in here?" He pointed to my back door that he must've kicked in. "David you gotta leave."

"Why didn't you call me? I waited for you." He walked towards me. "I'm making breakfast for you guys."

"David you gotta go." I said trying to pick up the bread he spilled on the kitchen floor.

He grabbed me by my hair. "So you're back with Malcolm? Why can't you ever just leave him alone?"

"David! Let me go!" I said trying to remove his grip from my hair.

He pulled me to stand up, "not until you tell me you love me. We're getting married Amber. We're moving to Florida where that black demon will never find us. We're gonna be happy just like we used to be. We'll have one more baby, a girl this time." I didn't want to scream and wake up the kids. "David, I'm not going anywhere with you."

He put his hands around my neck and started choking me. "If you're not with me, you're not with anyone!" His eyes were cold and although he was drunk, he seemed numb to what he was doing to me. He released his grip enough so that I could breathe. "I'm not playing with you Amber. We're leaving tonight! I was making breakfast for the road trip." He let me go. "What did I do with the eggs? Doesn't French toast sound good?"

I tried to run away from him but he got up, punched me in the face and I fell backwards. I kept crawling trying to find anything to hit him with; He kicked me in my ribs. "Good morning son, you want some French toast?" David said to Andrew. Andrew's eyes got big when he saw my face. Andrew's face changed rapidly, he went from surprised, to hurt, to angry in a matter of seconds. I told Andrew to go back, and that it was ok. Andrew reached for the phone on the wall. David threw my iron skillet at it and broke the phone. I hopped up right as David charged at Andrew, he was not gonna lay a finger on my baby. I grabbed the pan off the counter and I swung at him. "Amber, we gotta get rid of little Malcolm. He's too much like his father now." Andrew charged at David, you heard it when Andrew's fist connected with David's face. Andrew took off on David, he was moving too fast for him. I couldn't believe my baby had this grown man on the ground. I hit David in his right shoulder with the pan hard. Andrew kept kicking David and yelling,

"YOU DON'T EVER TOUCH MY MOMMA! I HATE YOU! YOU WERE MY
DAD! HOW COULD YOU?"
As I was running to the phone in the living room, I saw Derrick running down the
stairs. I told him to go back upstairs; he ignored me and ran in the kitchen. I dialed
Juan's number; it barely rang. I couldn't actually talk, I was crying so hard. Juan
hung up on me. The front door opened just as Juan chirped Malcolm's walkie-talkie.
Malcolm looked at me and then at the noise coming from the kitchen. I ran back to
the kitchen, Malcolm walked. Andrew and Derrick were still beating on David.
"Stop!" Malcolm said both of them froze. Andrew was crying, and Derrick looked
at me. He started punching and kicking David again. Andrew grabbed Derrick.
Malcolm took in the whole kitchen scene. "This is your last chance to live. Run
away!"
David hobbled up; his eye was swollen shut and as seconds past more and more
knots started appearing on his face. David hobbled as fast as he could out the door.
Malcolm looked at us, "you were distracted when I came in the door. He ran away!
Amber, go call 911!"
Malcolm chirped Juan on his walkie-talkie. Andrew asked Malcolm what he was
going to do. Malcolm just looked at him. Andrew was torn, he told Malcolm David
wasn't gonna be stupid enough to come back. He begged him to let him go.
Malcolm told Andrew not to be stupid, and that we all knew better than to think
David wouldn't come back. I didn't say anything, I had already been proven wrong
but it was breaking my heart to see how Andrew even with all this still had a
glimmer of faith in the goodness that used to exist in David.
When the police came, we all gave them statements about what happened. The
officers taking our statements knew Poppa and Malcolm. Daddy came over and he
was angry, he and Malcolm went out back and talked for a long time. Juan called
the house phone; his voice was serious but kind. He asked me if I was ok and how
the boys were. I told him we were fine, and then he asked to speak to Malcolm.
When he got off the phone, the officers went over their reports with Daddy and
Malcolm. Malcolm told them to wait until they heard from him before they turned
them in. Then they left, when Andrew pleaded one more time with Malcolm.
Malcolm lost it, which made Daddy lose it. They were all screaming. Daddy was
telling Andrew it was over. Malcolm was telling Andrew this was business. Andrew
was telling Malcolm it was personal. When Daddy had enough, he yelled,
"ENOUGH!" Both of them stopped immediately. "Malcolm, Andrew is right, this
isn't business it's very personal." Then he turned to Andrew, "family comes first!
This was his chance to prove that he was changed and he failed miserably. If we let
him go now he will come back with something. At the very least, we will lose you,
now that he knows what you're capable of, we cannot risk it." Andrew started
crying. "Malcolm don't fail me again!" Daddy's eyes were serious.
Derrick put his arms around Andrew. His face was serious, "it's for the best Drew."
In that moment, if I didn't know better I would've sworn that Derrick was Malcolm's
child. Andrew was more upset about David than Derrick was. We all stood there
staring at them. "Derrick, are you ok?"
He looked up from his big brother, "I'm fine." His face was nonchalant. He looked
at the question marks on all of our faces. "I don't like David."
"Why?" I asked
"Cause he doesn't like me."
"Why do you think he doesn't like you?" Malcolm asked.
"I don't think, I know."

"How do you know?" I asked.

"He told me, he always told me. He only cared about momma. Malcolm has been my dad."

Everybody looked at Malcolm; he was speechless. He put his hands out and he hugged Derrick. Daddy put ice in a towel and put it on my face. Malcolm hugged Andrew, Andrew pleaded with his eyes. Malcolm left; Daddy called Sophia and told her we weren't coming in today. Derrick got Andrew up and they went out back to play ball. Darryl came down and made a beeline out back. Connie knocked on the door as she pushed it open. Daddy had his arms around me while I was crying. I felt so stupid, my insides felt like they were being ripped apart. I couldn't believe that was happening under my nose and I didn't know about it. Connie asked if we were ok. I told her we were fine, David got out and broke in my house. She gasped and asked if we were all ok. I told her we were.

The phone rang and it was David's Auntie Lorraine. She was worried and asking if I had seen David. I told her what happened last night. She started crying; she said all he could talk about was starting over with me. She told him to give me space. She said he called her Friday upset because he thought I had gotten back together with Andrew's father. Her statement sounded more like a question than a statement. I let her question ride on the air. Then I told her the police are looking for him, and she should encourage him to turn himself in as soon as she sees him or heard from him. Then we got off the phone. We were sitting there and suddenly my heart sped up, I felt nauseous. I ran to the bathroom and threw up. I was in pain all over and then it was gone. Daddy came to the bathroom; he asked me if I was pregnant. "NO!" I said over tears. I was suddenly exhausted. I apologized to Connie and Daddy and then I went to lie down. Darryl came in my room.

"Momma I feel sad." He said

"Me too baby." I pulled back my covers for him to come lay next to me. "Why are we sad?" I asked

He climbed in my bed and shrugged his shoulders. I handed him the remote to the TV, and I rubbed his back. I could hear the guys who came to fix the door leave. Darryl said he felt better; he kissed my forehead. I dozed off for a while, I woke up to Malcolm undressing and getting in my bed. I looked at the clock it was after two in the morning. "When did my Daddy leave?"

"Around eight."

"You've been here that long?"

"Since about seven."

Tears were in my eyes. "I'm sorry I didn't believe you."

"How you feeling?"

"He's dead isn't he?" I asked. Malcolm sat on the edge of the bed. Even in the dark, I could see the look he was giving me. I started crying, "It's all my fault!" I started crying uncontrollably.

Malcolm pulled me into his lap. He kissed my forehead, "it's not your fault. He's been messed up for a long time."

"Yes it is! If it weren't for me, he'd still be alive. It's all my fault."

He rubbed my head, "baby it's not your fault. Ssshhhh! Ssshhhh! He did this to his self."

Chapter 34

"Oh my goodness! What are their names?" Darryl said completely excited.
"This is Skylar and that's Samara. They're both girls." Malcolm had two blue nose pit bull puppies. Darryl and Derrick were excited about the puppies, Andrew and I looked at the dogs. The dogs seemed to be drawn to us probably because we weren't responding to them. Malcolm took them through the house. He said they were house trained already, and that he was going to have a doggie door installed tomorrow. I didn't say anything; Andrew exhaled and went up to his room. Derrick and Darryl spent the rest of the evening playing with the puppies. Malcolm sat behind me on the couch; he cuddled me in a bear hug. I sat there being hugged. It's been months since they found David. They said his blood alcohol level was high, he had been beaten severely, but since his body had been in the water for so long, it was hard to determine the degree of his injuries. Malcolm and Daddy came with us to the funeral. The last picture they had with all of us together Darryl was a baby. I keep looking at the pictures. I may have been smiling but I wasn't really happy. I've been trying to wrap my mind around the fact that I'm toxic. No man should even look at me. Who was he kidding; Malcolm would never step up and be the man I need him to be. I can't even care anymore. Maybe having my boys is just what my life's supposed to be. I wished I could talk to my Momma just to get a glimpse of normality. Malcolm has been very affectionate, but that's as far as it's gone. I can't even imagine things going any further. I can see him getting frustrated with me but I can't fix it. I'm not happy, and I really don't think there's anything he can do to fix it either.

****

"Hello this is the principal at Andrew's school."
"Hello" I sighed not even surprised that the school was calling again.
"I know you're busy but can you please come down?"
"It's fine, I'll be right there." I huffed
When I got to the school, Andrew was sitting next to Toya. When they saw me coming, she scooted one chair over. I snapped my fingers at her and told her to stand on the other wall. She hopped up real fast and moved. Andrew's eyes were real big; he was searching my face to read my mood. The secretary told the Principal I was there. Ms. Boyd came out shaking her head. She called Andrew and I to her office.
"I know your family has gone through a lot over the past few years, losing your grandmother that you were close to, and then a couple years later suddenly losing your stepfather can't be easy on an adult, so my heart goes out to you Andrew but all this fighting has to stop. We had to have another parent come and take their child to the hospital. Amber last time we talked, it sounds like you've got him stretched pretty thin with school, after school activities, and working on the weekends. I don't know how you still have the energy. Andrew, you are our top student at this whole school. That's what makes it so difficult to discipline you. It literally hurts me to suspend you, but I have to. Please understand that this is the last suspension I can give you. If this happens one more time we're going to have to discuss expulsion, and I really don't want to have to have that discussion. Do you want to have to change schools this late in the year? Sasha and Tanisha will have to be here without you, and I know how close you all are."
"No ma'am." Andrew said looking at the floor.
"I have a question. What role does that little girl play in all of this?" I asked
"What little girl?"

"Nothing Momma, it's not her fault." Andrew said with his head down
"Who are we talking about?" Ms. Boyd asked
Andrew sighed, "Momma saw Toya talking to me. She was making sure I was ok."
I eyed Andrew cause I knew that wasn't the whole truth. She had something to do
with this. Lately she's had something to do with all of his fights. She's a pretty little
girl, but I don't understand why Andrew lets her manipulate him like she does.
When we left the school, Andrew nervously sat there not knowing how I was going
to react. I didn't say anything; I quietly drove back to the center. I sat down in my
office; Andrew sat in the chair in front of my desk. I wanted to yell, if I thought
hitting him was gonna help I would've done it but I had no energy to deal with this.
I put my head down on my desk and I exploded in tears. Ms. Boyd bringing up
Momma and David cut me to the core. Momma was traumatic enough, but then my
ridiculous excuse for a relationship tipped my baby over the edge. Now he's
probably gonna grow up to be some no good nigga who's always mad at the world
and missing out on opportunities because he can't control his temper. "Momma I'm
sorry." I could hear the surprise in his voice. "Please don't cry I'll calm down I
promise." Andrew was stroking my back and hair like he's done since he saw David
do it; that made me cry harder. "I'm sorry momma, please don't cry."
"I don't know what to do. I know you're upset, I'm upset too. But you can't go
around hurting people just because you're hurting." I said through tears.
"Yes momma."
I picked up the phone and I called Nana. I didn't know what else to do. Poppa
answered the phone; he immediately picked up on the tears in my voice. When he
asked me what was wrong I told him everything. He told me he was on his way.
When I told Andrew that Poppa was coming, he swallowed real hard. Nana and
Poppa came down to the center. They had Ryder with them; he was my Cousin
Sharon's little boy. They all came in my office. We chatted for a minute, poor
Andrew looked so nervous. He looked like my little Andy again, not this
blossoming preteen. Then Nana suggested that we take Ryder on a tour of the
facility and give them some space to talk. Andrew shot me pleading eyes as I
walked out of the room. We went to the theater and we let Ryder run all over the
stage.
Nana looked me up and down then she asked me what was going on with me. She
said she could tell I was depressed without a word. She said I looked "frumpy," that
made me cry of course. I unloaded like I normally do with Nana. She listened to me
then she told me that any man who makes me feel responsible for his choice to
become physical with me isn't a man. She said I didn't choose right by purposely
getting pregnant with Derrick, but he had a choice too. She reminded me that
everything that was wrong in our relationship wasn't all my fault no matter how
much he tried to make it seem like it was. She told me to stop painting the picture of
him like he was a perfect angel and I was the devil child that led him astray. I
exhaled while we discussed his faults in detail. Then she pointed out that he only
knew about Malcolm, and struggled to keep himself in line. She told me to imagine
how bad it would've been without Malcolm around. That thought kept echoing in
my mind. I told her how sweet Malcolm has been, and how he's really stepped up
with the boys but I know he's still going home to Yvette when he's not with me, and
how I can't get past it. She confided in me that Poppa has had at least one mistress
over the past however long they've been together. She said it wasn't something she
was proud of, or that she would openly tolerate. My mouth dropped open; if I
weren't sitting, I would've needed to sit down. She told me I couldn't tell anyone, I

promised not to say a word. I had fifty million questions; never in a million years did I think Nana would tolerate such behavior from Poppa. She told me there were rules; Malcolm needed to get smarter about how he handles his business. She said the mistress needs to know her place; she had to know and understand how disposable she is. She can't step out of line, and her presence has to be invisible to me, most importantly no extra babies. I'm the Queen and if I'm not happy then no one is. She said Malcolm still had some learning to do. I told her I didn't want to share. She understood and asked me if I thought she wanted to share? She said Poppa is a good man, and he has been good to her. She said every relationship has something to deal with.

Poppa and Andrew found us. Poppa informed us that Andrew was coming with them. Andrew's eyes looked like he just got scolded. He apologized to me for how he's been behaving and he assured me that he was going to be better. He said any fights at school from now on would only be because he couldn't avoid them after he exhausted all other options to resolve the issue. I asked about fights outside of school. He smiled and said those were different. I asked Poppa how long he was gonna be with them? Poppa said the duration of his suspension. They hung around for a while and then they left with Andrew. I was gonna miss him, but I knew it was for the best. I went in the bathroom and looked at my reflection. I needed a change. I could see the lack of exercise filling in my stomach and my thighs. My face was a little fuller. I pulled up my hair and I tried to imagine it different. Yea it was time to start over fresh, but before I did that, I needed to go see Auntie Lorraine. I needed some answers about David, so that I could put it all to rest. Staff was arriving for the afternoon classes; I said my hellos. When I popped my head in the Modern Dance class, Toya's neck almost broke when she turned to watch me. I could see the question all over her face. I eyed her for a minute and she backed down, I dared her to ask me where Andrew was.

I went home and Hubby and Dude were at my house with Derrick and Darryl. They were all sitting at the table doing their homework. They all held their breath when they didn't see Andrew with me. I told them he'd be back at school on Friday. When Connie came home, I packed up my boys and we rode to Richmond. Auntie Lorraine was surprised to see us. David's mother Dionne was there as well. I had only met her at the funeral. You could tell once upon a time that she was a very pretty lady, but like Malcolm's mother, hard lives had taken their toll on their appearances. Dionne kept her eyes to the floor mostly. The boys went in the study with Lorraine's husband. I asked Dionne how she was feeling. She nodded her head to say she was ok, her eyes wandered all over the floor and she kept her hands clamped like she was hanging on by a thread. Auntie Lorraine asked to what did she owe the honor of my presence. I asked her point blank how did she know David was hitting me. Dionne started rocking in her chair. Auntie Lorraine kind of slumped for a minute. She said she really hoped that it was just Patricia, who brought it out in him. She said we appeared to be doing well at first. I felt like Nana's words were embracing me. "So I didn't bring this out in him? I thought he became like that because of me." Tears poured out of my eyes.

In a moment of clarity, Dionne said, "no honey. My son has a lot of issues. His Daddy used to beat us both. I gave him to his aunt cause I knew she was the only one who could keep his dad away from him but he thought I was giving him away. I told him I wanted to meet you especially after you had the first baby, but he was so mad at me."

"Dionne you did the best you could in your situation." Auntie Lorraine said.

Dionne started rocking again; just that fast she slipped right back out.

I drove home so relieved; the weight of the world was no longer on my shoulders. Derrick turned off the radio and then he asked me what was wrong with Dionne. I told him she had a hard life, and she was in love with the wrong man. He asked me what made a man the wrong man. I told him it depends from woman to woman, but in general a man who bullies women, a man who doesn't make his woman his Queen. After that, it depends on the woman. He asked me if I would've ended up like Dionne if I stayed with David? I exhaled, then I told him it seemed like it didn't it. When we walked in the house, I told the boys to take their showers and to get ready for bed. I turned on the TV, midnight love was gonna come on in a couple hours. I cleaned the kitchen, hung up on Toya twice when she called, and vacuumed the entire downstairs. When she called the third time, I asked if she rode the yellow bus. She was quiet, I told her that Andrew couldn't have calls, and that he would call her when he could, then I hung up on her again. The girls watched me then they made their rounds around the house. They patrolled the house like they were officers patrolling their territory.

I had just laid down when I heard Malcolm come in the door. I was still watching TV when he came in the room. I was finally watching midnight love looking for inspiration for a new look.

"Good you're still awake. Have you ever thought about choreographing a video?"

"No."

"No you haven't or no you don't want to?"

"No I hadn't thought about it. What did you have in mind?"

He told me about a local artist who was looking for a choreographer for their debut single. He said he told them to come by the school tomorrow to see the investor video I had that showcases my work. It sounds like a good publicity opportunity for the school so I was in. Then I told him that Andrew got suspended again. He exhaled and started for the door, I told him that Andrew was with Nana and Poppa. He smiled and said that was a good idea; he was going to suggest my Daddy. Then he looked at me, I asked him what the look was for, he said I looked better, so I told him about my visit with Lorraine and Dionne. He said he was glad somebody talked some sense into me.

I asked what I had to do to extend my garage. He looked at me with a puzzled look. I told him I wanted a bigger garage so that I could park two cars in it if I wanted. Then I wanted a new car. He told me I'd need permits from the city, but he'd take care of it for me. Then he asked me what kind of car I wanted. I told him I didn't know, I wanted a nice car like his or nicer. He smiled, "you can't handle my car."

"Why can't I?"

"Well for one it's a stick, and you can't drive a stick."

"How do you know? I could drive a stick if I wanted to. You just like to show off all the time."

"How would you know, you haven't rode with me in a long time!"

"I'm just speaking from memory."

"So what are you saying?" He got in my face, "you wanna ride with me?"

I smiled, "depends."

He exhaled, "here you go! Don't ask me."

"Why haven't you handled that?"

"You showed no interest in riding, what was I supposed to do?"

"Oh well!" I said getting up to go to the bathroom. "All I've had time to do is work on my dance form, etc." then I slowly slid into the splits looking at him the whole time. Then I shrugged and got up.

Even though the only light in the room came from the TV, I could see that his mouth was open. I went in the bathroom, and then just to torment him more I got in the shower. When I came out the bathroom in only my silk robe he had turned on the light. He was standing with his back to the corner. His face looked mad, but I knew better. "Why are you messing with me?"

"I'm not messing with you." I said with a grin.

"Yes you are!" He barked.

I untied my robe, "no I'm not."

"I'm gonna go sleep on the couch." He said with his voice cracking.

The biggest turn on for me was seeing him weak for me. "Suit yourself, I'm not keeping you."

"Amber you play too much!" He said laughing.

"That's Queen Amber to you! And her highness is not playing but you have failed me. How should I punish you?"

He raised an eyebrow, "punish? I'm a grown man; you're not about to..."

"Hush! Her highness is thinking." I tapped my chin pretending to think. He stood there looking at me like he's never seen me before. "I know, her highness would like a royal massage!"

"A what?"

"A royal massage!" I grabbed my lotion off my dresser. "Here you go!"

"No," he said laughing; I love the sound of his laugh especially since he rarely laughs out loud.

"You dare to refuse Queen Amber? The penalty may be greater than you can afford to bare." Then I dropped my robe and commanded him to massage me.

He couldn't stop laughing as he came over to massage me.
****

"What would you charge me to choreograph my video?" Mister MC asked.

"I'd charge a flat rate for the choreography, and then hourly for rehearsals. If you'd want me on set, then that would be hourly as well." I said

"Ok, send me your proposal, and I'll get back to you." Mister MC said smiling.

"Malcolm wasn't lying."

"Excuse me?"

"He told me to come prepared cause you handle your business."

I blushed, "thanks I guess."

"So who are you to Malcolm?"

"We have a son."

"Really? Wow!"

"What's so wow about that?"

"You don't seem like the type to get your hands dirty like that."

"Looks can be deceiving," I said, "so tell me more about your concept for the video. I have some ideas just based off of what I heard."

Mister MC was a good guy. The rap scene was starting to really ramp up, and the Bay Area was starting to crank out some major players. Mister MC was our next great hopeful. Malcolm showed up as we were wrapping up. Mister MC was singing my praises about my professionalism, etc. Malcolm looked at Mister MC funny as he went into round four of Amber's so great. I was starting to feel like we got the point as well when he went into round three. Malcolm put his arm around me and moved me to his left side. He told Mister MC that he was gonna have to be present for our next meeting. I fought a smile, was Malcolm jealous? Mister MC put his hands up and said he could respect that and that he meant no disrespect. When Mister MC left, Malcolm locked my office door and asked me if I was in there teasing that poor guy. I said not at all. I told him what we talked about and what I was thinking I should charge him. Malcolm said I was giving him an exceedingly cheap rate, I told him since I didn't completely know what I was up against I wanted to be fair. I figured if this turned into an ongoing working relationship, I could always adjust my prices later; Malcolm agreed with my thinking, but he looked like he had other things on his mind.

"So last night we were talking about expanding your garage so you can buy a new car."

"Yes, I really do want to buy a new car. I've always driven used cars. I want a brand new high-end car. It's gonna be my special treat to myself."

"Are you dead set on buying it? Or can I buy it for you?"

I smiled really big, "you wanna buy me a car?"

"I'll buy you whatever you want. I've never had a problem with spending money on you; you're the one who acts like you're too good."

"I do not." I said smiling, "besides, you've been paying all my bills all this time. You set me up quite nicely."

He smiled, "you never said anything."

"I just did," I stuck my tongue at him.

"I took care of business today." He said giving me direct eye contact.

I got the biggest smile, "you did?"

"I did!"

"Ok, so now what?" Then he kissed me so passionately that my knees buckled.

"Well alright!"

"For real this time, I'm your King and you are my Queen! It's just me and you from today onward." He said holding my face.

I smiled real big, "I love you!"

His face frowned up and his face got real serious. "I've been waiting all these years to hear you say that again. Say it again!" He said kissing me.

"I love you Malcolm! I love you!"

We kissed for a long time and then we went to get the boys to go out to dinner. We drove in Malcolm's fancy car to Nana and Poppa's house to pick up Andrew. He wasn't enthusiastic about Malcolm coming with us to pick him up, but he was ready to come home. We had dinner at a little restaurant in Walnut Creek that Nana and Poppa liked going to. The food was ok, but the coziness of the space was nice. The owner came out, "Frank! I see you've brought company."

Poppa introduced us to his friend, and he introduced Malcolm as his grandson in-law. Andrew's eyes got big; Malcolm and I smiled at each other. Nana caught our smiles, she whispered to me asking if things had changed since just the other day. I nodded my head yes, and she smiled really big as she patted my hand. Andrew kept shooting me eyes from across the table. On the car ride home, Darryl was on a sugar high and he talked our ears off. I heard Derrick ask Andrew what was wrong, but I didn't hear an answer. When we got home, Derrick made a beeline to get in the shower first. Darryl ran in circles in the kitchen making the puppies so dizzy that they just sat and watched him. Andrew plopped on the couch.

"What's wrong Andy?"

"What's going on with you and Malcolm?" Andrew said giving me direct eye contact.

"What do you mean?"

"You guys are back together again?"

"Why does that upset you?"

"I don't know!" Andrew said throwing his body backwards.

"You can't be happy for me?"

"You guys are just gonna breakup again." He said uninterested.

"Boy! You don't talk to your momma like that! It's none of your business what's happening between your momma and I. What you need to concern yourself with is staying out of trouble, doing what I tell you, and making your momma smile! Let me hear you talking to your momma like that again and see what happens!"

"Ok, so then I'm talking to you!" Andrew said standing up. "That's my momma and you better not hurt her! Or I'm coming for you!" Malcolm's eyes got big, and then he fell out laughing. Darryl stopped running in the kitchen and he ran next to me. Derrick came out the shower, dripping wet to see what was going on. Andrew looked at me with the most sarcastic look. "I'm not playing! I'm serious!" Malcolm laughed harder. "Alright little man, I won't hurt your momma. I don't wanna suffer the consequences." He put his hands up.

Darryl whispered to me, "I never heard Malcolm laugh before." Then he said, "His teeth are scary white too!"

We all started laughing and Malcolm stopped laughing. "Give me a hug Andy." I said, "I love you baby!" I gave Andrew the biggest hug.

Malcolm smiled real big at Andrew, as Andrew mugged Malcolm when he walked past him.

****

"I like your concept, but I think there should be a lead girl in the video." Mister MC said.

"Ok, but you don't need me to choreograph that." I said going back to my bid.

"Yea but I want you to be the lead girl in the video."

I looked at Malcolm; I didn't know what to say to that. "What does the lead girl do in your mind?" Malcolm asked

"You would be the lead dancer, in the end you dance with me; nothing out of line, promise!" Mister said

"Do you want to do that?" Malcolm asked

"Only if it's ok with you." I said

"Why do you want her to play lead?" Malcolm asked Mister.

"Your woman is fine Malcolm! People will watch just to see me get the girl."

I blushed; I couldn't believe he said that. If he only knew how ugly I felt growing up, he wouldn't say that. No, I didn't think I was ugly today, but I didn't think of myself as all that like he was making me seem. "Let me see the contracts and we'll go from there." Malcolm said

"How soon is the shoot?" I asked

"A couple weeks, we'll get the contracts out this afternoon. Will you be at the center later?" Mister said looking at me.

"Have them delivered to the studio." Malcolm said directing his attention back his way. "We'll go from there."

Sophia brought three meatball subs to us. "Here's today's special, enjoy!"

"I thought you were gonna eat with us?" I asked her.

"I got a produce delivery. I'll be back." She said hurrying to the back.

Mister bit into his sandwich and you would think he was having an orgasm right there on the spot. I took a bite of my sandwich and it was very good. The bread was fresh, meatballs seasoned perfectly, the cheese melty and stretchy, and the sauce was so good you wanted to lick your fingers. The potato chips and the salad on the side added the perfect balance to this plate. Sophia had a gift for making you fat. I knew exactly why she had so many regulars and why her business was doing so well. She eventually came and sat with us for a little bit. Mister raved over his sandwich; she graciously took it all in.

The video shoot was a lot of fun. All of his dancers were local. I even snuck Melvin in amongst the dancers. It was weird watching me in the playbacks; I didn't seem like myself at all. Malcolm was right there from the beginning to the end, so everything was done appropriately. We didn't tell the boys, I received a tape of the final video. The boys were watching videos, when Andrew started calling me. I ran in the room and all the boys' eyes were big. They asked me how I knew Mister MC. I told them Malcolm knew him and set the whole thing up. My boys thought it was so cool to see me on TV.

****

I sat in Raynel's chair. "However you gotta do it, but I want my hair to come here." I said pointing to just past my shoulders. "And I want a perm, because I don't want to fight with it to keep it straight."

"Are you sure? You don't need a perm to wear it straight. You could blow dry and use your curling iron."

"Yeah and as soon as I go for a run my whole head will go right back. It will be easier this way." My hair had gotten ridiculously long, but every since that run in with Momma Shuga I rarely wore my hair down just because. Unless I was going somewhere, my hair was in one braid or a ponytail. I needed something different. Raynel cut my hair, permed it, and then trimmed it to my desired length. When Raynel turned me to face the mirror I cried, she had tears in her eyes. I could see Momma in my face. My curls were such a major player in my appearance that you didn't see my features all that clearly. I still looked like Daddy, but at this moment, I saw Momma. Raynel told me she saw Momma too, which made both of us cry. When I came home, the boys loved my hair. When Malcolm came later to take me out to dinner, he said he liked it, but he personally liked my curls better. Rosalind told me to pay him no never mind; she loved it. She said my shiny hair seemed like it added a couple shades to my complexion, I thought so too.

****

It was so busy at Sophia's that it seemed like everybody was rushing around. As soon as customers left a table the boys bussed it, and I was right back at that table in what seemed like minutes. I was moving so fast I wasn't looking to see who was sitting at the table before I approached them. "Welcome to Sophia's can I start you off with something to drink?" When I got no response, I looked at the person. It was Yvette and she was looking at me in total shock. "Why are you waiting tables?" I didn't say anything I could feel my blood starting to boil. "This is that girl I was telling you about." She said to her two friends.

They immediately started looking me up and down. "She's just light skinned, you made her seem like she was whiter than the whitest white girl." Her friend said "You should've seen her at the courthouse." Then she looked at Andrew at the hostess stand. "Your son has gotten so big! He still doesn't look a thing like Malcolm, but I guess some secrets a female will take to the grave with them." She said smirking.

28

I wanted to punch her in her face, but the restaurant was full of people, and the Piedmont police would have me locked up so fast. I walked away from the table; this was my opportunity to practice all that I had been telling Andrew about walking away and exerting self-control. I asked the other waitress to cover Yvette's table. Then I went to the hostess stand. I pointed out Yvette and her friends to Andrew and Sasha. I told them Yvette and her friends are not allowed in the restaurant ever again. Sasha and Andrew looked over out of curiosity. Part of me wanted Malcolm to come down to put any of her nonsense to rest but I told myself to take the high road. Then I heard music bumping outside. I smiled because I knew it was Malcolm. Like clockwork, he was bringing Tanisha. I was waiting on a table when he walked in. Little miss running her mouth wasn't talking any more. In fact, she looked uncomfortable.

"Hey baby," I said kissing Malcolm with my normal peck on the lips. "Your friend is here." I said pointing at Yvette's table. Her face was sour and it looked like she wanted to cry. I'm sure her friends weren't supposed to be looking but they were. He looked over at Yvette's table. "You don't say."

"Why does she constantly insist that Andrew is not your son?"

"I don't know, let's go ask." He took me by the hand, and led me to their table. "Good afternoon ladies."

"Good afternoon!" Her friends said Yvette shifted in her seat.

"So I hear there's a question about the paternity of my son?" Malcolm said looking at Yvette.

Yvette didn't say anything. "He doesn't really look like you Malcolm. Are you sure that's your son?" Her friend said.

If looks could kill that girl would've exploded! "Drew, come here for a second." As Andrew walked over one of the girls whispered, he walks like Malcolm. "You see this bitter woman right here?" He said pointing at Yvette, Andrew nodded. "This is the type of female you don't want in your life. She's so stuck on herself that she can't see past it." Yvette kept her eyes down. "Yvette you need to look at me for this." She slowly raised her eyes. Malcolm put his face next to Andrew's; "this is my son do you see it now?" Andrew had a lot of me in his face but everything that made him a man was just like Malcolm, I saw it.

"Whoa girl! I see it!" Her friend said.

"You did cheat on me with her!" Yvette said just above a painful whisper.

"No, I cheated on her with you! Get it right! I told you that, but you don't listen, you never have."

I told Andrew he could go back to his station but he wanted to hear.

"You're throwing everything away for her? What about us?"

"It was stupid for you to come here. Do you want me to embarrass you any more than I already have? I told you to never even speak to her, why are you here?"

"I didn't know she worked here."

"As soon as you saw her you should've left. You play too many games Yvette. Did you think I would go easy on you cause we had a past? You should first ask yourself if it meant anything to me."

"Come on Malcolm, she made a mistake." Her friend said.

"If you believe that you're dumber than she is! She knew exactly what she was doing by coming here. She didn't think I was gonna be here." Her friend frowned. "You're free to pay your bill and leave at any time or I could sit here and keep going."

"I can't believe you would embarrass me like this!" Yvette said

"You gonna cry now? Were you crying when you made your little comments to my woman? I told you before family comes first!"

"We were a family!" She snapped back.

Malcolm leaned forward, "you honestly expect me to believe that was my baby?" My stomach flipped. "It was your baby; you said you didn't want it." She said lowly.

"You are so full of it! That was Owen's baby." He said looking directly at her. Her friends flinched, and Yvette cried quietly to herself. "You didn't think I knew about him or the others did you? And I know about you pushing up on my cousin! You think he wouldn't tell me?" Yvette stood up in an attempt to capture any last drop of her dignity. "You haven't paid your bill!" Malcolm growled at her.

"I'm gonna pay it." Her friend said.

"Good," then he stood up, "ladies" he said as he bowed and then he led me by the hand away. I grabbed Andrew's hand so he wouldn't stay there. Yvette rushed past Sasha and Tanisha crying. Tanisha looked at Malcolm and she asked him what was wrong with Yvette. Malcolm shrugged and said she was stupid. Andrew walked back to the hostess station whispering to the girls, LJ and JoJo made their way over to hear as well. Malcolm led me to the back to Sophia's office. He put his hands on my face, "are you ok? Do you have questions?"

His concern for my well-being really touched my heart. "I'm fine Malcolm."

"She was pregnant that baby wasn't mine."

"How could you be so sure? As long as you were sleeping with her there's a possibility."

"I've been careful. Besides, I wasn't touching her when she got pregnant. That girl thinks I'm dumb. There's always a Momma Shuga somewhere." He said shaking his head.

"How long ago was this?"

"All her drama started coming at me in the last few years."

"So you were still messing with her with all this?" I asked

"No," he said looking at me.

"Do I even wanna know?"

"No."

"But it's over?"

"It's over," he said.

Chapter 35

In the mornings, I get up to see the boys off. Andrew is in Middle school and he and the boys, Sasha, and Tanisha all ride the bus to school together. When I offered to drive them, they all begged me not to. Plus I didn't have a car big enough to fit all of them at once. Sasha explained that they really liked riding the bus home all together. Their bus picked all of them up, and it dropped JoJo, Sasha, Tanisha, Hubby, Dude, and Andrew at my old middle school and then it dropped LJ off at Oakland High. After school, they all met up at the Bart station. If they decided to go to the library, they'd meet up with Derrick and Darryl and they'd all go. Then they'd all come to the school for their classes etc. Auntie Lauren would come and get her boys and most times Sasha from the school. Connie would get her boys, and most times Tanisha would come home with us. Tanisha has been having a really hard time ever since without any warning Benjamin popped up last summer. I guess when he called and Rosalind was in no hurry to call him back or rush to talk to him he remembered the family he sent away. When he came, instead of focusing on Tanisha like his family and everyone told him to. He couldn't get over the fact that Rosalind was dating Troy. He made a big deal out of their relationship to the point that little Tanisha had to tell him that Troy has been more of a father figure to her than he could ever be. She told him how much his being missing in action has devastated her, but she also ended up telling him to just leave. It was too much for a thirteen year old to go through or have to say but her rant refocused Ben for a bit, it was a day late and a dollar short. Tanisha's poor little eyes permanently glazed over at that point. I asked Andrew how Tanisha was doing because she and Andrew became very close after that. Andrew explained that she kind of felt like all this time her father was dead, then he comes back, not for her, the only person who was truly missing him, but for her mother who had finally moved on. She told Andrew it was like he died all over again. Most times, they'd all go out back and play basketball, sometimes they'd stop their game, and I'd see all my boys hugging Tanisha because she was breaking down. My poor baby was really going through it; puberty and these advance emotions.

Meanwhile Andrew was blossoming. He is taking on more and more of Malcolm's form. He started sprouting, his voice was starting to change, and these little girls have started losing their minds. I allowed him to have his own phone line, but he has to pay the bill. I take the actual phone from his room after nine o'clock ever since I caught him on the phone at all hours of the night with that little girl Toya. Andrew and the boys spend a lot of time with Poppa and Daddy, especially now that Jade and Sonny have moved back and into the house with Daddy. Sonny is working for a law firm in the city. Meanwhile Jade has her independent therapist practice. She works a lot with children, which makes her a wonderful help whenever she comes down to the school to help out. When she met Toya, she told me that little girl was deeply troubled. I told her to tell me something I didn't already know, but you couldn't tell Andrew anything. His nose is so open for that girl.

When I finally got my thoughts together to have a birds and the bee's conversation with my baby, he politely told me that he and Malcolm had already had a conversation. He said Malcolm gave him a ton of condoms and he told him which ones to get. I tried to mask my disappointment, so Andrew told me to continue but not to worry about the actual sex aspect of the conversation. I felt like I was gonna pass out, I asked him if he already had sex. He matter of factly told me yes. I couldn't believe it, I asked him with whom, and he looked at me like I was getting "too personal." He told me not to worry he was a gentleman about the whole thing. I gave him the whole lecture on how he's supposed to treat girls. He patiently listened then he told me that he had the whole conversation with Malcolm, Daddy, and Poppa already. I had to ask him if it was Toya, he smiled and said not yet, but he couldn't tell me who. Ok that killed me; every time his little phone rang I wondered if that was the one? I asked if Sasha and Tanisha were dating anyone seriously and he very protectively told me "absolutely not" he said he wouldn't let any boy get that close to them. He reminded me of Malachi in that moment but even Malachi couldn't be everywhere. I begged Andrew to be careful; I reminded him that I wasn't much older than him when I got pregnant with him. He assured me that he was careful. He said he didn't want any babies until he was married. I was relieved to hear a different tune other than the one his father sang at his age.

****

Sophia hired a manager for her restaurant and more staff now that it has taken off so well. She thought this would give her more time with Richard and Sasha but lately she and Richard have been having such a hard time, she ends up spending more time with me. Malcolm calls the boys his little soldiers; he has been taking them running, to firing ranges, and exercising the life out of my poor babies. Derrick and Darryl accept it and enjoy the time spent with Malcolm, but Andrew is always leery of Malcolm. Sometimes Andrew comes home mad at Malcolm but no one will tell me what's wrong. Even Darryl is tight lipped, and I used to be able to rely on him to tell me. Even when he did tell me it was things like Andrew still can't beat Malcolm at anything; and he gets frustrated or Malcolm would tell Andrew to "Man up" or "Suck it up." When I attempted to protest to everything Daddy was at the house, and he told me to leave them alone. He said they were doing "man" stuff and I couldn't understand what they were doing. Derrick and Darryl fortunately don't fight like Andrew did in school. They have fights on occasions, but I think Malcolm's driven home the whole make an example out of the ones you do fight point, and most of the kids are scared of them especially Derrick. Sometimes he acts so much like Malcolm I can't believe it. Most of the kids although they're older than Derrick, since we ended up skipping him up a grade, are afraid of my baby. They fail to notice that he's a year younger than they are. Darryl has his moments when he reminds me of David. Especially when he's telling me silly jokes or lightening the mood of a room but Darryl doesn't carry that gentleness that I loved about David. The gentleness that I wonder if anyone ever knew about based upon the way he's painted whenever I talk to Dionne in her brief moments of clarity or Auntie Lorraine who flips back and forth when she talks about him. One minute he was a sweet boy and obedient and then the next minute he had a real nasty side that you didn't want to know. She would tell me this like I didn't know it, and didn't live it for years.

But when I watch Andrew with his family and friends I see that kindness and ability to laugh that I know he didn't get from Malcolm. I want to say all my boys get that from me, but with Andrew, I know it goes a little bit further.

****

"NO! NO! NOOO!!" Malcolm yelled "AMBER! WHERE IS SHE???" He yelled again.

I put my arms around Malcolm and rubbed his arms. "Baby are you ok?"
Malcolm jumped out the bed like the bed was on fire. He looked confused like he
didn't know where he was. I waited for him to focus. "Amber?"
"Yes?"
"Where is she?"
"Where is who?"
"Our baby girl? Where is she?"
I swallowed really hard. "Our what?"
Malcolm laid back down and was knocked out. I thought he was awake but he was
still sleep. He tossed and turned for a little bit, he mumbled some, and then he laid
still. I was awake now, what did he mean by our baby girl? What was he dreaming
about? About an hour later, he was awake and trying to "wake" me. He put his arms
around me, and started kissing my neck. I moved over away from him as if I was
sleep but he was kind of persistent, when I rolled over and looked at him, he went to
town on me. Morning breath and all he kept kissing me, when my body was more
than ready he mounted me. Two extreme body shakes later, I was holding onto the
bed in hopes I wouldn't fall out. Malcolm fell back into a hard sleep, as I tried to
fight off sleep I wondered what was that. In the morning, Malcolm was up with the
kids hurrying out the door, he kissed me quick. I laid back down thinking about the
morning and I kept saying baby girl to myself. What did that mean? I laid there
racking my brain, but I couldn't put the puzzle together. I wished my Momma were
here, she'd tell me exactly what I needed to know. Malcolm was an open book to
her; I miss reading him through her eyes. I found myself stuck thinking about my
Momma. I pulled myself out of the bed. I showered with my expensive soaps,
trying to pull myself out of the funk I felt myself plunging into.
I got dressed and I went to Sophia's. She looked as upset as I felt.
"What's wrong?"
"Richard wants to tell Sasha." Sophia said looking devastated.
I sat down, "ok."
"He's got a job opportunity in Los Angeles, and it looks like he's gonna take it." She
inhaled and exhaled, "I can't believe he would leave me like this. I've been in love
with him since the eighth grade. I don't even know what life is like without him."
I rubbed her back, "why does he want to tell Sasha?"
"He still wants to be a part of her life. I can't tell her I've been lying to her this
whole time. I don't think she'd forgive me."
"But you know what, one day she's gonna look in the mirror and see Richard's face,
and she's gonna know. You're only postponing the inevitable. The sooner you come
clean the better it will be for everybody. You guys are also running on assumptions;
why not get a blood test? You could be surprised."
"That would just be a waste of money. I've always known that Sasha was
Richard's."
I put my hand over my mouth. "What do you mean?"
"When Richard and I broke up it was because I told him I thought I was pregnant
and he said he wasn't ready to be a father. Why do you think I slept with Charles so
fast? He was always a mark from the beginning. Kicking him out was supposed to
be his exit. My Daddy found out about what happened he made the call to make
him the mark for David. If I would've known all I had to do was tell what I knew,
maybe it could've spared his pathetic excuse for a life."

"Sophia! His inability to let the past go is what cost him his life. You can't carry that around with you. He had a choice in whether he asked you out, whether he dated you, whether he married you, whether he stayed with you."

We talked it out for a long time, I convinced her to be honest with Sasha. She still didn't know how she was going to tell her, but at least she was going to. Then she got dressed and we went over to the Berkeley Hotel's spa and got massages. My masseur said I was full of knots.

When I got to the school that afternoon, I went over the books. My programs were really taking off. The business that Mister MC's video generated for the school was amazing. Mister MC came back for a couple more routines for his on the road performances. Plus I hired a few teachers to travel to local elementary, Middle, and High schools. I used the money from the video shoots and the choreography to finance these programs. My classes were all full to date, and there was a growing waiting list. Mister MC said that he wanted to introduce me to a few of his colleagues, definitely a networking opportunity. I sat there with my notepad drafting out the help wanted ad that I planned to put in the paper. Then there was a knock at the door as it opened. I was happy to see that it was Malcolm. His face was normal serious and I smiled as he entered. I had hoped he would pop up at some point. He said he was dropping by to say hello. I asked him to sit, "I wanted to talk to you."

"Shoot."

"I'm going to hire a director for the school; someone to cover the day-to-day stuff here. That will give me more time to network and focus on choreography for any gigs that may come up."

"You're doing that well?"

I showed him my books and my profits from the last six months. I told him that North Star is definitely on the map and I wanted to keep my business moving forward. He nodded in agreement to everything I said. Then he asked if hiring a director would give me a little more down time. I told him that technically it would. He shifted in his seat. I asked him what was on his mind. He stood up; paced a little bit then he sat down again. When he sat down his face was sad, I braced myself for whatever he could possibly say to me. He asked me if I knew what today was. I looked at the calendar February 12th, I said the date out loud, and then I shrugged. He searched my face for recollection of the date. When I didn't get it, he got frustrated with me. He stood up and gave me evil eyes; "I guess it meant more to me than you. I gotta go!" He said, before I could speak he was gone. That whole scene irritated me. I'm not a mind reader; I didn't see the significance in the date. There was another knock at the door but this time the person waited so it definitely wasn't Malcolm.

"Hello Ms. Amber, can I talk to you for a minute?" Toya said, peeking her head in the door.

I nodded but I could tell this little girl was up to something. She had her hair pulled up in a ponytail and her dance clothes on. Something about her said she was being sneaky so I sat back in my chair waiting for her to get to it. She started talking in a mild baby voice. "How are you today?"

I looked at her with nothing but irritation on my face. "Now you know you better find your big girl voice or get out of my office. I don't have time for this!" I said She swallowed, I could tell she almost regretted coming in my office. "I just wanted to know how Andrew's doing."

I stared at her for a minute and watched her squirm in her chair. "What do you mean?"

"He hasn't been at school for two days. I was wondering if he's ok. Is he sick?" She asked trying to make herself look innocent.

"Aren't you the one who's been blowing up his phone? Why don't you know?" I asked

"He hasn't been answering. I thought maybe he was too sick to answer the phone." She tried to smile at me but my glare at her evaporated the smile.

"So, you want me to tell him you're concerned? I don't understand why you would be so bold to bring yourself in my office!" I said

She looked a little startled. I could tell she thought she was going to come in here and slyly tell me that Andrew has been cutting school to get him in trouble and that I would probably be so grateful to her for the heads up. This little girl is always plotting; I thought little boys are supposed to like girls that remind them of their mother and if that's the case, how in the world does this girl remind him of me? But the fact that I know he's been with someone else (oh lord I can't believe I'm thinking this about my baby) tells me she doesn't have as much power over Andy as she thinks she does. Hence, that's probably why she's in my office.

Her face flashed evilness. "I was just concerned about your son. I guess you don't like me so much that you wouldn't even pass on my concern."

"You're up to something, and I don't appreciate you bringing it to my place of business. Whenever Andrew decides to take your calls, you can pass on your concern then. YOU WILL NOT SEND MESSAGES TO MY SON THROUGH ME! Do you understand me little girl!"

She huffed and walked out my office. I was irritated with her but I wasn't a fool. I called the school and got Andrew's attendance records. It looks like sporadically he's been cutting school. I got irritated thinking about how I was trying to give him some space to spread his wings and look what he does. I got a lump in my throat remembering when I cut school. The only time I ever cut was to be with Malcolm. Otherwise, I valued my grades and attendance record too much to ditch. I wondered if he was cutting to be with this mystery girl. I wondered if all the other kids were cutting as well. So many questions raced around my brain, BUT I would not give this girl the satisfaction of knowing that she got Andrew in trouble. Acting on a hunch, I called Derrick's school and asked for his attendance records. He was at school regularly with only a few absent days but they corresponded to Andrew's absent days. I wanted to run out of that office and start swinging on those boys but I didn't want them to exactly respond to me out of fear. Besides, Andrew is almost as tall as I am, there's only so long that fear of his momma hitting him is gonna work. I needed more information and then there was the whole Malcolm scene; I really couldn't understand what that was about.

****

"So I'm gonna need you to do two more videos." Mister MC said.

"How extensive are we talking?"

I was meeting with Mister over the phone since we couldn't seem to tie Malcolm down so that we could meet. He only had to say it once, neither one of us were gonna test him. Besides, I didn't feel all that comfortable around Mister so it made me feel better when Malcolm was there but I haven't seen Malcolm in days. Ever since that afternoon when he came by the office, I haven't seen him. The boys have, but they say he's been in a mood. I don't know what's up with him, but it feels like the old Malcolm may be rearing his ugly head. I tell myself to keep calm and not panic, but I just don't know what to think.

"It shouldn't be more than what you did for the last video. I'll have the music dropped off at the studio, by the end of the week with the video concepts." Mister said

"Ok, sounds good."

I called Mister from home. I decided to pop up on my boys today. When I got to the elementary school, Darryl was in class but Derrick wasn't. Darryl looked so surprised to see me picking him up. He sat in the car very quietly. Darryl is not a quiet child, so his lack of noise led me to believe he was aware of whatever was going on. When we got to the Middle school Darryl kept his head down. In the office, I asked to speak with Tanisha, Sasha, Joseph Wallace, and Andrew Wallace. Of course, JoJo and Andrew were not there. Tanisha and Sasha froze like deer caught in headlights when they saw me. Holding Darryl's hand, I had them step in the hallway with me.

"Somebody better spill it fast! Where are they?" Tanisha and Sasha looked at each other. Neither one of them were going to cooperate. "Fine! I guess everyone's getting in trouble then! I'm signing you out of school; we'll lay you all out." Both of the girls huffed but neither would talk. I signed them out of school. Then they got in the back of the car and sat as quietly as Darryl did. I asked Darryl in the rear view mirror if he knew, and he looked at the girls and then he shrugged. I saw Tanisha rub his back like he did a good thing. I went to Sophia's house and she was coming home at the same time that we pulled up. I was pissed as I explained how they were all sticking together and I needed to go find the other three maybe four of our little posse. Sophia picked up where I left off as I walked out the door. On my way to Oakland High, I decided to drive by the shop and just make sure that they weren't there. When I pulled into the parking lot Malcolm's, Daddy's, Uncle Jeff's, Uncle Frank's, and Poppa's cars were there too amongst other cars. It was a Monday so the shop should be closed. The front door was locked and no one was in the front so I walked around to the back door LJ was coming out as I walked up. He turned red when he saw me. I nodded my head for him to move so I could walk in the door. All the men down to Derrick were in Malcolm's office and the break room. When I stepped in the door they all stopped talking and looked at me. I even spotted Malachi and Sonny amongst the men. "What is going on?" No one said anything they all looked at me like they were all busted. So I repeated myself, I looked at Andrew who looked at Malcolm, who looked back at Andrew. Malachi stood up, but Poppa told him to sit. Poppa inhaled heavily then he exhaled. He announced to everyone we'd be back and they all kind of stayed motionless like they were watching my face for a reaction. Poppa opened the door for me to step backwards. Poppa's eyes were sad but he walked towards his car and I knew he expected me to follow. He got in his car and I got in the passenger seat. "What's going on Poppa? Why aren't any of the boys in school? Why is everybody here? You guys normally meet at Uncle Frank's."

He started the car and drove slowly out the parking lot. A car followed us as Poppa drove slowly to the lake. He parked the car and told me to come on. We sat on a bench facing the lake, Juan and another guy followed us and stood not too far from us with their backs to us.

"In the beginning it was just me and my dad making things happen, providing for our family. We were legit you know, so money didn't come as fast, but it came all the same. Then I met your Nana, I wanted to give her everything, and so I made

moves that allowed me to give her whatever she wanted. My Queen wanted for
nothing, and that made me feel like a man. Then our family grew some of our
children showed more heart than others. Those that had the stomach were promised
that their children would not know this life. You know who I'm talking about?"
"Daddy, Uncle Frank, and Uncle Jeff." I said
"Right!" Then he paused, "what it boils down to is that I have to make sure I keep
my word. I'm not gonna be around too much longer, they found something in my
prostate. Your life especially has been touched the most by all this."
"No it hasn't Poppa!" I said over tears.
He looked around trying to avoid his emotions. "Well, that's the way I see it." He
inhaled and exhaled. "We're pulling out of the game as an entire family. Please
don't be mad at the boys or Malcolm. They've come up with some pretty good
ideas."
"Derrick's only eight."
"And a firecracker! Out of all of my grandchildren and greats, and great greats, your
boys are the brightest! I like watching their minds work. I hate that I won't be here
to see how they turn out."
"Poppa why don't we all know about this? Why do the boys have to miss school to
brainstorm?"
"Sweetheart I've always gone to the men, don't take it personal. Plus during school
is the only time we thought we could pull this off without the women noticing, so
much for that idea." He hugged me. "This summer will you come on the camping
trip? We're going to strongly encourage everyone to come."
"I'm gonna be there!" I said through tears.
He squeezed me tighter. "I'm gonna need you to be strong for your Nana. She's
gonna need you." I cried harder. "Don't cry this is just a part of life. I've had a good
and long run."
As we drove back to the shop, I pulled myself together. I got in my car and left, I
went to Sophia's. I told Sophia everything then I told her we had to pretend we
didn't know. We cried together, and then we took the kids to Bob's.
Tanisha asked me what tipped me off. I told her Toya must think that Andrew's
cheating on her. Sasha and Tanisha exchanged looks. I asked them if they liked her.
Both of them said no immediately, even Darryl said no. I asked why and they all
started talking at once. In the end, they said she brought too much drama. I asked
why they thought Andrew liked her. "Cause she's pretty and she puts out." I cut my
eyes at Tanisha's frankness. "It just happened" Tanisha said realizing what she just
said.
"So who's the other girl Andrew's been with?" Both of the girls dropped their eyes.
****
"Are you avoiding me? Call me, when you get this message." I couldn't put my
finger on the exact malfunction here, but Malcolm and I never seem to last too long.
It's always something with us, but we've never made it three complete years without
breaking up. Who am I kidding, we could barely do two years, and we were doing
great if we made it past a year still together without any interruptions. I'm preparing
myself for the worse but hoping for the best.
"Let's go you guys." I called out to the boys, "Sophia's outside, figure out who's
riding where." The kids hurried outside. Every Sunday we take the kids skating, it
tends to be the highlight of their weekend. They've gotten so good that management
looks forward to whenever we bring them. Sophia and I skate as well, but Ms.

Connie sits over to the side talking to the other parents talking most of the night. It's a good night for me if that little girl Toya doesn't show up.

It's something watching your baby as a teenager. Watching LJ, JoJo, and Andrew flirt with girls is crazy. The boys and their friends break out in one of their extra fast routines; most people leave the skating floor to watch like we did, but a few people stay on the floor. Darryl tries to keep up, which pulls away attention from Derrick being the littlest one out there with perfect execution. They skate forward then at the same time, the all do a fancy turn and they're going backwards. They do all that and more on cue around the floor. On their third lap around everyone is cheering them on when a little girl accidentally skated in the line of fire. Derrick and the little girl collided and fell hard to the ground. Derrick bounced right up, but the little girl looked hurt. My baby rushed back to the girl, he asked her if she was ok all while he continued to apologize for not seeing her. He helped her up and off the skating floor. The little girl was totally embarrassed. Derrick went to the snack bar and he got her a soda. The sweet little girl was very thankful. Her family and friends came to check on her and make sure she was ok. Derrick stayed with her for quite awhile. I was smiling at my little gentleman until he lingered too long. I was getting ready to tell him to focus on skating when Malcolm walked into the skating rink. My mind shifted so many gears and suddenly no one else existed. I saw Bernadette and a ton of cousins following him. All the kids got happy as there were now more of them, the boys came off the skating floor, and Andrew and Darryl introduced their friends to their other cousins. As Malcolm walked towards me, he caught a sight of Derrick talking to the little girl. He stopped and looked at Derrick, and then he looked at me and smiled. When I didn't smile, he caught himself and he went over. He talked to them for a minute then they both got up; the girl went back to her little group; she was giggly. Derrick actually almost had a smile on his face as he skated off to catch up with the other boys. Malcolm smirked and said, "that's my boy"! He said hi to Sophia then he asked her where Richard was.

She looked at me, "Malcolm hasn't been around. I didn't tell him."

"Tell me what?" He said giving me a hug.

"Nothing, where have you been?"

He pulled me on my skates to a bench and then he sat me on his lap. "Working. You miss me?"

"Of course! Working has never stopped you from calling or coming home before." I pouted

"I should've called; can we talk about it later?"

"You're coming home with us?" I felt like my younger self who just wanted Malcolm and nothing else mattered. I spent the rest of the night talking to Bernadette, Tiffany, Penny, Renee, Connie, and Sophia.

When we got home, I told the boys to go to bed. I took Andrew's phone and pretended not to notice that Derrick had gotten that girl's phone number. Malcolm played with the dogs for a little bit. Suddenly I heard one of the dogs yelp, we all ran to the stairs. "What happened?" I asked

"Samara growled at me like she done lost her mind." Malcolm sounded irritated. "Have they acted like that with any of you?"

"Maybe they growled because you've been missing." I said in a smart aleck tone.

"Maybe they growled because you've been missing." He said mimicking me as he came up the stairs. "Goodnight son," Malcolm said to Darryl.

When Malcolm came in the room he looked like he was trying to make, my clothes fall off by looking at them. I waved my finger at him. "You've been M.I.A. for two weeks. You're on punishment." Malcolm blew air. "Whatever!" Malcolm took off his clothes, and I hopped in the shower to freshen up. When I came out the shower, Malcolm was standing there completely naked looking at my birth control pills. I put on my nightshirt, and wondered why he stared at my pills like he was in a trance. "You ok?"

"You really don't remember what February 12th was?" He asked putting down my pills and getting in the bed.

"No," I couldn't remember for the life of me.

He put his head on my stomach. "That's when our little girl was gonna be born." Then he kissed my stomach. Suddenly I felt the impact of Sammy's car and the other car hitting me. I instantly broke out in a sweat. I probably blocked the date out of my mind on purpose. "I want a little girl." He said kissing my stomach again. Suddenly I didn't want him to touch me. "Stop Malcolm!"

He looked at me with completely red eyes. I didn't realize he was crying until that moment. "I want a little girl Amber."

"Malcolm!"

"Amber! Don't tell me no, I can't handle that right now. Stop taking those pills, I'll give you whatever you want." He kept kissing my stomach. "Please!"

"Malcolm! Please stop!" My skin was crawling.

"Amber!" He rested his head on my stomach.

"I can't keep having babies and it will most likely be another boy. Where is this coming from?"

He rested his head on my stomach. "I want my little girl back."

"I hate being pregnant." I tried to laugh him off.

He popped up, "I'm not kidding! I'm very serious little girl!"

"Malcolm can we talk about it later?"

"Fine" he kissed me. Then he laid back down.

We fell asleep with him laying on my stomach. In the morning, he hurried out with the boys as usual. When I reached for my pills to pop my morning pill, they were gone. I sucked my teeth.

Chapter 36

Every night that he's spent the night, he's had a nightmare, and he wakes up in tears. Last night he tried to stay awake as long as he could, and when he finally passed out sure enough, he had another nightmare. Andrew knocked on the door; he asked if Malcolm was ok. Last night was worse than any other night, his scream was so loud, and I had no idea his voice could get that high. Malcolm got up and he threw his arms around Andrew. He was crying very hard and he kept saying, "I thought they got you Drew! I thought they got you!" Andrew looked completely confused, as he's never seen Malcolm like that. I recognized it though, that's the way he was when we came to see him at the police station, and how he erupted when he saw me. Andrew patted Malcolm's back and he told him he was right there. Malcolm kissed Andrew on the cheek and he told him he loved him. Then he went and laid back down, he was sobbing his eyes out. Andrew looked at me in shock. I could tell their relationship turned a corner in that moment. Andy struggles to understand Malcolm cause he's unlike any other male in his life. Andy gave me a hug and kiss then he went back to bed. I did my best to comfort Malcolm the rest of the night, but neither of us got very much sleep. I just don't understand the complete 360, now he wants a baby when before he didn't "want no babies."

****

"You aren't asking me, you're basically telling me this is what's gonna happen. I've got a lot going on right now, and having a baby just isn't part of that." I said opening the car door.

Malcolm stood there with an angry face. "I'm asking you to choose me. I'm asking you to do this with me, and you say no?"

I walked over to the next car. "Baby I've chosen you. We have a family, and now we're both making moves that are too fast to have a baby hanging around slowing us down." I sat in the car, the interior felt like butter. Then I looked back at him, "why do you keep making it seem like money is the issue?"

He grimaced, "money?"

"Yea, you keep saying stuff like you'll pay for it or something like that. When has money ever been the issue with us? I really just don't want to have any more babies."

"So that's just supposed to be it? When do I ever ask you for anything? And I'm not just asking you, I'm begging and you just say no? All these females constantly throwing their selves at me, I'm turning them all down cause I'm with you. What am I supposed to do"?

"Why does it have to be a baby Malcolm? Talk to me, what's going on?" I said watching his face.

He started to speak and the salesman came over with the biggest grin on his face. "Do you see anything you like?"

"I like that one," I said pointing to a black car I sat in moments ago.

"Aw yes, that's our W126 model." Then he looked around as if there was somebody around who didn't need to hear what he was going to say next. "In August, we're getting the new W140 model. It's going to be nicer." He raised his eyebrows at me. "Of course I don't know how much you're looking to spend either?"

Malcolm's face was very serious. "She can have whatever she wants. Tell her more about the car; if she wants it she can have it."

The salesman got very excited and he invited us into his office. He went to the sales manager and they both came back with a brochure. The sale manager was very happy to meet us, but I could see the curiosity on his face. Clearly, we were a very

40

young couple, and we were talking about buying the most expensive car they had to offer. I knew he was coming to make sure we weren't wasting their time, and that the actual sale was legit. As the salesman went over all the available options for my new car, the sales manager chatted with Malcolm. The manager relaxed when Malcolm gave him his business card for Drew's. I chose all my options, and then they haggled back and forth about the final price. Malcolm was firm about the final cost. He told them he would put so much down, and pay the rest upon delivery. They were still making a wonderful commission on the sale. The salesman drove us to the bank in one of their lovely cars. It rolled down the street like butter glides down a pancake. If we hit a pothole on those downtown Oakland streets, you wouldn't know it in that car from the way it glided down the street. Malcolm got a cashier's check for the up-front deposit. The salesman was so excited he talked our ears off.

When we got in Malcolm's car to leave, I kissed him on the cheek and thanked him. Then I asked him to swing by the school. Jade volunteered to work part time as my director, and we just hired an assistant for her to cover when Jade couldn't be at the school. I told Malcolm I wanted him to meet Summer; she was really sweet and on top of her business. Plus I wanted to pop in and see how things were going and verify that classroom space had been blocked off for my rehearsals with Mister MC's people. Jade and Summer were in what used to be my office, but now was Jade's office. When I introduced Malcolm to Summer I could see the recognition in her face, Malcolm appeared to be unaffected by her presence, but he knew I was gonna ask him about it. Jade whispered to me, asking if everything was ok with Malcolm. I don't know how she could see anything different in his face, but clearly, she did. I told her I'd call her. Then I asked Summer if she was gonna be ready to hold down the fort by end of May. She was very confident that she would be.

"Melvin's still sick." Jade said

"The sub is still on standby right?" I asked

"Yep, I just thought you should know." Jade said moving on to the next thing.

On the car ride home, Malcolm was completely silent. His demeanor wasn't its normal hardness he seemed wounded. I didn't say anything either. When we got inside the house, I sat on the couch and I patted the seat next to me. "Talk to me." I said as gently as I could.

He sat down and put his head back. I could tell he was exhausted. He exhaled real big. "I'm ready, I wasn't completely ready before."

"Yea, but you don't even understand what you're asking me to do." I said

"What am I asking you to do other than choose me? I don't see why it's so hard to say yes. I'm not tricking you; I'm not plotting on you. I'm asking us to be on the same page, let's do this together. We were babies when we had Drew. Let's do it for real!"

"You're not plotting on me? What happened to my pills?"

He smiled, "ok except for that. I brought them back though. Give me points for bringing them back; temporary slip into my old self."

"Malcolm we have a family, three of the most amazing little boys."

"Amber!" He bucked his eyes at me.

"Malcolm!" I bucked mine back

"Three boys are not the same as a little girl."

"We've got Sasha and Tanisha, both of them need you."

"Stop playing I'm serious! Neither one of them came from you, it's not the same."

"Where are the nightmares coming from?"

He exhaled, "when you lost the baby, that really hurt me. You were so distant and cold. I really wanted that baby, I felt like that was our little girl." He inhaled and then exhaled, "but I was still young and not looking at how I was affecting you. By the time you warmed up to me again, well you know; I so was wrapped up in my feelings, what I thought I needed. When I came home and saw Leonard laid out like that... I thought you guys were dead. I have never been so heartbroken in my life! I knew that when I got out I was gonna make it up to, you... you chose David." He exhaled again. "I keep seeing her face. She looks just like you or more Andrew actually; the perfect combination of you and me. We'll be driving and she's calling me daddy. Then out of nowhere, a car crashes into me. Sometimes she's thrown from the car, other times its worse. I can't save her! I can't save her!" He said rubbing his head.

"Malcolm maybe you should see Jade. Maybe she can help you. I don't think the answer is to have another baby."

He got irritated. He stood up and stormed around the room. "How could you have TWO babies with that...? That! But for me!"

He was so mad he looked like he was going to fly away. "Malcolm please! Come sit down." I needed him to calm down.

He waved me off and sat in the chair across the room. "I've been good Amber!"

"Yes, you have. But I don't think having another baby is the answer for us."

"You're still choosing him over me!" Malcolm barked

"Malcolm, why are you trying to compete with a dead man?"

"Please Amber! David was never competition for me, and you know it!"

"Ok so why whenever I say no, you keep reaching back to him? You have no idea what I went through with him except for the tidbits you pry from everyone else. Neither one of you appreciated or considered what I went through behind you. Being pregnant with Derrick was the only pregnancy I chose, and even that was because I felt like you forced my hand! Being pregnant and the deliveries have been traumatic. I don't want to do that again!"

"But I'm here; it will be different this time."

"Really, according to whom? Not for me it won't! As soon as my belly gets big, you lose interest. What if I get fat again? On top of every other emotion I'll be going through to be ignored by you is torture when all I wanted was you! You still don't give me all of you, but I'm compromising here."

"How you figure?"

"Seriously? Where were you for two weeks after your nightmares began?" He just looked at me. "Exactly! I'm over here turning a blind eye to the things you do just to have you in my life. You can't go longer than three days!"

"You don't know where I was." He growled.

"I know you weren't with me. I don't even have a key to your place. For all I know someone could be living there. You've just gotten better about keeping your dirty laundry away from me, but I'm not stupid!"

He was quiet for a minute, "what if we got married?"

"Married for what?"

"I'm not going anywhere Amber. I want to have a baby."

"You wouldn't want to marry me without the baby?"

His face turned evil. "Like you just said, married for what?"

"Because you want me!" I sucked my teeth, "you just want me to continue to feel trapped! Why not just be good to me? Why not just love me unconditionally? I don't want to be pregnant! I hate how repulsive I become to you. I don't want my body all out of whack. I'm good with the three we have!"

"I'm not!"

"So what are you saying?"

"What I just said, I'm not!" He said

Everything in my body burst into flames. "Seriously how do you think I'll respond to that?"

"I honestly don't know, but I can't care. I asked you, I begged you, and I pleaded with you! No! No! No! So what does that leave me with? You're not the only female in this world. Since I want a baby and you don't, I'll go have my baby and everybody is happy. You get what you want, I get what I want." He shrugged the whole thing off.

"How is that a solution?"

"Do you see another option? We're at an impasse here. I want; no, I need to have a baby. You don't want to be the one. I get what I need, you get what you need."

"How is that giving me what I want?" I asked

"You get to keep your body!"

"Ok, that's a good idea. I keep my body. You can run around polluting your body. Maybe you'll catch what Melvin's got, and then maybe then and only then, for once in your life you'll slow down. But you don't need to touch me anymore. You just turned me OFF!"

"Is that supposed to be a threat?"

"Oh my goodness no, I would never threaten Malcolm Latour!" I said sarcastically. "It's just a promise!"

He flew across the room; I closed my eyes and told myself not to flinch although my insides were screaming! "You think you could deny me? You cum when I say!" I shook my head no, "not anymore." I inhaled and exhaled; his breath was in my face. "I'll find somebody else. You are not the only man in the world Malcolm."

"Yea, you tried that already. What did it get you? Two kids and your butt kicked regularly."

"And you keep messing with these hoes who only want you for your money and or your clout, when they hit that wall with you they start screwing everybody around you. The big dick is good, but it's not enough!" I said still keeping my eyes closed. Malcolm screamed! "You crave me. You can't move past me!"

"It scares you that I can and you know I will. Yea so, David had some major red flags. I was a kid and I didn't know what to look for. I'm almost thirty, I think I could manage just fine to find someone who loves me, someone to be good to me, and who acknowledges that they don't need more than me." I opened my eyes and looked at him. "I'm a good woman Malcolm, and I don't have to settle for someone who cheats on me and has the audacity to tell me they're going to have a baby with someone else as if I have no choice but to accept it! You won't marry me fine, but I will not accept you having children with anyone else! If you think you can live without me, be my guest!" I stood up, "if you think I'm playing TRY ME!" I walked upstairs. I didn't have to look; I knew he was watching me. I knew he was gonna be downstairs going crazy! I laid on my bed, with my fingers interlocked behind my head looking at the ceiling, listening to him screaming and cutting up downstairs. When he came upstairs, he stood in the doorway. "Did you really just punk me?" I shrugged at him, "call it whatever you want. I don't make idle threats."

He started laughing, "I've created a monster." I nodded in agreement. "This isn't fair Amber!"

"It sucks when the person you love won't let you do what you want to do doesn't it?" I said flatly.

He gave evil eyes, "yes!"

"I guess this makes us even."

"How you figure?"

"I don't get a husband, and you will have to win Sasha and Tanisha over to get your baby girl fix."

****

As we drove on the freeway, I had butterflies. The sun wasn't up yet, but I barely slept anyways. Sophia and I sat up on the phone crying our eyes out, trying to get it out of our systems before we saw Poppa and Nana. Everyone was coming together for this trip. Timothy and Grace flew out with the kids. Andrew asked Poppa to invite Troy and Rosalind so that Tanisha could come and they could all be together. Our caravan to Nana and Poppa's was long. We rode in Malcolm's car, Troy followed us, Timothy followed in a rental car, Richard and Sophia followed, Uncle Jeff and Auntie Lauren followed, Daddy rode with Sonny and Jade. When we got to Nana's, cars were everywhere. Poppa stood at the top of the stairs that led to their house. He explained the directions to the cabins where we were going to all the drivers. He gave everyone flyers with the number to the front desk and directions. Darryl hopped in the car with Timothy. Derrick hopped in the car with Daddy and Jade. Andrew hopped in the car with Uncle Jeff. Malcolm held my hand while he drove. "You gonna be ok?"

I blew air, "I'm really trying to be."

"Anything I can do to help?" He asked

I know he was thinking a foot massage once we got there or telling me a stupid knock knock joke but my mind went as far away from the pain as I could imagine. "I want you to make my eyes cross! I wanna lose my voice! I wanna have to bite you to make sure what you're doing to me is real and not just a dream! I want..."

"WHOA! Ok!" He started blushing, "let me know how you really feel!"

"I feel horrible Malcolm, and the best feeling in the world is being under you." He smiled, "next to you." He kept smiling. Then I rolled my eyes and moaned deep, "on top of you!"

"You keep that up and we won't make it out there." He said still blushing.

"I need you in the worse way right now!" I said licking my lips.

"Stop it Amber!" He said blushing and trying to keep his eyes on the road. "We still got a long drive ahead of us; let's change the subject for now."

"Fine!" I huffed crossing my arms and pouting. Then I smiled, "why do you like having sex with me?"

"We should've kept one of the kids in the car with us." He said grinning

"Tell me!"

"Why?" He couldn't stop blushing.

"I'm curious. You've been with so many, why do you keep coming back?"

"Because I love you!"

"Loving me doesn't equal loving sex with me."

"You curve to me; you fit me like a glove. I know your body like I know my own. I can feel everything that you feel. I know when I excite you, and I know how to excite you. I love how you respond to me. I love when you come after me. Do you remember the first time you did that?"

"Yes! You were bucking so hard the first time I rode you." I smiled at the memory.

"Yea, you were brand new to sex huh. I was sprung then trying to act like I wasn't."

"Remember that time at the drive in?" I closed my eyes at the memory.

"Yea but remember that time right after we realized you were pregnant? You had cooked something for the family." He inhaled deeply, "we could play remember that time over our entire relationship. I was born to be inside you basically."

"Aw! I love you too!" I said kissing his cheek. "It didn't feel weird after Andrew?"

"Naw! Just tighter if that makes sense. After Darryl it was dang near like you were a virgin again."

"I was there! I don't like that part."

"Oh really? What's that like?"

"Sweet torture! But since I knew what's on the other side, I held on until we got there." Then the cloud rolled in, "if sex with me is so good, why did you have to go anywhere else?"

Malcolm's smile dropped. "I knew this conversation couldn't last!"

"Oh come on." I said

"I honestly don't know." He scratched his head.

I stared at him, "you know you're gonna have to do better than that!"

He blew air, "well it's gonna have to do cause I don't know."

"And here I was thinking we were gonna have an open and honest conversation." I rolled my eyes.

"I got one for you." His face was serious. "How long before I went in did you reconnect with David?"

Ok now I didn't want to talk. "What do you mean?" I said shifting in my seat.

"One time I came over and you and Drew were gone. Momma said you guys left early in the morning. You didn't come home until later on. Drew was knocked out when you pulled up to the house." He said

"I could've been anywhere, with Sophia, Cassondra, Tammy, and Stefan."

"Yea, but I checked all those places that day, except for Tammy's, but I would've known if you were at her house that day. I think you said something about the zoo." My face dropped. "What's your question? We weren't together at that time."

"Yea, but that doesn't mean we weren't together when you found him." Malcolm shot me evil eyes.

"I don't know." I said irritated.

"Un huh! You are such a hypocrite! You wanna ask me hard questions, but as soon as I throw some back at you, you act funny."

"Whatever!" I said rolling my eyes.

"Ooh! Ooh! I got another one! AND IT'S GOOD!"

"I don't wanna talk about David!" I shot back.

"Not about David."

I eyed him, "what?"

"What happened between you and the white boy? Whatever happened with him was while we were together." I sighed real loud. "You know you're gonna have to do better than that!" He said mimicking me.

"He taught me to run; he wanted me to go out on a date with him. I told him no."

"Un huh, did you kiss him?"

I took a deep breath, "yes."

Malcolm swerved in our lane. "AMBER!" He looked at me in disbelief.

"Seriously?"

"Yea" I didn't see the point in lying about that part any more. I would never come clean about the rest.

"How could you... Wait a minute.... Hold on! Hold on! You're messing with me aren't you?" He said trying to grab his bearings.

"No I'm serious. I knew you were at home with Yvette and who knows who else. Call it a moment of weakness or curiosity, but I did."

"I KNEW I WASN'T CRAZY!!!!" He started shaking his head. "All of a sudden you were too good for a room at the tele, making a nigga have to put in work just to get some! Females!"

"And you stepped up which I appreciated. Are we done with this question and answer session?"

He laughed an irritated laugh. "You started this."

"Yea, and I don't like the way it's turning on me so let's change the subject."

Malcolm squinted at me, "so it's only ok when I'm getting busted out?"

"I won't go trying to kill nobody; you on the other hand have serious anger issues."

"Please! If you had a gun, and you saw Yvette you wouldn't be tempted?"

"Temptation and execution are two different things."

"Yea right!"

I changed the subject. I suggested that we take a family vacation. Even if it was only to Southern California, we should do something as a family annually. Malcolm was quiet and he had a weird look on his face. When I asked what the look was for, he said he's never been to Amusement Parks and the thought of a family vacation made him feel soft. He said it was bad enough that Andrew saw him cry the other night, now I was trying to turn him into Mr. Mom. I told him Andrew needed to see his human side. He didn't agree, he felt like Andrew saw him in a completely vulnerable state and that that was something he wasn't comfortable with. So then, we debated back and forth about that. I asked him if something happened to me would the boys see him cry. He gave me evil eyes and said it depends. I asked what it depends on, and he said depends on whether he did it or not. I gave him evil eyes, "you're not funny." I didn't like the vibe in the car, I couldn't tell if it was my nerves because of Poppa, or there was an argument we were both trying to unsuccessfully avoid. "Malcolm what's wrong?"

"Nothing, what's wrong with you?"

"I know I'm upset about Poppa. However, is that the only emotion in this car? Is there something else?"

"Nope!" He said with an attitude.

We had courteous conversation after that but neither one of us was very conversational. As we arrived at the cabins, the once empty parking lot filled up quickly. Poppa went to the front desk and told the staff that the Wallace Family has begun to arrive and that they should set up for our breakfast, cause we'd be ready to eat in an hour. The boys were sleeping in tents and the girls were still sleeping in the campers. The cabins were for the parents and grandparents. Daddy opted to sleep in the tent with Poppa instead of sleeping in a cabin alone. Poppa and Nana booked out the whole facility. They had a huge banquet hall where all our meals would be prepared. You could eat in doors or outside on the picnic tables. They had water activities, even jet skis, inner tubes, a banana boat, and so much more. Once everyone were checked in and put their things in their cabins, we all went to the banquet hall for buffet style breakfast. There were twelve chairs to each round table, and the tables had simple settings with water glasses, orange juice glasses, and Mimosa glasses. Poppa thanked everyone for taking time out of their busy lives to come together as a family. He put his arm around Nana; he told everyone that everything was prepaid so to please eat until they couldn't eat any more, and to take advantage of all the excursions provided by the facility to make sure they got their money's worth for the weekend. He told us what time breakfast and lunch would begin and end each day. For dinner they asked that everyone come on time, and dressed up for the farewell dinner, and he warned that especially that dinner would be videoed so if you look crazy it's your fault. Then Monday morning no later than lunch, we'd all say goodbye as we went back to our daily routines. Troy and Rosalind, Malachi and his girlfriend Denise, Jade and Sonny, Sophia and Richard, Timothy and Grace sat at the table with us. The vibe at the table was polite, but everybody was holding back. Denise said that it was nice that our family got together like this, and then she asked if we did this on a regular basis. Everyone at the table said no in unison, which made us all laugh. Jade explained that every summer our grandparents got all of us kids together for their annual camping trip and general time spent with them, but as adults we kind of fell off except for weddings and funerals. Everyone kind of relaxed and started talking. The kids were finished and taking off to go play. Tanisha and Sasha were stuck to each other, and Sasha introduced her to all her cousins. We were laughing and joking at our table when Malcolm put his head down and mumbled a curse. Immediately everyone looked up and turned around to see what rubbed Malcolm the wrong way. Gwen was walking in late as usual, but she was holding Tag's hand. I swallowed, I would've NEVER admitted to kissing him if I thought there was a chance he would be around this weekend. I looked at Sophia who had a big question mark on her face. When Gwen saw Troy, she made a beeline to our table with Tag in tow. I wanted to melt.

"Hello everybody!" Gwen said, the table said a unified hi. "This is my boyfriend Tag for those of you who don't know him already. He's been around our family for years." Her eyes went from person to person. "Amber! I love your hair!" I thanked her. Tag's eyes landed on me, and immediately you saw longing in his eyes. I looked at Malcolm whose eyes were glued to Tag. "And who do we have here?" She said towards Denise. Malachi introduced Denise, while Sophia, Jade, and I exchanged looks. We knew she just wanted to know who Rosalind was, and suddenly it didn't seem like such a good idea for them to be there. "Who's this lovely young lady?" Gwen said to Troy. Troy introduced Rosalind as his beautiful girlfriend that he was very happy with and looking forward to spending a drama free weekend with; everyone erupted into laughter except Gwen.

"How's everyone doing?" Tag asked the table. Everyone said fine and I nodded my head.

"Let's go make our rounds." Gwen said taking Tag by the hand to meet family. Malcolm shot me a look and I innocently smiled at him. I was just as surprised as he was. We all decided to go explore the area. Malachi convinced the men to go one way and to let us go the other. As soon as we were out of ear shot Rosalind asked who Gwen was. I looked at Jade in hopes that she would have a good explanation. Jade struggled with her words for a moment, then Sophia, "she's the black sheep of the family. She's had a thing for Malcolm and your man since we were teenagers. When you take men out of the equation, she really is good people, but it gets murky when there's men involved. Even with her showing up here with Tag is so wrong. I wonder how Uncle Tim is gonna respond when he sees him." Sophia said with a grin.

"Why should Daddy care about him?" Jade asked

Sophia told her about the dinner after my performance in the twelfth grade. I had completely forgotten about that. I hoped for once in his life Daddy would forget a face. I didn't want any problems. As the morning progressed, it got warmer and warmer. By lunch just about everyone had changed into cooler clothes, which also meant most of the men were shirtless. Even Uncle Frank had his shirt off letting his belly hang out. I brought a couple of bikinis and a couple of suits. I was so happy that I packed both, because I didn't want any problems with Malcolm, he doesn't handle jealousy too well. But then again neither do I. I put on my simple black suit, and white shorts. Everyone came out of their cabins in suits and some sort of cover up. As we made our way down to the lake, we saw Sasha and Tanisha playing with Tina in the water. They were having a good time splashing around. We found a spot over to the side and we all kind of laid out in the sun. Grace said she missed California weather. We asked if they would consider moving back. She said they've been talking about it lately, but she didn't know.

"Where are the men?" Gwen said taking her seat next to me.

"They're out exploring, where's Tag?" Sophia said

"Talking with Nana." Gwen said, and then she turned to me. "What did you do to your hair? I want to copy."

"I went to Raynel's and I had her perm it."

"That's where Jade used to work?"

"Yep."

"How do you take care of it?"

"You'll have to rewire your brain as to how you care for your hair; like you shouldn't wash your hair everyday."

She gasped, and then she touched my hair. You could see the surprise on her face when it wasn't dirty. The men came by, Malcolm asked where Tag was, and Gwen told him that he was talking to Nana. Malcolm told the group they should go get him, and then he shot me another look. Their group size had gotten so big it was as if they were collecting men along the way, the men were exploring and marking territory. "I tell you, he is a beautiful man!" Gwen said watching Malcolm walk away

"What do you mean when you say stuff like that?" I said trying to check my jealousy. Everyone looked at Gwen with evil eyes waiting for her answer.

"Just what I said, he's beautiful!" Then she looked at me, "does that bother you?"

I sat up to look her in the eyes. "Coming from anyone else it probably wouldn't, but coming from you it does." I inhaled to calm myself cause I felt my blood start to boil. "You are so disrespectful! I had only given birth hours ago and you were throwing yourself at him. Any time there's any guy around that we aren't related to you're all over him. You don't even stop to consider how that makes anyone feel or how it makes them feel about you. Your dad, Nana, they've tried to slap some sense into you, but given the opportunity you would do it all over again and then you show up here with Tag! What is that about?" I blew air to try to calm myself.

"Gwen I love you! You're one of my closest cousins. And we are good as long as men aren't involved." I blew air one more time. "So let me just say this. This weekend you will not speak to Malcolm or Troy...."

"Or Richard!" Sophia chimed in.

"Right or Richard unless they've spoken to you first, do us all a favor and steer clear of them. This is Poppa and Nana's weekend and I would hate to ruin it by having to put my hands on you! Even though it would break my heart, I'll do it!"

Gwen looked like she was going to cry. A reaction I wasn't expecting. "I honestly don't see what the big deal is. In the end, it's only sex, and it's natural to be attracted to someone. I would never tell you that you couldn't date my ex, especially if it's over. However, if that's how you feel, thank you for saying something."

"Malcolm is not my ex, he's my man. And even if we did break up he's still off limits!"

"What's the big deal about Tag though? You guys never dated." She asked

"Hello! Did you see how the man looked at her! He still wants her!" Sophia said

"He's a man, they may like what they see, so what. I didn't think it was a big deal; him chasing you was so many years ago. You've had two kids and a fiancée since then. I honestly didn't think it was a big deal."

"Ok, I'll give you that but please keep him away from me. I don't want any trouble."

"Clearly I have a different viewpoint on all this, but I have to respect what you're saying as your feelings. I'll keep my comments to myself, and I won't converse with your men. Does that include Sonny too?"

Jade's eyes turned evil. "My husband! Are you kidding?"

She snapped her fingers, "darn!" She said jokingly.

"That's not even funny! If Amber puts fear in you, you don't wanna mess with me!" Jade said laughing in a scary laugh.

Her laugh did kind of send chills through you.

We spent the whole day, girls on one side and guys on the other but we were catching up, and getting to know each other. Our cousin Sharon came over, she ended up having to put Gwen in her place as well. Goodness that girl! At dinnertime, it was buffet style. Malcolm came by me and he whispered that he was missing me in my ear. I smiled, then he said we were gonna have a night to remember. I made him promise as he kissed my cheek. When I looked up Tag was watching us from across the room. I acted like I didn't see him. We all spread out at dinnertime. Malcolm ate with the boys and they were all hooping and hollering over sports. A lot of my family was San Francisco fans so they were all about the Giants and the 49ers. Malcolm and the boys including LJ and JoJo were all about the A's and even though they left us, the Raiders. It was funny watching them for a bit but every time I looked up Tag was looking or looking away. Then I felt another pair of eyes on me, I searched the room until I saw Daddy burning a hole in me. He put his finger up and told me to come as he walked out of the banquet hall.

"Yes Daddy?"

"I see that boy giving you eyes. He don't know how to leave well enough alone."

"Not that I care, but why don't you like him?"

"Any boy stupid enough to keep pressing the issue in front of your father, Uncle, and Grandfather is a red flag."

"Is that why you like Malcolm?"

"I like Malcolm" he paused, "mostly, but he does have my respect. He never really had a family, and he respects ours but you are my daughter first! And that FOOL in there is gonna make me lose it. I see him in there staring at you- No respect! Do you understand?"

"Yes Daddy!" I gave him a hug and a kiss.

When I walked back into the banquet hall Malcolm's searching eyes found me, he smiled when he saw that I was with Daddy. Andrew was over to the side talking to Tanisha and Sasha. I went over to their table and asked why they were over to the side. They smiled and said they were talking about school stuff. I gave them a hug and a kiss each. I told them it made me feel good to see the daughters of my best friends so close to my first born, it's almost like they were brother and sisters. Andrew and Tanisha kind of frowned. Andrew asked if that meant they were like triplets, and I said exactly. They all gagged, Sasha said they were fine just as they were. Andrew shot Sasha a look and she smiled an innocent smile. When they realized I was watching them, they all smiled at me. I didn't know what was going on, but I told them to go join everybody else. Derrick was playing chess with Uncle Frank. I didn't even know my baby knew how to play. He had a smile on his face while he waited for Uncle Frank to make his next move. I asked who was winning; all the men said in amazement that Derrick was. They said he was fast and killer. Uncle Frank kept laughing he couldn't believe Derrick was beating him so easily. Uncle Frank finally made his move.

Derrick smiled real big, "you know you messed up don't you?" Uncle Frank watched in disbelief as Derrick made his final move. Uncle Frank couldn't believe it and Poppa put his hands on Derrick's shoulders telling him that he did well. Uncle Frank demanded a rematch; Derrick told him he'd play again for the fifth time. I never learned how to play that game but it was always pretty serious when Daddy and Malcolm played. I gave Derrick a congratulatory hug and kiss. Then I found Darryl at the other end of the banquet hall with Ryder, little Tim, and Tina, they were talking to the cameraman who was filming everyone. He was showing them how he works the camera etc. Sharon and Grace were right there with them. I gave Darryl a hug and kiss and he actually got embarrassed. After I made all my rounds, I asked the bar keep if he had a special. He didn't know what I meant, I asked him to put together something nice but with a kick, and if I liked it I would come back and ask for his special. He thought about it for a minute, pineapple juice, orange juice, grenadine, a splash of sprite, and rum. I tasted it; I gave him a thumbs up. I took it to the table and I had Sophia taste it. She went to the bartender. I brought one for Jade. Grace said she doesn't mess around; either she drank screwdrivers or straight liquor. Before long, all the cousins were drinking the "Amber special" all the girls anyways. The men swore they needed manly drinks. Malcolm came over and asked how many had I had. I shrugged cause I didn't know, but I felt nice and numb. Malcolm had me wave bye to everyone, when we got to our room, he kept his word. Amazing!

All Sunday afternoon all of us women, or girls sometimes I forget I'm grown so excuse me, did each others hair, makeup, and nails. We were all looking good, and Gwen had been on her best behavior all weekend, everyone was amazed. Tag on the other hand kept looking but he kept his distance. Besides when Malcolm wasn't watching him, Daddy was. Other than that, we had a good time Rosalind and Troy got on the jet skis. So of course that meant Malcolm and I had to do it. Before long, everyone was on the jet skis and the banana boat.

When I walked into the cabin to get dressed, Malcolm stared at me. He asked me to go easy on the drinking tonight. When I asked why, he said he would like to lay with me sober at least one night while we were out there. Then he told me I looked very pretty. I sat on the bed watching him dress. He had on his black slacks and no shirt standing in the mirror debating whether to touch up his hair. I've stared at him millions of times before, and each time I just sit there in Aw! I don't think I've ever seen him ashy, which is a good thing; his skin is so smooth it looks like black velvet. Even his old battle wounds dresses him wonderfully. My eyes slid over each muscle ripple with appreciation. I don't even know when he finds time to workout, but his body shows it. As if he could feel me watching him, his eyes looked at me through the mirror. I could tell he was trying to get a good read on me. He smiled and said I needed to get dressed. I shook my head no. He lightly chuckled then went back to doing what he was doing. I carefully took off my shirt and then I waited.

Without looking at me, he said no, and told me to get dressed. I took off my pants and I leaned back on the bed. He chuckled again saying no. I scooted back to the middle of the bed; he was watching me in the mirror. I looked directly in his eyes, and then I slowly brought my legs up in front of me. I pointed my toes to the ceiling then I slowly let my legs fall into a full split. His face looked angry but I knew better. I had won this battle; I put my finger up and told him to come over. As if he hadn't just told me no twice he moved quickly to me. "You are so beautiful!" I said as I kissed him. This was my show, so I drove.

We weren't the only ones who made it to dinner just in time to be on time. We had to sit where there was space so we ended up at the table with Sharon and her husband Thomas, Gwen, and Tag, my cousin Ryan and his girlfriend Stefanie, Jade and Sonny, Troy and Rosalind. Since everyone at our table were the late ones, we all looked at each other with guilty but satisfied grins. Malcolm didn't even seem concerned that Gwen and Tag were at our table, which was a relief. Honestly, I was too relaxed to care either. The banquet hall was decorated beautifully. Everything was decorated in a beautiful crimson red, gold, and pearl. All except the children's table had real crystal and china place settings. There was a menu card in each setting. Poppa asked us to make our meal selections immediately and then make selections for the children who couldn't read, he gave us a few minutes to do this. He spared no expense there was lobster, crab, shrimp, clams, oysters, filet mignon, and chicken all over the menu. Malcolm pointed to the oysters and smiled at me. Everything sounds so delicious; everyone concentrated hard on his or her selections. Out of curiosity, I went over to the teenager table to see what Andrew's menu looked like. His menu was almost identical except his menu also had simpler choices like hamburgers and hot dogs. Of course my baby had lobster checked on his menu; his choices were all very rich, he was very excited. Derrick who was also at the teenager table selected everything Andrew selected. Andrew told him he would not be sorry.

When I sat down Malcolm was checking on Darryl and chatting with Daddy. Jade and Sonny were still at the table and so were Gwen and Tag. Rosalind and Troy were talking to Sophia and Richard. Tag smiled at me and I smiled back, and then I started talking to Jade. Each table had its own server, and the servers came and took our numbered menu cards away. The bartender personally brought over an "Amber Special" for me. I thanked him and then I told him I was told to go slow tonight. The bartender laughed and said he'll wait for my queue before bringing another one. As I took a sip of my drink, Tag asked if it was good. I nodded yes, and then I started talking to Jade about anything. Poppa said that he and Nana put a picture slide show together of almost all the pictures they had of all of us. He said the tricky part was putting them in order. Then they dimmed the lights and our salads and appetizers came out at the beginning of the slide show. Everyone said aw at pictures of Poppa and Nana's parents. Poppa always looked serious even as a baby. Nana was absolutely gorgeous, pictures of them with their families, pictures of them when they started courting. Poppa was so proud! Pictures of them as the babies started coming. Nana's big belly, their children from babies on; Daddy, Uncle Jeff, and Uncle Frank stood out from all their siblings. It was something in their eyes. I forgot how pretty Gwen's mother was. Gwen instantly fell into tears when she saw her mother. I reached over and grabbed Malcolm and Jade's hands on either side of me cause I knew Momma was gonna come up. Daddy was sitting by Nana, when the first picture showed of Daddy and Momma, Daddy smiled like he was reliving the moment. Momma was gorgeous and she had on this hat that perfectly complimented her outfit. She looked like a model Daddy was pretty dapper himself. I was surprised to see a cigarette in his mouth. I didn't know he ever smoked. Uncle Jeff and Auntie Lauren looked great too. There was a picture of the six of them out somewhere, everyone looked so happy and young. Pictures of Gwen and her brother when they were each born and them as a family, then Sophia, LJ, and JoJo. Malcolm slightly squeezed my hand, I saw him swallow hard as he looked at Momma. Then there were pictures of every camping trip we've ever taken. I immediately recognized the trip when I was pregnant with Andrew. There were pictures of Andrew's first camping trip, Derrick's, and Darryl's. It seemed like they were always snapping pictures, weddings, and even funerals. By the time the picture slide was over, they had this one picture of me with my arms around Malcolm and we were both smiling at the camera. Darryl gasped and yelled, "MALCOLM! YOU'RE SMILING!" That made everyone laugh Malcolm lightly chuckled but I knew I needed that picture! The pictures they showed could sum up my life, they didn't hide anything. They had pictures of Sophia with Charles and Sasha; Sasha's body language stiffened when she saw it. Then pictures of Sophia with Richard and Sasha, it was there clear as day. Sasha turned and looked at her mother; you could see the question mark on her face. Richard whispered to Sophia and I could tell she was agreeing in defeat. I was surprised that with all the pictures they had they barely had any of David and I. The few they were always pictures of someone or something else and we were on the side. They were pictures of Tag and I running when I was trying to lose weight, he and I when I lost weight. Tag and all the cousins running, Tag at our camping trip talking to Timothy a picture of Tag holding Andrew and me holding Sasha. We were talking in that picture; I had no idea Nana took it. Malcolm showed no reaction but I know he didn't like it. Our graduations, high school, and College, different cousins at work. I could go on and on; Poppa and Nana held hands watching the pictures go by. Dinner was served and everyone was talking about the pictures. Gwen was very sad. Jade went over and hugged her and she started crying again. Uncle Frank came over and hugged Gwen. He had a little coldness in his face, but he still was concerned for his daughter. They walked out the banquet hall together. Then Malcolm nodded at Tag, "so he helped you lose weight?"

"Yep, he taught me how to run. He taught all of us." I nodded towards Sharon and Ryan for backup. They both agreed.

"So what do you do now?" Malcolm asked Tag.

"I'm a football coach at CVC, and I still offer personal training sessions."

"And it looks like you used to have a little crush on Amber too."

Everybody dropped their forks. I looked at Malcolm with pleading eyes, but he ignored me. "Does it look that way?" Tag asked

"You saying you didn't?" Malcolm asked then he put a fork full of food in his mouth and stared directly at Tag.

"Amber is a lovely young lady, who wouldn't have a crush on her back then?" Tag said then eating a fork full of his food.

"So what about her today?" Malcolm asked

"Come on Malcolm." I said

He cut his eyes at me and returned his stared to Tag. "She's still very lovely, but I have no idea who she is today."

"Good answer." Malcolm said, "If you haven't noticed I'm very protective over my Queen."

"That's understandable; I would be the same way." Tag said looking at me.

"We're on the same page right?" Malcolm tilted his head at him.

"Got it," Tag exhaled. Then he excused himself and went out the door in the same direction Gwen went in.

"I wish I could have that kind of presence." Ryan said admiring how Malcolm thinly veiled his threat.

"He was born that way." Jade said making light of the situation.

"So Queen Amber when are you going to send me these contracts you want me to look over?" Sonny asked

"Contracts?" Malcolm asked

"I told you, Mister wants to put me on payroll."

Malcolm paused for a minute. Then he shook his head. "Not a good idea. You need to remain as a freelance consultant. Besides you don't want his business affairs tied to your school."

"Ok you guys, I know tomorrow we have to return to our day to day lives. But for right now let's stay in vacation mode." Sharon said

"Here! Here!" Jade said

Malcolm shot me a look like, "you heard what I said." Once dinner was over a live band came and played music for us to dance. My cousin Stacy showed everybody her version of a square dance. Once we got the steps, everyone had a blast.

Malcolm and Sonny sat on the side talking while the rest of us were out on the dance floor. When Poppa and Nana took the dance floor, everybody cheered. Then they slowed the tempo to a nice slow dance. All the couples filled the floor. Then I saw Sasha dancing with JoJo, Darryl dancing with Tina, and Andrew dancing with Tanisha. Everyone was dancing like cousins should dance. But when Andrew saw me looking it was a quick little panic that flashed over his face. I kept watching to see if he would do it again, but he knew I was watching now so he kept his game face on. Troy and Rosalind were dancing right next to them so I let it go. The night was wonderful although Gwen never came back inside. Tag came and got cake for her and took it back to their cabin.

At breakfast, Rosalind was looking for Troy. She said he got a page and he went to use the phone, and thirty minutes later, she still hasn't seen him. I told her he was probably talking business and to come and have breakfast and that he would show up. As Troy was coming in the front door, we all noticed how Gwen came in the back door. Troy tried to look casual, but he looked guilty. Poppa stood up to address everyone and Troy sat next to Rosalind. We all look at him, and he just shrugged and asked "what?" Rosalind looked like she was going to blow. She walked out of the banquet hall. Sophia asked him if he was going to go after her, and he said no she probably went to the bathroom. I was so disappointed in Troy; I couldn't stop staring at him. Then Malcolm redirected my attention to Poppa. Poppa got emotional and then he couldn't finish. Nana stood up and thanked us all again for coming. Then she said this would be our last family trip on this grand of a scale. She explained that they were both getting older and they couldn't keep up with the young ones any more. She said she hoped everyone had a good time and all that they asked was that everyone hold on to the memories as tightly as they could. Jade asked me why that felt like a goodbye. I told her she needed to go talk to Poppa. She looked at the tears in my eyes and she hurried to Poppa. Sharon and all the cousins Aunties and Uncles were right behind her. One by one, Poppa gave them the news. I snapped my fingers at Troy and I told him to go to my friend. He huffed, and then he got up and went to their cabin. I stared at Gwen and she wouldn't look at me. Tag was across the room talking to a cousin. I walked over to Gwen, I grabbed a fist full of her hair, and I took her outside. Gwen wasn't fighting back or even trying to defend herself. She was already crying. "What is wrong with you?" With tears pouring out of her eyes, she stood there waiting for me to hit her. It was like she wanted me to hit her. "Why are you trying to get my friends killed?" She stood there crying with her eyes closed waiting for me to hit her.

"She's acting out because of her mother. You beating her up would feel better to her than having to deal with what's going on in her head that's why she sleeps around and constantly wants every man's attention. None of that will bring your mother back Gwen and you constantly hurt people by being this way. Rosalind's never done anything to you. And now there's another broken heart behind something she doesn't even know about." Jade said coming out of the banquet hall. "You really need to talk to your father. Ask him the hard questions you need answers to. Doing stuff like this is gonna get you killed. Maybe that's what you're hoping for, but you don't do this to family. And Rosalind and Troy are family."

Andrew and Tanisha came flying out of the banquet hall. I asked them where they were going. Andrew explained real fast that they were leaving and he was making sure Tanisha had everything she needed. Tanisha was crying very hard I hugged her, she looked at Gwen, and then she spit at her. I wanted to tell Tanisha that she shouldn't act like that, but I couldn't blame her honestly. Andrew put his arm around Tanisha's neck telling her it was gonna be ok as they walked away and she cried her eyes out. I looked at Gwen and she was beet red, "you have to live with yourself knowing what you did to that little girl!" I said

Chapter 37

"I LOVE THIS CAR!!!" I screamed as I flew down the freeway. I picked up Sasha and Sophia to take them for a ride with Rosalind, Tanisha, and I down the highway. Rosalind and Troy broke up, and Tanisha took it very hard. She became introverted like Jade did so many years ago, except her outlet wasn't actually school. She just kind of pulled away from everybody. Richard and Sophia came clean on the drive home from the camping trip. I don't know what was worse for Sasha, finding out that her parents had lied to her all these years or once she finds out her father really isn't dead, but he's moving to Southern California and would no longer be a part of her daily life. Without her best friend to help her through her emotions, Sasha was breaking down at home. Andrew worries about both of them and neither one of them wants to see him or talk to him. I tried to explain that they just needed some space but Andrew didn't get it. So unfortunately, that meant I was seeing more and more of Toya. I'm not a religious person, but dealing with that girl made me look up to the heavens and ask what I did to deserve her in my life. A couple of times Andrew has broken curfew running behind her, and he's always fighting somebody. She is completely bad news. Therefore, when Malcolm said he was taking the boys, I brought my new toy out and convinced everyone we needed to run away. We didn't even know where we were going just that we were getting away.

"Hey" Tanisha said to Sasha

"Hey" Sasha said sadly back

"You ready for school?" Tanisha said dryly

"I guess so, you?" Sasha said in a dry tone back.

"I guess so." Tanisha said then she sighed.

"Light bulb!" I said excitedly, "let's go school shopping, my treat!" I said hoping that would cheer them up.

Sasha forced a smile, "ok."

"I don't want new clothes." Tanisha said full of pain.

"Why not baby?" Rosalind asked already hurt by her daughters tone.

"I don't want anyone looking at me." She said plainly.

"People look at you when you have new clothes?" Rosalind asked

"Guys do! You change your hair, they notice! You start developing, they notice! They notice everything but how they hurt you! I HATE THEM! I HATE THEM ALL! I just wanna be left alone!"

Sasha and Sophia reached over and hugged Tanisha as she cried very angry and hurt. "Tanisha sweetie, not all guys are like that."

"No disrespect Auntie Amber, but Malcolm cheats on you all the time. It's like you've turned a blind eye to it, but I know it hurts you. Andrew can say all he wants about Malcolm but he's just like him. And he can't even see it."

"What Andrew does affects you?" I saw the shocked look on Sasha's face in the rear view mirror.

"I'm a female and I have to sit back and watch it. It's sickening to watch." Tanisha said

"Ok, by the look on Sasha's face I thought there was more to the story." I glanced at her in my mirror. Sasha was shaking her head no. Tanisha blew air and turned her head. "What does that mean when you guys do that?"

Tanisha opened her mouth, but Sasha said "nothing!"

"Is somebody in trouble? Do we need to be worried? "Sophia asked Sasha.

"Everybody's fine Momma, we just have stuff that's between us." Sasha said

"Un huh!" I said, "but I would still like to buy you guys some clothes or something. It doesn't have to be extra, extra. Is that ok with you Ms. Tanisha?"

"So where we going?" Sophia said

"Corte Madera!" I said, now armed with a destination I stepped on the gas. The car felt like it floated. I liked the feeling of pushing this car faster and faster. As we drove through Richmond on the freeway, I found myself thinking about David. Suddenly I could see his face clearly, and he was my sweet and gentle David, not that monster that used to hit me. Although I slowed to pay the bridge toll, it was like all of a sudden I was alone. So Malcolm wasn't doing a good job of being discreet after all. I don't blame Tanisha for being angry; it would've angered me to see stuff like that at her age. I needed to decide what to do with that tid bit of information. When we walked in Macy's juniors department immediately, Sasha went from rack to rack. It took her no time to acquire a nice little pile of clothes to try on. Where Tanisha rejected everything Rosalind held up. The good part was that the girls were talking with their moms while they went from rack to rack. Everyone was crying and communicating. I waited outside the dressing room while Sasha and Sophia were inside. Everybody had a daughter but me. I did feel a little left out, and yes, it was different when the child isn't your own, but I really didn't want to be pregnant AGAIN! My Momma was with me each time, even when she wasn't feeling well. I couldn't do it again without my Momma. The thought of being pregnant or the first two years without her sound completely ridiculous to me. Without Momma who's gonna support me? Malcolm says he will, but I don't trust him. The first sleepless night and I bet he's out the door. I told myself to stop being ridiculous, I said no more babies and I meant it. Matter of fact as a thirties gift to myself I'm gonna get my tubes tied. Even though I see the blessing in it now, when he wouldn't let me marry David, that broke my heart, now it's his turn to bleed. Although I wouldn't put it past him to defy me.... He better not!

I was surprised to see Tanisha come with a pile of clothes, she looked happy as she headed to the dressing room. Rosalind plopped down next to me; tears were streaming down her face. I waited for her to share but only if she wanted to. She put her head on my shoulder. She told me that Tanisha said she wanted to wear boy clothes. She said they argued about it, but their compromise was that Tanisha wouldn't cut her hair off or do anything overly masculine as long as she could wear baggy clothes. She told me that she and Tanisha had been having this struggle for a long time. At first, it was little things here and there. Then Benjamin's visit didn't help the situation at all. She said for a minute, things were good and Tanisha was actually interested in a little boy. I asked her who, and Rosalind gave me a "you know who" look. I felt very bad when I asked her if Tanisha was the other girl. She nodded, I felt horrible, and I wanted to go upside my son's head. Rosalind assured me it wasn't Andrew's idea. She said it was all Tanisha, but Tanisha didn't want the whole relationship and then enters Toya. We both rolled our eyes, that child was a pain. I asked why she didn't tell me before, and she said Tanisha swore her to secrecy. Rosalind assured me that Andrew was a gentlemen and he was actually the only calming factor in Tanisha's life for the longest time. Then she told me that Troy was trying to come around. It took him a minute to realize what he had done, but it's been really upsetting to Tanisha because she doesn't understand why Rosalind would forgive him. I told her it might be a good idea for him to continue to lay low for a while, just in case Uncle Frank finds out about him and Gwen she didn't want to be around for that. "You don't mess with the Boss's woman or daughter!" Rosalind said

"Exactly!" I said

****

"Andrew I promise if I have to come down to this school one more time cause you put one more stupid kid in the hospital, I swear!"

"It wasn't my fault!"

"It's never your fault!"

"You don't understand momma!"

"What? I don't understand what?"

"They're always testing me! Calling me names." He said

"I wouldn't understand? Even to this day people say the stupidest stuff to me. They want me to identify myself or prove who I am. If you guys didn't all look like me, people probably wouldn't believe we were related. I still don't get credit for being your mother. Tell me what I don't understand."

"You don't understand what it's like to be Malcolm's son. People are scared of me!"

"So.... You help that by putting people in the hospital?" I asked sarcastically

"When people are scared they do stuff out of fear. They wait 'til JoJo and Hubby's not around as if they think that this time their ambush is going to be the one to put me down. What am I supposed to do? Let them jump me?"

"No"

"Then what? I'm not walking around starting stuff, or looking for a fight."

I thought about it for a minute, this boy! "So the boy you fought today, he tried to jump you? But you only fought him?"

Andrew gave me a busted look. "No!"

I smacked him upside the head. "Today was about that girl wasn't it?" He put his head down. "Andrew she's bad news. What girl makes you fight this much over her? She's gonna get you hurt; right now these little boys are bringing their fist. Once they realize no one can beat you, they're gonna bring something else."

"I hear you momma. But I care about her."

"Why?" He opened his hands and closed them. "If you ask me, she's just a replacement for whoever the mystery girl is. What do you think?"

"I'm not gonna tell you who, momma I promised."

"Ok, but tell me about her."

His face got sad. "She..." He searched for words. "She's mad."

"At you?"

"No," he exhaled. "Maybe.... I don't know. I thought she loved me."

"You don't think she loves you now?"

"She says she does, but she's so mad. She doesn't want to be my girlfriend. I wouldn't need anybody else if she wanted me. It hurts you know?"

"Did you do something to make her mad?" I asked trying to mask that I knew who he was talking about.

"I don't know. She's mad about a lot of stuff. She talks to me still, but she doesn't want to be with me. So I'm with Toya, at least she wants to be with me."

"Are you faithful to Toya?"

"No, but that's because she does stuff. She makes me mad! So to get back at her I do stuff."

"Why not break up with her?"

"We break up all the time. When we get back together she's good for a little while."

"Why do you get back together with her? There are other girls."

Andrew smiled at me, "cause I care about her."

"I don't like her Andrew."

"I know momma."

****

"Derrick and his little girlfriend are so cute!" Sophia said
"Yea, yea!" I said unenthusiastically. "At least she's no Toya. She's actually quite nice. She's respectful when she calls, and they're not on the phone all hours of the night either. I like her." I told Sophia as we watch Derrick and Raquel skate by.
"Uh oh! We got an audience." Sophia said pointing out Toya who was watching us from across the floor. Toya was watching us as she stood by the skating floor entrance. "Something is wrong with that little girl." Sophia said
"What little girl?" Malcolm asked as he walked over. I pointed Toya out. "What's wrong with the Hershey kiss?"
"Everything, take your pick." Sophia said.
Bernadette and the cousins all said hello then disbursed through out the skating rink.
The DJ announced that the next couple of songs would be for the couples. Andrew grabbed Toya's hand and pulled her out on the floor. Darryl, Tanisha, and Sasha came by us. LJ and JoJo were skating with girls too. Malcolm said hi to Tanisha and she said an unenthusiastic hi back. We watched the floor as the couples skated round and round. Toya wanted Andrew to twirl her, you know put on a show. It angered her that we weren't watching them and going ooh and ah! When the couple skate was over Derrick and Raquel came off the floor, and she came over to say hello. Derrick introduced her to his dad, I looked at my baby standing there looking all proud, Malcolm was surprisingly nice to Raquel, we were all impressed. I think he was more or less touched that Derrick viewed him as worthy to be introduced; Andrew never introduced Toya, but could you blame him? Toya hit Andrew on the arm and pointed in our area. Andrew shrugged and went back to talking to LJ. Toya stormed away, she went over to her little group fussing and carrying on. Tanisha and Sasha were watching her like a hawk. I heard Sasha say to Tanisha that Toya was going to try something. Sophia looked at me because she heard it too. Derrick was thoroughly into his conversation with Malcolm and Raquel, he wasn't aware that there was anything else going on. Raquel excused herself and skated off to the bathroom. Sasha and Tanisha popped up and followed her in the bathroom. Sophia looked unconcerned; she said Toya wouldn't be that stupid. Obviously, she doesn't know the monster that is Toya. As the girls walked out of the bathroom one of the cousins came to hug Tanisha and Sasha, as they were introducing Raquel, Toya and her group of girls walked past. As soon as Tanisha saw them coming she got ready. Sure enough, Toya pushed Raquel. Poor Raquel wasn't prepared at all, and being on her skates she fell into Sasha, but Sasha caught her and they fell. I was on my way; I hopped that rail so fast. Tanisha connected a fully charged left to Toya's face. Toya's whole body flew backwards. Her friends started to go for Tanisha and the girls. Suddenly the skating rink came alive. I grabbed two little girls, one by her hair and I told them to back up. These little girls called their selves looking like they were going to come at me when the little one in the back got their attention and told them to look around. Suddenly this group of six girls, well now that Toya was laid out five girls, realized they were surrounded by almost the entire skating rink. The manager came to my side and asked what was going on. Derrick was helping Sasha and Raquel up; the anger in his face was scary. I explained that Toya tried to start a fight. The manager asked Toya and her friends to leave immediately. Andrew was with Derrick and they were talking, Derrick was furious as Raquel explained that she didn't know what happened and Sasha filled in the blank. Andrew looked at

Love Is Just Enough

Tanisha with sad eyes as her eyes were still fixed on Toya as if somehow that girl was gonna try something else. Tanisha had laid her out with one punch, and I know it was killing her not to go in and finish her. A couple cousins asked Derrick if he wanted them to handle Toya for him. Andrew and Derrick kept going back and forth about it. I couldn't hear their conversation, but I could tell by their demeanor Andrew was trying to calm Derrick down and Derrick wanted vengeance for Raquel even though Toya was pretty messed up from that one hit from Tanisha. Andrew walked outside with JoJo and Hubby, more than likely to check on Toya. Skating resumed and Malcolm sat back watching me. Something was up but he wasn't saying anything, he was watching me. For whatever reason, in that moment I didn't feel like dealing with Malcolm, so I skated on the floor with Darryl the rest of the night, while Malcolm sat back watching me with his serious face.

****

"Thank you for getting this fixed before everyone arrived." I said to Summer.
"I can not apologize enough, I am so sorry." She said
"How is your family holding up?"
She sighed, "We will be ok, thank you for asking. My mother said my grandmother will be coming home very soon so we're excited that she's pulling through."
"That's good to hear." I said, I waved to Jade and then I headed to the larger classroom in the West wing of the school. A couple of Mister MC's regular dancers were waiting inside the classroom with Melvin. I had two weeks blocked off for rehearsals in this classroom; I guess because of the distraction with her personal life Summer confused the bookings and she booked a hip-hop dance instruction class in here. Once we realized the error, Summer scrambled to fix it. She was so stressed that I think her head was about to blow off. Not to mention whenever she sees Malcolm she becomes clumsy and nervous. I asked him if he knew her, and he said he's seen her before but he wasn't dating her if that's what I was getting at.
A few minutes later, Mister and the rest of his dance crew arrived. As we were warming up, Malcolm walked in the room. He didn't speak to anyone and he pulled a chair to the opposite side of the room to watch us. I broke down the routine to them, and then we went through the routine a few times. Once I was comfortable with their execution, we went over placement. Mister had Sophia cater lunch for us. Malcolm didn't touch the food, and he wasn't conversational. He just watched with a serious face quietly the entire time. Something was up but he wasn't saying. When we were done for the day, Mister was telling me how much he enjoyed today's routine. Malcolm came over and gently put his hand in the small of my sweaty back. It made me stop talking. I looked at Malcolm and he asked who the artist for this song was. When Mister said some name I hadn't heard before, Malcolm asked where he recorded. Mister told Malcolm that the rapper lived out towards Fairfield so he recorded in Malcolm's Vallejo studio. Malcolm was taking mental notes, but his face was beyond serious. Then he asked me what the contracts looked like on these two videos, cause I may have to decline the next job that we would start next week. I felt a little disappointed but I figured it was for a good reason so I told him I would ask Sonny and Ryan to look at them. Mister put his hands up and asked what was going on. Malcolm told him if the artist is who he thinks he is, I couldn't work with him. Mister got irritated and looked at me. "So he speaks for you?"
I was surprised he went there. I couldn't believe he put me on the spot like that. Malcolm looked at me, waiting for me to answer Mister. "When hasn't he? I only know you because he brought you here. If he says no, it's for a good reason. I trust Malcolm." I heard myself say.

"Look Brad, it's nothing against you personally but some of your artist have their own agendas and you're gonna need to clear your requests through me before presenting them to Amber, if you don't choose to go work with someone else."

"Some of my artist? What that mean?"

"Exactly what I said; you can choose to continue to work with Amber, but not all of your artist can be around my woman."

"Amber's your woman? I could have sworn..." He caught himself. Malcolm waited for him to finish. "Excuse me." He took a deep breath. "Look I've already budgeted my video expenses according to Amber's prices. You're messing with my money, you sure you wanna do that Malcolm?"

Malcolm put his hands out like he was weighing something. "Your money... My Queen..." He looked Mister in his eyes to make sure his point was felt. "Family comes first! If this presents a problem for you, we will refund whatever you've paid for this project, and cut our losses now or... You can finish rehearsals here, and rely on the skill of your dancers on the actual day of the shoot. But Amber will not choreograph the next video for this specific artist or any others without my approval." One of the hardest things for me to do, was stand there quietly while they discussed my business. It's not like we were talking chump change here. We were talking about over fifteen thousand at least for both videos. I figured it had to be serious for Malcolm to do all this but the hardest part, which I know I shouldn't be focusing on, is, even this fool knows about one of Malcolm's sidepieces? Is he only exercising discretion in keeping her or them away from me? This is getting old.

Mister stood there trying to read Malcolm. "I need to look at some numbers." He said angrily. "I'll page you." Then Mister started walking away.

"Oh yea and Brad", Mister stopped and looked at him. "Don't let me catch you around here without my prior approval.... You understand!" Mister continued walking out the door.

"What was that?" I said as soon as Mister was gone.

"What part?" Malcolm asked because he knew I heard the reference.

"First my business, and second the hoe?"

"The guy's name is Ricky." He waited to see if the name jogged any memories. Of course, it didn't so I waited. "Back in the day we got the best of him. Once he figures out who you are, if he does, there's gonna be problems. You can't work with him. Whether or not Brad knows is the question, and the way he's slithering around here these days I don't know where he's at, but I'm gonna review the tapes from the Vallejo studio to be sure. You don't need Brad's money anymore; you've done a few other videos. You got a good name behind you, build on that plus, I'm still talking you up. You don't need him, he needs you. Plus you are working way cheaper than you need to be."

"Fine and second?"

"What about it?" He said instantly getting irritated.

"Who's the hoe?"

Malcolm exhaled real big. "Nobody!"

"Nobody? Seriously that's how you gonna play with me?"

"Nobody worth all of this."

"How do you manage to be so good about business, but like Troy you get caught up as soon as a female opens her legs?" He just looked at me. "You are getting on my last nerve. If one more person comes talking about what they know for a fact about you! Got me up here declaring that I trust you with my life, and then I gotta hear about some other females!" He didn't say anything he just looked at me. "Now you have nothing to say?"

"What do you want me to say?" He said looking at me. I sucked my teeth and rolled my eyes. I grabbed my towel and my bag. "Is my baby girl still off the table?" He asked as soon as I reached the door.

I squinted my eyes at him. "Why would anyone have a daughter with you just so she could turn out like Gwen? One in my family is good enough." I knew my words did their job and hit him in the heart. I let the door slam as I walked out of the classroom.

I went to the office and I told Summer to tentatively release next week in the classroom and that, I'd confirm tomorrow. Malcolm walked in the office fast paced with his pager in his hand. He picked up the phone and dialed the number. When the person picked up, "what's the 911... Are you sure... Where is he?.......... I don't know... I don't know... I told him not to be so stupid!" Malcolm growled, "I don't think I can fix this... I know! I know! .... Whoever finds her first tells her. Alright!" Malcolm wasn't hanging up the phone good before he was telling me we needed to talk. Summer's eyes were big as she tried to pretend like she wasn't watching Malcolm. We left the school and he told me he was gonna follow me home. As we pulled up to my house, I could hear commotion coming from the backyard. It was definitely the sound of girls arguing. As I walked around the corner, I saw Toya with her finger in Derrick's face. He looked beyond angry and Raquel was pulling him away. He had a fed up look on his face. He pulled his arm away from Raquel, slapped Toya's finger away, and in a very defeated manor started choking Toya. Toya's whole reaction showed she was surprised. Raquel begged him to let go, Derrick looked like he had been pushed beyond his limit. Malcolm's voice boomed telling Derrick to let Toya go. Raquel didn't realize we were there and she jumped. Derrick was so gone he didn't hear Malcolm. I walked over to Derrick because honestly, although I didn't want my sons putting hands on any female, if there ever was one, I could understand the sensation with, it's her. I lightly slapped Derrick, which surprised him, and he dropped Toya.

"Where's Drew?" Malcolm asked

"I don't know." Derrick said calmly as he proceeded to hug Raquel who was a mess about the whole scene.

Darryl came running to the door, and the dogs came out. Raquel's reaction to the dogs explained why they weren't out here in the first place. The dogs didn't like Toya, and merely tolerated her presence when Andrew brought her around. Raquel was clearly scared of the dogs otherwise, I don't think Derrick would've kept them off of Toya.

"What's going on?" I asked dryly

"Your son attacked me!" Toya said holding her neck and crying.

"Why?" I asked

"He's crazy!" She said

"Like a fox!" Derrick said sarcastically

I looked at Raquel and I asked her what happened. She said she and Derrick were sitting on the front porch waiting for me to come home. Then Toya came looking for Drew. She said Derrick wouldn't even acknowledge her, so Raquel told Toya he wasn't home. She said Toya went away for a little bit then she came back. But Derrick had them go in the back yard because he didn't want to deal with Toya. Derrick was showing Raquel how to play basketball when Toya walked back there asking for Drew again. Raquel said she told her again that he wasn't home yet. Then

Toya started going off talking about Drew was home and they were covering for him with some other girl. Toya tried to push past Derrick to go in the house and he told her she couldn't go inside. She got mad and started cursing Derrick, he didn't care, or listen until she acted like she was going to get in Raquel's face. Derrick pushed her and told her to leave, and then she put her finger in his face saying what she was gonna tell Drew and as soon as Derrick wasn't around all the things she was gonna do to Raquel as she beat her up. "Derrick snapped and then you guys came out of nowhere!" Raquel said

"Son you couldn't think of another way to handle this female?" Malcolm asked

"That's not a female!" Derrick barked. "I don't know why Drew keeps her around! I can't wait until he breaks up with her for good!"

"Drew and I are in love! He's gonna kick your butt when he finds out what you did to me!"

"Wait a minute!" Malcolm's voice boomed again. "You honestly think Drew would turn on his brother for the likes of you?"

Toya's eyes got big, and she started shaking; Malcolm did look and sound scary, her reaction was warranted. "Yes, he loves me." She said in a real low voice.

"Listen to me little girl! The day my son turns on my son, is the day you had better run for your life! Let me find out that they even looked at each other cross and you had something to do with it! That's it for you!"

Toya's mouth fell open; she started crying. "But he attacked me!"

"Did he invite you back here?" Malcolm said

"Ms. Amber, please!"

"Girl if you don't go home. Oh and Malcolm, I think that promise should include Raquel. I don't care if I can prove it or not, the day something happens to Raquel that's your butt!" Toya got up and ran away crying. "Darryl baby, please page your brother for me. Tell him to come home, he's probably with JoJo and LJ."

Raquel stood there wide-eyed trying not to stare at us. "You ok?" Derrick asked her. She shook her head yes. He opened the door so that she could go inside. My rule was no girls in the house when I wasn't there which is why they had to stay outside and then absolutely no girls upstairs even if I was there.

Darryl was sitting at the table working on his homework. I gave him a kiss then I answered the phone. It was Andrew, I asked him where he was, and he said the library. I rolled my eyes and said un huh. Then I told him he needed to come home because Derrick just choked out Toya, and then Malcolm threatened her. Andrew laughed; he thought I was playing. When I assured him I wasn't, he said he would be right home. LJ dropped him off about fifteen minutes later. Andrew asked what happened; Raquel told him the whole story. Then he looked at Malcolm, "I know she can be difficult but, there's good in her too."

"You need to let that one go son, she's no good." Malcolm said. Andrew remained quiet. "Whatever Drew, I guess you're gonna have to learn the hard way. The only one that you should turn your back on family for should never make you." Andrew nodded his head but he didn't say anything. Malcolm exhaled then he reminded me that he needed to talk to me. We went upstairs and he closed the door. "When was the last time you talked to Gwen?"

"Not since the camping trip, why?"

"She's pregnant and not telling your Uncle who by. Naturally, everyone's assuming it's the white boy but why keep that a secret if it were true. I'm going to have to have Troy lay low until the baby comes. Troy and Rosalind were on the road to reconciliation. They're gonna have to stop that for now. I'm gonna need you to find out as much as you can. If that's Troy's baby this will not end well."

"Troy is grown, why does this involve you or me?"

"I know Troy can be a knuckle head, but he's my closest family member."

"But we told him to leave Gwen a lone. He made the choice."

"You wouldn't plead for Sophia?" He asked

"Of course I would!" I said

"So why all the attitude?"

"I guess I'm just mad at you so I don't want to agree with you." I said exhaling. "I'll call Gwen and see if she tells me anything."

"Hold on, why are you mad at me?" I could tell he was offended.

"I feel like we're back in high school. I'm looking the other way and you're running around with whomever. I don't like having to be faithful while you run around with whomever you like. This isn't working."

"Oh come on Amber we went over this. Every year or so we gonna argue about the same thing?" He said throwing himself on the bed.

"I can't help how I feel." I said

"You're the one who will have anybody's baby! Anybody's but mine!"

"I had yours first! And I do recall getting beat down for it too. Being pregnant is a head trip I don't want to go through ever again!"

"How did Darryl happen then?"

"I wasn't on the pill, and things were out of control. I don't even know when he happened. I have an idea, but I'm not certain. It wasn't planned!"

"Imagine," he put his hands up to paint the scene. "Our little girl! Your credit cards will say Mrs. Latour! You could have as big of a wedding as you want; your Daddy walking you down the aisle looking all proud."

"We don't need a baby to have that. We could have that now."

"Not until I know for certain I'm getting what I want."

"I don't wanna get fat again!" I whined.

"You didn't get fat with Derrick you were all stomach."

"Yea, but I also forced myself to stay active and finish school. I would make myself sick worrying about when Troy was gonna pop up at the house."

"But my point is each pregnancy is different and you popped right back in shape after them. You could do it if you wanted to."

"Malcolm as much as I love you I don't want to have any more babies. I really don't!"

"So again what's your point? He got up angry. "

"Just because I won't have another baby doesn't mean it's ok to cheat on me."

"You can't have it all Amber! I have feelings too."

"Maybe we should break up."

His whole body tightened. "What?"

"You heard me." I was frustrated, "that way you can see whomever you like. And you wouldn't have to hide it."

"And what about you?" He asked

"Well look at that, I'd be free to see whomever I wanted too." I smiled.

He stared at me for a long time. He pointed his finger at me. "Keep playing!"

"I'm not playing, I'm serious!"

"You're mine! The only person who's ever belonged to me."

"But you don't belong to me!" I could feel my eyes tearing up; I shook my head trying to stop the tears. "Why do you need a baby so bad?"

"I already explained all that. We're not breaking up so you can get that out of your head. You're right; I could stand to exercise more discretion. Got it!" He said like he was done with the conversation.

"You can't make me stay with you if I don't want to be with you."

"The HELL I can't!" He had that same crazy look on his face he had when he was in prison. "Is there someone you have in mind?"

"What?"

"Last time you couldn't wait to get away from me so you could lay up under David. I'm asking who's the guy now." He said giving me evil eyes.

"There's no guy Malcolm but I want someone who views me as all they need. You're always reaching over me. Beyond me, how do you think it makes me feel? It's just in my face, I'm not good enough for you, and that hurts." The look on his face scared me. I got up and went to the bathroom. I had nervous energy I needed to do something with before it made him mad. I put lotion on my hands as an excuse to rub my hands together but I was sweating now. When I came out the bathroom, he went right back to staring at me. I stood there rubbing my hands together, and he kept staring.

I reached over the bed and I picked up my cordless phone. I dialed Gwen's number she answered on the second ring. I asked her how she was, and she said she was good, once she realized it was me I could hear excitement in her voice. She kept apologizing to me for the way she behaved on the trip. She said she's been in therapy per my suggestion. It's been really helping her sort out her feelings and understand why she does the things that she does. I told her that was good. Then she said that she's not seeing Tag anymore, and that it was obvious that he still has feelings for me. I told her that was good and she deserved better. Then she told me about the new guy she was seeing, she said he's a good guy. I asked her if she heard wedding bells. And she said definitely, and then she told me she was pregnant. I did my best to sound surprised. I asked her how far a long was she. She said they told her about six weeks, I silently exhaled. I asked if there was any chance she could be further along. She paused, and then she assured me it wasn't Troy's baby. I asked her how she could be sure. She said they didn't sleep together, she said she gave him head and that was all. I sighed in relief. Malcolm was still sitting there staring at me. I put my hand over the mouthpiece and I said it couldn't be Troy's baby. He shook his head ok, but his expression didn't change. Gwen was so excited about her baby. Her plan was to have her Dad meet her boyfriend first then they'd tell him, but the cat got out the bag. So now, she's waiting for him to calm down before they meet. We talked for a while; Malcolm sat there the entire time watching me. When I got off the phone, he kissed my forehead, and then he walked over to my dresser. He picked up my birth control pills then he looked at me. "I'm taking these and you better not refill them. When you're ready call me."

"What?" I said in disbelief.

"You heard me. I've tried to be nice about it. This is what I need; I know it's selfish and all that. But I told you, and you're not listening so I have to take matters into my own hands."

"You can't do this to me!"

"All I'm doing is taking your pills. You call me when you're ready."

"I don't have a choice?"

"You get to choose when." He squeezed his hand and my case crumpled like paper in his hands. Then he put it in his pocket.

"This is the club all over again!"

"You get to choose when. That's the difference."

"Malcolm please!"

"What do you expect me to do? You're over there talking crazy! We're not breaking up! We're never breaking up!"

"You're bullying me!"

He thought about it for a minute. "I guess I am." Then he smiled

"Malcolm!"

****

"This is Travis," Sophia proudly said

"Nice to meet you." I said

"Likewise, Sophia talks about you two all the time." Travis said

"Amber and Jade are the closest things I got to sisters." Sophia said proudly.

Travis looked at his watch. "I gotta get back over to the office. I'll see you later on tonight?" He said giving Sophia a kiss.

"Definitely, Sasha's making your favorite for dinner."

He smiled real big, "I can't wait! It's nice meeting you two."

Jade and I waved bye. "How did you meet him?" Jade asked

"He used to come in the restaurant all the time. We were both cordial, but you know I wasn't interested because I was with Richard. Sasha and I bumped into him at the grocery store a few months back. Sasha was convinced that he liked me. I thought he was just being nice. I know this sounds weird but I hadn't ever considered a white guy. But Travis is great!"

"Um! What's wrong with white men, our fathers are the best men ever and they're white." I said

"Right, but I just never pictured myself with one." Sophia said

"Men are the same no matter what color they are." Jade said. I huffed and twisted in my seat. "What is wrong with you?"

"It's been six months!" I said twisting in my chair.

"He hasn't given in yet?" Sophia said

"No! He's come home every night; he's taking me out on dates. He's been very attentive. He's calling me at all hours of the day. HE'S DRIVING ME CRAZY!" I said

"I don't see what the big deal is." Sophia said

I looked at her, "seriously? Our children are in high school. I don't want to go backwards."

"I would do it. Matter of fact, Travis and I were talking about babies last night. He doesn't have any and he would like to have at least one."

"Are you guys gonna get married?" Jade asked

"Ugh! I've been there done that. I don't need the paper. We said we'd give us some time and then see what we think. But the way it looks today, I'd have Travis's baby."

"Really?" I said in disbelief.

"But the reason I asked you guys to come here is because I have some news." Sophia said

"Other than Travis?" I laughed

"Yes you nut. Poppa is almost gone, and I worry about Nana being out there by herself. I discussed it with Nana, and Sasha and I are going to move in with them."

"What about the restaurant?" Jade asked

"This location is a well oiled machine. I'm going to expand to a location in walnut creek. One of Poppa's friends owns a restaurant, he's gonna sell it to me."

"What about your house?" Jade asked

"I'll probably put it on the market."

"Or Sonny and I could buy it."

"You don't like living with Daddy?" I asked

"It's kind of weird sometimes. Normally he goes out, but every once in awhile he may bring someone home. I'd rather he have his space. Besides Sonny and I plan to start our family soon. It would be nice to have our own space to do that."

I wiggled in my chair again. "For crying out loud Amber, go to the drug store get some spermicide and go do the man!" Sophia said

"That works?" I said feeling like there was hope for me.

"Most times it does."

"But what if Malcolm has terminator sperm? Are you ready to have a baby if it doesn't work?" Jade asked

"I don't know how much longer I can hold out. If he would just go away, it would be easier. But he's gotta be around every day, looking good, being good, making me feel WONDERFUL! I'm bursting at the seams over here."

"So go try it. Push come to shove you'll have another baby with a man that loves you." Sophia said

"Let's go find this stuff you're talking about." I said bouncing out of my chair.

"How soon is all this gonna take place, you moving and all that?" Jade asked

"We started the paperwork on the Walnut Creek location. Sasha and I are moving at the end of the month. But she won't transfer schools until next year."

"The boys are not going to like not being able to watch over her." I said

"Maybe that's why she's looking forward to it." Sophia laughed.

Sophia took us to the drugstore and she showed me the stuff she was talking about. I felt empowered; I drove home on a mission. I made dinner, and then Derrick came home with Raquel in tow. Then Andrew came home with Toya; even she couldn't spoil my mood. Malcolm came home with Darryl. When Darryl came in the door, he was happy to see Raquel; he huffed when he saw Toya. She was sitting in the chair when Darryl walked past her; he smacked her upside her head. She whined, Andrew told him to cut it out. All in all, it was a pretty normal evening. I kept looking at Malcolm, after awhile he started staring back. That night was amazing, armed with my spermicide I felt ok. By round three, I was nervous. It seemed like he had been patiently waiting on me. Saving all he had for this moment.

Six weeks later when my period was nowhere to be found, I finally accepted the inevitable. I did everything but curse Sophia out. That heifer laughed at me and said "oops."

Malcolm and I went to the doctor and sure enough, I was pregnant. Malcolm was so happy he kissed my forehead and said "thank you." I told the doctor that I had been spotting and having a sharp pain in my stomach. The doctor got a funny look and he gave us a referral to go down immediately to the ultrasound department. Instantly worry was all over Malcolm's face. I tried to convince him that everything was gonna be fine, but I didn't really know either. When the technician took pictures of the baby it didn't look like a jellybean like I expected. It was kind of stretched out. I got a sinking felling that this wasn't gonna end well. Malcolm asked the technician questions but she said she wasn't authorized to give out information. She said she was sending the pictures back up to my doctor, and that they needed to go over the results right away. Malcolm's hands were sweaty as he held mine and we walked back up to the doctor's office. They brought us to the back immediately. The doctor had a nurse take my blood, hospital administration came in, they were talking so fast, I looked at Malcolm and he had sad eyes as he was taking it all in. The doctor explained that I had and ectopic pregnancy and they needed to perform surgery right away before my fallopian tube burst. The doctor explained that scarring may result from the surgery which would make it more difficult but not impossible to get pregnant in the future. My heart started racing, I squeezed Malcolm's hand I felt like I failed him. They had me give them a urine sample and sure enough, there was a little blood in the urine. Everything was happening so fast; they asked who was my in case of an emergency contact, I told them that everything should be directed to Malcolm. As they took me to the hospital on the other side of the building, Malcolm told me he'd call Jade and Sophia. He was so stressed and serious about the situation that I tried to make light of it. I told him we'd have matching battle scars. My joke caught him off guard, so I kept going. Eventually he smiled through sad eyes. The orderly pushing me couldn't help but laugh. I told Malcolm to relax and that we would get to try again. He kissed me and he told me he loved me. When I woke up my mouth was dry, and the doctor said everything went well. He told me to come back daily for blood work over the next week, depending on how that went he'd tell me when it was safe to try again.

Chapter 38

"Momma I need to talk to you," Andrew said looking completely defeated.

"Shoot baby, what's going on?" I asked patting the bed so he would sit down.

"I just wanna say up front that I'm sorry, and I never meant for this to happen." My heart started to flutter as I anticipated what he was going to say next. "Toya's pregnant." He said then he hung his head low.

I sighed disappointedly. "Seriously Andrew? How did this happen?" He gave me a goofy look. "Did the condom break? That's how you got here."

"No, we were messing around and things went too far."

I sucked my teeth, "what are you going to do?"

"Her mother wants her to get rid of it, but she says I have to pay. I don't want her to kill my baby. What if you would've killed me?" He was clearly upset.

"I understand how you feel. I was thankful Daddy didn't make me do that with you. Although it seemed like Momma was trying to beat you out of me." I ran my hand through his curls. "Maybe it's for the best. Children are forever and I have better hopes for you than you throwing your life away just to be with Toya. You have the money don't you?"

He sighed, "yes."

"Good, do the right thing." Then I gave him a hug, and thanked him for telling me. He didn't have to tell me. He asked me how I was feeling, and I told him I was good.

"You and Toya would've been pregnant at the same time." He flashed his dimples.

I gasped. "That wouldn't have been pretty!" I said shaking my head.

"Do you think I would've made a good father?"

"Yes, but not this young baby, and not with her; you've gotta protect yourself. You don't want to get caught up like your Uncle Melvin."

"How's he doing? He doesn't come around as much." Andrew asked

"His health is getting worse and worse. It seems like death is all around these days don't it?" I said

"Yea" then he exhaled real big. "Momma why do you love Malcolm? I try to understand it, but I honestly don't get it."

"He's got some rough spots doesn't he?" Andrew nodded yes. "He's a good man; I've never met anyone like him. We've been together so long sometimes I forget why myself."

"I think you can do better." He said

I gasped. "That's your father!"

"I know, but I'm saying. I wanna see you happy."

"You don't think I'm happy with Malcolm?" I asked

"Not all the time."

"Are you happy with Toya?" I asked

"She's my first real girlfriend but I know you don't like her so that makes it hard sometimes. What's the difference between Toya and Raquel?" He asked

"Day and night! Everywhere Toya goes, drama and mess follow. Raquel is a sweet girl. I want someone like that for you. I honestly think the poor child can't help being like she is. Life can be calm and peaceful with the one you love. I just don't see you having that with Toya."

"Do you ever miss David?" His eyes were full of tears.

"Oh honey!" I said giving him another hug. "David started off real good didn't he?" Andrew nodded his head yes. "He had issues deeper than I allowed myself to see.

Sometimes I think about how good everything started, and how wonderful he was with you. But the man in our kitchen that last day, I try everyday to forget."

"Did I kill him?" Andrew burst into tears.

"NO! Absolutely not! Sweetheart, we know what happened to him."

"I HATE IT WHEN MALCOLM'S RIGHT! I HATE IT!!" Andrew yelled with his deep voice

"Me too sometimes!" I said

"David felt like a real dad to me. Until I saw with my own eyes, I would've never believed anyone! I HATE HIM SO MUCH! Until I saw him grab you, I would've defended him to the grave even against Malcolm. Now I feel empty, at least I know up front with Toya what's going on with her. I don't like it, but at least it's not hidden. No pretend fathers, no pretend girlfriends, she is who she is."

I threw my arms around my baby, the one who's been with me the longest. I kissed his cheek. "Just because she doesn't hold back who she is doesn't mean you have to accept who she is. You deserve better than that, than this."

"I know you're right, but I can't see past this for now. Maybe I'll meet a good girl one day. But for right now, I just don't have it in me to believe whole heartedly that the person I love and trust isn't who they say they are." He said drying his face.

"I hear you baby, I understand. And thank you for explaining cause I was starting to feel like that's the way you saw me."

"Like Toya?" He blew air. "When I meet a girl like you that's gonna be my wife!" Andrew said

I smiled.

****

RING! RING! RING!

I swallowed hard. Phone calls at this hour were never any good. I thought for sure it was Poppa. "Hello?"

"Amber!" Rosalind said, she was crying so hard.

I sat up, "Rosalind? What's wrong sweetie? Are you ok? Tanisha?"

Malcolm was sitting at the foot of the bed. About an hour ago, he popped up out the bed holding his chest. I asked him if he was ok, he said he was but something didn't feel right.

She was trying to compose herself. "Somebody car jacked him.... They shot him!" She was crying uncontrollably.

"Who? Where are you?" I said trying to understand through her tears.

"Troy! Troy is dead! They killed him!"

I looked at Malcolm even in the dark he could see how wide my eyes were. "It's Troy?" His eyes pleaded with me to say no.

I shook my head yes. "I'm on my way, stay there!" Malcolm didn't yell or scream, but his hands were shaking. I grabbed his pants, and shirt. Malcolm couldn't move. He kept rubbing his chest. "Baby come on." I said

He couldn't move. I knocked on Andrew's door; his head popped up, "Poppa?"

"No baby, something's going on with Troy we gotta get to the hospital."

"Ok, you want me to call Bernadette, Tiffany, Penny, and Renee?"

"Yes, and Fuzzy too. Tell them we're at the Main hospital."

"Is Tanisha and Rosalind there?"

"I know Rosalind is, but I don't know about Tanisha."

"After Darryl gets up we'll come to the hospital. I'll pickup Tanisha too."

"You think you gonna be able to drive?" I asked

69

"I'll be ok. See you in a little bit." Then he stood up and walked to my room. Malcolm was sitting there still in shock. Andrew put his hand on Malcolm's shoulder that brought Malcolm back. Malcolm stood up and hugged Andrew. Andrew is almost as tall as Malcolm is now. Malcolm inhaled and then exhaled then he slowly put on his clothes. Malcolm told me to drive his car. When we got to the hospital, Rosalind had bloodstains all over her clothes and she was doing her best to talk to the police. Malcolm asked where Troy was and Rosalind pointed to a curtain in the ER. You could see blood on the floor; Malcolm asked her if he was gone. She tearfully said yes, his face was stone. He walked to the back, when Malcolm came back; he asked the officers who they reported to. Then he pulled out his huge cellular phone and walked away. The officers asked who Malcolm was and Rosalind said Troy's cousin. I asked her where they shot him, and she pointed to her chest right where Malcolm was rubbing his. Bernadette came bursting in the emergency room with everyone else in tow. As soon as they saw Rosalind's clothes, they all started crying and wailing. A little while later, Andrew and the boys and Tanisha walked in the emergency room. Tanisha was already crying saying she already knew. Everyone went to them. Then Daddy walked in, he gave his condolences to everyone then he asked where Malcolm was. I told him out by his car. Daddy walked quickly over to Malcolm. I saw them talking, and then Daddy came back inside. Call the mortuary take care of everything, I'm gonna take Malcolm. I looked at Daddy's face and I knew better than to ask any more questions. I said ok, and I asked Rosalind where her car was. She said she rode in the ambulance with Troy. We all went back to Renee's house. All the cousins were still on the porch; most of them were drinking and crying even though it wasn't noon yet. When I stepped inside, I realized it had been years since I had come to this house. Renee had made this house a home. There were pictures all over the walls of all the kids and some current. She had nice furniture and each room had a theme. It didn't seem like the same house, she even had the kitchen remodeled. I told her the house looked beautiful and she said, "thank you cousin," as she hugged me. Renee looked so much better; she put on good healthy weight. Her hair was neatly combed; she looked one hundred percent better. We pulled out the yellow pages and we made all the arrangements. Sophia brought over food from the restaurant. Sasha and Tanisha cried together, while my boys were out on the porch with their cousins. Sophia took Rosalind home to change and then they came back. I gave everyone the date, time, location of the funeral. Then we went to Troy's apartment. You could still smell him in the air. He didn't have any suits; I don't know how I didn't notice that before. When we went out to nice places, I think I always glanced over his clothes. I never took stock of his clothes or his appearance. I told them we needed to get him a suit; we didn't have to go today. Rosalind laid on Troy's bed she started crying because she said she could smell him in the sheets. Sophia asked her what happened cause she hadn't heard the story. Troy was supposed to be staying over which was nothing new, but at the last minute he decided he needed to make a "run" to help him sleep. Rosalind asked him to stay and they'd find another way for him to fall asleep, but he said he'd be right back. She said he wasn't even gone five minutes when she heard the gun. She took off running; she didn't see the guy as he was driving away in Troy's car. Rosalind cried, she said he put his arms around her until he couldn't. She said he was losing too much blood and they tried real hard to revive him and stop the bleeding. We both hugged her and told her we were sorry.

That night Malcolm didn't come home. I called Daddy, but he didn't answer either. I called Uncle Jeff and he said that this crack head was trying to sell Troy's car to someone they knew who owned a shop. The guy was able to keep the crack head there until Daddy and Malcolm arrived. Uncle Jeff said I might not see Malcolm tonight.

****

Malcolm wasn't taking losing Troy well at all. His moods kept running hot and cold. We were all very patient with him, but he kept leaving. I took the boys to Drew's to get haircuts. Everybody offered their condolences and said they were going to be there Wednesday.

Wednesday morning, when I came downstairs to make breakfast, Malcolm was sitting on the couch with a crisp black suit and shades on. He was sitting there like he was afraid to move. I came over and hugged him, his body was stiff, and he didn't move. I could see tears streaming beyond his glasses, but he didn't move. One by one, the boys came downstairs, each one came and hugged him, and then they gave him space. I made breakfast, but Malcolm refused to eat. He just sat there. When we were all dressed, Malcolm put his keys in my hand. When we got to the mortuary, we were the first ones there. They opened the doors to Troy's room. We all stood frozen in the doorway. Bernadette came next with her van full of kids but she had a woman with her I had never seen, I could tell by the pain in her face she had to be Troy's mother. The woman was crying and she looked like she had lived a hard life. She came and hugged Malcolm then she went into the chapel. She looked down at her son's lifeless body and she cried out. The limo brought Rosalind and Tanisha. We found our seats in the front amongst the family. Uncle Frank, Uncle Jeff, Auntie Lauren, Malachi, Daddy, Jade, Sophia, Sasha, and Sonny came as well. After the service was over, I noticed Summer as I walked out of the auditorium. I waited for her in the lobby.

"Summer I didn't know you knew Troy."

"He used to come by regularly. This is my sister Shonda."

I stuck my hand out, "hello."

Then she pushed a little boy forward with Troy's face and long hair pulled into a ponytail. "This is her son Yussef."

I looked at Summer in shock. "Why didn't you say anything?"

"I didn't want to lose my job." Summer said

"We live in Fresno anyways." Shonda said, "We just wanted to pay our respects."

"Why would you lose your job?" I asked

"I don't know. It's a sensitive topic. I know how close he and Malcolm were and Malcolm has his hand in everything you do. Malcolm didn't say anything so I figured that meant to just be quiet. So I was."

Then Malcolm came over and told me to come with him. He didn't even acknowledge Summer or Shonda. He brought me over to people who were obviously family but I didn't recognize any of them. "This is Amber," he said and then they introduced their selves one by one. Some of them said they came to the hospital when Andrew was born, but there were so many of them I couldn't keep track. I saw Melvin and as I waved him over Malcolm saw him, even though he had shades on you could tell he was mad. Melvin froze and waved me over. Malcolm grabbed my arm, this situation felt too familiar. I grabbed Malcolm's hand and I brought him with me. Melvin walked outside, and Malcolm's hands got sweaty.

"What's going on?" I said once we were outside.

"I just wanted to offer my condolences. I just got the story this morning." Melvin

said
"What story?" I asked looking at the both of them.
Melvin was really sick and shouldn't have come outside, but apparently, this was important enough to bring him out. "The crack head who shot Troy was Stefan."
I looked at Malcolm and he locked his jaw, he squeezed my hand but he didn't say anything. "Did he know it was Troy?"
"No, he was trying to get some money to support his habit." Melvin looked at Malcolm, "I know my apology won't bring him back, but I am truly sorry. Troy was a good man and he didn't deserve this." Melvin hugged me then he hugged Malcolm. Malcolm didn't stop him, but he didn't hug him back. Melvin told me to give everyone his love then he left. That was the last time I saw Melvin, he succumbed to his illness a few days later.

****

When it rains, it pours. Summer quit after the funeral. I tried to find her, but I couldn't. It was like she vanished into thin air. I eventually replaced her with Tony; he was good and got along with Jade, so I had no complaints. I got the call about Poppa and I know we were expecting it but it still hurt all the same. I'm tired of funerals and services. Nana was so strong, a pillar of strength so it seemed but six months later we lost her too. I think she missed Poppa more than she let on. Like Poppa and Nana wanted, provisions were made for everyone of us. If my boys wanted to be career college students, and live high on the hog, we could afford it. Some cousins decided to live off their inheritances; more power to them, but the rest of us did like Nana taught us, we diversified our assets, and then watched our money grow. I updated my kitchen and all three of my bathrooms. I had my house painted and re-landscaped the front and the backyard. Andrew begged me not to get rid of the basketball hoop, so we left it.
Malcolm hasn't dealt with losing Troy. He stays gone for days; the only one who can get him to come around is Derrick. It's like they speak a secret language or something. Rosalind and Tanisha had to get out of Oakland, fortunately they didn't move too far though. They moved to Richmond and Rosalind works out of the shop out there. I miss her but I understand why she had to go.
With Sophia in Concord, and Rosalind in Richmond, that only leaves Jade and she and Sonny are in baby making mode. I dare not go over too often; I might feel like I'm interrupting. Malcolm rarely comes around and when he does, he never stays. The question isn't if I can even get pregnant any more, it doesn't matter cause he doesn't touch me. I busy myself with work. I've been working with different artists and really creating a name for myself, which has been fun. The kids enjoy the perks; backstage passes, concert tickets, awards ceremonies. We're B list celebrities in our own right, which is fine with me. When I finally saw Mister MC's artist, he didn't look familiar, and his name didn't ring a bell until I saw Jade's reaction to the video. She said that he was the guy who Malachi and Sonny fought in high school. Once she said that it all came together. I hoped I didn't cross paths with either one of them.
With all the stress, my hair has been shedding like crazy. Raynel suggested that I stop perming my hair for a while. After three months, I cut off the remaining perm and I dressed my short curly fro up with headbands. Fortunately, for me African print scarfs are in right now. With my scarves and bamboo earrings people keep mistaking me for the boy's sister and not their mother. Andrew said he liked my haircut, Darryl didn't, and Derrick didn't care.

Chapter 39

"We have news!" Uncle Jeff said

"You're pregnant!?!?!?" Sophia joked

Everyone burst into laughter.

"Absolutely NOT!" Auntie Lauren said as if she was offended.

"No, after Joseph graduates next year, my lovely wife and I are moving out towards Sacramento."

"Sacramento? Why?" Gwen said holding her daughter Peyton.

"Because they're building some pretty nice homes out that way and we'd like a new house."

LJ or Jeff as he prefers to be called now just graduated from high school. We were celebrating at Uncle and Aunties'. It was so weird not having Momma, Poppa, Nana, or Malcolm here. Malcolm's been kind of missing in action. He leaves indications that he's still around, but yea, I haven't seen him or even heard his voice in forever. The boys see him; after all, they're still his soldiers in training but they say he's all about business and growing his empire. I don't know why that's translated to avoiding me, but whatever.

"So what's been new?" Gwen asked

"Nothing just working, how about you?" I said

"Where's Malcolm?"

"I don't know."

She was quiet for a minute. "Did you guy's breakup?"

"He said that would never happen, but lately it surely does feel like it. Why are you asking, you're married?"

She smiled, "not for me silly. The assistant coach for the NINER's asked about you. I told him I didn't know if you were single or not."

I blew air, "I don't know if I am or not either."

"Would you at least like to go to a game? Preseason starts in August."

"Who is this guy?"

"Let's do this, if you still don't know by preseason, just come to the game. You're under no obligation to date anybody. Deal?"

"Deal!"

****

Of course, I haven't heard anything from Malcolm. I don't know what I've done for him to throw his hands up and just be done with me. My mind is spinning from all the loss in one year's time, I really need him, and I guess he's done with me. Who am I kidding, let me be honest, I know he's not done with me, he can't just walk away from me like this and expect me to hang on the sideline waiting for him to remember me. That's not how this works. I think a year of waiting is long enough, whenever he comes back he better hope I'm not into whoever this new guy is. Gwen got tickets for us to go in a large group that made me feel good, cause if this guy was ugly or not my type I could just fade to the background. Our seats were excellent; Gwen really knew how to work her marketing into anything. I sat next to Andrew; my boys were reluctant to come because Malcolm groomed them as Raider fans. They've even flown out to LA to watch more than their fair share of games but I begged them to go like only a mother could. Once I turned Darryl to the dark side, it was only a matter of time before the other two would give in. When they saw how good our seats were, they were impressed. Just for the sake of football, they got into the game. My heart dropped when I spotted Tag with the players looking like a coach. I shot Gwen a look like, "no you didn't bring me down here for your leftovers!" She laughed and said not Tag. So then, I was confused, although some of the players were down right FINE their selves, I wanted to know who this guy was. I felt eyes on me, I looked around our seats, and I saw no one. I looked out to the players and there he was or at least I was hoping this was him. This man had serious eyes, a feature I realize I like in a man. He was caramel brown, and he looked like he could be a player himself. When our eyes met, he grinned, and I blushed. Suddenly it was hot out here in Candlestick Park. I crossed my legs and suddenly the game became all that more interesting. When the guy kept looking back at Gwen and me, she confirmed he was the one. I almost slid out of my chair. What would he want with me? Wait stop doing that, I'm taking my ugly duckling garb off for the moment. Andrew saw the guy and I exchanging looks and I could tell he didn't know how to react, he looks confused. When the NINER's scored a touchdown, suddenly his face lit up and I thought I was gonna die when he smiled. Gorgeous, beautiful smile, good job, and he liked me first!!!! Whoa! Whoa! Whoa! There has to be something wrong with this guy. Eventually Derrick noticed the guy too, and he didn't take it so well. He stared the guy down; respectfully he turned his eyes away. Derrick wanted me to switch seats with him and I refused. This little boy is not my daddy. When I refused to move Derrick proceeded to stare at me just like Malcolm would. I told him if he didn't cut it out I was gonna bop him out here in front of everybody. Andrew and Derrick spent the rest of the game going back and forth. When the game was over, the players and the coaches went to the locker room. Gwen snuck over and whispered, "So what do you think?" She asked with a knowing smile. I told her he was gorgeous, but I wanted to know what was wrong with him. She said nothing as far as she could tell. Then Derrick came over very rudely and said he was ready to go. So I had to go Annette style (minus the beating) on him and put him back in a child's place. I told him we were going to meet the players and he could sit out here and sulk if he wanted to, but he better not bring his attitude to the back with us. Derrick said he would wait at the seats, stubborn little mule. Darryl was gonna stay with him, but he changed his mind at the last minute and came with us, but you could tell he was guarded.

Andrew was the only one of my babies to have my back. Although it was two years away, the thought of him going away to college like Malachi and Jade did made me sad. We had been together more than half my life; I couldn't imagine him being so far away. Andrew picked it up so naturally when he and Malachi restored Malachi's old car. That car purred when they were done it was like it was brand new. They gutted the car put everything in it brand new. The car even got that paint job Malachi never got around to getting. Malachi said that Andrew had a natural mechanical mind, and he was trying to influence Andrew to look into The Technology Institute of Cambridge. I was trying to be a good sport about it but I could already tell in moments like this I was gonna miss him dearly.

There was a lot of media talking to the players and the main coach. As the players came out, they said hi to Gwen and her husband, who would in turn introduce them to us. Darryl got a little star struck when he met the quarterback. He was a nice guy. Then the cutie came out, he had that million-dollar smile on as he approached us. He said hi to Gwen and her husband, and then he looked at me. He dropped his smile and the serious eyes came as he shook Andrew's hand. You could hear how strong their handshake was. "How you doing Dwayne."

"Andrew" he said in a deep voice

Then he turned to Darryl, "and you are?"

"Darryl" my baby said matching his big brother's stance.

Then he turned to me. "And I know who you are. It's nice to finally meet you Ms. Amber Wallace!" He said using both hands to shake my one hand.

"How do you know who I am?"

"I've been following your work."

"Really? That's interesting."

"I was watching a video station and they were showing a making of a segment for one of my favorite videos. That was the first time I saw you. I made it my mission to meet you. Even if you had a man, I just wanted the opportunity to meet you." Then he looked around "I thought you had three brothers?"

I turned red, "you mean sons, and yes there's one more. But he wasn't feeling coming back here for the meet and greet."

His eyes bucked as he looked at Andrew again. "Wow! I thought you guys were siblings." He regrouped. "Ok well, are you guy's hungry? Can I interest you in an early dinner? My treat!"

"Sounds good to me." Gwen said.

Andrew and I nodded in agreement; Darryl gave in being out numbered. "Are you parked by Gwen, I can meet you guys at her car." He asked

"Amber, Andrew can drive. Why don't you ride with Dwayne?" Even Andrew frowned at Gwen's suggestion.

"If that's ok with you." Dwayne said giving Andrew serious eyes as if to say he understood if he said no.

"Where exactly are we going to eat?"

"Well that's up to you." He said pointing at us. "Wherever you'd like to go."

"We don't need anything fancy. A pizza joint would be fine."

Everybody looked at me and said in unison, "Pizza?" Then they all started laughing.

"You know what I mean a laid back environment." I said trying to clean it up.

"Ok, how about the All-Stars Pub on the wharf? They got pizza, burgers, and hot dogs, if you're in to them, video games, hoops, it's a cool place."

"Beer?" Gwen's husband asked

"Yes, a full bar if you so desire." Then he smiled that beautiful smile again. Then he explained the exact route that he was going to take to the wharf. Andrew told him he had it, but he would prefer that I didn't go with Dwayne until he brought his car around. Dwayne said he understood and he would be right around. We laughed at my boys. Gwen said I had three pit bulls guarding me. Derrick was not happy to hear that we were going out to dinner with Dwayne. His face got real serious and he looked at all of us like we were crazy for going along with it. I gave Andrew my keys, as Dwayne pulled around in his nice but not flashy car. I liked that, there's nothing worse than a man who has to have all the flashy and over the top stuff. Darryl wanted to ride with us, but Andrew made him ride with them. Dwayne got out the car and opened my door. Andrew was nodding his head taking it all in, while Derrick and Darryl shot him daggers with their eyes.

"So three boys huh?" He said

"Yep, you have any kids?" I asked

"Yea, two girls." He said

"They don't like to come to your games?" I asked

"The oldest loves to, but the youngest is like their mom and not really into the game." He said watching the road

"So where's their mom? What's your status; let's get that out the way right now." I said feeling good about asserting myself.

He smiled that beautiful smile. "It's hard to explain. We are not together, but she's the mother of my kids."

"I get it. I haven't spoken to the boy's father in a year. He's going through something, but we have three boys you know."

He nodded his head, "so are you looking for a relationship?" The question made me nervous. I opened my mouth then I closed it. He smiled and put his hand on mine. "It's ok, believe me I get it. What were you guy's high school sweethearts, never actually dated outside of each other, and started your family early. Am I right?"

"For the most part."

"Ok so we're just getting to know each other no harm in that right?" He said

"Right" I said. I don't know how to get to know somebody. My first real date was with David and we ended up almost married. I started feeling like I bit off more than I could chew by agreeing to come meet this guy. He's FINE! But am I even ready for this? Like he could hear my thoughts, he smiled and then he shared his story. He and his ex wife met in high school. She got pregnant while they were in college so they got married. He said he got a job coaching and it was fine while he was in town, but whenever he traveled, she became insecure to the point that it ruined their relationship. He didn't want to get divorced but she insisted. He said that was when he met her boyfriend. He said that was a hard pill to swallow; seeing some other man play daddy to his girls, but what could he do? He said she'll always have a special place in his heart, but everyone can't handle being in a relationship with someone who travels. I thought about David. It never bothered me that he traveled, but he never gave me reason to think he was doing anything other than working. "But you did cheat on her on the road though right?"

He laughed; he didn't expect me to ask. I guess I was supposed to be caught-up in the beauty of the story and not look at it realistically. "Not at first, but it did happen eventually. Does that make me a bad person?"

"Makes you human; I just wondered if you were gonna be straight with me or lie about it."

"I HATE to be lied to!" He said emphatically

"Me too!" I said matching his excitement.

"Alright then! That settles it! No lies between us even when the truth hurts. Deal?"

"Deal! But I know this is gonna hurt later." I said laughing.

Andrew pulled right next to us in the garage. All three of them were looking at us with serious faces. I smiled at them and Andrew was the only one who returned my smile. "You got some serious men on your hands."

"Aw! They're nothing compared to their father."

"Oh yea, what's he like?" He asked

"Like that one" I said pointing to Derrick, "but bigger, blacker, and ten times scarier." I said with a grin.

"Figures! Of course, he'd be scary. Of course." He said, we both laughed.

Derrick opened my door while giving Dwayne evil eyes. The restaurant was really fun, the staff wore jerseys, and it was all neon lights, scoreboards, big screen TVs, and arcade games. The place was a lot of fun, even though Derrick vowed to stick next to me giving Dwayne evil eyes. His brothers were having fun throwing three pointers. Eventually Derrick went to play with them, but he made it a point to look Dwayne up and down one more time.

I asked how I came up, how did he find out that Gwen knew me. He said it was a late night at the office and an awards ceremony was coming on. They showed me with an artist, and he started going on and on about me. Tag told him he knew me.

He said he begged Tag to point him in the right direction. One day Dwayne saw Tag talking to Gwen, when she introduced herself as Gwen Wallace he didn't think there would be a link but he asked anyways and the rest.... He said Tag was very tight lipped about me and he really thought it was a slip up that he told him he knew me. Then Dwayne sat back and gave me that gorgeous smile. "I jumped through hoops just to sit this close to you. You are my celebrity crush."

"That's flattering." I said, I liked that smile; it seemed to make my insides bubble up. But I think he knows he has a nice smile.

A couple of games over from the boys, there was a quarterback toss game. You had to throw the ball and make it in the hole where a player's hands were painted around it and it looked like they were in the in zone. So every time the ball went in, the board lit up signaling touchdown. Dwayne walked over to this game and put his token in. Derrick was watching him like a hawk. He gave Derrick serious eyes and Derrick shot them right back. Dwayne threw the first of his three balls, and it was way off target. Dwayne locked his jaw, replanted his feet and he threw the ball. It went into the hole. The board went crazy, "touchdown" fake cheerleaders cheered on the screen, the hole moved backwards. Dwayne nodded at Derrick, Derrick stared, his final ball, he threw, and it missed. Dwayne hissed and put his portion of the tokens from the table on top of the game. Apparently this is where he was gonna be. By the way, Derrick was watching, you could tell he knew he could do it better. Eventually he walked over to Dwayne's game, picked up the next ball and fired directly into the hole. Derrick's precision was so spot on. So now, it was war. Dwayne against Derrick, who was gonna win. Gwen leaned over and asked me what I thought of Dwayne, so first I had to ask her if she ever slept with him, dated him, kissed him, gone down on him, everything. She laughed and asked me if she was that bad. I gave her a look like you must be kidding, and then she said no. They met just like he said. She said, "Tag isn't happy, but who cares what he is right?" I didn't even acknowledge her question. I told her he kind of seemed like a playboy. She agreed, but she said he put a lot of effort into finding me and meeting me, so the ball was in my court.

When the food came, they came back to the table. Dwayne was very impressed with Derrick's ability to throw accurately. We all smiled knowingly, he looked at all of us like he didn't understand what he was missing. I explained that all three of my boys can do whatever they want, they're athletically inclined, they can dance like you wouldn't believe, they can run, jump, throw, Derrick especially could play any instrument put in his hands, all except sing, you name it, they can do it. Then I explained that I'm not forcing them into any particular mold. If they wanna be athletes, they can. They can be whatever they wanna be as long as they're happy doing it. Dwayne said that was a good model, but you could tell he had no idea who my three soldiers were. After we had eaten dinner and all the nice conversation had kind of died down. I saw a twinkle of Malcolm flash in Andrew's eye. "So Dwayne, you're interested in my mother?" It was a question but it sound more like an accusation.

Dwayne returned Andrew's serious glance. "I've been a big fan of your mother's for some time now."

Andrew nodded his head. "Kind of like a fantasy of yours to meet her?"

"You could say that." Dwayne said

"Well what would you say?" Andrew asked directly.

"I'd say I've admired her from a far, and now we're finally meeting."

"You do understand that she may just be a beautiful face to you, but she's also my mother. I don't want to have to come after you." Andrew was dead serious.

Dwayne started to laugh until he saw the expressions on our faces. "I wouldn't want my mother disrespected either. I can understand that. However, your mother is a grown woman, nothing happens here without her consent to it."

"Just make sure you put everything up front." Andrew's voice rumbled the table.

Andrew and Dwayne were then locked in a stare down. Then Derrick said to Andrew, "we already know what he's gonna do. Why would we even play this game?"

"Remember you gotta give him a chance, even if he only ends up hanging himself." Andrew said

"Is he the pawn?" Darryl asked

Then they all three looked at him with serious eyes like they were reading him. "That remains to be seen." Andrew said

I lowered my head, I am gonna end up a lonely old woman cause these boys will be blocking me at every opportunity. The boys went back to playing their games and Dwayne and I exchanged pager numbers. We all said our goodbyes in the parking garage, and then we went our separate ways. Andrew drove us home and Derrick ranted in the backseat the whole time. We all went back and forth; Andrew was defending me although really no one would be good enough for me. Derrick was absolutely against it and Darryl my little mess starter, had to mention that he worked for the wrong team. The car exploded in lively chatter. I told them my Daddy is a NINER fan and that the NINER's were fine. Darryl brings his face to the front, "but you live in Oakland!" Darryl said

"But they're not even in Oakland" I said

" They are coming back though!" Darryl said, I know we were debating but that boy makes me laugh! Timing is everything, and he's always right on top of that. "My point is pretty clear; he is just trying to get over. Throw that one back momma."

"What if I don't want to?" I said with attitude. "I know you guys want me to be with your father."

Andrew blew air, "speak for them!"

"Why you always gotta be like that with Malcolm?" Darryl asked

"They're too much a like." Derrick said matter of factly.

"Um, you are little Malcolm. I'm just Drew!"

"Ok, so I might have his mannerisms and act a lot like him but you are just like him. When you try so hard not to be, you still are." Derrick said

"Not true! You are little Malcolm!" Andrew said stepping on the gas a little harder. "Who's always directing stuff? Bringing everybody together? Who's always running stuff from behind the scenes? Who's always gotta be one-step further? Who has to beat somebody down for flexing at them?" Derrick shot each question rapidly.

"Who gotta have at least one female on the side at all times?" Yea! His mouth ran away from him, the car turned to ice and there was no way for him to pull that back. I didn't wanna react, but hearing this information matter of factly hurt me. I started crying, even though I was trying to pull it back I couldn't. "I'm sorry momma I didn't mean it." I could tell Derrick felt horrible.

"Cheating doesn't make you a man! All it does is breaks hearts. You guys please! I don't want to talk about this anymore. I don't know why Malcolm's not talking to me or even seeing me. He knows there's only so long I will idly wait for him. Before you guys tell him he will already know. How he takes it, is how he takes it. Please try to be nice at least at first. I'm not saying I'm gonna fall in love with

Dwayne, but I deserve to be happy too don't I?" You could've heard cotton hit the floor. "Don't I!"

"Yes, momma you do. We just don't know how happy you'd be with a forty-niner. Think of the family get togethers, and functions. I mean I know we are a close knit family but could we survive you bringing in a NINER?" Darryl said

"My Daddy is a NINER fan!" I yelled while laughing.

"And we've already forgiven him for that!" Darryl said

I pushed his face as I chuckled. Andrew grabbed my hand, as he apologized with his eyes.

****

Things have been interesting to say the least. Naturally, Dwayne would like to take me out to a nice restaurant in the city. However, I avoid the city as much as I possibly can. Whenever they have a home game and Dwayne wants me to go, I can't drive. Andrew came a couple of times. Against my better judgment I let him bring Toya the last time we went, and that was a disaster. It's always the same question, "what is wrong with that girl?" So for the next game Dwayne sent a car service to bring me over, which was a nice touch. But this meant he would have to bring me home. He thinks he's so slick. When Tag saw me sitting alone, he came over at halftime to say hello. He couldn't hide his jealousy and I don't think he was trying to. He said hello and then he cut to the chase. "Why are you here for him?" He said

"He invited me to the game. Why does that bother you?"

"Come on Amber, you know why, we have unfinished business." He said with longing in his eyes.

"I guess you closed the door on that the day you decided to do whatever it is you were doing with my cousin. What makes you think I'd even consider you after that?"

"That was years ago we were all young."

"Yea, but clearly you guys were at it for awhile. You were at our last family gathering with Gwen. It wasn't that long ago, but it doesn't matter." I blew air, "I'm not trying to be a witch. Tag you're timing has always been off. That's not a reflection on you, just on when you've shown up in my life. I can't get past you and Gwen, so for me, you and I ended when you and Gwen began. I know you're a sweet guy, and whomever you're dating is a lucky girl. It just can't ever be me."

"Amber! We would be good together, don't throw it away because I made one mistake. Please just think about it." He was staring in my eyes.

"What do you want from me? Do you want me to sleep with you? Is that what will make you go away? I don't know why it's such a big deal that we never got together."

"If you could only see you from where I stand. You'd beg you too. I already know I was your first." Then he gestured with his tongue and instantly I started tingling. I couldn't believe how my body betrayed me. "I want more than just your body."

I scrunched up my nose, "Tag. You're nasty!" He stood there smiling. "If you feel I'm all that, then you'll just have to wait."

"Are you kidding me? We both know eventually you're gonna get back with Malcolm and then it'll be years before you surface again. Get rid of him, let me date you."

"I like him Tag."

"And you like me, so he and I are on an even playing field. But! You and I have history! This could be our last chance." He clasped his hands together and he begged. "Please!"

Ok, ok so I think it's safe to say that seeing ANY man beg is a turn on. It makes me feel powerful and like I would imagine a Goddess would, dealing with peasants. When I look in the mirror I don't see anything special, but who am I to say what beauty is. I sat there looking at Tag change colors as he tried to convince me to see the light. What he didn't understand is I already told him no and that wasn't changing. I don't know everywhere Gwen's been but I will never go behind her. Maybe if it weren't for Gwen I would've given Tag a try.

Dwayne walked out the tunnel with serious eyes. He walked over and hugged me all the time staring Tag down. "Why weren't you in with the team?"

"I was talking to Amber." Tag said shooting serious non-budging eyes back.

"You're here to work! They want you in the office." Dwayne said

"Think about what I said!" Tag said to me completely serious.

I nodded my head. Dwayne watched him walk away. Then he looked at me like he was trying to read me. "After the game can you wait for me in the office? It's right next to the locker room."

"Of course." I said with a smile.

He looked in the direction Tag walked in, and then he went back to the sideline. The game was exciting, and the die-hard fans all around me, made me forget I was sitting alone. After the game, I waited for the crowd to die down then I made my way to the office. The coaches and assistants were finishing up. When their meeting was over Dwayne hugged me again, and his colleague asks, "who's this pretty little lady?"

"This is Amber, Amber this is William." We shook hands. Tag walked out the office slow at first and then fast like he was mad. Dwayne held my hand as we walked through the tunnel. Then he grabbed me spun me around and kissed me. The element of surprise was in his corner, but his kiss was kind of sloppy and all over the place and if he knew how close he came to a black eye he'd never do that again. He flashed that smile at me. "This is the first time we've ever been totally alone."

I thought about it and he was right. "You're right."

"What would you like to do? You hungry?" He asked

"I could eat, but you know me. I don't want to stay in the city no matter what."

"San Jose ok with you?" He asked

"As long as you don't mind driving me home from there." I said

We had nice conversation all the way down to San Jose. As we were eating our meal, I felt eyes on me just as Dwayne put his hand on mine. I started looking around, I saw someone move out of eyesight on my right as I turned my head. I saw the wavy black hair and instantly knew it was Juan. I rolled my eyes cause I was having a lovely evening then here we go. Dwayne stopped talking when he saw my expression. He asked me if I was ok, I assured him I was ok; I just needed to go to the bathroom. He had a puzzled look, but he nodded anyways like he understood me. When I rounded the corner, Juan was standing there with a big smile. "Having fun?" He asked

"I was until I saw you! Why are you here?" I barked

"You know why I'm here."

"Whatever Juan! You have a whole agency of employees. Why are you here?"

"Sometimes you gotta get back in the middle to remember how it is. Plus others may assist me, but when it comes to you, I'm the point man."

"Whatever! Just lay low ok. As long as he doesn't realize you're around I don't care." I said

"I haven't seen you date a skinny man yet. You prejudice or something?" Juan smiled

"Shut up!" I said as I smiled, gave him a hug, and then kept going into the bathroom to at least, wash my hands.

When I came back, my smile had returned. Dwayne asked me if everything was ok and I assured him everything was fine. He wanted to go dancing, but I couldn't go because I had an early flight in the morning to LA. I was only flying out for the day; I did that a lot. If I had to stay out in LA, I'd ask Daddy to hang out with the boys so they didn't get any ideas.

Dwayne was disappointed cause he was enjoying our time alone. I told him since he handled this one well, there would be more in the future. He liked the sound of that. When we pulled up to my house, he leaned over and kissed me. I was a little reluctant because the previous kiss didn't do anything for me but he redeemed himself and I told myself it had to be that he caught me off guard. Then he asked me what the deal was with Tag earlier. So I explained how I met him, and how he's been around my family sporadically ever since that summer. I even told him how Tag has always wanted to date me, but like I told Tag his timing was ALWAYS off. Dwayne listened then he told me, that in so many words, I was bad for business. I told him I didn't have to come to games anymore if that would make it easier. He told me not to worry about it because the season was winding down and then we'd have more time for other things. We talked for a few minutes more, and then you could see eyes peeking out the window until Derrick got in the window and opened the blinds completely so we could see him standing there with his arms folded. We laughed and Dwayne insisted on opening my door for me, so I waited. It felt nice to be doted on again and to be appreciated, even if in my heart I was wishing he was Malcolm, it didn't matter, it was the attention I needed for now. Derrick opened the door as we approached and I closed it. Dwayne laughed and said he didn't know why Derrick didn't like him. I told him that Derrick is very loyal to his father, whether he's around or not. He said he could understand that. So we hugged good night on the porch and then I went inside. As I watched him pull off that's when I noticed Malcolm's car following Dwayne.

Chapter 40

I don't know why Malcolm was following Dwayne that night. I don't know if he followed him for dramatic affect or if he even really followed him. However, knowing Malcolm, he followed him all the way home and did something scary. I paged Dwayne later that night and he called right back, so if he says nothing we're good right? We talked for a few hours that night, which left me, tired the next day but it was ok, I had the adrenaline of a new relationship to fuel me forward. It did seem a little weird that every so often, I would hear a click on the line, but eventually we said good night.

"Momma! Let's go!" Andrew called from downstairs. I put my cap on, grabbed my fanny pack, and ran down the stairs. Andrew gave me Skylar's leash while he held on to Samara's. Derrick and Darryl were warming up with Hubby and Dude by the curb. A car pulled in front of the house with tinted windows. The boys looked at the car, and then we took off. Skylar and I were in the front because we're the slower runners. We ran around to Joseph's block and he joined our group. Now we didn't do this run every Saturday, but we did it often enough. Malcolm told the boys since we did it so often we should have someone watching the house while we were gone. We would run so long we'd end up at The Bakery by Merritt for breakfast. The puppies would be tied up on the side of the restaurant with water and whatever treat we brought them. The boys were having a ball being silly, but I kept thinking about the dress for tonight. Dwayne asked me to be his date for a black and white ball that the entire team was invited to, amongst other high profile guests. I found the perfect black dress. It was long and straight formation, it has a halter neckline and a split up my right leg to the middle of my thigh, very sophisticated and sexy! I could not wait to wear it. Jade was coming over to fix my hair, and Rosalind was gonna do my makeup. I was in my own world when Derrick tapped me and asked me if I was ready to go. We were almost home and my legs were on fire. We were at that burning point where I wanted to stop, which meant I had to dig deep and push. I was so happy to see our house. Ms. Connie was on the porch waiting for us. Andrew and Joseph went to talk to whoever was in the car. I gave Skylar to Darryl and I caught my breath. Ms. Connie and I hadn't chatted for a while so I invited her in. She told me there was nothing new in her drab life, and then she asked how things were going with Dwayne. I told her it was going along fine, I knew she was looking for dirty details. I hated to disappoint her but we haven't crossed that threshold. I was in no hurry to put myself out there like that knowing about what took Melvin away from me. I value my life even if other people don't and the fact that Dwayne hadn't complained said to me he was getting it from somewhere, which was fine with me. It was a little surprising how long this had gone on without any interference from Malcolm. I knew if Juan wasn't around often, the boys were telling him everything. I guess he really didn't care, so oh well. When Rosalind called to tell me she was on her way, the phone kept clicking which was weird. We got off the phone because the clicking got so bad. Then I got a page from code 49, the code I gave him. Original idea right? When I called him, that clicking was still there, it was starting to get on my nerves. Dwayne said the party may run late and he wondered if we should get a room. My insides screamed I hadn't prepared my mind for anything like that. I made my voice smile as nicely as I could, then I told him more than likely I was gonna wanna come home regardless of how late it was, but I could always take a cab or figure something out if it got too late for him. Therefore, he suggested that he reserve two adjoining rooms so there wouldn't be any pressure, just in case we decided to stay. YEA RIGHT! However, I couldn't believe myself, when I heard myself agree. He said he'd be at my house by seven. I felt giggly as Ms. Connie and I went up to my room to discuss what to pack for my sleepover. Rosalind and Tanisha came up to my room. Tanisha seemed to have gotten a lot taller in the past almost two years. I gave her a huge hug. Then she went to the backyard to play basketball with the boys. Rosalind told us about her new boyfriend and how wonderful and patient he's been with her; he helped her track down Benjamin to serve him with divorce papers. Then she showed us her very modest, but you could tell it came from the bottom of his heart, engagement ring. She wore it proudly. She said Bernadette and Renee really like him, but she hasn't seen Malcolm long enough to introduce him. She said Malcolm normally swings by the Richmond shop whenever her man isn't there. I told her to feel fortunate that she's seen him, because I hadn't laid eyes on him in forever. She said he's been strictly business and never creating a routine about anything these days. She said it's like they know he's coming they just never know when. I changed the subject back to my overnight bag, and Rosalind couldn't believe it. She couldn't believe our relationship had lasted this long without Malcolm interfering for one and for two, me not touching Dwayne, if he's as fine as I describe him. I told her to stick around to see him when he picked me up. We went back and forth, over what to pack. I was on the fence about how tonight was gonna go. Scared out of my mind, but kind of excited cause it was all new. I didn't know what to expect and that was driving me crazy. Could anyone be better than Malcolm? Naw, I think the mold was broken when Malcolm was created. Ok, so how far from second am I willing to go? David didn't compare, but what I thought we had was different. So now that I'm thinking about it, I'm curious to know where Dwayne would fall. I couldn't pack my silk robe that was for Malcolm, I left that in the closet. I packed a satin gown, jeans, and a T-shirt, toiletries, etc. Then I threw my stinky booty in the shower while Rosalind and Ms. Connie went downstairs. I washed my hair, which was at my shoulders when it dried in its naturally curly state. All my life my hair has been curly but it's not until now, that I realize how long my hair actually was all my life in its curly form. I have a newfound appreciation for my hair.

Jade told me what to put on it and to let it air dry and she'd be over in a minute to style my hair. She was in her last trimester so she moved slowly these days. I lotioned up and put my undergarments on. Jade wobbled up the stairs and into my room. I rubbed her belly and talked to my nephew who I couldn't wait to meet. He liked the sound of my voice. Then Jade pulled my hair to a side ponytail. She brought out her container of hair accessories, she looked at my dress, and she pulled out a black flower. When she pinned it, it was perfect. Rosalind came up; she said Ms. Connie said she'd be back to see me off. Rosalind did my makeup and I was completely impressed. I told her she had to come with me on some of my shoots, etc. She smiled and said cash will do nicely.

Jade went home, but she made Rosalind promise to take pictures of the finished look. Around five thirty, I heard the front door, I assumed it was Ms. Connie or Joseph coming over. I put on my terry cloth robe and bounced down the stairs to get some juice, and show my face Rosalind created. Nobody was in the living room; I saw the light under the bathroom door. I went in the kitchen and poured a glass of juice. The boys and Tanisha were still in the back playing basketball. I heard the toilet flush and then the water run. The light turned off and I spit juice all over my counter when Malcolm stepped out the bathroom. His face was serious; he scanned me from the top of my head to my feet and then back to my face. "Why are you wearing so much makeup?"

"GET OUT!"

"It doesn't look bad, I'm just asking."

I rolled my eyes, "your boys are out back!" I said waving my hands behind me as I tried to storm past him.

"I know where they are, but I'm here to see you." He said blocking my path.

"It's not a good time Malcolm, I have a date." I said trying to go around him.

"Oh yea, your little coach. How's that going?"

I crossed my arms and squinted my eyes at him. "Get out of my way!" I said through clinched teeth.

"I'm just asking you a question." I started tapping my foot, but I didn't respond. Then he looked me in my eyes, "are you still my good girl?"

That question hit me like a ton of bricks. He hadn't asked me that since he was in prison. I stumbled past him and I took off running up stairs. I ran in my room and as I fell against the door, Malcolm pushed it open to my surprise. I didn't know he was chasing me, Rosalind jumped, and her eyes were wide like what's going on. He looked mad, "answer the question!"

I'm not gonna cry! I'm not gonna cry! Rosalind stood up and walked downstairs. Malcolm slammed the door behind her; I jumped when the door slammed. The dogs came running and barking. I hadn't seen Malcolm in forever and even though this scene was scary, I just wanted him to hold me but there was no way I was gonna let him know that. Andrew knocked on the door, "momma, what's going on?"

Malcolm opened the door, "do you mind! I'm trying to talk to my woman!"

Andrew looked confused, "your woman?" Malcolm slammed the door again.

Andrew opened the door shaking his head. "This is not your woman, and this is not your house!"

"Andy, baby please! I'm ok! I'm ok!" I said trying to calm my baby. I knew that look in his eyes, and I know Malcolm. Derrick and Darryl were standing next to Andrew looking confused but like they were waiting on Andrew to tell them what to do. "Andy!" I put my hands on his cheeks. "Look at me baby." Andrew reluctantly looked at me, although his eyes kept going back to Malcolm. "Baby, this is Malcolm! I'm ok!" Andrew's eyes went back to Malcolm. "Look at me!" His eyes turned red. "That's Malcolm, and I'm ok. It's ok. You hear me?"

"Yea" he said very slowly.

"Ok, I'm gonna close the door. I'm gonna talk to Malcolm. Then he's gonna leave." Malcolm blew air, as if to say he wasn't. "Ok, Andy?"

"Ok!" As I closed the door, my babies definitely looked like soldiers.

"Answer the question Amber!" Malcolm barked at me picking up right where he left off.

All my anger and neglect came bursting to the surface. I slapped Malcolm as hard as I could! My hand was numb it stung so badly. "HOW DARE YOU BUST UP IN MY HOUSE DEMANDING ANSWERS FROM ME THAT ARE NONE OF YOUR BUSINESS?" I blew air trying to keep the major heart felt sob I felt begging to come from my knees at bay. "I haven't seen or heard from you in two years! I didn't do anything to you! Now you show up with this drama! You don't own the right to ask me anything! I don't belong to you!"

He was still mad and he acted like my slap didn't faze him. "Answer me!" His voice grumbled

"Get out of my house!" I said in a low tone. His eyes glazed over and a tear fell which I wasn't expecting. He grabbed my face and kissed me passionately. I lost myself in the kiss for three seconds. I pulled away, "get out!" I said loudly this time.

He walked past me, opened the door, and pushed past Andrew down the stairs and out the front door. All three boys followed him to the porch. Derrick and Darryl stayed on the porch watching him leave; Andrew came busting back up the stairs. My baby looked eight feet tall when he came back in the room. He was looking me over. He asked me if I was ok. I told him I shouldn't have run from him. Andrew's eyes were serious, "why did you run?"

I shrugged, "I choked! I wasn't expecting him." I said with nervous energy. "He wasn't gonna hurt me. He's never hurt me."

"That's not the way it looked from where I was standing." Andrew said

The phone rang, Andrew looked at me, I shook my head no; he answered the phone next to my bed. Then he hung up; he looked at me like there was no point. I asked Andrew why Malcolm showed up today of all days if he's known about Dwayne all this time? Andrew looked at me and didn't say anything at first. I could tell by the look on his face he knew something, so I asked him again. He got up and shut the door; he whispered, "Did you and Dwayne talk about anything over the phone?" The horrified look that flashed over my face; "The clicking on the phone, did he just put a tap on my phone?"

"Just?" Andrew made a confused look. "Momma it's been there for years!"

"WHAT?" I couldn't believe it. "You knew about this?"

"I know about a lot of stuff I don't speak on." He said

"Like?" I said

"Like why does he have complete access to your house and you never even go to his place? I'm not telling you to go over there, but he shouldn't have free reign over your house like that. Whether he's your man or not. You're always waiting on him, move on and be done with him." Andrew said as if he could even comprehend Malcolm and me.

I put my hands on his face and I kissed his cheek. "I really hope you never understand the dysfunctional relationship your father and I had." He gave me a knowing look. "Ok, ok. Have. But baby as long as you're with Toya, get back with Toya, or have Toya in your life. You are in no position to judge your father or me. Your relationship is way more toxic." Of course, I could tell he didn't understand yet but he would.

He shook his head, "are you still going on your date?"

"You think I should? Malcolm seems a little unstable."

"Don't ever let Malcolm stop you from doing anything! If the only reason he's even come around is because of some other guy, you go on the date."

"Ok then I'm going." I exhaled. I looked at my makeup. I called down to Rosalind. She came in the room real slow, "is it safe?" She came in with her hands up. "Gurl, I don't miss drama like that." She said chuckling

I know she meant no harm by her comment but it did hurt my feelings. Her comment made me feel like she was saying she has risen above my lifestyle. Andrew looked at me to see if I had a reaction to her comment. When I didn't say anything, he politely excused himself because he was still upset and needed to go calm himself. I looked at my makeup and decided it was fine, and I didn't need her to do anything else. At six-thirty, I put my dress on, and at six forty-five, I heard the doorbell. Rosalind had spent so much time gushing over her man, that she failed to notice I hadn't said two words. The only thing that quieted her is when she looked out the window and saw the driver waiting next to the car Dwayne arrived in. I

guess she had no way of mentioning how her relationship compared to that. I don't know what happened to my friend, or maybe I was just sensitive about the scene Malcolm created but I was taking my sensitive behind out of this house. Darryl knocked on the door and told me that Dwayne was downstairs. I knocked on Andrew's door; he was listening to music so he didn't hear me knock. I cracked the door and he jumped he was writing something. I told him I knocked. I told him it was going to be a late night, and I may end up spending the night. He nodded and told me to have fun. I grabbed my purse and my bag, and Rosalind followed me downstairs. Dwayne's smile spread so wide when he saw me come down the stairs. Derrick was standing in the dining room; he didn't look as annoyed as he normally did about Dwayne's presence. I gave Dwayne a hug then I introduced him to a very speechless Rosalind. I mentioned everything, I told her he was fine, but I failed to put the necessary emphasis on how FINE HE IS! I knew she was shocked to see me with such a pretty boy. "It's very nice to meet you." He said in a very charming manner, and then he turned his attention back to me. "Are you ready?"
I handed him my bag. "I'll meet you outside." I said
Dwayne said goodnight to Rosalind, Ms. Connie, and Tanisha. Tanisha smiled at her mother and Ms. Connie blushed.
I put my arm around Derrick and we went in the kitchen. I asked him if he was ok and he said he was, it wasn't eight o'clock and he already had a lot to digest. I kissed him and told him I loved him. Then I went out in the backyard, hugged, and kissed Darryl and Joseph goodnight. I took deep breaths as I walked along side the driveway to the front of the house. I didn't know if I was making a mistake or not by still going and what was with the tear. That man is so weird, and I'm tired of trying to figure him out. He needs to open his mouth and just say what's going on. I would still rather be with him tonight, after he apologized for deserting me at the worse possible point in my life of course. Dwayne was surprised to see me coming from the side of the house. The way his eyes danced around my body, he approved of my appearance. I was quiet in the car. He asked me what was wrong, I started to say nothing, but we said honesty. So I told him about Malcolm popping up out of the blue. He listened and then he said Andrew was right. In my mind I was thinking, of course he sides with Andrew because it benefits him. I left out the part about Malcolm having a tap on my phone.
We got to the banquet early, which was good because everyone was early. I met a lot of the team members and their wives and girlfriends. Even Tag had a date, she was very nice, but that still didn't stop Tag from trying to find an opportunity to corner me. I decided to widen out beyond the teammates in the room. I started introducing myself to anyone; Dwayne was stuck talking to the team owner, and some other people in a conversation that looked non-appealing. Dwayne got sucked in before he realized that everyone was avoiding that conversation, and I knew better than to join him.
"Hello" a woman said as she came over to meet me. "You're Amber Wallace."
"Yes, very good." I said hoping she wasn't hitting on me, because I was not in the right mind space to deal with that.
She stuck her hand out to shake mine. "Talia Lewis, it's very nice to finally meet you." Then she gestured towards the room. "Ten thousand a plate" she said pointing to the table, "it better be good!" She said
"I'm sure it will be lovely, I had no idea it cost that much to be here." I said
"Oh yea, but stuff like this will become common place now that the season just ended." She said unimpressed.

The light bulb clicked. This is Ron Lewis' wife. I guess I was supposed to catch that by her giving me her name. Ron and Dwayne hang out a lot during the off-season. Talia went on and on about how unimpressive the night was gonna be, then she gasped and stopped talking mid-sentence. "Who is that delicious specimen?" I looked up, could this night become anymore cruel. Malcolm and Juan were walking directly towards us. Fresh hair cuts, custom tuxedos that looked like they were born to wear. I was frozen and couldn't move; Malcolm had his eyes on me. As if we didn't just have a huge emotional scene hours ago, he walked over to me. He grabbed my hand and raised it to kiss it while looking me in my eyes. "Amber." The touch of his lips on my hand, gave me goose bumps.

Talia cleared her throat. "Talia this is Malcolm Latour and Juan Ramirez, this is Talia Lewis she's married to Ron Lewis." I said

I could tell Talia wanted Malcolm to kiss her hand but he didn't reach for her hand. "I love this dress!" Malcolm said taking a step back to take me in. "This dress deserves a Tango!"

"Thank you," I said trying to remain even. "Juan, why didn't you bring your wife?"

"She was going to come originally, but our son got sick at the last minute."

"Malcolm you're filling in for Gloria?"

"No, Juan is filling in for you." Malcolm said giving me serious eyes.

Then the MC took the microphone and asked everyone to take their seats. I patted Malcolm's hand then I walked away. As we walked to our table, Talia was going on and on about how fine Malcolm was. He did look good in his tuxedo, smooth and crisp. However, why does it always take the attention of another man for him to remember me? How was Juan filling in for me when he hasn't spoken to me until tonight? Oh well, right? Dwayne stood behind my chair as we approached the table. He scooted my chair under for me. Our table was a huge round table, Ron and Talia sat next to Dwayne. The rest of the people at our table looked like high-end professionals. When I saw the last two chairs at our table were empty and next to me I whispered to myself to be cool and of course Malcolm walked up to our table to the two seats. Malcolm and Juan greeted the table, and then Malcolm sat directly next to me. Juan excused himself and then went to talk to the hostess. As I'm watching, I realized that Juan knew her. Immediately everyone wanted to know who was at the table. So as our salads and then soups were being served, everyone introduced themselves and what they did for a living. The introductions started on the other side of the table. One guy was with his wife and he was the head of the whole East Bay Cable Company, there was a banker and his fiancé, the CEO of a grocery franchise and her husband, Ron was a former 49er and now trying his hand as a sports commentator. Then there was Dwayne the professional assistant coach, one-day Head Coach Hopeful. Then there was me, the only arm candy at the table with her own business. I was curious to hear what Malcolm would say; Juan sat down as I finished my share with the table. As soon as Dwayne heard Malcolm's voice, he sat forward to get a good look at him. Dwayne looked at me and I nodded my head yes slowly. Malcolm charmed the entire table; he called himself an entrepreneur extraordinaire! He rattled off so many businesses I counted about six well-known ventures. It seemed like the women would've loved for him to continue regardless of the topic. As I watched him talk, I remembered what it was like to hear Malcolm speak for the first time. His manner of speaking seems to draw you in. A lot of the time, he had me convinced that he had no idea he had this affect on people, but moments like this let me know that even if he wasn't doing it on purpose, he definitely used it to his advantage. Juan who is charming in his own right shared that he is the CEO of Mitigated Staffing Services. Almost everyone at the table was familiar with his company, as they've all hired from them. My body temperature shot up as I knew that his company was huge and that let me know they had minions all over the place. Juan smiled at me when he was done. I didn't hear anyone else at the table. I ate my salad, and tried not to notice the pensive expression on Dwayne's face. Malcolm was here to stop me from moving any further with Dwayne tonight. Dwayne wasn't stupid enough to dismiss Malcolm as a non-threat but with the argument, we just had before Dwayne showed up, how could he not know that there was still something between Malcolm and I? I felt so stuck in the middle cause Malcolm was gonna get mad if I put Dwayne in front of him but there's no way I could choose Malcolm even though my heart wanted to run to him. I guess Juan was his wingman tonight. I hope he has some kind of a calming affect on him. Cause if Malcolm pushes the issue he will leave me with no choice but to reject him.

Oh, my goodness this bread was so good. I told myself not to eat anymore. Malcolm rubbed his leg against mine under the table. I moved my leg but he just moved his with mine. I wished he'd stop messing with me, especially before someone realized what he was doing, but knowing Malcolm he didn't care and if someone did notice, he dared them to say something to him. The presenter went over their presentation as we were served dinner. Everyone looked forward, the presentation was very lively and attention grabbing although when I glanced at Talia she looked board stupid, I guess when all you do is attend events like this, it would seem extremely boring. Malcolm started rubbing my thigh. I took my fork and stabbed his hand. He kept his hands above the table after that, Dwayne whispered in my ear asking me if I was ok. I nodded yes. Once the presentation was over, our table erupted with conversation. The cable guy wanted to know what Malcolm thought about the presentation. In a way, it felt like a test to see if Malcolm belonged here, in my opinion. Malcolm eloquently explained the plight of the everyday man and how charity events like these were nice and appreciated; but there was still so much more that could be done to benefit Aids research. By the time he was done, the whole table was eating out of his hand. Dwayne listened but he didn't say anything, he more or less kept watching me for a reaction to Malcolm. A lot of people had a ton of questions for Malcolm and Juan about the presentation, their businesses, and any other charity events they were aware of. Business cards exchanged hands, and future plans to golf, etc. were made.

The band opened the dance floor, and Dwayne invited me to the dance floor, Malcolm showed no reaction as we stood up, he continued his conversation. On the dance floor, Dwayne didn't have any special dance moves. He asked me if I was ok, I told him I was. I told him I didn't know what was the point of Malcolm and Juan being there. He asked me if I wanted to leave, I told him that wouldn't make Malcolm go away, Dwayne didn't look happy, but what could he do? We stayed on the dance floor for a long time. Eventually Dwayne was called off the floor to network. As we left the dance floor, Tag asked Dwayne if he could dance with me. I guess Dwayne thought Tag was a better alternative than leaving me open for Malcolm to slide in. Fortunately, for Tag, he's a good dancer, but I knew our dance wouldn't last long. Once Malcolm saw that I was dancing with Tag, he came to the dance floor and interrupted our dance. Tag had no idea Malcolm was there. He was not happy about relinquishing my hand to Malcolm, but he knew better than to do anything but that. My body stiffened as soon as I transferred hands to Malcolm.

"I need to apologize about earlier." I blank stared at him. "I was wrong for barging into your house like that. I'm gonna go apologize to the boys in the morning." I felt like I wanted to cry; only the boys deserved an apology? "What?" He stared at me for a minute. "I apologize for barging in on you too. Do you forgive me?"
I clinched my jaw, he's gotta be kidding right? The song ended and I stopped moving. "Clearly I'm an after thought to you, so why don't you leave me alone." I said then I started to walk away from him. Music started and Malcolm grabbed my arm and spun me around.
"Why are you in such a hurry to get back to him? Do you want me to go tell the pretty boy he's dismissed?"
Knowing that he would do it and not care, I lowered my head and said, "No."
"Then let's give this sexy dress what it's asking for, a real dance with a real man." I didn't respond. "The longer you remain unresponsive the longer I'm gonna keep you out here on the floor." His face was very serious. People were starting to watch. Now I didn't know Malcolm knew how to Tango. His lead, like everything else he does was strong and I didn't have to guess where his was taking me or when he was going to dip me. He kept staring into my eyes as his strong hands told me which way to go. I felt like I was going to explode, but I kept my face serious and screamed at my body for tingling. When the song was finally over, everyone applauded for us. Talia stepped in as soon as I created space between Malcolm and I to request the next dance. Malcolm looked at me, and I told her she was going to enjoy every moment of their dance. Malcolm squinted his eyes at me and I smiled as I faded away from him. Dwayne met me at the table. "I'm ready to go." I said lowly. Dwayne grabbed my hand and we walked out of the auditorium while Malcolm was dancing.
Dwayne asked me if I wanted to go to the hotel. I didn't care; I just wanted to get away from Malcolm. As promised, Dwayne got adjoining rooms; I took a shower and washed my face. I put my gown on with my hotel provided robe. I opened my door and knocked on Dwayne's, he told me to enter, and of course, he was shirtless having just got out the shower himself. He asked me if I felt better, I shrugged. He suggested that we order dessert and a movie. I frowned because the guy who came to deliver our desserts looked familiar. We ate some of our rich desserts, Dwayne stretched across my bed shirtless (nice), and he patted the bed for me to join him. So I took my robe off, his eyes danced around my gown. We both yawned at the same time, and then started laughing. I laid in front of him and he snuggled in close. He turned on the movie and I yawned again. He cuffed my breast as he started to yawn again. I guess during the movie he was planning to make his big move, he started kissing my neck and rubbing my body. It felt good but I felt like I was fighting to stay awake. I hopped up, "is the heater on? Why am I so sleepy?" I stumbled over to the thermostat and it actually said sixty-five.
Dwayne stood up, "yea I feel tipsy, but I didn't have anything other than wine with my dinner. What's going on?" He sat on the bed, and then he laid down. Then I heard him snore. What is going on? I was sleepy and was not winning the battle to stay awake. I stumbled back towards the bed. There was a small knock on the door but I fell asleep before I could get up to answer it.
I woke up to the sound of my pager going off, Dwayne jumped when I moved, I opened my purse, and it was Sophia's code. When I talked to her the other day, she said she'd text me a 4 for yes and a 0 for no. She texted a four for yes, she's pregnant. I sat towards the top of the bed and picked up the phone. Dwayne got up and went to the bathroom. I called Sophia and we giggled, I told her I was really

happy for her. She said Travis and Sasha are excited. Dwayne came out the bathroom, and I told her I would call her back. He came and sat on the bed and I hurried to the bathroom. I brushed my teeth and then I came out. I looked at the clock, it was a quarter past ten, and checkout was at eleven.

"We need to get moving if we're gonna checkout on time." I pointed to the clock. He looked at the clock, he was debating, and "You sure you won't come back to my place?"

"Not as long as it's in the city."

"What do you have against the city?" He asked

"Not a topic you wanna get into right now. We could get dressed and then go have breakfast. If you don't have plans we could spend the day together." I said changing the subject.

He thought about it quickly. Then he got a big smile. "How does a kind of late brunch sound?"

"Sounds good to me." I smiled.

Then he kissed me long and passionately. His kiss was fine, no; it was good, it just didn't send electricity into my toes like Malcolm did every time. When I came out the bathroom dressed and ready, Dwayne looked disappointed that he didn't get to see anything. I asked him where we were going and he said it was a surprise. The car service took us to the San Jose airport and we caught a flight to Los Angeles. We had brunch at the Vine in Los Angeles. There were a ton of celebrities here dining and networking. I was so surprised and impressed. I called the house from the restaurant and talked to Andrew. I told him where I was and that I didn't know when I'd be home. He said Malcolm came over at about noon, and he's been hanging around ever since. He said Malcolm was waiting for me. I got a little tickled by that, but I told him to tell him only if he asked that he didn't know when I would be home.

When I came back to the table, Dwayne suggested that we go on a trip somewhere. That put butterflies in my stomach. Because that definitely meant at some point we were moving forward. I let that swish around my brain for a while; I kept asking myself if I wanted to do this, and how badly did I think Malcolm's response would be, after all I'm not in the business of getting people killed. I told him I've never been to Hawaii and I wanted to go one day. He smiled real big and told me to consider it done. He said we could compare calendars and make it happen. After we finished shopping, he had a cab take us to Tiffany & co. When we walked into this jewelry store, I felt confused as to why we were here. He led me by the hand around the store. When he spotted what he was looking for he asked the salesclerk if he could see a pair of diamond studs. When she took them out, he asked me to try them on. I pushed pass the awkward feeling I had and I put them on. The clerk held up a mirror for me. They weren't very big diamonds. With both earrings together, they came to half a carat. But the way they sparkled and caught the light, it wasn't like I cared. He asked me if I liked them, and I said yes. He told the salesclerk that we'd take them. Now they weren't like oh my goodness look at the ice dripping from my ears, but they were special to me. I planted the biggest thank you kiss I could muster on him. He turned a little red and had to think real hard about what he was doing even though he had his wallet out and his card was in his hand to pay for them. The salesclerk smiled as she helped him out by taking the card from his hand. He looked at me for a minute, and then he told me I couldn't kiss him like that anymore, he said flashing a beautiful smile. I said thank you again as I admired my earrings in the mirror some more. When we left the store, Dwayne held my hand all proud. Then he looked at his watch, he said we had four hours before our flight back. He asked me what I wanted to do. Feeling drunk off the appreciation of my earrings I kissed him and said I didn't know whatever he wanted. His eyes got big as he clarified what I meant by whatever, because we both knew what he wanted. He had us power walking to the curb to flag down a cab. We went to the airport Hilton; he got a standard nonsmoking room. He gave me a room key as he went to the gift shop to buy condoms I assumed and I was right. The first time with someone feels awkward and clumsy at best. But Dwayne and I had a good time, and the awkwardness only lasted the first few minutes when he walked in the door. We actually turned out to be very compatible in this space. That was a relief; the only thing was afterwards he wouldn't let me go. I could tell he was trying to hold back from showing how emotional he felt. I thought to myself, oh no what did I just do. We showered then we had dinner and drinks at the hotel. Dwayne looked like his eyes had been opened and he was fighting very hard to hold on to any cool points he had earned before. As soon as we boarded the plane, he wanted to know when he would see me again. I explained this week was gonna be a busy week for me, and I was gonna need time for my family. He started to look disappointed; I told him we'd figure it out. I told him to spend as much time as he could with his girls. When the car service pulled up to my house, Malcolm's car was still out front. Dwayne asked whose car, and when I said Malcolm's I could see insecurity flash across his face. "Oh no!" I thought to myself. Please don't let Dwayne get any ridiculous thoughts that it ever would be ok to confront Malcolm. I gave him a huge kiss and thanked him for the beautiful day we spent together. I told him I'd call him soon or he could page me.

When I walked in the door, Malcolm was talking to Darryl, Derrick was in the kitchen, and Andrew was upstairs. Darryl smiled when he saw me but returned to his conversation. Malcolm barely looked at me, but I didn't care. I kissed both of my boys then I went upstairs. I knocked on Andrew's door; he got off the phone once he saw it was me. I came in the room and I asked him how things were around the house. He repeated that Malcolm came over. He said Malcolm apologized for the way he behaved the night before, something he's never done. They accepted his apology and then Malcolm hung around. Andrew said they all knew he was waiting for me, and Malcolm got more and more annoyed the later it got and I wasn't home yet. After I called, Malcolm's pager started going off. I asked him if anything else happened. He asked me if I heard from Sophia and I told him I had. He said there was nothing else other than that. I went in my room and I started pouring a hot bath. I wanted to relax and soak. It had been two years since my last piece; my body was a little in shock. I turned on my stereo in my room to soft music and I lit my candles in my bathroom and turned off all my lights. I had the best bath salts and bubbles from this little mom and pop specialty shop in the Rockridge shopping center. Expensive soaps and body stuff have become my guilty pleasure. Especially when I had my new fancy tub installed when I had my bathroom remodeled. This was one of my gifts to myself. I had the shower and tub separated and I had the fanciest tub that could fit in my bathroom put in. I laid back in my tub and my mind ran back to that hotel room. I didn't have high hopes for Dwayne just because our first kiss wasn't grand. But he was quite good actually, and I'm happy I waited this long to find out. He seemed vulnerable now; I didn't know how much I liked that. I hoped he got that in check, because I could see myself dating him for a while.

I opened my eyes as Malcolm walked into the bathroom. He asked if I had a good time. I said I did, he was staring at me so I looked at him. Then he asked why I left so early last night. I told him he irritated me and I didn't feel like staying. He looked confused and asked me how apologizing irritated me. I looked at him and told him to think about it. I could tell he couldn't put his finger on what I was talking about. I tried to calm the fire that was starting to burn within me.

"YOU DROPPED ME LIKE A BAD HABIT! I haven't seen or heard from you in two years. You suddenly pop up and I'm supposed to swoon upon sight of you. AND THEN!!!! You've got the nerve to ask me for the loyalty that you don't have to me! You left me out here hanging on waiting for you. I'm not doing this with you anymore Malcolm. I don't even know why you're in here." I wiped the tears that fell.

Malcolm was quiet for a few minutes. Then he sucked his teeth. "You're trying to use me as an excuse for being with that fool?"

"No, I like him. I don't need an excuse to be with him. I'm telling you that your cameo appearance was too little too late." Then I thought about it. "No, I'm saying that you just disappearing on me and then reappearing like you have the right to demand anything of me is a JOKE! I've spent more than half my life waiting on you, I'm done with that."

"I'm hurting what do you expect me to do?" He barked

"YOU ARE NOT THE ONLY PERSON WHO LOST TROY!!!! HE WAS JUST AS MUCH MY FAMILY AS HE WAS YOURS! You forgot about my pain! You wouldn't even let me be there for you or even thought that we could've grieved together! Plus I lost my friend, AND MY GRANDPARENTS! You don't care about how you hurt me and continue to disappoint me. I can't keep doing this with you Malcolm; I'm too old for this high school mess."

"What are you saying?" He looked at me with a weird look on his face.

"I don't belong to you; you said before that you weren't husband material. Some how I thought after all this time that would change. You've turned out to be an excellent father; your sons never wonder where you are. Everything else in your life seems to be going so well. Then there's me! I'm so serious Malcolm I love you! I'll always love you but you need to leave your keys to my house. Even if you don't, I'm changing the locks."

"You think there's a lock that can keep me out?" He growled

"So what are you gonna do kick in my doors? I'm not running from you, I'm not even hiding. I'm just saying the whole I belong to you thing. I can't do that right now, and it is unfair of you to ask anything of me with the way you've behaved."

At first he looked like he wanted to argue with me, but he started thinking about it. "Fine, for now, but if you ever try to put me to the side for some fool. We're gonna have a problem."

"Don't pull that flexing your muscle stuff on me and we won't have a problem."

"Ok so come on." He said

"Come on what?" I said

"Get out the tub and come see me off properly. I need you to remember that pretty boy ain't got nothing on me!"

"You're joking right?" I asked in disbelief.

"Do I look like I'm joking?" His face was dead serious but that wasn't a fair question; it was very rare when he didn't look serious.

He stood me up, wrapped me in my towel, and carried me to my bed. I felt like I was about to get in trouble. I watched his face for a reaction upon entry, his expression didn't change, and he watched my face. I guess I expected him to hop up and curse me out, but he never did. Instead, he went deeper and harder, I thought he was trying to kill me a sweet death, but death nonetheless. At one point, I didn't know if those were tears or sweat dropping on the back of my neck. Then he told me I'd always be his good girl and I about lost it. I cried my eyes out, and he kept kissing me telling me it was ok. When he held me, I didn't want him to let me go. When he laid on his back to sleep, I climbed on top of him and fell asleep listening to his heartbeat.

I didn't sleep good though. My subconscious kept calling me names like whore and hooker. Two guys in one day, that was so unlike me and I hated the way I felt. When I sat up Malcolm looked at me, he wasn't sleep either. He asked me if I was ok and I shook my head no. I told him I just spent the day with Dwayne and then he stopped me from talking. He kissed me and told me he already knew. He made me lay next to him and he spooned me. Then I had a thought. So I asked him, "Did you drug us?" He started laughing and said I had a very active imagination but that wasn't a no either.

In the morning, Malcolm asked if he could hang out with me for the day. I didn't want him to leave so I happily agreed. We went by the school and I introduced him to Jade's assistant who was new to him. In my newly renovated conference room, we met with a new artist to go over contracts and concepts for my choreography services. I keep Sonny and my cousin Ryan on retainer, so Ryan came to go over the contracts while we discussed the concepts, etc. This artist Torrie was a dancer herself, and that excited me, I loved working with artist who could move. The video took on a whole other life. Torrie kept looking at Malcolm, and then she asked if he would be willing to be in her video. Malcolm looked surprised; I needed to know what she meant. Torrie had a whole storyboard concept for her album. She explained that she was telling a story through her songs and they all interlinked. One of her songs was about big bosses, and in her eyes, Malcolm was that. He blushed so hard, I didn't like it, but this is business, so I asked Malcolm if he would be willing to do it. I thought I was doing a good job of staying even, but Malcolm knew me better. He told Torrie he wasn't about being on TV or even being seen. Then he thanked her for the consideration and tried to turn the attention back to our meeting, I could see it in her eyes, she wanted Malcolm. Malcolm excused himself from the conference room after that. If this contract didn't have a six-figure profit return on it, I would've kicked all of them out. I picked up a glass of water and chugged on it hoping to calm the fire inside of me. When the meeting was over, I escorted Torrie and the group back to the parking lot. I could tell by the way she was looking around she was looking for Malcolm. This little girl needed to slow down and ask herself why Malcolm was even there. Maybe then, she'd realize he wasn't available. Then she put her arm around mine and asked me how she could find Malcolm and I said "my Malcolm?" Trying to feed her the clue to leave it alone, she laughed and said if it was meant to be it was meant to be. She said she was looking forward to working with me.

Malcolm was in Jade's office on the phone when I walked in. He finished up his conversation with Juan, and then he asked me if I was hungry. I was more annoyed than hungry, but I went along anyways. When he pulled up to the deli, he handed me two twenties and told me to go inside and get some food. We both fell out laughing, I put the twenties in my pocket, and I got out the car. He held my hand as we walked in the door. I went up to the counter and Rita came out the back. She said, "I'll be right with you in one second." Then she turned around. "What can I....?" She searched my face, "Amber?" She got very excited and ran around the counter to hug me. She picked me up actually. "You haven't aged one bit! How are you? I've been seeing you on TV! Your school is doing really well! How's Malcolm?" She was very excited to see me.

I pointed to Malcolm and she screamed and took off running. She jumped on Malcolm and wrapped her legs around him. I didn't like that either, but for Rita, I wasn't gonna have an attitude about it. They hugged then Malcolm put her down. She made us monster-sized sandwiches, and then she packed big pieces of cakes and cookies.

She asked how Andrew was doing, and I told her he was so tall now, and that he was about to graduate from high school. Then Malcolm showed her a picture of all three of his sons. She pointed to Darryl and said he comes in there all the time, she should've known he was Malcolm's son. Rita said their business wasn't doing too well and that they were thinking about closing up the shop. She said the days of mom and pop stores like hers were becoming less and less of a reality but she said on the bright side, she'd have more time to travel, depending on when she got out of the business. I told her she couldn't disappear on us and she would have to keep in contact. Then she said Malcolm knows how to reach her and the whole family whenever. I know I shouldn't have but I shot Malcolm a look like really. Rita got up and packaged up the whole cake and a couple of pies. She put a bunch of cookies in a pastry box she said it was all for the boys. She gave me a big hug and a kiss on my cheek, she told me to come back as soon as I could. She gave Malcolm a hug and said the same. When we got in the car, I couldn't let it go. "You slept with her before haven't you?"

"I told you that when you met her." He said matter of factly.

"You did?" I was jogging my memory.

"Remember I told you she likes dark meat."

"She was a grown woman then."

"Your point?"

"You don't think she's doing that with Darryl?"

"Amber! No!"

"I had to ask." Then I thought about it, "Are you still sleeping with her?"

He blew air, "no!"

"When was the last time?"

"Years ago. Before Darryl."

I gasped, "You guys carried on for that long?"

"You asked," he said.

"Ok so what about..."

He cut me off. "If we're gonna play fifty questions, I'll play, but then you'll have to answer mine."

I knew he was just gonna ask me questions about David or Tag and I didn't want to discuss them. I crossed my arms and said fine. We went back to my house and hung out in my room for a while. We made the slowest sweetest and most passionate love. I asked him why he disappeared on me. I asked him what I did to make him go away. He said I didn't do anything, but he couldn't talk about it yet. I could tell the whole topic made him emotional, and maybe feel a little unglued but not answering me felt worse. I turned my back to him and scooted away from him. I silently cried myself to sleep, and when I woke up, he was gone. I hated that feeling, but he wasn't ready to come back to me yet so I held on to the memory of him. Then my pager went off, 49 was paging.

****

"Girl! I don't know how you've done this three times!" Sophia said

"Girl me neither! I know how much that hurts. Are you guys going to have any more?" I asked

"No! We're good! One is good!" Sophia said

Travis smiled looking at his beautiful baby girl, "one is good."

I laughed, "I give you guys six months before you start talking about more."

Travis laughed Sophia did not, "you can leave now if you want!" She said pointing at the door.

Then, beautiful tall and long legged Sasha came in the door holding the diet cola her mother had asked for. She was so happy to see me. She told me that she got into Berkeley, ULA, Spellman, and NYU. I was so happy for her. I asked her which school she was leaning towards and she said ULA mostly because Joseph (her Uncle) was at the school, and that it would give her some alone time with her dad. I told her it sounds like her mind was already made up. She smiled at her mother and said she was still debating. I could tell Sophia was rooting for Berkeley without even talking to her. Sasha asked me if Andrew had decided yet, I told her NO! I told her he was driving all of us crazy.

This past summer Malachi, Daddy, and Malcolm went with him on his college tours. Malachi was really talking up The Technology Institute of Cambridge; Andrew said he liked everything he saw there, he wasn't sure that he wanted to focus on a technical background. He said he didn't like the vibe at Princeton. He said more of the students seemed like snobs just because they were there. He actually liked Stanford, and the proximity to home he liked even more. I know he worries about us, but we all try to assure him as much as possible that we will survive four plus years without him. I know I say it, but he reads my face, and my face says please don't go.

I told Sasha to call him and maybe they could all figure it out together. I asked what school Tanisha was going to and she said Tanisha was going to take some classes at Contra Costa, the Junior College in Richmond until she decided because she had no idea right now. I told myself to call Tanisha when I got home.

Eventually, Travis gave the baby to me; she was so precious and tiny. At that, exact moment it seemed like both of my miscarriages hit me at once. Tears poured out of my eyes; everybody was startled, I startled myself. I asked Sasha to take the baby from me. I was going to leave, but Sophia asked Travis and Sasha to give us a minute. I couldn't stop crying, I laid on Sophia's bed next to her, and both of us cried together she rubbed my head and I apologized for ruining that moment. She told me there was no need to apologize. What I love about how close Sophia and I are, is that she knew exactly why I was crying; she asked me if I had seen Malcolm lately. I shook my head no. I told her how we saw Juan when Dwayne and I were in Hawaii, how he "happened" to be on a family vacation on the same island and at the same resort. We even had dinner with them a couple nights, but no Malcolm. She told me it was going to be ok, Malcolm was just going through some things right now, that made me cry more, what about what I was going through? What about what I needed? It never seemed to matter. I asked her if they finally agreed on a name for the baby, she said just as they were leaving the hospital they both agreed on Sabrina. I told her I liked that name. I cried so hard, instantly my eyes puffed up, but at least I was calm enough to drive. I apologized for scaring everyone and then I came home. Andrew and Derrick were home. They told me Darryl was with Malcolm. Derrick was upset and Andrew was trying to talk him through it. I sat on the couch next to Derrick and I asked what was wrong. Derrick said that Raquel's father lost his job; the company shut down. Her family is moving to Atlanta at the end of the month. Derrick was devastated. I put my arms around him and for the first time since he was a baby Derrick cried in my arms. The sight of his little brother crying was too much for Andrew. He got up and went to the kitchen. Derrick told me he loved her and he didn't want to let her go. I could feel my baby's anger, disappointment, and broken heart in every fiery tear that dripped from his eyes. I told him they'd see each other again; maybe she could come back out here to go to school. He shook his head; he liked the idea of coming up with a game plan. He hugged me and kissed my cheek. Then he grabbed the cordless phone and went upstairs.

"What did Malcolm do now?" Andrew said walking back in the living room.

"He got me pregnant."

Andrew froze in place. "He did what?"

"Not now. You were two." Andrew exhaled and sat next to me on the couch chewing a Popsicle. "The day it was confirmed that I was pregnant I got in a car accident and I lost the baby." My eyes watered up. "I was so angry with Malcolm about the whole thing that I couldn't allow myself to feel like I needed to feel. There was too much going on at that time that I never got a chance to grieve losing that baby. Then I lost this last one, and yes, I was scared to have another baby, but I wanted it. That baby was gonna set everything right or at least that's how I felt. I was so worried about your father's disappointment that I never dealt with mine. I wanted to try again, but I don't think your father could withstand the disappointment if yet again, it didn't happen. I went over Sophia's and she has the most precious baby girl, that's all I want is a little girl of my own."

Andrew put his arms around me. He pointed at my leg. "That's when that happened right?" I shook my head yes. "Momma you gotta know it was for the best. Look what happened each time. If I understand the story right, you would've had two kids to raise by yourself. And look what happened this time, you still would've been alone."

"He hasn't deserted you guys; he would be there for his baby girl just the same if not more."

"Yea but momma what you need is a man who's gonna be there for you. Where's Dwayne?"

"It's mid-season he can't be babysitting your whacky momma."

"Lucky him." Andrew laughed.

"Speaking of babysitting have you decided where you're going to school?"

Andrew exhaled, "I haven't gotten all of my acceptance letters yet."

"How come Sasha has most of hers?"

"Sasha's graduating in January. I enjoyed my summers off. As soon as I have it down to five I'll let you know."

"I just want you to know even though I will miss you; it's ok if you need to go far away. I have two little you's. By the time it's time for me to lose another one you'll be back."

"Who says I could stand to be that far away from my momma?" He smiled at me.

"You are a momma's boy aren't you?" I said

"Until the day I die!" He kissed my forehead. "Now I hope you feel better, because I gotta take Toya to the mall."

I sighed. "You had to destroy a perfectly good moment by bringing up that girl."

Andrew hugged me then he bounced out the door. Malcolm was dropping Darryl off, it's as if he heard my heart begging him to notice me. He parked his car. He hung up his phone; before he hit the walkway, he was asking me what was wrong. I simply said I just got back from seeing Sophia's baby. He came inside.

Chapter 41

"You guys are the cutest couple!" A very tipsy Torrie said.

We were at an after party. Torrie won three awards and she was definitely feeling herself. "Thank you Torrie. Let me introduce you..."

"No intro necessary for the HOTTEST coach of the Hottest team who just WON THE SUPERBOWL!!!!!" She screamed!

"Ok, well were gonna walk this way." I said pointing to Dwayne to walk the other way.

"I BET YOU HE'S A GOOD LAY TOO!!! BRING ON THAT SUPERBOWL BOOTAY!!!" She screamed

My thing is I think she would've said that even if she weren't drunk. Nana said that in a person's drunkenness, their truth comes out. Hence why I NEVER wanna be drunk in front of Dwayne. The Super Bowl was just the month before so everywhere we went people were recognizing Dwayne. Little kids were asking for his autograph and females were drooling left and right. He was the man of the hour, the one every female wanted to be trapped on an island with. I don't like all the attention personally; I know he's FINE! I know females throw themselves at him all the time and I'm pretty sure he goes for it sometimes. I don't care; I just don't want to talk about it. On occasion, I still see Malcolm and I'm not about to declare that. So as long as he stays out of my business I stay out of his. However, tonight I can't wait for the night to be over. Everywhere we turned; it's a guy wanting to go over the Super Bowl, or some female throwing herself at the gorgeous assistant coach. I told Dwayne his face should be hurting from smiling so much. Dwayne was talking to a very drunk record executive when I heard, "Amber!"

I turned around to see Mister MC. "Hey Mister!" I said as we hugged.

Dwayne's neck snapped in our direction. Now I've been hugging people all night, but there was something about Mister's hug that felt wrong. Maybe because Malcolm would've never allowed him to touch me. There had to be something about this man because Dwayne did not look happy about Mister's long embrace. He made his way over quickly, and he introduced himself.

Mister pointed at Dwayne, "what happened to Malcolm?"

"I'm here with Dwayne."

Mister started laughing. "You went from Malcolm to this pretty boy?!?!"

Dwayne gave Mister a serious look. "What's seems to be the problem." He said walking up on him.

"Oh pretty boy's got heart!" Mister said looking Dwayne up and down. "Anyways, Amber I wanna get with you regarding some of my artists."

"Mister you know you gotta run that by Malcolm."

"Seriously? Even when you got pretty boy Floyd right here, I still gotta go through Malcolm just to do business with you?"

"Amber lets go!" Dwayne said grabbing my hand.

Mister got mad and as he reached to hit Dwayne, Dwayne spun me out the way and moved before the hit connected. He came back with a right that could be heard throughout the party. Security was there lightening fast. Dwayne was ready to keep going, I was impressed. Outside of my boys, I never seen or met a pretty boy that could fight. I didn't assume that just because he was solid and built like a workhorse that meant he could fight but the fact that he didn't back down from Mister, something I only saw Malcolm do, was impressive. Media was all over it; I don't know where the cameras came from. Our driver happened to be right at the door when we exited the building. Cameras were snapping like crazy. We were in our room maybe twenty minutes when my pager went off; it was Malcolm, I ignored the first page. Then he paged again 911, and he started blowing up my pager. Then the room phone rang. Dwayne was walking out of the bathroom when I picked up the phone.

"Hello." I said sounding annoyed

"WHAT PART OF 9-1-1 DON'T YOU UNDERSTAND?" Malcolm barked at me. I frowned at the phone as I pulled it from my ear. "Ok"

"You can't stay there! You gotta come home now! Get your stuff, you had thirty minutes, but your playing cost you ten."

"What about Dwayne?" I said

"Amber!"

"Malcolm!" He knew I wasn't gonna leave Dwayne behind.

"Fine whatever, you're coming home by car, so if that's too much, tell him he can try to get out of there by plane, but Brad's gonna be looking for him." Then Malcolm hung up.

Dwayne had serious eyes. "How did he know where we are?"

"I don't know," I got up and started grabbing all of our stuff. "We've gotta get out of LA. Malcolm said Mister's gonna send people after us. Someone's gonna drive us back to the bay, flying isn't safe." I said still getting our stuff together. Dwayne started to question me. "Baby, they're gonna come with guns. Stay if you want, but I have to go." I took my dress off, and then I put on jeans and a shirt. I put on a cap and shades. Dwayne grabbed his bag and his stuff out the bathroom. The phone rang again; Malcolm said Todd was at the door and to go with him, I told Dwayne to open the door and to make sure the guy's name was Todd. Dwayne said yea it was him, I hung up, and we were out. Todd was as big as Dwayne was, with no smile. He took my bags. We efficiently but casually walked to the garage. Todd put our bags in the back of the black car with tinted windows. I got in the back with Dwayne. When we pulled out of the garage, media was from all over and more was arriving at the hotel. Dwayne said Malcolm wasn't kidding Todd looked at Dwayne.

"Todd will you be ok driving? Will you need help?" I asked

"No, I'll be fine."

"But it's like two in the morning. Feel free to let us know if you need help, either one of us could help." I said

Todd smiled, "I got it but thank you." Then he picked up the car phone. "I got her, we're getting on highway five now; provided that we don't stop we should arrive just after seven am. I will check in at the halfway point... Yes, he's here too.... Ok... Ok" then he hung up the phone.

I snuggled into Dwayne and he put his arms around me. I closed my eyes and dozed off. I could hear Dwayne and Todd talking, it sounded like they were talking about sports. Major bore I wasn't waking up for that, but then I had to use the bathroom. As we pulled off the road at a rest stop, Todd picked up the phone and called it in. It was five o'clock in the morning and my pager started going off. First, it was Andrew, then Uncle Frank, then Uncle Jeff, then Daddy. When I got in the car, Andrew asked where I was because the fight was all over the news. I told him that Malcolm sent a car and I was guessing I was two hours away from the bay. He calmed down and then I called Uncle Frank and Uncle Jeff explaining the same thing I told Andrew. When I called Daddy, I explained the same thing but Daddy also wanted to know who Dwayne was. When I explained that he was my boyfriend, Daddy said he wasn't happy that he had to find out this way that I was seeing someone. I was in trouble, I tried to explain that we hadn't got to the meeting parents stage. Then Dwayne gave me a look. He asked to speak to Daddy. I knew Daddy was mad, and I didn't think it was a good idea but Dwayne was insisting. So I huffed then I asked Daddy to hold on. I tried to tell Dwayne that this wasn't a good time. The thing was Dwayne wanted me to meet his daughters and his family. I didn't think we were ready for that step yet even though we had been seeing each other for over a year and a half now. "Hello Mr. Wallace this is Dwayne Reed, I apologize that we have to meet under such circumstances... Yes sir... I would like that... Yes, I do... I'll have to check with Amber but I believe we can... I look forward to meeting you as well... Ok, you too sir.... Ok here's Amber." He smiled and handed me the phone. I rolled my eyes at him because I already knew they were making plans to meet up. When I got back on the phone Daddy informed me that the three of us were going out to dinner and we were going out to dinner in the city. Daddy's voice was very firm, I knew better than to argue with him but I knew better than to be afraid when I was with my Daddy, so it wasn't the worst-case scenario. Dwayne was very excited, where I wasn't. Todd looked back and forth between our expressions. I knew he was gonna report everything to Malcolm. I remained quiet and on my side of the car the rest of the car ride. Dwayne frowned when Todd pulled up to his community gate entered a code, and pulled into his driveway. "How do you know where I live?" Dwayne asked Todd. Todd pointed to Malcolm's car, which was waiting across the street.

"Oh boy!" I thought to myself, "Here we go!" I took a deep breath as I got out of the car. Malcolm got out of the car and Dwayne walked over. I got nervous, as I didn't know how this was going to go down. "Malcolm what are you doing here?" I asked "What's going on?" Dwayne asked not taking his eyes off Malcolm.

"What happened last night or should I say this morning?"

As I explained the situation, Todd took Dwayne's things and put them on his porch. Then he put my things in Malcolm's trunk. I kept talking hoping that there wouldn't be a scene as Todd drove off.

Malcolm looked at Dwayne, "I know you were defending Amber but do you know what you just did? You could lose your job. You can't be fighting at after parties, especially with everyday common thugs. Not to mention Brad is HOT that you got the best of him and it's all over the papers. It makes him look soft and that's not going to blow over easily either. Are you prepared to deal with this?"

Dwayne's pager went off. "There's my PR rep. I gotta figure this out." Then he looked at me. "You coming?"

Malcolm looked at me. "Oh um, Malcolm's gonna take me home. I'm going to go shower and get some sleep. I'll be back with Daddy."

"Daddy?" Malcolm said

"You can shower and sleep here." Dwayne said giving me serious eyes.

Malcolm looked at me like "what are you going to do?"

I walked over to Dwayne, I took him by the hand, and we walked to his porch.

"Dwayne I need to talk to Malcolm about the whole Mister situation. Plus, I don't have anything here to wear. You need to talk to your publicist and the team. It's damage control time."

"I hear that but I don't feel right about watching you ride away with your ex." He said

"I know, believe me I understand but nothing's gonna happen I promise. I'll call you as soon as I walk in the door if that will make you feel better."

"It'll make me feel better if you spent the night tonight." He said

My stomach dropped. "You know I hate being out here!"

"It will be ok; I don't know why you hate the city I'll die protecting you if it's a dangerous factor. I need you to ride with me."

If I didn't say yes, he was going to give me a hard time about leaving. So I said yes then I stepped inside his front door. We kissed long and good, I felt a little lightheaded.

Then I walked back out to Malcolm who hadn't moved. He was looking around the community. "This is a cute little spot." Malcolm said, and then he opened my door. As soon as he got in the car, "What's happening later with your father?"

"Daddy paged this morning. They made a date to meet."

Malcolm was quiet for a minute. Then he started his car. "You know we were gonna have a problem if you stayed."

"I know," I huffed, as I didn't feel it was fair but whatever.

"What are they meeting for?" Malcolm asked trying to mask his jealousy.

"Dwayne has wanted to meet Daddy for some time now. I've always had an excuse for why they couldn't meet. I couldn't avoid it this morning." I said feeling helpless.

"You think they'll like each other?"

"You met him, they're both NINER fans. It's a love affair waiting to happen." I laughed Malcolm didn't. "Why do you care?"

"I don't actually!" Malcolm said with an attitude. "I was just asking."

"You'll always be Daddy's little man!" I said pinching his cheek. We were stuck in commuter traffic in the city. He looked at me unamused by my little tease. He leaned over to kiss me and I backed up. "What are you doing?"

"Kissing you!" He said grabbing my hair and making me kiss him. Then he kept his hand in my hair. "I'm so happy you brought your curls back." I didn't say anything. My hair was falling out, and I had to stop perming it. If he had been around maybe I wouldn't have stressed as much, and I wouldn't have lost all my freaking hair. I was quiet the rest of the car ride. We got to the house as the boys were loading up in Andrew's car.

"So your boyfriend's got a little heart; that was dumb but ok." Derrick said unimpressed.

"Good morning to you too." I said kissing his forehead.

"Good morning Ms. Amber" Hubby said with a huge grin on his face.

I smiled, "morning Hubby."

Andrew shot Hubby a look. "Don't talk to my momma like that!"

Mrs. Hall came out her front door. "Andrew, Derrick, Conrad, and Darryl. I'm gonna need your help this afternoon, what time do you think you'll be home? Hello Amber." She waved

"We should be here around four at the latest. Andrew said

"Perfect I'll see you then." She said sitting down on her stoop.

Malcolm and I walked over and gave her kisses on her cheeks, and then we sat down. "How are you today?" Malcolm said

"Oh I'm kicking! Listen honey," she was talking to me. "Tell your friend he's got to be more careful; he's got that good job, and this morning it's all over the paper how he fought that low life thug. He ain't worth it!"

"I think he's getting an earful of that this morning." I said

Then Mrs. Hall looked at Malcolm long and hard. "You are so handsome!"

Malcolm blushed and thanked her. "You are a classic handsome though. I bet women throw their selves at you all the time." Malcolm blushed harder. "You gotta be careful son, all that glitters ain't gold; and I know it's none of my business, but I

don't get you young folks today. Clearly, you two love each other, you've got a beautiful family together, but yet you two are with other people? That doesn't add up to me. I can only guess where the hiccup is, but you don't have to let the conditioning of those slave masters continue to affect our future generations."
"Slave masters?" Malcolm asked

"Yes sweetheart. They would use a handsome young man like you to impregnate a few slaves and then sell him off kind of like a breeder. A lot of young men grew up never knowing their fathers, and this disconnection keeps getting passed down even to this day."

"But my sons know me." Malcolm said

"Yes honey they do, but what kind of relationship example have you set for them? You are doing so much better than so many, but there's so much more. You want your youngin to be men in a full circle. Now I talk to Andrew, I don't know why such a nice young man is with such a demon child. I've talked to him about her; I hope he gets rid of her before it's too late."

"You and me both!" I said

Then she pinched my cheek. "So good you take after our side. You still look like a child." She laughed. "Love you guys! I gotta go get ready to take my seniors aerobics class with my friends down at your school in an hour."

"Ok, have fun." I said. Malcolm and I walked back towards my house. Malcolm was quiet; I didn't want to discuss it. As soon as he opened his mouth, I started talking over him. I know he doesn't like that but I was tired and still needed to call Dwayne. He shot me evil eyes; I could feel the argument coming. I walked inside the house. "Look Malcolm I heard what she said. I don't want to talk about it right now." I said matter of factly

Malcolm frowned. "So that's just it? You don't want to talk about it so we don't?"
I smiled, "well look at that, the shoe is on the other foot for once."

"You're trying to piss me off on purpose."

"Call it whatever you want! I don't want to have this conversation right now. I have a boyfriend!"

"I don't care about him!"

"You never do! Funny how whenever I'm not available, you want to have these life changing conversations, you have the gumption to be the man I have been begging you to be for years, And then, as soon as you have the chance, you blow it! I don't want to have this conversation again! I don't want to have it until you can actually deliver and knowing you, that will never be! I'm tired of having these conversations with you. How come Mrs. Hall can look at you and know you're out there? I don't want to do this!" I yelled

He started to say something, but then he stopped himself. "Fine! Whatever! I'm putting somebody on the house, the boys, and you. You know the drill. I'll be in touch!" Then he stormed out the house.

I brought a big purse to hide the fact that I was carrying an overnight bag. I wore a nice dress, hubby's eyes got big when he saw me coming down the stairs. Andrew smacked him upside the head and told him to come outside to play basketball. Daddy told me I looked nice then we left to the city. We met Dwayne at Thanh Thanh in the city for an Asian themed meal. Dwayne was there before us and we arrived early. Daddy liked that, one point Dwayne. Daddy came out guns blazing asking Dwayne hard questions. Dwayne didn't back down from any of them. Oh no, Daddy was falling for him. I needed a drink; I asked what the house special was. It was some cute little foo-foo drink. I asked for a Long Island iced tea. Daddy and

Dwayne were in their own world talking when they noticed me finish my second drink and pick up my third. I smiled at them, and then Daddy eyed me. He started reading me "CRAP!" He started asking me a bunch of questions so I put down my third drink and I talked with them before Daddy dug into me with extremely hard questions.

"I don't know why Amber has kept us apart so long Mr. Wallace; I think tonights gone well." Dwayne said sipping on his cocktail

"Yea, why is that? Were you ashamed of him or something?" Daddy asked me.

"I'm just trying to move at my own pace." I said

Daddy looked at me. I knew he could see Malcolm written all over my face. Then he turned to Dwayne. "So I assume you've met Malcolm." I wanted to melt away. Sweat beads appeared on my forehead.

"She's never formally introduced us, but I am aware of him." Dwayne said

"Honey, why haven't you introduced them?" Daddy was being a snot. I shot him a look that said leave me alone. "Ok, little Annette. Ok." He laughed. "Do you plan to introduce Amber to your ex wife?"

"I want her to meet my girls and everybody. She has cold feet."

Daddy looked at me. "I see." He took a swig off his drink. "So your nose is open." Daddy said to Dwayne.

"I wouldn't say that...."

"No! No, that was an observation not a question. But you haven't had the talk." Daddy looked at me. "We're all adults here, put your big girl panties on."

"Eeewwllll! Daddy!" I frowned.

Daddy started cracking up laughing. "You know what I mean. Handle business!"

"Business I can do, this is emotional." I said

Daddy nodded, Dwayne leaned back in his chair letting Daddy, and I's words hang over him. I slowly sipped my third drink while Daddy and Dwayne discussed the position that he and his publicist decided to take. At the end of the night, Daddy said he was gonna knock off. He didn't even ask me if I was coming with him. He gave me a hug and a kiss, and then he told Dwayne he enjoyed meeting him. That sealed it; Daddy liked him. Dwayne was feeling good about himself. I was very relaxed having had four Long Islands. Dwayne gave me a tour of his house. Each of the girls had their own rooms in his house, and he still had two guest rooms, an office, home gym, a fabulous kitchen, huge pool, hot tub, sauna, and three-car garage. This house was fabulous! His master suite was huge and beautiful. My little house didn't compare to his but my Nana bought my house, I wasn't gonna ever just leave it. He told me he had the maid put satin sheets on the bed because he knew how much I loved them. I smiled; the bed was huge and beautiful! He had to have had the sheets custom made, which probably meant he's been waiting for tonight for a long time. I told him his house was beautiful and he thanked me for the compliment. Realizing how tipsy I was, he asked me why I drank so much tonight. I blurted out because I didn't want to marry him. Then I asked him if that made me a jerk. He said it would've if he were asking. He wasn't ready to get remarried, although I don't know if he was saying that to save face. He said it wasn't fair to talk about any of this in my current state of mind. I apologized then I blurted out that I hated the city! He asked me why; I told him if I answer, he might not get lucky. He really wanted to understand, so I told him my mother's family lives out here. I told him about Uncle but a cursory overview, I said I hated him. Then I told him about the club and the fight the next morning. I showed him the scar on my left leg, which then prompted him to ask about the bigger scar on that same leg, so I told

him about the miscarriage and the accident, I didn't go into the details about Sammy. I was crying nonetheless as I told him all of this. I was crying most about my child that never was because someone else decided my life wasn't worth sparing. Dwayne really comforted me and for the first time in a long time, I felt like someone cared about how things/stuff affected me. Ok so then the alcohol kicked in. "You better not fall in love with me! I heard what my Daddy said about your nose. You had better close it up! Staple it or cement it shut! Just promise me you won't fall in love with me!" He started to say something. "Ah! Ah! Ah! Promise!" He asked me why. "It just never works out! I don't want to fall for you! And I'm not going to! I don't care how cute you are or if my Daddy likes you! Shoot! Malachi could love you and I'm not going to!" He asked me who Malachi was. "Shows how much I talk to you! Malachi is my beloved big brother! I have two you know but Timothy is old! Old! Old! Old! Malachi is my protector! He always looks out for me and Jade." He asked me who Jade was. "Only the best big sister a girl could have. She always took care of me when Momma would go crazy." Then I heard myself and I sat on the bed. I patted his hand, "just do us both a favor, and don't fall in love with me. If you can't agree with me, we need to cut ties now. I can't be more than your girlfriend, and I'm so sorry I had to be drunk to say this to you."
"Again Amber, I didn't ask you to marry me."
"Yea, yea, and I'm telling you not to let the thought enter your mind. Don't even think about it."
"Is that why you don't want to meet my girls?"
"You shouldn't have them around just anybody."
"You're not just anybody."
"See! See! See! How could you do this to me? You're supposed to be the ultimate bachelor. Why? Why? Why? "I took a deep breath. " I need a drink!" I got up heading towards the bar I saw somewhere around this room.
"The last thing you need is more alcohol. Come here!" He pulled me into his lap. "That was a lot to take in."
"I'm sorry! I'm just really emotional! A lot has happened and it's only Thursday!"
"Thursday?" He laughed. "We have a problem." My body stiffened. "Your dad called it. I am already really...."
"No! No! No!" I tried to wiggle free.
"Hold on! Let me talk." He said tightening his grip on me. "Are you even coherent?"
"I'm lucid Dwayne, none of this is coming out like it should, but I know what I'm saying." I said
"Amber I like you a lot, way more than you want me to. I don't know why you wouldn't want to marry me, but I think I have an idea." I blew air because I didn't want to know what he thought. "I want you to meet my daughters because they are very special to me and you are very special to me. I want you to meet my parents and my whole family, for however long you'll have me in your life."
"No! No! Dwayne! Did you not hear me?"
Then he kissed me long and hard. "I heard you! But I can't help how you make me feel!"
"You're supposed to be a playboy! What is wrong with this picture?"
"I was and then in walks Amber!" He said I smiled.
"That's not even funny!"
"No it's not. However, I'm gonna help you out. You care about me too. You know how I know?" I shook my head. "Otherwise you wouldn't try to push me away so

much." He took a deep breath. "I also know you're still in love with Malcolm. I don't like it, but you have three kids. Ties like that don't just go away over night. I just want to be with you, please don't run from me, not now, not after all this."
"Falling for me is bad for your health, just ask D...." I caught myself before I said his name. I broke out in a sweat, and that sobered me up real fast.
"Who?"
I took a deep breath. "During my off again on again relationship with Malcolm. I started dating this other guy, but I don't want to say his name right now. Not yet. Things were going really well with him. He wanted to marry me and everything but I couldn't marry him. All the things I loved and admired about him vanished. He became this horrible monster. He's the only guy I've dated outside of Malcolm until you. And I really only agreed to you cause I never saw it going this far."
"Gee! You had a lot of faith in me."
"You know you come across as a playboy." I exhaled. "We can date, for now! As long as you don't turn into a monster. This is important Dwayne! My family is not to be mocked or not taken seriously."
"Ok, but that just means we continue as we have right?" He asked
"Right." I said
Although that night, I'm no fool. I know we made love. Is it bad that I loved it?
****

"Why do I have to come meet some little girls?" Darryl said as if he was too cool.
"Because they're closer to your age, and it would take the pressure off of me to have at least one of my babies there." I said.
Darryl looked out the window. "Here we go! They're here." He said unimpressed.
I looked out the window and I saw two little girls with hair like mine with the sweetest faces. I told myself to be cool. Both girls walked in holding hands, they looked just as nervous as I was.
"Tiffany and Crystal, this is Amber, and this is one of her sons Darryl." Dwayne said standing proud.
They said hello in unison.
"Hello ladies it's nice to meet you." I said wanting to scoop them both up.
Dwayne clapped his hands together. "So let's get this show on the road."
We got into Dwayne's car and within minutes, Darryl had the girls talking and sharing stories about their schools, their crazy cat, and goofy stuff. As usual, Darryl had everyone in stitches. I was so thankful that he agreed to come with me. Otherwise, I would've made Derrick come and that would've been uncomfortable for everybody. Watching Darryl with the girls made me think of Jade and I with Malachi. I guess it was time for Dwayne to meet Malachi. I just didn't want him to think anything had changed within me. Since it was a nice and hot day at the theme park, we decided to get on the water log ride. I rolled both girls' hair up into buns and then I did mine. I told them we'd take them down later so we wouldn't end up looking like bush women. Going to a theme park was a good idea. We had the excitement of the park, the wait in the long hot lines to talk, and the thrill of the roller coasters. Darryl feeling himself in the big brother role took it upon himself to buy the girls anything they said ooh to. He kept saying they were just so cute he had to buy them stuff. I had to remind him he wasn't exactly two years older than Tiffany, but he said all that mattered was for once he wasn't the baby.
Dwayne asked us to come with them to drop the girls to their mother. The girls cheered, they told Darryl they wanted him to meet their cat. Everyone got out of the car while I waited inside. The girls took Darryl inside as soon as their mother

opened the door. Dwayne and the mom started walking towards the car so I got out. She looked me up and down as soon as I got out the car, but I did the same so hey it was what it was.

"Michelle this is Amber, Amber this is Michelle." Dwayne said

"It's nice to finally meet you." Michelle said coming in for a hug.

"Likewise" I said feeling relieved that she didn't seem catty.

"Was that your little man that the girls were towing in the house?"

"Yes, that's my Darryl. The girls wanted him to meet their cat." I said

"They must really like him. The girls only introduce Mocha to people they like." I looked at Dwayne, "I think they hit it off pretty nice."

"Definitely!" Dwayne had a huge smile on his face.

"So I take it we'll be seeing more of you?" She asked

"I guess so." I smiled

"That's good; well it was nice meeting you. I'm gonna get back inside."

"Nice meeting you too." I said. Darryl hugged the girls' goodbye and then he bounced into the car. "So you like the little girls?"

"Yea, they're cool for little girls." Darryl said

****

"And that's a wrap!!" The director yelled

Whew! I have never been so ready for a project to be over! Everyone is hugging and saying their goodbyes and I am ready to go. I hugged a few of the dancers' goodbye. Here she comes with that camera crew, ugh!

"This is the woman responsible for choreographing all of our moves. She's the one who makes us all look good. Say hi to the camera Amber!" Torrie said

"Hello everyone in TV land." I said waving to the camera.

"I really think this video is going to make video of the year. What do you think Amber?"

"Oh I'd definitely say it's a contender." I said wanting to get away.

"Amber is THE choreographer to get these days. She has quite the resume built up for herself. Amber what do you think makes you different from other artists?"

I blew air. "Torrie has talent and she has a clear vision for her music. It's not just about writing the songs for Torrie. She knows her lyrics, her music, and concepts for her videos. You can't just come to her with something you picked up off of the street. You must come with that same depth, love, and respect for your craft. I can see Torrie going all the way."

The camera guy took the camera off his shoulder. "That was beautiful!" He said staring at me like I actually said something when all I wanted was to go home. I had a graduation party to finish up.

"Aw! Thanks girl!" Torrie said hugging me.

I stood there letting her hug me. "Alright! The director yelled cut so I'm out! Until we meet again," I said to Torrie, I grabbed my bag and I headed for the airport. I called Jade on my way to the airport and she got me booked on the next flight out of LAX in twenty minutes, from the time my foot hit the airport. I ran through the airport and checked in at the gate. I smiled a huge smile when I realized Jade booked a first class ticket. I could use the space, but I wouldn't have cared if I were in the back as long as I was going home. I sat in my chair and closed my eyes. I felt someone sit next to me, but I was listening to my CD Walkman so I was oblivious to the outside world. When they touched me, I was prepared to be annoyed, I opened my eyes, and it was Tag. I was actually happy to see him that surprised me too. He gave me a hug and sat next to me. The flight attendant asked him if he had a first class ticket. He told her he would pay any price to be upgraded to that specific seat. He handed her his credit card. The flight attendant happily hurried back to the main gate. She returned with a receipt requiring a signature. He signed the receipt not in the least bit concerned with the price. I told him his bonus must be nice. He smiled, then he asked me what business venture had me leaving LAX. I told him about the video that completed my sixth video obligation with a client, now I was on my way home to Andy's graduation ceremony and party. He couldn't believe he was graduating already. I told him if it felt like that for him to imagine what it felt like for me. He asked what school Andrew was going to, I told him Andrew hasn't told us yet, and that he was waiting until his party to reveal it to us. We talked about the family a little more, and then he asked me how Dwayne was doing. I told him Dwayne was fine. Then he went on and on about how we never got our chance to see how we fit as a couple. I told him I've never known a person to be rejected so much and to still keep coming back for more. He smiled and said he can be persistent when it was worth it.

"Not that I don't enjoy the attention sometimes, but you're really gonna have to let that go."

"What about now? We could go in the bathroom, I'd never tell. You know I'm good about keeping secrets." He gave me a knowing look.

"What does that look mean?"

"I've never said anything about the camping trip."

"And I thank you for that. I don't have to carry the burden of your death on my shoulders." I laughed.

He moved in closer, "I won't tell a soul, just say yes. Please! Please!"

"Tag, I'm not a hoe. I'm not gonna screw you in a bathroom."

"I will be anywhere you want me to be."

"Don't you have a girlfriend?"

"Come on Amber! You must know what you mean to me. I would marry you right now! Will you marry me?"

I started laughing. "Tag! You are a very handsome man. I'm sure women throw their selves at you. That black hair, piercing blue eyes, you could have just about anyone else. Why do you waste your time lowering yourself to beg me? I don't understand you."

"First you were too young, now I'm too handsome. You always have some kind of a flaky reason for why we can't be together." He said sitting back.

"Sorry. You won't accept that I have a boyfriend, a crazy baby daddy, and a father who isn't crazy about you as reasons to stay away. So I guess I have to resort to you're too handsome to be selling yourself too short."

"I've been in love with you since you were fifteen years old. Although I'm not giving up, I want to enjoy this alone time with you. So what project do you have coming up next?"

"I'm taking the summer off actually. I want to spend time with Andy before we get him settled wherever he ends up." I blushed. "Plus Dwayne wants to take all the kids on a family vacation."

If looks could kill! "You are killing me! I tell you I've been in love with you for" he did the math in his head. "Eighteen years and you tell me you're taking family vacations with my sworn enemy!"

"Since when is Dwayne your sworn enemy?"

"From the moment you were willing to give him a chance."

"Not cool Tag!"

He shrugged like he didn't care. The closer we got to Oakland airport the more agitated he got. Then he asked me if we would ever have a chance. I told him honestly I didn't know, but I told him more than likely it would never happen. He looked disappointed, but that persistent look flashed on his face, and I just shook my head. When we exited the plane, Tag made sure he was on my heels. As soon as I hit the corner, I spotted Dwayne waiting for me. I was so happy to see him. He had a sign with my name written in a heart. His smile was huge and then he saw Tag walk out behind me, and his smile dropped and he instantly started frowning. I hurried over and gave him a huge hug, while he stared down Tag. Tag gave him an evil glare back and I grabbed him by the hand and told him to come on. He asked me why Tag was on my flight, I told him I didn't know. I told him how I had my eyes closed and then all of a sudden there he was. He asked me what we talked about, and in a very bored and over it tone I told him that basically, Tag badgered me about giving him a chance. He didn't like that but it was the truth. I asked him where his car was and he said it was at my house and that Drew dropped him off. Suddenly he stopped walking, pointed at a guy, and asked who he was. Seeing the slim walkie-talkie in his back pocket, I knew it was one of Malcolm's guys. The guys in LA were less obvious, but I guess it's hard to be discreet in an airport. I shrugged and told Dwayne I didn't know him. Then I told Dwayne he probably worked for Malcolm. Dwayne stopped in his tracks and asked me to explain what I said. So I explained that with everything that happened with Mister, Malcolm wants to make sure that we're safe so he has bodyguards follow us. Dwayne was quiet for a minute, and then he asked if that's how Malcolm knew what room we were in that night? I said it's more than likely but I never asked directly. I could tell he was thinking about it. Then he said that whole thing with Mister is supposed to be squashed, "especially after we apologized to each other publicly." Then I told him that whole thing with Mister wasn't even about him, and Malcolm doesn't trust Mister. Dwayne was quiet again, when we got in my car Dwayne asked if something had happened before so I pulled over and explained that the car accident I had was the result of someone lashing out at what they thought was him. I told Dwayne even though Malcolm and I weren't together he would never let anything happen to me. Dwayne asked me who Malcolm was, I told him he's just Malcolm, and you either hate or love him, but don't cross him. Dwayne changed the subject. We started talking about our family trip. We decided to go back to Hawaii as a family. I volunteered to help pay for it, but Dwayne wasn't having it. When we walked in the door, Jade and Lil Sonny were there. Jade told me to let her know when I was ready then we could go over Andy's party plans. I put my bag in my room. I picked up the baby and then I told her to shoot. Lil Sonny reminded me of Andrew when he was a baby, he was very smart already; he observed everything you did, Jade was already pregnant with baby number two. I think she was making up for lost time or something. She didn't even wait to get her body back she just dove right in. Sonny didn't seem to notice or care. Andrew said he liked Jade with the weight, and he kept hugging her saying she was so cuddly.

Jade told me that Timothy and Grace come in tomorrow. Then she asked if Dwayne was bringing his girls and he said he was. She said the caterers had confirmed the menu, and that the table, chairs, and dance floor were arriving to Daddy's house on Friday. She said the temporary workers from Mitigated would be there to setup Saturday morning so as long as we had our example table setup by the time they came they would handle the rest of the decorations and set it up. We hired a celebrity DJ for his party. Jade had everything laid out perfectly. I thanked her ten million times over, and then I had her sit on the couch while I rubbed her feet and legs. Dwayne sat back and watched us. He said he hoped his girls were that close when they became adults.

Timothy told us that his Chicago firm was shutting down and he felt it was a good time to move back to California. Daddy insisted that they stayed with him until Timothy found a job or whatever. I already knew as soon as Uncle Frank heard he was going to tell Timothy to start his own firm. He was disappointed that Timothy chose to work for someone else in the first place. Grace was so excited to be moving back, she said she missed California especially the Bay Area so much. She was over the snow and wind chill. Friday night before Andy's graduation we rented out Gonzalez's for dinner for just the family. Malcolm was quiet in the corner the whole evening not saying too much. We all celebrated Andrew and then we convinced him to tell us tonight rather than wait a whole day where he was going to go to school. Andrew informed us that he was going to Berkeley and I cried. I wouldn't have to love my baby from afar. I hugged and kissed him excessively. He pretended like he didn't like it, but he was eating it up. He told me he still wanted the college experience so he wanted to get a little apartment close to campus. He said as soon as Derrick was legally driving he'd give him Malachi's car, and then he'd get something else. Malachi liked that idea. Derrick loved the idea especially since Andrew had put hydraulics in the car, which just put the car over the top. I pulled Andrew to the side and I asked him what was going on with him and Malcolm. He told me nothing I needed to worry about but we both knew I'd ask him again. When we got home, I followed Andrew to his room and I asked again. He said that he and Malcolm got into a big argument. He said it started about Toya, but it just went into everything else. He said they even argued about me. When I asked him what about me, Andrew's voice was booming as he expressed how he felt Malcolm constantly disrespected me and strung me a long. I told him I was the only person Malcolm argued with, he didn't argue with people especially men. Andrew did say it started because Malcolm was really trying to explain to him why he needed to leave Toya alone. He said he knew Malcolm was right, but it still made him mad that Malcolm thought of himself as any kind of expert when it came to dealing with females. When I asked him what he was gonna do about her Andrew blew air. Then he told me that he loved her. I couldn't take the disgust off my face. Andrew said he already knew what everybody thought of her, but it didn't matter to him. So I let it go, my son is brilliant in regards to everything else, at some point I hoped he wised up regarding the woman he chose in his life.

I went early to the ceremony to block off a huge section for our family in support of Andrew. When we pulled up those little girls were batting their eyes and anything else they thought would get his attention. All I heard was "Drew! Drew! Drew!" Girl after girl was running up to my baby saying their goodbyes and pressing their goodies up against him. Bernadette and her large family got there next and she and I sat back and watched the shameless patrol of female after female. I asked her if Malcolm was that bad and I just didn't see it. She belly laughed, she said that they're on different levels. She said Drew was approachable so it's more in your face. She said only the girls who were more turned on than afraid of Malcolm acted that way, but she said if you took Malcolm's scariness out of the way, he, and Andrew were just a like. Family arrived and we packed out not only the space I chose but also more. Dwayne and the girls sat next to me. Everybody kept giving me thumbs up and pats on the back. Bernadette said her eyes hurt because Dwayne was so fine. Penny said the girls looked like they could be my girls. I guess we did look like a family, but I definitely was not trying to take their mother's place. Malcolm sat on the opposite end from us. As the class valedictorian, Andrew has to speak to his classmates and the audience. I got a little teary looking at the charisma of Malcolm and the charm of Malachi up on that stage. Andrew was such and eloquent speaker, I could've listened to him speak all day. I looked over at Malcolm and I smiled at him. He nodded his head, but he gave me no smile. When they called Andrew Wallace, everyone stood up and cheered our whole section and just about all the graduates. We were so loud they had to wait for us to settle down before they went to the next student's name. Toya looked at our section and I could see sadness in her eyes. I think only the faculty courtesy clapped for her when they called her name. When the ceremony was over, I told everyone to go back to Daddy's house and we'd meet them there. Daddy was so happy Dwayne was there; Dwayne invited Daddy to ride with him back to the house while I waited for the man of the hour. Andrew came busting out of the auditorium with his diploma in his hand. His eyes were red and he was looking for someone. I instantly felt heat on my neck, as I wanted to know who did it. When he spotted me, he walked very heavily towards me. When I asked him what was wrong as a tear rolled down his face. He picked me up in the biggest bear hug and told me he loved me so much. I asked him what happened, he said nothing, he was just sitting there thinking about me, and he felt overwhelmed with emotion. Andrew and I stood there hugging for a long time. Toya stood next to us looking annoyed while people walking by ooh and ahh'd because they knew Andrew loves his momma. I felt so loved and appreciated in that moment. I thought Andrew would be embarrassed to let people see him cry, but he didn't care. He kept telling me how much he loved me and how thankful he was for me. Toya looked like she was gonna snap. Then a lot of Andrew's classmates asked how to get to his party so we told them to follow us. As we walked to the car Toya was fussing with Andrew because she didn't want to party with anyone from the school. Andrew told her to calm down and to just go with the flow. She sat in the back seat pouting. When we got to Daddy's house Andrew got so excited seeing Hubby, Jeff, and Joseph he hopped out the car and very loudly and excitedly ran over to his best friend and cousins. Toya screamed and threw her body across the backseat. "Um little girl! I know you know better than to act a fool in my car!" I said Toya sucked her teeth, "yes ma'am!" She said sarcastically. Then she got out of the car. She walked over to Andrew, the guys looked at her, and I could only imagine what she was saying. Andrew grabbed her by the arm and led her down the street. The guys started laughing at her. She was wiggling her neck trying to respond but Andrew continued to pull her. I took a deep breath then I got out of the car. Hubby looked at me, smiled real big; he said something that made Joseph smack him upside the back of his head. I gave my cousins and the graduate a hug. Hubby held on a little longer than he should. Jeff and Joseph growled at him, Hubby blushed. I gave him a pat on the shoulder and told him he was a goofy kid. The boys erupted into laughter. Hubby said real low that he was 18 and that he was a man now. I smiled and walked inside the backyard. You saw a ton of caps and gowns, even some from other schools. I spotted Tanisha with Lil Tim, Tina, Tiffany, and Crystal demonstrating with Darryl how to play basketball. Once she was done, she gave me a huge hug. I asked her why she hadn't called me back. She looked embarrassed, then she wrapped her arm around mine, and we walked to the far corner. She said she wanted to accept my offer to pay for her college tuition but she felt weird about it. I told her I had no idea why, she was my baby just as much as any of the others, Berkeley was such an expensive school, and she felt like she would be taking advantage. I had to make her stop talking. I put my hands on her face and I looked her in her eyes. I told her how much I love her and as long as I can help her, I was going to. Then I asked her what did she want to do, she wanted to go into law enforcement. I told her having an education would help her to go forward. She started crying and she put her head on my shoulder. Then she told me she brought a friend. I told her to make sure she introduced us before the day was over. I asked her if her mother came, she looked at the ground. She said Yuri wouldn't let her come. I sucked my teeth; I patted her head and told her it was ok. I guess maybe because I had been through a dysfunctional relationship, I saw the signs a little faster. However, that man that was all drama free eventually brought his controlling drama to the frontline. Rosalind had put her foot in her mouth so deep I don't think she could figure out how to get out of it. I popped up on them once and she told me Yuri said not to do that anymore. So I left them alone.

Daddy had Dwayne with him talking to Uncle Jeff, Uncle Frank, Ryan, Timothy, Malachi, Travis, and some of my other cousins. Dwayne and I made eye contact and he smiled, I could tell they were all talking sports by the looks on their faces. Over in the opposite corner of the yard was Malcolm. He was talking to Renee and a few other cousins but he was watching me. I knew that look in his eyes so I looked the other way. FINALLY, Andrew graced his own party with his presence; Toya was clinging to his arm. Sasha bounced from across the yard in her cap and gown. Andrew and Sasha bounced together, and then Tanisha joined them. Everybody was cracking up, we had always seen them do this, but until they did it just then we didn't realize it was on purpose. Before long, Jeff and Joseph joined in the fun, then Derrick, Darryl, and Hubby. Next thing we knew, all the teenagers were bouncing, and the DJ put on a record that seemed to fit perfectly with their crazy movements. Everybody started dancing except Toya. She was on my nerves and the party had just begun. Toya found a chair at a table and sulked while Andrew danced with everybody; even the girls from his school and other schools that he invited. I thought that was very bold of him, but Hubby told me they were on the verge of breaking up again. Then Tanisha introduced me to her friend Amanda. Amanda was very pretty and a sweetheart, I thanked her for coming then they all went back on the dance floor. After a couple of hours, I noticed Andrew dancing with Amanda. Tanisha was right there dancing with Hubby but Hubby looked like he was trying to get Sasha's attention all day. Any who, I was sitting holding Sabrina with Jade, Sophia, Bernadette, Gwen, Renee, and a few others when Toya came storming over talking about my son was the most disrespectful so and so she ever met.

"Little girl! Don't bring that mess in here. We need one day where you don't go ruining things for everyone."

"You're always defending him! Maybe, if you let him suffer the consequences of his actions just once he'd grow up and finally become a man!" Then she stood there looking at me like yea I said it now what you gonna do.

Sophia reached over and grabbed her baby as I stood up. "Toya, I'm gonna have to ask you to leave. You're not gonna ruin this day for my son or me. I'm only gonna tell you once!" I said through clinched teeth.

"YOU ARE SUCH A BI..."

Before I could stop myself, my fist connected with that little girl's face, as she fell backwards I lunged on top of her. Her face was so surprised and I could hear myself saying don't hurt the baby too badly but every time I looked at her I got more and more angry. Bernadette picked me up and did her best to hold me back. Toya

looked scared stupid; Renee helped her up and then told her she needed to go home before the cousins' came to finish the job. Toya was holding her nose and she rolled her eyes at Renee. Penny grabbed Renee to stop her from going in on her. Toya yelled that we were always picking on her. She couldn't spot Andrew in the crowd and when she called out his name, he didn't answer. She stormed out the yard and the guys with the walkie-talkies out front pointed at her and laughed. The music came back on and Andrew walked over, he was trying not to look sad. He apologized to us for bringing her. Penny told him he better not let that crazy girl spoil the day. Then she made him go out on the dance floor with her. She was dancing so retarded he had no choice but to laugh and enjoy the moment. Although all the men went back to talking Dwayne was looking at me all concerned. He mouthed asking me if I was ok, and I said yes. Then I looked at his girls who didn't seem to notice so I thought. Then Sophia said as soon as she saw that glimmer of Auntie Annette in my eyes she knew she needed to grab her baby and duck. As the evening progressed I danced a couple songs with Dwayne, danced with the kids, showed them a few things then I went inside to see about the cake. There was cake but no ice cream. I decided to walk over to Bob's like Momma used to send me to. When I opened the front door Malcolm was talking to one of the walkie-talkie guys. He stopped talking when he saw me. When I was almost past him, he turned and started walking with me. Neither one of us said anything at first.
"So he's gonna go to Berkeley you gotta be excited."
"Are you kidding? I'm ecstatic! Not only is he going to my old Alma Mater, but also he'll be close by. What about you? Our baby graduated today! He's going to college aren't you happy?"
"I'm excited can't you tell?" His face was stone and his eyes were serious.
"Good grief Malcolm."
Bob was just putting the closed sign up when he saw us coming. He opened the door for us. "We've come for the usual!" I said
Bob said he'd drop it off. Malcolm took me by the hand and led me to the back. He kissed me long and hard in Bob's office. I knew I shouldn't have been back there but I wanted to kiss Malcolm badly. He started pulling at my dress and I told him I couldn't. He said he didn't care about Dwayne, I told him I was on my period. He looked so disappointed, he knew he wasn't gonna be alone with me again for a long time. We locked up the shop and walked back. He told me he heard about our upcoming trip. "I guess you get to have your family vacation after all." He said looking at me.
"I am so excited! I think the boys are gonna love it!" I said
"Just so you know it's not that I didn't want to do that kind of stuff, I just didn't know how. The boys will love it. Give Derrick some space to adjust, he'll come around." Malcolm said.
As we approached the house, Dwayne was outside talking to Bob. He stared at us as we got closer. I thanked Malcolm for walking me to Bob's. Malcolm grabbed my hand and pulled me into a bear hug while staring at Dwayne. Dwayne's expression remained blank. I told Malcolm to cut it out, and then I walked away. "What's up Dwayne?" Malcolm said putting his hands out.
"What's up?" Dwayne said walking towards Malcolm.
I grabbed Dwayne's arm that he tried to move out of my reach, and pulled him back towards the house. Uncle Jeff was standing in the doorway cracking up. He told Dwayne to never let his temper ever make him that stupid. Dwayne looked back at Malcolm, and Malcolm waved the finger at him with a smile.

Chapter 42

"This is the dumbest argument I think I've ever had with ANYONE!" I said

"Maybe if you said something worth saying we wouldn't be arguing!" Dwayne said

I took a deep breath, "I'm not gonna argue about this. You've got three choices when most people are fortunate to have one. Either Juan goes, some random guys we don't know, or my boys or I will go on our own vacation. It's simple!"

"And I'm saying we will be fine! We don't need Malcolm in our bed out there!"

"So I guess we're not going then!" I crossed my arms. Dwayne walked away. I turned around, I was trying to think of where I was gonna go. I opened the sliding glass door. My heels clanked on the marble tiles as I walked into the kitchen. I looked for the phone book. I called the SF cab company but I didn't know the address to Dwayne's place. I told them I would call them back. I was looking for an envelope or a magazine with his address on it. I heard him coming right when I found what I was looking for. I called back, "it's me again. Can you send a cab to 498 riv....?"

Dwayne hung up the phone. "For real Amber?"

"I didn't come over here for this. I'm going home!"

"Ok so, I'm not a man? The only person who can protect you is Malcolm?"

"Dwayne you don't even understand what you're up against! I'm sorry I value my life too much to play these games with you. This is not an attack on your manhood, but I do value my life and that of my children. If you can't understand where I'm coming from I'm so sorry, but I'm not playing this game to make you feel like a man."

"Help me understand." He said trying to calm down. Even though I didn't want to, I explained how Sammy came around, then the next thing I know a car is crashing into me. I thought I was going to die! Then about Momma Shuga and Pam, I told him I was a little bit traumatized and how if Malcolm felt like I needed someone watching over me I listened. I told him my family didn't worry about me because they knew no matter what Malcolm was watching over me. "Who is Malcolm? Who is he? To hear you talk about him, he's like a god!"

I blew air, "do you think I'm making this up? I'm not a liar!"

"I didn't say that. I just realize there's more to you than I thought. You looked crazy going after that little girl. It was business as usual for everybody else. That was crazy! You guys got your own little secret service standing outside watching over the house while you party. I know your Uncle Frank at least was packing. Who brings a gun to a high school graduation party? I just wanted us to have a family vacation away from all that noise."

"It's not noise when it's been your life. You have no idea who I am!"

"Then tell me!"

"No!"

He threw his hands up in the air. "I'm trying!"

"Maybe we should just call this whole thing off!" I said

"What is wrong with you? You're looking for a reason."

"No I'm not!"

"Yes you are!"

"Whatever!" I picked up the phone to call a cab.

He hung up the phone. "You want to go home, I'll take you home." He walked towards the garage.

I had to pee so I went to the guest bathroom. I was moving as fast as I could, but he was still standing by the door with his arms crossed. I dried my hands on the towel, then walked heels clanking on the marble tiles and got my jacket and purse off the chaise lounge sofa in the living room. I rolled my eyes as I walked past him into the garage. I stood in the garage waiting for him to indicate which car he was driving. Of course, he picks the sports car. I stood still; when he looked at me, I shook my head no. "You gotta be kidding me!" He yelled.

"You're mad! I'm not getting in that death trap with you!" I said

Dwayne was mad and his patience was running thin. When he got out the car, he slammed the door on his car very hard. I never seen him this angry with me, I started feeling scared. David would've snapped along time ago. He was walking towards me to go to the car but I thought he was going to grab me so I squared off. "Now you wanna fight me?" He walked up on me, "what is wrong with you?"

Ok Amber you're playing your crazy card I might as well let it all hang out, I told myself. I got on my tiptoes and stuck my chest out in an attempt to get in his face. On my tiptoes, I reached his neck but so what. "Don't walk up on me when you're mad! I'm not scared of you Dwayne Arthur Reed!" I kept bumping him with my chest. My fist were balled and I was ready to grab the broom next to the door to use as a weapon if he tried to catch me off guard like David used to try to do.

He smirked, "so now you're using my middle name?" He fought to hold on to his serious look although he was starting to laugh, I backed up and looked at him and he stopped laughing. "You're serious?" I glared at him. "Amber, we need to talk."

"I don't want to talk to you! I want to go home."

"Why don't you want to talk to me?"

"Because!"

He rolled his hands. "Because?"

"Because you just want to get me out in the open, away from Malcolm's protection just so you can hurt me!"

"Why would I want to hurt you? I love you!"

"You're lying!" I screamed. "You don't love me! You might like me. You might like me a lot, but you don't love me!"

He was mad all over again. "I haven't lied to you ever!"

"Cause I don't ask you questions. It's easy to tell the truth with easy questions." I barked

"Like?"

"Like when was the last time you hooked up with a groupie?" His eyes hit the floor. "Or when was the last time you and Michelle hooked up?" He exhaled. "I could go on, but I don't ask. I'm telling you my life could be at stake and all you can see is how I'm threatening your manhood. That's not love!"

"Why don't you ask?"

"Why should I ask you a question I don't wanna know the answer to?" I said

"Why don't you want to know?" He asked

"Because I don't want to care."

"Why don't you want to care?"

"Hello! I just told you."

"Tell me again I was distracted by your little fist." He smiled

"Little?" He smiled bigger. "You just want to get me out side of Malcolm's protection so you can hurt me."

"Hurt you how?"

"However you plan to do it I don't know!"

"Amber! I don't want to hurt you. I don't want you thinking of me that way." I
rolled my eyes. "You are so tight lipped about everything. Then you're over here
freaking out; how can I redeem myself if I don't even know what's going on?"
"But when I'm telling you that I feel it's a matter of life or death to have certain
things, just back off, and let me have it. Don't take it personal."
Dwayne took a deep breath, "Come inside?" He gestured towards the house.
I stood there thinking about it. I wanted to go home but I only wanted to go home to
run away from Dwayne. Him telling me he loved me made me feel funny. Like I
knew he meant it, and there was a part of me that loved him too. I definitely cared
for him. There was a bigger part that is still in love with Malcolm and is hurt that
there even has to be a Dwayne. I exhaled and walked back towards the house. He
opened a bottle of wine, and we went back out in his backyard. He lit the fireplace
and we snuggled next to it lounging in a chair. I love being out under the stars. It
makes me think of the time when Malcolm took me to the beach and pointed out the
constellations and then we made love under them. I was missing Malcolm but that
wasn't an unfamiliar feeling. Dwayne was right he was trying, and he has been
trying. I just don't want to open up to him to experience anything I experienced with
David. I don't want to go through that again. I'm so scared to feel what I could feel
for him. For one he's too dog gone pretty! Malcolm is handsome and I hate dealing
with that, but Dwayne is pretty! It's even worse that he's so high profile, women all
over the country drool over him. It's getting to the point where he needs the security
of the front gate.
"So how do you want to resolve this?" He asked me.
"Juan was there last time and he's a good guy, I like his family. I vote for Juan." I
said
He exhaled. "Fine. Whatever makes you happy."
"Feeling safe makes me happy." I kissed his arm.
"I just wish you could feel that way with me." He said kissing my head.
"Um, hello? I'm here aren't I? I HATE the city, but I've been coming here to be with
you. I'd say that's progress."
I could hear his heart beat speed up. "That's true; you do love me don't you." I didn't
say anything. "One of these days you're gonna slip up and say it."
"Honestly Dwayne I won't. I've asked you too many times before not to go there
with me. I don't want to love you, and if you can't handle this we can stop now."
He hugged me a little tighter. "Stop trying to pick a fight." I didn't say anything
because that's exactly what I was trying to do.
****
Hawaii was beautiful! Rosalind braided the girl's hair as well as mine just before
we left. We got in the water every day. I taught the girls how to swim and we did
some lightweight snorkeling. The boys went parasailing, we ran like crazy on jet
skis. We ate like pigs; we had a good time with Juan and his family. What I like
about Juan is he does his job. He makes sure we're safe and covered at all times no
matter what we do. Other than that, he minds his business; he wasn't in our personal
business or mentioning Malcolm to make us feel uncomfortable. Even when
Derrick had his fill of watching, Dwayne and I interact and he called himself
storming off. Juan didn't try to talk him down or change his mind. He just did his
job and made sure my baby was safe. Even though my boys did have, an altercation
with some of the locals behind a girl that Derrick was talking to, Juan let them have
their little brawl to an extent but he stopped them before my soldiers went too far.
Dwayne's eyes were big once he caught a glimpse of what they were capable of.

Again he was looking at me like who are you? Fortunately, the girls and I were out shopping with Gloria and her daughter Juanita. The girls had fun playing nurse to Darryl and Derrick. Putting ice on their heads and making them lay down. Darryl ate it up, Derrick tried to resist but the girls broke through his hard exterior; and just like Darryl, he was putty in their hands. Andrew came out with us during the day, but at night he and all but two of the guys Juan brought hit the clubs. Andrew would come back to the suite sometimes after four in the morning. Rest for a few hours and then get up with the rest of us. He told the girls he couldn't lie down; he said he might not wake up.

Our suite had three bedrooms. We had a cot brought in the boy's room so that each person had their own bed inside a bedroom. They each had their own bathrooms. The master suite was on the opposite side of the suite and it was huge. Our balcony over looked the water; we had a hot tub in our room. Dwayne and I had the best sex that whole vacation. So good, I almost called him Malcolm one time. I caught myself almost telling him I loved him more than once. Outside of my babies, beating up on some locals it was one of the best vacations yet. Even Derrick had to admit he had a good time. Andrew told me he liked Dwayne but even he could tell I was holding back.

When we got home, we immediately began our search for an apartment for Andrew. I threw out the idea of Tanisha and Andrew being roommates but they both shot down the idea as quickly as it came out of my mouth. We found nice little one-bedroom apartments for both of them in the same building. They weren't extravagant at all, but Andrew wanted to start off fresh. Even though he never flaunted it, many of his high school classmates knew, because he was Malcolm's son, that he had money. None of them could understand why he drove an old school car when he could have something brand new, or why he didn't wear name brand clothes, where Hubby on the other hand, was always wearing the latest and newest stuff. Thank goodness for his modesty, otherwise my baby would forever be ridiculous. We got simple and small furniture, he took his bedroom furniture from my house however, and he did upgrade his mattresses. He was barely out of his room when Derrick started moving his things in; he was so excited to finally have his own room.

Sasha decided to go to ULA although she almost changed her mind when she found out that Andrew and Tanisha were going to Berkeley. Sophia insisted that Sasha have her own place out there even if she planned to spend most of her time with Richard. Joseph was happy to have family out there with him. In the end, Joseph asked Sasha to move in with him, partially to keep a close eye on her, but mostly to have family close.

Since I was funding Tanisha's college education and lifestyle, we set up a checking account for her. I explained the structure to her. I decided to use some of the money Malcolm still put in that savings account weekly to fund Tanisha. At the beginning of the month I would deposit her rent money and a set amount for her utilities, since I gave her my everyday car she didn't have to worry about a car note, the insurance that she got on her own would be included in her utilities. On the fifteenth of each month, I would deposit a set amount for her food and spending money. I was paying her full tuition and books, anything associated with school needed to be brought to me directly. I told her anything lower than a B- was unacceptable, and her spending money would be lowered. Tanisha asked if Amanda could stay with her. I told her the decision was up to her but if their relationship affected her schoolwork etc., she knew the consequences. Tanisha decided it was better for her to live alone. Smart girl.

****

Torrie's record sales soared, and the label attributed her success to marketing which covered her expenses for her videos. The label threw her a huge release party right here in Oakland although her record had already come out. They made a big deal out of me being there although I didn't really want to go. I kept telling them no, until at the last minute Sophia convinced me to go provided that she came with me. Dwayne was out of town and I didn't want to go alone. When Sophia got to my house, she called my outfit frumpy. I told her she sounded just like Nana. She hated my pants; she went in my closet and found a green dress I had completely forgotten about. We went back and forth about my hair. I wanted to wear it down but she convinced me that it set the outfit off nicely to wear it up. Darryl was playing a video game, and Derrick was on the phone. He didn't talk to Raquel all that much anymore. He said they mutually agreed to break up but to keep in contact. I would see Derrick talking to girls, but he wasn't as girl crazy as Andrew was/is. I told Derrick to order pizza and to make sure whoever was watching the house got some too. Then Sophia and I bounced out the door like two teenagers. This was her first time out since she had the baby, and my first time out without a man wrapped around my arm in I couldn't remember how long. We took my good car, as I hadn't bought another everyday car just yet. We went to Club Twilight in Jack London Square. The line was wrapped around the corner of people waiting to get in. When the two guys following me didn't want to come in, I should've known it was gonna be bad, but I figured maybe it was too crowded. I showed the bouncers my VIP tickets and Sophia and I floated right in. The music was bumping and there were a lot of life size cut outs of Torrie all over the floor; Sophia laughed at them, I just rolled my eyes. I knew Torrie loved all these shout outs to her. We went to the VIP section and claimed our booth. Sophia and I asked for the house special in unison and we both laughed. A couple of drunken execs came over to our booth. One of them offered Sophia something and she firmly declined. The look she gave me, I didn't even want to know what it was. After our second drinks, we were ready to dance. The dance floor was packed so as soon as we stepped on the floor it was like it swallowed us up. I couldn't even tell who I was dancing with. Sophia and I made sure we stayed close to each other, but we had so much fun breaking it down on the dance floor. People from the label kept getting excited that I changed my mind and came out. I didn't realize it was such a big deal that I was there. When Sophia and I made our way back to our booth we asked our waiter for another round. Matthew one of the younger big wigs came to our booth. He was about business, and he was commending me on my work with Torrie. He was telling me that he had some other clients that they wanted me to work with, but Torrie was really fighting to hog me all to herself. I told him I didn't belong to Torrie and that I'd love to hear more about the other artist. The crowd started going crazy, Matthew said Torrie and her entourage finally arrived. He sighed probably from her diva persona and she was only one album in. The Torrie crowd sat in the booth next to ours. I could hear Torrie's voice as she took in the whole scene in the club. She was so touched by the layout of everything. I gave Matthew my card, and then I told him to come dance with Sophia and I. Again, we were back in the middle of the dance floor having a good time. Suddenly girls were staring over my shoulder. They looked hungry which meant they had to be looking at a guy. After having, enough I told Sophia I was gonna sit down. She was following me when I noticed a familiar silhouette dancing in front of me. Sophia recognized him at the same time that I did. I know I shouldn't have been surprised to see him, but I was. I tapped him on the shoulder, and Andrew turned around. He had such a busted look on his face. He said a surprised hello as he hugged and kissed Sophia and I. Then he tried to tell me something but I couldn't hear him. I pointed to our booth, and I told him Sophia and I was going to go sit down. He watched us walk to our table and then he nodded and went back to dancing.

"Ooh child the apple doesn't fall far from the tree!" Sophia said

"Yea but we were younger than him in places like this." I said

I noticed that the noise level over at Torrie's table had dropped significantly and I was thankful, because I didn't want to listen to that drama all night. Andrew started towards our table and the bouncer looked to us for approval. I waved him on. Andrew was holding hands with a girl and he had the biggest smile on his face.

"This is Rachel." He said all proud.

"Hello" I said looking the girl up and down.

The girl looked Sophia and I up and down clearly he didn't tell her who we were.

"These your sisters?" She said unimpressed, and not acknowledging my hello.

Andrew's whole demeanor changed. He dropped her hand and he looked disgusted.

"This is my cousin, and my mother."

Then we watched as her whole everything changed. She put her hand over her mouth. "Oh my goodness, I am so sorry!"

It was too late the damage had been done. All three of us blank stared at her, as she stood there apologizing for two minutes straight. Andrew told Rachel she could leave. She walked away with her tail between her legs. Andrew plopped down next to me. "Oh well, cross her name off the list! NEXT!" He laughed

"Boy are you drunk?" Sophia said laughing.

"Maybe just a little bit, but I know what's going on. I'm good!" He said grinning from ear to ear.

Sophia smiled at me. "You're smiling, but what do you think yours is doing right at this moment? You better hope all she's doing is drinking at a club." Then I smiled back at her.

"He's here! He's here!" Torrie was too excited.

Like a shark fin, you saw a black fedora moving through the crowd. I didn't think anything of it at first until I saw the side profile, I grabbed Sophia's leg, but she was already looking. Malcolm glided through the bouncer and he almost passed our booth without seeing us. He stopped mid-step. "I thought you weren't coming out tonight?"

"You thought?" I said with attitude.

Malcolm sat down next to Sophia. "Yes" then he pointed at Andrew, "what you doing here?"

Andrew smiled, "I'd like to ask you the same thing old man!"

"Old man?" Malcolm smirked. "I'm 34, how is that old?"

"Just is" Andrew said smiling.

"Your momma is only a year younger, is she old?"

Andrew blew sloppy air, "Naw! My momma ain't ever old, you on the other hand." Andrew waved his hand.

"You need to learn to handle your liquor or you won't be able to get into too many places like this." Malcolm said but you could see a sense of pride in the way he looked at Andrew in that moment.

Torrie came storming around the corner. She was looking for someone but she stopped at my booth. She paused as soon as she saw him, she was about to go diva until she spotted me. "I thought you weren't coming!" She said looking busted. I looked her up and down. Her micro-mini dress clung to her perfectly, leaving nothing to the imagination. Her weave was nice and full, and her makeup was flawless. She looked good.

"I changed my mind at the last minute." I said crossing my legs so she could take me in. I didn't care how good she looked; she'd never look as good as I would.

"Malcolm honey, I have a booth for us over here." She said pointing next door.

"Honey?" I said looking at Malcolm

Malcolm shook his head, "why would you say that?" He said to Torrie.

"Malcolm!" She said through clinched teeth.

"I'm talking; I might get over there eventually. Go talk to somebody." He said shooing her away.

Her mouth fell open like she couldn't believe he just treated her that way. Andrew's exaggerated laugh didn't help the situation. "Who are you?" She said eyeing Andrew.

"His son!" Andrew said trying to calm himself

"How is that possible?" She said in shock.

"He is" Malcolm said, "Now get!" The look on Malcolm's face stopped any more questions from her. She turned on her heels and walked away.

"Seriously Malcolm!" I said

He leaned back, "what?"

"So my business means nothing to you?" I was angry.

"Of course it means something. It was my idea."

"Then what are you doing here?"

"You weren't supposed to be here." He said trying to be cute.

"That's not funny!" I yelled but it was so loud it seemed more like I was saying that's funny.

"Come on baby lets go dance." Sophia said to Andrew, who looked like our reality was getting to him.

They went to the dance floor and the crowd of people swallowed them. Malcolm walked over and sat next to me. His eyes went straight to my thighs and then my cleavage. "What difference does it make? Your boy will be home soon anyways." He said not taking his eyes off my chest.

"The difference is I've never dated any of your colleagues or employees."

He blew air, "and I know you know better!"

"But you don't?"

"You're blowing this way out of proportion!" He said sounding irritated.

"Am I? I don't want to be in the same room with any of your whores let alone work with any of them." I said

"If that's the case you'd never go anywhere." He chuckled to himself.

"You think you're funny!"

"Yea, I think I am." He grinned.

I crossed my legs in the opposite direction; his eyes were glued to my thighs. "Fine! Have fun with your slut; ruin my business behind pleasing a temporary curiosity you have. I'm done with you!" I said then I stood up and walked back to the dance floor.

Malcolm sat there watching me. Torrie walked over to my booth; she put her hand on his thigh. My blood boiled, Malcolm looked unmoved. He picked up her hand

and moved it. She stood up and it looked like she was trying to get him to stand. He waved her off and she stood there looking hurt. When the waiter came to collect our empty glasses, Malcolm said something to the waiter. Torrie stood there staring at Malcolm. He wasn't paying her any attention then she said something he didn't like. His head jerked in her direction and she jumped. Malcolm was glaring at her and she moved quickly out of the booth. The waiter came back and said something to Malcolm, Malcolm handed him what I can assume was money. Then he stood up and walked on the dance floor straight to me. The song ended and then MJ music poured out the speaker. He put his hands out, "you're done with me?" Torrie looked like she was going to fall over the railing looking at us. I rolled my eyes and then I put my hand in his. Whenever this song plays, Malcolm becomes someone else, he sings the song, and the Malcolm who's in love with me is undeniable. Torrie looked like she was going to cry, and I wondered if this is the first time she experienced rejection. Yep this working relationship was ruined. I saw Torrie talking to Matthew and I could tell by her body language that she was upset. Matthew kept shrugging I wish I could hear what they were saying. Then Malcolm turned my chin back to him as he sang the words to me. This song was the only time he sang to me, or really acted like this. It was weird because he hadn't drunken anything, so no this wasn't the alcohol talking. I decided to stop questioning it and enjoy the moment. It's not like I'd be hurting for money once this whole thing dies down. Meanwhile I am enjoying the ride. When the song ended, Malcolm stayed out on the dance floor with me. I asked him if he needed to get back to Torrie, he acted like he didn't hear me. Then I danced with Andrew while Sophia and Malcolm danced. We spent the rest of the night together. Torrie called herself dancing with everybody else. What did she expect? I told her he was "MY Malcolm!" I guess she thought she had enough pull.

Chapter 43

The label really wanted Torrie and I to work together on her next set of videos but Torrie fought it and I flat out refused. Kimmy one of the execs there, and someone I'm starting to consider more of a friend has been giving me the scoop over there. She said Torrie told them I'm just a choreographer and there are plenty of good ones out there. I agreed with her, and felt they could get anyone else. So they went with one person for three videos, they didn't like him. They tried someone else for the other two, and they didn't like them. They tried one more person, and that video was never released. Although her records sales were still good and they played her songs on the radio all of the time, something was missing. The second record was almost all love songs, heartache and pain, and a couple about loving a man. I had no doubt who her muse was, so unless I was forced to, as soon as I heard her voice I changed the station. Kimmy said she was already working on her third record and the label is putting pressure on her to agree to me. I told Kimmy it didn't matter if they convinced her cause I wasn't doing it. She told me I would be able to name my price, within reason of course, but I had a pretty high ceiling to play with since they were projecting high sale volumes from the couple sample songs she submitted. Meanwhile I had been working with their other artist; Matthew said I had the Midas touch. He said my choreography turned their mediocre artist into superstars. Kids were buying records because of the videos these days. The story told within the video was as important for records sales as the actual music it's self. The director Corey that Torrie liked to work with told them that the chemistry was off when I wasn't there so for the other artist that could afford him, he was so happy to see me there. His goofy self would even get in there and try to do some of the moves. It was constant comedy, and if Dwayne was on the set forget about it, in between takes they would be clowning around talking about they had it. Serious dancers they were not, but we had a lot of fun. Even Corey told me to make them give me more money, but not to turn the label down when they came to me. Corey didn't like Torrie either but he said this was business.

So when the label approached me about Torrie's new album, they wanted to sign me to a six video contract. I had Sonny look at them before I decided on a price. Jade suggested that I ask for so much up front and then a percentage on the royalties' side. She said they were coming to me and depending on how crucial they felt I was to the project they'd either go for it or counter. I kissed Jade and thanked her for thinking outside of the box. Sonny, Ryan, and I flew to LA to haggle over my final price. I could tell by the reaction and how long we haggled this was not common practice for this label. Kimmy said the Execs would say there was a recipe for Torrie and if they wanted to watch the money, pour in they couldn't stir the pot too much. She said I was like the salt to that recipe, some people could eat without salt, but whether or not they enjoyed it was another question. In the end I was paid a pretty hefty fee up front to do all six videos, and what they called a minute' kick in on the back end. Sonny and Ryan explained that it would amount to a few thousand every so often, but it was good to have in case the songs lived on I would see royalties from it.

Kimmy told me that Torrie threw such a fit when she found out the label came to me. The label almost put her record on the shelf because it got that bad. At least I knew the feeling was mutual. I had worked with almost all of her dancers before so they were so happy to see me on the set. I told myself to remain professional and I did my best. At first, Torrie kept her distance, but after a while you could tell, I intrigued her. I tried to pretend not to notice how she was studying me, but I'd be lying if I said it wasn't pissing me off. I knew she was probably still seeing Malcolm and probably figured that if she couldn't beat me she'd try to be me. I did my best to remain professional, but I wanted to knock her out. I calmed down a lot as payments started hitting my checking account though. No matter how hard she tried, she could never be me.

Dwayne surprised me on the set one day. I was happy to see him but I was not happy that he was around Torrie. She started flirting immediately; Dwayne looked at me with the biggest question mark on his face. I asked him to wait for me back at the hotel. Corey came with me back to the hotel. Corey called Kimmy and she picked us up, we had dinner in Beverly Hills. We had a good ole fashion we can't stand Torrie dinner roast in her honor. Kimmy said Torrie has calmed down a lot from the way she used to be. She said Torrie has to know that every man wants her. Kimmy said she forbid her man to come to her office. She said Torrie isn't the only one like that and that a lot of the people in the business are that way. Dwayne said she just looked tacky throwing herself at him like that so I had to ask him if he thought she was pretty. He said Torrie was gorgeous but all that took a back seat when she knows that he's there for me and she feels the need to throw herself at him. He said it makes her look desperate and dirty and dirty wasn't appealing. I wondered if he meant that, and if he did why wouldn't Malcolm see the same thing.

****

Corey called out, "that's a wrap!" That was it! Sixth video wrap and I was happy this was over. Torrie kept testing me and trying to push me to react. I would have dreams about beating her face in. They couldn't offer me enough money to put up with this again. My sanity is important. Torrie kept giving me sad eyes like she wanted to say something to me. I wanted to say something to her too, but I had more choice words to share with her. I said bye to Corey although I'd see him in a month back in Oakland. He was coming to North Star to discuss the concept for a different artist's up coming video. I was going to get to be home for the video, I was so excited to be with my boys. This final shoot ran over on time and I was missing my babies. Ok, ok and I was missing Dwayne too. Things were still going surprisingly well with him. The problem is that he keeps trying to tell me he loves me and I try to avoid it or let the comment ride on the air. Every time his parents come around, he seems to feel it more. His mother is the sweetest, and she gets so excited every time she sees me. Dwayne's dad and Daddy hit it off from day one. The three of them go golfing when they come into town; they've even taken my boys, Sonny, Malachi, Timothy, and little Tim with them a few times which was only weird for me. Well I take that back, I could see jealousy in Malcolm's face as Darryl told him about it but I refused to talk about it. I won't really discuss anything with him since I know he's still seeing Torrie. Torrie called herself trying to buy him a car, and he made her take it back. It was some new fancy car; he told her he'd dump it in the bay if she didn't take it back. She was so hurt and not understanding why he wouldn't take the car, but he accepted money, jewelry, and she paid for mostly everything they did. Her friend was explaining why Torrie was so grumpy a few months ago to one of their friends, that's one of Torrie's dancers. They had no idea I was in earshot listening to everything. At least I know Malcolm was still taking these females for everything he could but it still didn't make me feel good that they even had to be.

I said my goodbyes and then I was off. I returned my rental car and then I went from ticket counter to ticket counter trying to find a flight out tonight. I told Jade I would handle my arrangements when I had to cancel my first flight arrangements and I had no idea when I was getting out of here. She had two babies to look after; I didn't want to burden her with making my arrangements. I FINALLY found a seat on a flight but it didn't leave for an hour and a half. There were only first class seats left, I guess that was gonna have to do!!! I sat on the far end of the seating area of my gate. I took out my book, the collection of Jane Austen stories and got lost in the story again as if I hadn't read it before. It was almost boarding time and then I noticed a crowd of people. Torrie was signing autographs and trying to make her way to my gate. Fortunately, the crowd kept her over there while first class boarded. I was in the back and the corner of first class. The coach passengers boarded and still no Torrie. I wondered if she was on my flight at all. I bent over to get gum out my purse I heard her very diva persona arrive. The flight attendants were so excited to have her on our flight. She sat down in front of me, and immediately they started doting on her. I smiled because she had no idea I was behind her.

"Anyways so I asked him who she was and he said they hadn't spoken in years, and they just recently ran into each other."

"You don't need to be worried about some old woman. He was probably just missing you too much, and settled for her company until you came back." The girl next to her said.

"I guess!" Torrie sighed. "I don't get him sometimes. I do so much for him and he still acts like its nothing sometimes. And I HATE every time Amber's around, he acts like he doesn't know me."

"He probably does that to keep the peace." The girl said

"I don't understand why. Being with me is always an upgrade. Amber is just a behind the scenes wanna be. She has a boyfriend so I don't know why he acts like he does about her."

"How does he act?" The girl asked

"He won't talk about her but then he told me I better not try to confront her or even talk to her. I tried to ask him what was so special about her, but he wouldn't answer me. She may be cute, but she's not me. Besides I'm younger and way more talented."

"But without her your videos wouldn't get the rotation they get. She is good." The girl said.

"Yea she can dance a good jig like the rest of the house niggas. But she'll never be as fine as me!"

"You think Malcolm still sees her?"

"Probably, I know he sees somebody besides this old lady but Amber could never do for him all the stuff I do. He probably gives her pity sex." Torrie laughed

"You're ok with that?"

"Malcolm stays strapped up. I told him I was on the pill and he told me he didn't care if I had a hysterectomy he was staying strapped up. So if he's like that with me after all this time I'm not worried about it." She said proudly.

"But condoms can break."

"He's always checking to make sure. But she's with Dwayne Reed, you know him right?" Then she moaned.

"Girl who don't know him, he is so fine!" The girl said

"Isn't he! I'd trade Malcolm for him if I was her too." Torrie said

"Why?"

"Girl! Girl! Girl! For one he's a freak, my girl knew him before Amber. He's FINE! At least he spends money on Amber, Malcolm may drive a kind of nice car, and his

house is nice but he ain't got no money. He lives like he's on a tight budget, that's why I pay when we go out. But Dwayne got some change and he spends it."
"You trying to trade up?" The girl asked.
"Dwayne's not biting for now."
"How you know?"
"I told you about when I went to his game against Atlanta. He's like a lovesick puppy right now. He wasn't feeling me or anybody else. He ate with his team mates then he went back to his room."
"Didn't you try to go in though?"
The girl and Torrie laughed. "You know I did but he wasn't having it, so I'll wait until he's had a chance to get tired of her. I was watching her; I don't know what makes her so special."
"She's really pretty, she's nice and sweet." The girl said
Torrie shot her evil eyes. "Get off her nuts! She ain't that pretty, and she ain't that nice. I'm so happy this project is over. Watch as soon as I have a chance I'm rearranging that so called pretty face of hers."
"But Malcolm said..."
"Yea! Yea! He ain't my daddy. Besides what he gonna do if I do? Break up with me? He's not the only big dick out there. I'm kind of getting tired of paying him anyways. As soon as he realizes how much money, he'll be losing by losing me I bet you he'd deal with it. Besides, little Miss Amber needs to learn her pretty little lesson. She needs to see how Berkeley girls get down anyways!"
"I don't think that would be fair. I don't think she can fight." The girl said
"That's not my problem. I can't wait to get my chance!"
I heard enough! I stood up and went to the bathroom in the front of the plane so they could see me. As soon as they saw me, they both shut up. I kind of laughed in the bathroom; because half the stuff they said tickled me, but Dwayne never told me about Torrie throwing herself at him. Does he really act like a lovesick puppy? I can't wait for her to run up! When I came out the bathroom Torrie and her friend stared at me. When I sat down they didn't utter another word but they had already said everything I needed to know. Except, who is the old lady? Please don't tell me Yvette is back, I hate that name! Didn't matter because my heart was fluttering over Dwayne at this moment. I could feel that inner battle happening within me. When it was time to exit the plane Torrie and her friend kept looking at me. I blew Torrie kisses then I went on to my car. I can't wait for her to run up! I can't wait!
When I walked in the door, Derrick was on the phone and he cracked probably his first smile of the year when he saw me. He got off the phone and gave me the biggest hug. As much as Derrick tries to hide it, he's a momma's boy too. We sat at the table talking, Darryl was with Malcolm, and Derrick had just finished his homework. We talked about each other's weeks. Derrick said that he's been having problems with this kid at his school behind a girl. He said he doesn't like the girl but she likes him. Her ex boyfriend is jealous and he seems to think Derrick is encouraging her. Derrick sat there laughing saying no one has been crazy enough to challenge him since elementary school. I told him to be careful because people rarely fight these days. He said he was aware of that, but he looked forward to the challenge because this guy was a little bigger than he was. Derrick was built like David, tall and solid, but unlike David, Derrick had Malcolm's muscular tone. Derrick was fast just like Andrew, but Derrick was scary like Malcolm. Speaking of Malcolm, I heard a key in the front door. Darryl was talking about something and laughing. Malcolm called out to Derrick, and he told him he was in the kitchen.

Darryl lost it when he saw me, they were both surprised, but Darryl was caught off guard and got emotional. He put me in a bear hug, "no more than a week momma! I can't keep doing this! Malcolm doesn't cook! Grand Dad only makes steaks and baked potatoes! Derrick is withholding the vegetables! I came home momma! I was dying for broccoli. That nigga!" Darryl said pointing at Derrick. He shook his head like the memory was painful. "That nigga had a whole veggie platter! I asked for some broccoli. HE SAID NO! He said no momma!" Darryl shook his head. "So I asked for one broccoli or a carrot. Something! He said no! I tried to take one, and that's when the fight started."

I was laughing so hard. Malcolm was even smiling, but I think he was smiling at me. "Darryl, why didn't you just cook your own?" I said

"That's what I said!" Derrick said rolling his eyes.

"WHO WANTS TO COOK WHEN HE'S SITTING THERE WITH IT???" Darryl said dramatically

Derrick looked at me unmoved and not amused. "This is what I've been dealing with. You can't leave this fool longer than a week."

"Ok, I think I got it." I said

"When did you get in?" Malcolm asked

"About an hour ago." I said unenthusiastically

"What's wrong with you?" Malcolm asked

"Nothing, nothing at all." I said standing up.

"Uh oh Darryl lets go." Derrick said grabbing Darryl by the shoulders.

"But I just got here, I want my momma!" Darryl said trying to be funny but he looked at Malcolm who was very serious; he kissed me on the cheek and hurried out the kitchen.

Malcolm folded his arms waiting for me to speak. "So I sat behind your girlfriend on the plane today. She didn't know I was there."

He frowned. "Girlfriend?"

"Torrie!"

"She's not my girlfriend." Malcolm said

"She surely seems to think so. The point is that you have completely disrespected me for the last time. That one female Malcolm, you couldn't leave that one alone out of respect for my business or just because I asked you to. I'm tired of playing this game with you. It actually hurts to look at you." I didn't yell I just spoke matter of factly.

Malcolm sighed, "Are you on your period or something?" I picked up the saltshaker and I threw it at his head. He ducked. "You better be happy that didn't hit me!"

"Get out Malcolm! Next time I won't miss!"

"Since when do you think it's ok to threaten me?"

I picked up the peppershaker and threw it. It hit the wall next to his head. He looked at me in disbelief. "Get out Malcolm!"

"Why do you always let those females affect you?"

"Get out!"

Malcolm threw his hands up. The boys were sitting on the couch acting like they weren't listening.

****

"Ok close your eyes." Dwayne said, and then he placed a small square box in my hands. "Open them." He was excited.

I looked at the box, it wasn't a ring box. I had no idea what was in it. Dwayne was too excited for me to open it. To torture him I opened the box extra slow. Dwayne kept stopping himself from helping me open it. He was excited like a big kid. I opened the box and there was a key and a paper that said codes with numbers for the front gate and the home alarm system written on it. I looked at him with a huge smile on my face. "Is this what I think it is?"

He shook his head yes. "Now get out!" He said too excited. I hopped off the couch giggling to the front door. I went out the door and closed it behind me. Then I used my key to open the door. "Baby is that you?" Dwayne called out.

The scene was corny, but I was so in love with the gesture. I jumped on Dwayne when I came back in the family room. We started kissing, and I told him to come upstairs. He wanted to stay downstairs, so I ran upstairs to get a condom; I grabbed an extra just in case round two happened right away. Afterwards we laid on the couch cuddling. I could tell something was on Dwayne's mind by the way he was acting. "Penny for your thoughts?" I said laying on his chest.

"Do you want more kids?"

"NO!" My body stiffened.

He rubbed my back. "Calm down, I was just asking."

"Why are you asking?" I said

He exhaled, "don't freak out." I didn't say anything but my body was still tense.

"Sometimes I still want to try for a son. I figure that you're a sure thing."

"Why?"

"Cause you only have boys." Then he laughed, "I know that's silly to think. But my mind keeps going back to that."

"I don't think I can have any more even if I wanted to." I said lowly, I couldn't believe that the idea of having Dwayne's baby wasn't as off putting, as I would've thought it would have been.

"Really? Did you get your tubes tied?"

"No, I had an ectopic pregnancy. The doctor said that there might be scarring which would prohibit pregnancy."

"Ectopic?"

"A tubal pregnancy."

"Oh, but why are you still on the pill then?" He asked

"Cause honestly when I think about it; that wiped out only one tube. I still have a healthy tube. I don't want to have anymore so I'm not taking any chances." I said

"Then why do you think you can't have anymore?"

"Because after the tubal we were still trying and nothing." Tears filled my eyes. "Besides, do you really wanna be linked to Malcolm for the rest of your life?"

He hesitated. "The rest of my life? Darryl will be a teenager soon."

"Your point?" I asked

"Once the kids are grown wont he step back some, If not completely?"

I hadn't thought of that. I had gotten so used to him being around even if it was only for the boys. "I guess so. But, you don't think of Michelle as a permanent factor in your life?"

"Not really. Once the girls are grown maybe, I'll see her at the girl's weddings, interacting with our grandchildren from time to time. But not like she is now."

The thought of Malcolm not being around made me sad, but he's barely around as it is. Maybe then, I could move on officially and actually get married. I guess that was the silver lining in the whole thing but it made me sad. "I guess I figured you guys would always see each other."

"As much as I care about her, I care about you more." He said sincerely

"See! That's crazy to me; I don't know how you could even say that. She's the mother of your children. She was your wife."

He exhaled again. "Yea, and with all of that we couldn't make it work. I actually like being married. I didn't like how insecure she became. How many times can someone accuse you of cheating before you actually do it?"

"I understand why she felt that way though." I said honestly

"Please explain it because I don't." He said

"Have you looked in the mirror? Knowing how females respond to you can be intimidating for any woman. Seeing how you respond sometimes can be sickening."

He chuckled. "How do I respond?"

"You get off on it."

"I don't!" I could hear the smile in his voice

"Stop your lies! Yes you do." We both laughed.

"How does it make you feel when guys fall out all over you?"

"They don't." I said matter of factly.

"Oh yea right! You trying to tell me you don't see it then. Because I'm there and I know they do."

"I guess I don't see it, because I sure as heck didn't grow up with a of bunch guys following me around. Girls didn't like me but for their own petty reasons. Most of the time they called me names and poked fun at me." I said not liking the feeling of remembering my childhood

"What about Malcolm, he never went on and on about you being beautiful?"

"No, but he doesn't go on and on about anything. He told me he thought I was pretty, I know he was attracted to me. We weren't about appearances. "

"What about the other guy you dated?" Then he paused, "you've never said his name. What is it?"

I felt a heat wave come over me. "David"

"What about David? He didn't go on about you?"

"David thought I was pretty. It even made him very jealous. But I don't know, he didn't make me feel beautiful." I hoped he didn't ask me anything else about him.

"You ok? You started sweating."

"I don't like talking about him, let's just keep moving."

"Ok" he was quiet for a minute. Then he pulled me up so that we were face to face. "Let me be the first to explain to you how gorgeous I feel you are." I turned my head; he moved my chin back to face him. "The first time I laid eyes on you, time stopped. I was glued to the TV watching you. To talk myself out of crushing on you real hard, I told myself that someone that beautiful has to be stuck on herself and high maintenance. However, everything I saw about you painted you as a down to earth person. That drew me in more. Television does you no justice; you are even more gorgeous in person! I don't know how you don't spend all day staring at yourself in the mirror! Your eyes, their shape, and the way they put emphasis on your words, thoughts, and ideas. I could spend all day kissing that mouth." Then he kissed me passionately. "I cant get enough of those lips. I love everything about you. I don't know how someone as gorgeous as you are can be so down to earth but I'm grateful that you are. My girls love you, my parents love you, and they see in you the same things that draw me in. I'm not saying that I always do the right thing but even with that, you've given me the space to grow up. I thought my life was going to be an endless stream of women until the day I died but the moment I laid eyes on you, my life changed. Being with you makes me feel alive; talking to you makes me feel real. Looking at you makes me feel like I'm going to explode!"

I don't know why his words made me want to run and hide. I couldn't even look at him anymore, I wanted to lay back down, but he wanted to stare at me. "What am I supposed to say to that?" I said with my eyes on the floor.

"You love me too!" His eyes were pleading for me to say it.

I closed my eyes and slouched until he let me lay on his chest. I tried not to but I cried anyways. "I'm not gonna keep coming over here if you're gonna keep making me cry." I said through sobs.

Dwayne hugged me and rubbed my back. "I know you love me, why you won't say it." He exhaled. "We both know why you won't say it. One day he won't matter and you'll be free to live life in my heart." He kept rubbing my back.

****

"Momma this is Jennay!" Andrew said proudly

I shot Andrew a look because I just saw him last night at the club with Toya but Jennay was a nice girl. She was pretty; I was impressed that she was thick. "Hello nice to meet you." I said reaching to hug her.

"It's nice to meet you as well." Jennay said returning my embrace. "Drew talks about you all the time."

Andrew blushed, "ok, we've got plenty of time for small talk. You ready?" Andrew said flashing his dimples.

"You're riding with us then?" I asked.

"Yes" Andrew said grabbing her hand.

I put food and water out for the dogs. I gave Skylar a hug, and then I locked the door behind me. Andrew was introducing Jennay to Derrick and Darryl. Derrick said hello, and of course, Darryl blurts out, "ANYBODY IS BETTER THAN TOYA!!!! I'M SO HAPPY TO MEET YOU!" Andrew popped Darryl upside the head. He smiled at Andrew and when Jennay got in the car, Andrew smiled back at him. In the car, I drove us to Dwayne's house as we all asked Jennay question after question. She seemed sweet and like a nice girl. I could tell Andrew was quite taken with this girl, but I didn't understand why he was with Toya the night before. When she saw me, they moved out of the way real fast. She looked very pretty with her hair down and they seemed to have a drama free evening. Maybe the drama was that Andrew belonged to someone else. I kept looking at Andrew in my rear view mirror. Driving over the Bay Bridge no longer gave me anxiety, a few butterflies but nothing that I paid too much attention to anymore. I entered my code to the gate. I parked in front of the garage. Derrick and Darryl got the charcoal out the trunk and the other stuff I brought. Dwayne and his parents were in the backyard. Andrew introduced Jennay to everyone; Dwayne said the girls would be there shortly. I put my potato salad and Derrick's peach cobbler in the refrigerator. Betty got excited seeing the dishes. Then Daddy, Malachi, and his girlfriend Denise, Timothy and his family arrived. I buzzed Michelle in the gate, and I opened the door for her and the girls. As usual, the first thing Michelle did was look me up and down and of course, I returned the scan although I'm sure it was surprising to her to see me answering the door. I gave the girls hugs and I stepped to the side so Michelle could enter. We said our cordial hellos, and then I told her that Betty was in the kitchen. Betty had all the women in the kitchen drinking wine and helping her construct her salad while she also had pork and beans on the stove. Betty said a cordial hello to Michelle and then she told her the men were outside at the barbecue pit. As soon as she closed the door behind her Grace asked Betty why she didn't like Michelle. Denise and I leaned in to hear, Jennay did her best not to get overly familiar right away, but her ears were perked up too. At first, Betty tried to act like

128

that wasn't the case. Then she said she just didn't care for the way Michelle conducted herself during the divorce. She said she knew Michelle trapped her son in the first place by getting pregnant, and then she tried to get everything in the divorce. Dwayne and Michelle walked back in through the sliding door. She was telling him something about one of the girls. Dwayne looked at me and said he would be right back. Tiffany, Crystal, and Tina came in the kitchen all smiles. Jade and Sonny buzzed at the gate, I buzzed them in. Dwayne walked back inside with them, and then he told Crystal he needed to talk to her. Crystal had a busted look on her face as she followed her dad up the stairs. Tiffany gave her grandmother sad eyes. Betty asked her what was wrong. Tiffany said Crystal's been slipping at school and that their mother was very upset about it. Malachi came inside with a beer in hand. He said we were gonna need more meat. Denise pointed at the sauce in the corner of his mouth and told him to stop eating all the meat before we got a chance to eat any. Malachi smiled a busted smile then he gave Denise a kiss getting sauce on her face. When Dwayne and Crystal came downstairs Malachi asked Dwayne where he could get some more meat. As Dwayne was explaining where to go, I volunteered to go with Malachi since I understood where he was sending him. Derrick walked inside as I grabbed my purse. He walked out the door with us; he didn't even ask if he could come with us. We got in Malachi's car and drove down the hill to Geneva Street, as we passed the Cow Palace I watched the surroundings change then we made a right on Mission. We were definitely leaving Dwayne's neck of the woods, Malachi was telling me how Denise was putting pressure on him to marry her. I asked what was holding him back. He couldn't say what but he just didn't feel ready. We pulled into a parking lot next to a market just like Dwayne described it. When I got out of the car, the guys outside the store noticed me right away. The way one of them looked at me instantly gave me the creeps! Derrick's face turned to stone as soon as he saw all the gazes my way. He stood next to me, and then he walked next to me. He stared the guys down as we walked inside the store. Malachi grabbed a number in the butcher section, then he told me to get more sauce, and he told me which one to get. Derrick was glued to my hip, I was thankful he was there. The guys from outside were now walking around in the store. When Derrick and I went down the chip aisle, I saw a woman with a cart full of barbecue items as well. The closer I got the more familiar she became. Her face lit up when she saw me. "Amber!" She said excitedly.

That's when I realized it was Emma. She looked at me with Momma's eyes.
"Emma?"
"Yes sweetheart!" She gave me a big hug. "What are you doing out here?"
"We're at a friend's house. This is my middle son Derrick. Derrick this is Emma my Momma's sister."
Emma hugged Derrick he didn't have a choice he was getting hugged. Then the main creepy guy walked up to Emma. "Who dis?" He said with his eyes gliding all over me.
"Oh" Emma said excited like this was gonna be a happy family reunion. "This is Annette's baby girl Amber. Amber this is your Uncle Raymond." She said happily. Raymond licked his lips at me. "Oh snap! This is who Preston was talking about!" Hearing his name sent me spinning. Raymond reached to hug me and I stepped backwards. Derrick took a step forward to block me. "Who are you, her man, or something?"

Derrick didn't respond he looked at Raymond like he was the stupidest person alive. I saw the light bulb go off in Emma's head. "Raymond go away! Let me talk to my baby."

He was staring at me as if I was a piece of meat. "Naw! I wanna say hello too." Emma turned to Raymond, "I will leave this cart, and no one will have anything to eat. Is that what you want?"

He gave her an irritated look, and then he looked at me one more time. "Fine! Whatever!" He walked away.

Derrick watched him walk away then he started looking up at the aisle mirrors watching which way Raymond went.

"Baby, I'm sorry I forgot about Preston." She reached to touch me and I flinched. Derrick looked at me. "I'm sorry honey, I'm sorry." She said with tears streaming down her face. She hugged me but my body was stiff. Then she walked away. Derrick asked me if I was ok. I shook my head yes, even though I wasn't. I started putting almost a bag of each chip in the cart. Derrick just watched but didn't say anything. I put ten bottles of barbecue sauce in the cart. Then I stood there trying to pull myself together. Derrick put his arms around me, he didn't know what was going on, but he hated seeing me upset. Then I looked up and Raymond was almost on us, he was coming from behind Derrick and I didn't know another guy was coming from behind me. Before I could say anything, in one swift move Derrick pulled out his gun and had it resting on Raymond's temple. He had Raymond's arm twisted behind his back, he was pressing one of Raymond's fingers, which made him say ouch and go down on his knees. "You know better than to sneak up on people!" Derrick said

"Aaaaaa man!" The other guy said. "That's not even necessary!"

"What do you want?" Derrick barked

Raymond had his free hand out to show he was surrendering. "Um, um!" Is all he could say.

"What do you want with her?" Derrick barked

"Nothing!" Raymond said, "Ouch! Ouch!" He said as Derrick pressed in more on his hand.

"Niggas is trying to buy stuff for a barbecue, we ain't here for this!" Derrick said. Raymond looked at me with pleading eyes.

Malachi walked around the corner with arms full of meat. "Whoa nephew! What's going on?" He said putting his stuff in the cart.

"Blood ain't always thicker than water." Derrick said with cold eyes. "Ya'll go pay for this stuff up front while I talk to my man right here." Derrick said

"What about him?" Malachi said gesturing to the guy who was standing there wide-eyed. We all turned to the guy. He raised his hands higher to say he was no threat. "You cool?" Malachi asked him. The guy shook his head yes. "How about you walk with us, we'll let them resolve this back here." Malachi said real calm.

I looked at my baby; there was no fear in his face where Raymond looked scared. Malachi put his arm around me and told me to come on. I didn't want to leave Derrick with that man even if he had the upper hand at the moment. Malachi assured me that Derrick was fine and that we needed to hurry. Malachi chatted with the cashier real calm and charming even. Then Derrick walked ever so calmly to the front of the store. Malachi looked at him and asked if everything was cool, Derrick nodded yes; he leisurely pushed the cart to the car. When we walked out the other guy looked nervous. Emma was calling them to her van. As we slowly drove away, two guys were helping Raymond walk out the store. Malachi hit the breaks when he realized he was looking at Emma. He backed up next to her car and he got out the car fast slamming his door. I called after him but he ignored me. Derrick got out the car to stand next to his Uncle. Malachi went from zero to sixty in point five seconds. He got in Raymond's face asking him what he did. Raymond's finger was clearly broken as he put his hands up. I tearfully pleaded with Malachi to get back in the car. Emma touched Malachi's face just like Momma used to, he instantly stopped yelling, and he looked at Emma like she was Momma for a minute. Malachi cursed then he got back in the car. Derrick got back in the car and then Malachi drove off. We drove back up Geneva a few blocks up then Malachi pulled over. He hugged me, I was sobbing uncontrollably. He was trying to calm his self down; I didn't want to walk in that house this rattled. Derrick asked Malachi who they were. Malachi couldn't explain he kept yelling because he was so mad. We sat there a good hour; Dwayne started blowing up my pager. I started blowing air trying to calm down. Derrick was quiet watching us and watching the cars that drove by. I told Malachi I was ok to go to the house. Malachi drove real slow down the street. When we pulled in the gate, Dwayne was in his car. He was about to come find us. Malachi pulled in front of the door and I ran up the stairs to Dwayne's room. I went in the bathroom and I sat there trying to calm down. Derrick knocked lightly on the door. I opened it so he could come in. He gave me a hug then he sat there on the floor watching me. I know he wanted to know but I couldn't talk about it and be ok the rest of the day. "I'll explain later, but I can't go into it right now. You understand?"

Derrick nodded as we heard Dwayne and Malachi talking. Malachi was explaining that we saw my Momma's sister and it messed us both up for a minute. Dwayne opened the door he looked at Derrick then at me. He gave me a huge hug. Derrick got up and walked out. Dwayne asked me if I needed anything. Malachi came back with a glass of Hennessy. He told me to sip slow cause he knew I wanted to throw it back.

When I finally came downstairs, Daddy was talking to Jade and they both read me when I came down the stairs. Daddy looked me in my eyes, "you saw Emma?" I nodded yes. "Was she alone?" I shook my head no. "Sibling?" I nodded yes. Daddy's eyes glazed over. "Malachi handle it?"

"Derrick" I said lowly

Daddy grinned at Derrick, then he gave him his glass of Hennessy and they walked outside together. Jade asked me if I was ok, I told her the truth when I said no. We sat in the living room away from everybody and Jade hugged me like she always has. Timothy came in the living room to tell us the food was ready but he paused when he saw we were upset. He asked what was wrong, Jade told him Malachi, and I saw Momma's brother at the store. My biggest brother picked me up like I was a paperweight and hugged me, which made me cry all over again. Malachi refilled my glass, and the four of us sat silent comforting each other just like we used to after they took Uncle away all those years ago.

Chapter 44

"I don't want to talk about it!" I said

"You never leave the house when you go out there. I dropped the ball! Are you ok?" Malcolm asked

"I don't want to talk about it!" I said as I fixed my hair.

Malcolm stood there staring at me. "You're still upset."

I looked at him through the mirror. "If your guys would've been there it wouldn't have changed anything. I still would've seen him; he still would've been a disgusting pervert! My fourteen-year-old still would've pulled out a gun I didn't know he was carrying to protect his momma from something he's still waiting for her to explain to him. And who gave him the gun?" I looked at Malcolm. He just stared at me. "Why do you think a fourteen year old needs to carry a gun?"

"It's not the same out there. Besides I carried a gun at his age." Malcolm said.

"You give my baby a gun without even discussing it with me!" I said shaking my head.

"I gave my son what he needed at the time. Andrew was strapped at his age as well." Malcolm said matter of factly.

I shook my head. "How does that teach them to resolve anything?"

"They're good kids; they're not trigger happy morons. If that guy hadn't snuck up on you guys, you wouldn't know about the gun." He said

"Whatever Malcolm, you continue doing whatever you want whenever you want. There's no point in even talking about it. Are the guns clean at least?"

"Of course!" He said like I insulted him. "They're mine."

"Whatever Malcolm. It doesn't matter." I said rolling my eyes.

"What's up with you?" Malcolm said sitting on my bed.

"Nothing's up with me!" I said pinning my side bun.

"You don't talk to me anymore. Now you keep saying *'whatever Malcolm'* like I'm nothing!" He said mimicking me

I rolled my eyes. "I just don't see the point in wasting my breath. You're always gonna do what serves you and what you want first. So why tell you how I feel about anything it doesn't matter."

"Your feelings matter." He said quietly.

"Yea right! That's why you discussed the guns with me?"

"That was the decision I made for my boys. I had no idea you'd freak out about it. But I guess if I would've thought about it, I would've discussed it with you."

"Right Malcolm, whatever!"

He squinted his eyes, "this isn't about the guns. What are you mad about?"

I turned around and gave him evil eyes. "Nothing!"

He stood up and he came to kiss my cheek, and I moved out of the way. "I can't kiss you now?"

"HELL NO YOU CAN'T KISS ME!" I said

"Hell no? Woman if you don't just tell me and stop this game." He said annoyed.

"I'm not playing with you. Don't kiss me, don't touch me!" I growled

He stood there staring at me; I could see him flipping through his mental Rolodex. "Is this about that girl?" I stared at him. My body temp went up and my breathing got heavy. He exhaled and sat on the bed. "Why do you let them bother you?"

"Even after all this with Dwayne you don't get it?"

"What is there to get? You're having fun with the pretty boy for now. I don't care about him."

"So it doesn't bother you that my family loves him?"

"You trying to tell me you love him?"

"I'm saying that no matter how much you try to say his presence doesn't bother you, I know it does. You're not stupid you see how long he's been around, this is not just a crush."

He stared at me. "What are you saying?"

"You keep telling me not to put anyone ahead of you; but you keep creating these situations where someone else gets close enough to me to matter. When all I ever wanted was all of you. You're not capable of giving me you. Fine! But move out the way. Why do you insist on keeping my life in limbo because you can't get it together? Then to make it all worse, you deliberately mess with someone I ask you not to, I tell you about it, and it changes nothing. You do what you want, and you don't care how it affects me. I don't want to spend the rest of my life like this. If you ever cared about me, let me go."

Malcolm shrugged, "go where, to do what, and with who?"

"Let me go find happiness, or something close to it that I can live with."

Malcolm chuckled and exaggerated laugh. "We've had this conversation, that's not gonna happen. If you feel like things are getting too hot and heavy with the pretty boy, then break up with him. I already told you."

"Told me what?"

"You belong to me! You're in love with me! You may actually really like him, but he'll never be me!"

"He's been hinting around marriage."

"Get rid of him then. Why are we even talking about this?"

"Because I don't see the point in hanging on to you, when there's someone who wants to offer me something real!"

"Realer than what? What we have is real!"

"We don't have anything Malcolm! We got history! Currently we don't have anything. You have your whores, and I have Dwayne. The only reason I see you is regarding the boys. They'll be grown one day then what? I'm gonna end up being an old lady waiting for you to tire of your whores. Maybe one of them will burn you up real good, but you'll be no good to me then. What am I supposed to be hanging on for?"

Malcolm stared at me, the left side of his face twitched. "You really letting that fool get to you aren't you?" He sat back down on the bed. "Okay, you wanna play the what if game. What if I said ok fine Amber, you go your way and I'll go mine. You go running to that fool like a dumb idiot, say he even marries you, then what? He doesn't even know who you are. Your temper flares, he gonna demand that you choke that back. You can't be you and have your righteous anger fits anymore. Okay maybe that's for the best, maybe you need to calm down a bit, although Momma went to the grave having her righteous fits being true to herself to the end. Anyways, so there's that. How long you think the pretty boy is going to hang out with the family when he finds out your cousins and aunties and uncles maybe white but they just a bunch of niggas in the end. Pretty boy don't want his daughters around that. Then you going to have to choose him or your family. Like a dumb idiot, you'll choose him sighting love as the reason. So let's keep track, now you've given up ME, the love of your life, a very important aspect of who you are, and your family another important lifeline. THEN here's the best, you realize he's not all that different from me. He's still creeping because he's too pretty not to. I know how them tramps be throwing it at him. A man can only be so strong Amber, so what do you do, tuck your tail between your legs and accept it. You'll get depressed and probably get fat again, then he'll really be done, talking about he loves somebody else because you gave up on the relationship. No me, you lost your family, and most importantly YOU LOST YOURSELF! That's what you want?"

My head spun! I wanted to tell him that none of that was even possible, and that his imagination was wild but some of it was true. "I want someone who loves me enough to accept me as me and who doesn't make me feel like I'm not enough for them. I haven't been hiding who I am from him, but he doesn't know me like you know me either. When you love someone, you accept the good with the bad. I tried accepting your wandering eye, but I accepted a little and you took it too far. I didn't want to have another baby, but I did it for you. It was beyond my control that it didn't happen. I still get kicked to the curb because of something beyond my control." His eyes turned sad. "I didn't take Troy away from us, why am I being punished for his death? I..,"

Malcolm hopped up as if fire was under his butt. "I don't wanna talk about this!" He headed for the door.

I jumped up and threw my back on the door. "Why can't we talk about him?"

Malcolm was livid, "Amber, baby I need to leave. Please move out of the way." He was trying to speak calmly.

"No! You wanna talk so let's talk." I said not moving.

Malcolm spun around in a complete circle. "Baby! I'm at the end of my rope. I don't want to hurt you. Move out of the way!" I never heard his voice that deep before or his eyes that evil. I opened my mouth to speak and then he very firmly picked me up and tossed me on the bed. He opened the door and walked out. I tried calling after him but he kept walking. He got in his car and drove off.

When the phone rang, I thought it was Malcolm, I dove across my bed, it was Sophia telling me she and Travis were almost at the house. I told her Malcolm just left and that I was running late. I could hear her smile through the phone. I assured her it was not like that. I heard her smile drop. I hurried to finish dressing; tonight I was going to be the lady in red. How dare he say I would end up fat again! I stood in the mirror taking myself in. Nana said I didn't have to be anything I didn't want to be. Thus far, she was right; as long as I stayed active, I was fine. Besides what was so wrong with me, getting fat? Just because he wasn't attracted to thickness doesn't mean my love life would be over! Forget Malcolm! He doesn't know everything.

Sophia came inside she smiled real big when she saw me, she said I looked sizzling hot. Then we picked up Daddy, while Timothy & Grace followed us with Sonny &Jade. We were meeting Dwayne and his brother Dwight, Uncle Jeff and Auntie Lauren at the Oakland Theater. We were going to see an Old School revue of the classics. Daddy got excited when he heard about the concert so we made plans to go. At the last minute, we added Dwight on to the group since he was out visiting. Daddy made all the arrangements, and of course, Daddy got us front row seats. As we were being escorted to our seats, I saw Torrie sitting a couple rows back from us. Her mouth fell open when she saw me, because yea I looked that good! I sat in the third chair from the aisle so Dwayne and Dwight could slide in when they got there. I felt eyes on me and I knew they weren't Torrie; the heat wasn't coming from her direction. I looked to my left and I started looking at the people, then I saw her, way back there I saw Yvette. She looked bitter, old, and sad. I smiled at her and she rolled her eyes. Torrie hung all over the seat in front of her until she figured out who I was looking at. When she saw Yvette, the question mark was all over her face. Just as the lights were dropping, Dwayne and his brother slid in. Dwayne in a dramatic fashion grabbed his chest, and then he told me I was ravishing. I smiled and thanked him for the compliment. I waved hello to his brother. As the show started, it was good, we sang along with most of the songs. As the intermission started, waiters walked up to our row and started passing out champagne glasses filled with champagne. Then they put champagne buckets filled with ice and champagne in front of us, a bucket every second person. A waiter came with a menu and asked us if we would like anything else. Since we planned to go out to eat afterwards we only ordered strawberries. Then I asked the waiter where this was coming from, and he pointed up and said it was all compliments of Mr. Latour. We all raised our glasses up to say thank you. Malcolm who was sitting above the stage in a private booth, he nodded at us. As the ladies, all rose to go to the bathroom, I looked up and Malcolm was staring. I couldn't pinpoint the look on his face but it was serious as usual. Torrie was having a fit in her seat as we walked past. We got in line for the ladies room; we were about four ladies back from Yvette. She looked nice, but she looked tired, like she was just tired of it all. Torrie and her friend got in line two ladies behind us. Then our special waiter came over to us and told us that we weren't supposed to wait in this line. Torrie turned purple as she watched us walk up the stairs and get escorted behind a velvet rope. We walked down a hallway to a nice and very clean bathroom. It smelled wonderful in there and there were no lines. A few of the performers were in the bathroom sitting in the lounge area. As we came out the bathroom, we told them how much we enjoyed their show. I guess it must've been the woman's granddaughter but she started jumping around. "Oh my goodness it's you!" She said pointing at me. I was caught completely off guard by her recognition of me. She explained to the woman who I was and I said a very embarrassed thank you as the girl squealed with excitement. She ran to get her camera. She asked the woman to take a picture of us. Everybody was smiling at us. Then we made our way back to our seats. I could see the young girl peeking at us from behind the curtain when we sat down. I waved at her and the curtain started bumping around. She was cute, I told Dwayne what happened, and he smiled brightly at me. The second half started and just before the woman we met back stage started to get into her groove she stopped the music. She said, "Amber honey, I'm so sorry but my grand baby has to know if that's Dwayne Reed sitting next to you. I smiled and said yes. Then she asked us to please come backstage again so her grand baby could get a picture with us. I told her we would and then the she went on with her show. The show was even better in the second half. Malcolm's eyes stayed glued to us the entire time. It didn't look like he was with anybody either. When the concert was over, instead of walking out of the auditorium our special waiters came again and escorted our entire party back stage. We met all the performers and we complimented them on a job well done. One woman asked me if I had any label connections, I told her I had some but if she were looking for studio time her best bet would be to contact Silent Chaos Studios and lay down some tracks for a solid demo first. When she asked where the studio was I told her they have several locations all over the Bay Area and quite a few in Southern California as well. I handed the woman a general card for the studio. We chatted a little more then we told them we had to go because we were all starving. As we walked out of the theater, I couldn't help but notice Torrie's over priced vehicle waiting out front. We got our cars out of valet and then we drove to the Shylight restaurant and lounge in Berkeley. Again, all of our cars went into valet custody, and then the manager greeted us at the door. We were escorted to the VIP area. This area sat above the rest of the restaurant, you could clearly see in and out of the area, but this area had its own everything. I saw Torrie and her friend enter the restaurant. I couldn't believe she was that pathetic to follow us here. Since we had an elevated view, we could see the lounge area from our area as well. We were people watching when Malcolm walked in the door. At first, I thought he was following us when I realized the manager was reporting to him. I leaned over and I asked Daddy if this was one of Malcolm's spots. Daddy nodded yes, I had no idea. I couldn't believe it; I saw my son's silhouette bouncing around on the dance floor with Jennay. I pointed Andrew out to Daddy, we both smiled. Malcolm went over to Andrew and then he pointed us out in the restaurant. Andrew and Jennay came up to say hello. He said they already ate and they couldn't wait for all of us to join them on the dance floor. Torrie's head was whipping around trying to keep up with everything that was happening. Andrew and Jennay stayed with us until our food came then they went back on the dance floor. I didn't drink too much because I wanted to be alert just in case that girl felt Froggy tonight I was gonna be ready. Although I didn't want to chance messing up my three hundred dollar dress, if I had the opportunity to, it was gonna feel great beating her in her face. Malcolm eventually came upstairs as we finished our meal. He sat on the end where Daddy and Uncle Jeff had migrated. Dwight asked who Malcolm was; Dwayne explained he was the father of my boys. Dwight just said "whoa!" as he sat back to watch everything play out. I took Dwayne by the hand and led him to the dance floor. We danced to quite a few songs, every so often, I looked up, and Malcolm was watching every time. Then I looked over and Torrie was looking as well. After a while I told Dwayne, I was ready to go home. Dwayne wanted me to come back to his house but I couldn't because I had a meeting in the morning at the school, and he had his brother with him so it was ridiculous for him to come home with me. He told me that he had to be with me tonight. I told him to leave his brother at the lounge and he could pick him up from Daddy's. Torrie sat there trying to figure out what was going on. She kept trying to talk to Malcolm but he wasn't having it, he wasn't in the mood for female company etc. Andrew said that Torrie came over to chat with him and Jennay. He said she wanted to know why Malcolm was there. He said she seemed surprised when he told her that Malcolm owned the place. I asked him why he told her, he said he wanted to give her what she wanted so she would go away. When Dwayne and I left Malcolm was watching, and Torrie was watching him watch us. I couldn't put my finger on my interpretation of his expression. It was a little before midnight when we got to my house. Derrick and Darryl had already gone to bed. I told Dwayne he couldn't be loud like he normally was, I didn't want my boys hearing all that. He promised he'd try but he made no guarantees. I turned on soft music and Dwayne and I had a wonderful couple of passion-filled hours. I kept biting my tongue cause in that moment I wanted to tell him that I was in love with him too. I wanted to declare it from the rooftop, but the reality of Malcolm stopped me from saying anything. A little after two, I walked Dwayne to the door. The dogs weren't by the front door like they normally are, but that didn't exactly standout to me. I looked out the window and I watched Dwayne get in his car and drive away. Then I noticed Malcolm's car parked across the street. I called out to Skylar and Samara, but they didn't come. When I stepped in the kitchen, someone was in the kitchen sitting at the table. I had a flashback of David trying to make French toast in the middle of the night. I hit the switch and Malcolm was sitting there drinking. He looked at his glass until his eyes adjusted to the light then he looked up at me. His eyes were red. Which was scary with his black skin, he looked crazy. "You done already? That has to be disappointing!" He said taking another drink. "With the way you looked tonight, I wouldn't be done with you yet."

"Is that supposed to be some kind of a compliment?" I asked feeling a little scared because this scene felt too familiar. I moved over by the knife block, I didn't know what to expect from him. He left here angrier than I've ever seen him, he gave me weird looks all night, and now he's sitting in my kitchen waiting in the dark.

He watched me move to the other side of the counter. He took another drink. "My name is Malcolm not David. Come sit down."

"I need to go to bed I gotta get up in the morning."

"SIT DOWN!" He barked

My insides screamed. "No! I'll stand."

"Amber either you sit on your own or I will make you sit!" He gave me evil eyes.

"I don't want to sit!" I said trying not to sound scared.

He got up fast and he stood in my face. "You're standing over here with your hand on those knives like you're scared of me and it's pissing me off! I'm not David so stop acting like it. SIT DOWN!"

"I'm gonna sit down only because I want to." I said trying to see how angry he was and why. "But you only have a few minutes I have to go to bed."

He sat down, he stared me in my eyes for a minute. "You let me down." He might as well have punched me. His words winded me. "I remind myself why, but it still doesn't take away from the fact that you let me down." I gave him a question mark expression. "David!" I slouched a little. "You won't tell me when you guys began, but I know it was before I went in. I don't know how, but I know it. I can feel it! You wanted to marry him and give him everything, everything that is mine. When did he start hitting you?" His eyes were evil.

"Malcolm, why do we have to rehash all this?" My back was dripping with sweat.

"Answer the question!" He stared at me.

I blew air. "The day you came to take Andy to the Raider game."

Malcolm shifted in his chair. "You mean to tell me that he had the balls to put his hands on you after I was out and you said NOTHING!"

"Malcolm there's no way you can understand what I was going through. You can't understand what that time was like for me."

"You put him before me! I haven't completely forgiven you for that. It's hard because I really do love you. But sometimes I feel like anyone can come a long and your head will turn."

"At least the feeling is mutual."

He stared at me. "Troy was always in your corner. When I wanted to break your neck for cheating on me in the first place he calmed me down. There would be no Darryl if it wasn't for Troy. There would be no you if it wasn't for Troy!"

"What?"

"You have no idea how quickly I tend to fly off the handle. Your Daddy and Troy were forever calming down my temper. I am angry he's gone! Half of me is gone. I don't want to open up to you, when you're open to someone else."

"Dwayne came a long two years after you left me dangling."

"Doesn't matter, he's here now, and I don't like it. I want him gone."

I felt a lump in my throat. "I'm not ready to give him up."

He cocked his head to the side. "Why?"

"He loves me, and I care about him."

"I don't care!"

"What would I be giving him up for? Are you going to fill the void left behind?"

"No, I just want him gone."

I blinked my eyes at him. "So you're telling me, you want me to give up someone who loves me because you're tired of them, but you're gonna continue as you are? Are you high? Why would I give him up especially if I can't have you? "I exhaled. " This conversation is dumb! There never would've been a David or Dwayne if you would've done right by me in the first place. You sleep with whomever you want whenever you want. You're not even sorry about it either. Some how you think I'm supposed to just accept your indiscretions and not feel anything about it. My babies even know about the stuff you do, they probably think that's the way it's supposed to be." Then I looked at him. "You're drunk and talking out the side of your neck. Talk to me when you're sober."

I turned in my seat to walk away. "Do you still love me Amber?" A tear fell from his eye.

"Of course I do!" I said grabbing his hands. "Nobody means more to me than you do. But right now I don't like you very much."

"All that I have left are you and my boys."

"You have family Malcolm, plenty of people love you."

He shook his head. "I only have you and my boys."

"I don't agree, but ok."

"I'm not ready for you yet but I'll let Torrie go. She doesn't mean anything. Don't marry him!"

"Ok"

"Promise me!"

"I promise!"

"Don't have his baby either!"

Tears fell out my eyes. "I can't have anymore, you know that."

"Just don't do it!" He said

The liquor was talking, in a person's drunken state the truth comes out. "I'll make a bed for you on the couch." When I stood up, he hugged me tight. "I miss Troy!"

"I do too!" I led him to the couch. I had him lay down. I took his shoes off. Then I got a couple blankets out of the linen closet. He was knocked out when I put the blankets on him. I took his car keys off the table. I looked out in the yard and the dogs were sleeping outside. I thought about putting his keys under my pillow. Instead, I put them in my closet on the top shelf in the back under sweaters; I was sleep for a little bit when he came and got in my bed. He put his arms around me and his hands on my breast then he fell back asleep.

When I got up in the morning, I got in the shower. Malcolm came in the bathroom. He said his head was killing him, I told him to get medicine out of my medicine cabinet. He took some then went back in my room. I came out the bathroom in my terry cloth robe. He was going through my jewelry box. "What are you doing?" He was looking at the ring David gave me. "I didn't know you still had this." "What are you doing?"

"I was looking for my keys. I figure you hid them." Then he looked at me in my robe.

"Go out so I can get them."

"Or..." He raised his eyebrows

"Or nothing! The penis that touches Torrie's will not touch mine!"

He frowned at me. I pushed him out the room. I got his keys, when I opened the door he pushed his way back in. He kissed me deep, and then he started untying my robe. When I started to protest, he looked me in my eyes and gently pushed me back on the bed. He got on his knees and proceeded to kiss me. As I gasped for air, I realized his purpose in life is to keep me in a constant state of confusion.

****

"Do you understand?" I asked Derrick

His face was angry. "So what was he supposed to be doing sneaking up on us like that?" He growled

"I don't know baby, but whatever he thought he was gonna do obviously back fired on him." I said

"So who is Emma?"

"My Momma's sister. She was at the hospital and the funeral, I think. That day was such a blur I couldn't tell you everyone who was there but I think she was there. If he was there I don't know, but I doubt it."

"He better hope he never sees me again!" Derrick said

"Derrick we don't go looking for trouble." I said

"I know momma. I'm just saying. All of you guys were pretty upset and when I told Malcolm, he almost lost it. I just wanted to know what was going on."

"That's understandable."

"Since you're in a sharing mood, if it isn't too upsetting for you I have some questions." Derrick said

"Shoot, you can ask me anything."

"What happened with you and David?"

My stomach dropped. "What do you mean?"

"I can't imagine that he was always the way I remember him."

"No, he started off as a good guy. I really thought he was too good for me in the beginning."

"Do I act like him?"

I smiled, "you have always acted more like Malcolm than any of my sons, that's always been amazing to me. Even as a baby, you didn't cry much. You've always been serious."

He smiled, "why did he hate me?"

"Baby I didn't know he ever said anything like that to you."

"Maybe the more of Malcolm he saw in me the less he liked me." Derrick exhaled. "That's the way I imagine it anyways."

"I think you might be right." I said

"Are you sure Malcolm's not my father? Should we get a Blood test?"

I touched his face. "Baby Malcolm is whoever you want him to be. But I know exactly when you were conceived, Malcolm was still in jail."

"I'm saying though, sometimes me and Malcolm be looking at Drew like what's his deal. Drew and Darryl, sometimes they be they goofiest somebody's. Drew loses it over females I know you know he's still creeping with Toya. I don't get that, Jennay seems cool, drama free and he seems like he cares about her." He shook his head. "I don't care how fine she is, she ain't worth no headache."

"I agree. How's Raquel?"

He made a wounded sound. "You know the saying out of sight out of mind. She's moved on, we're done, ain't no sense in holding on."

A light went off. "Derrick did you guys, you know?" He smiled and looked away. "Eeewwllll! Boy! I knew you guys really liked each other and were always together. Now your tears make so much more sense." Derrick sat there blushing. "Do her parents know?"

"No! Her dad would've lost it." He said still blushing.

"Did you use condoms?"

"Of course! Malcolm made sure I had everything I needed."

I gasped, "He knew?"

Derrick put his hands up. "No he didn't know. After he met her, he told me he could tell I really liked her. We had a long talk and he told me to be prepared for anything. And I was..." He said shaking his head.

"Eeeeewwwwlllll!" I said as I playfully hit him. "So I can assume that since I didn't get a phone call from an irate parent there's no little Derrick running around Atlanta?"

"No way! I'm not married!"

I smiled real big, "you want to get married?"

"Yea, I want a wife and kids. I just don't want any drama. Most of these girls bring drama. I don't have patience for drama. It's so bad that every time I see Toya I want to choke her again. I do not want a female like that even knowing my name."

"I know the feeling."

Derrick blew air. "When was the last time you talked to Drew?"

I thought about it for a minute. I hadn't talked to Andrew in a minute. "It's been a minute. What's going on with him?"

"You should go drop in to see him, but don't tell him that you talked to me."

"When should I go?"

"Go now!"

I went and got my purse and then I left. I got off the freeway made a right and then a left, down Telegraph, being near my old school always made me think about David. When things were good and when things went bad. I thought about Blawndee's Pizza and my mouth watered. I decided I'd tell Andy I wanted some pizza and ask him to walk with me. Ooh and then we could top it off with some frozen yogurt that could definitely do the trick. I pulled into Andrew's garage; his car was there as well as Tanisha's. I parked in the visitor parking space. I could hear arguing and the closer I got to Andrew's door the louder it got. I rolled my eyes and said "Toya." I knocked on the door, Jennay snatched the door open, she couldn't pull herself together; I knew that look in her eyes. She stepped to the side so that I could enter. Andrew slouched in his chair when he saw me. Not the reaction you want from your child. "Andy what's going on?"

"Momma its just relationship stuff." He said

"Your mother doesn't know does she?" Her Chicago accent was real thick in that moment.

"You gonna bring my mother in this?" Andrew barked

"She might as well know!" Jennay said

"There's nothing for her to know. We can move past this!"

She blew air at him. "Your son is going to have a baby!"

"Jennay!" Then he looked at me. "No I'm not momma."

I had to sit down, I plopped on the couch, Jennay started screaming at Andrew; Andrew was trying to calm her down. Her heart was broken, she couldn't calm down.

"Jennay! Jennay!" I yelled my ears were bleeding. She stopped screaming. "Let's go get some pizza!" Jennay looked insulted. "I came over to ask Andy to come with me, but clearly he needs some time. If you don't want to eat just walk with me. Please!" I stood up and took her by the hand. Andrew put his hands on his head as he slouched over on his chair. As we walked out the door, Tanisha was leaving her apartment. She glanced in our direction, she nodded at me, and then she kept walking. When she got close she gave me a kiss on my cheek, then she kept going. I grabbed Jennay by the hand and we started walking again. We walked in silence while tears streamed down her face. When we got to Blawndee's I asked her if she changed her mind. She shook her head no. I got a slice of pepperoni; I piled on a thick layer of red pepper flakes. Jennay stared at the floor. I touched her hand. "Toya?"

Tears started pouring out of her eyes again. "Amber how could he do this? I thought we were in love! I thought we would be together forever." She inhaled and then exhaled. "He knows she's evil! Why would he let her hurt us like this?" She cried. "I hate her!"

"I know baby! There are not too many people who do like her." I said

"It's so hard to find a good man. One who accepts you as you are, appreciates your mind, doesn't make you feel self-conscious, and is good to you but he comes attached to an evil person. I worked too hard to get here to end up rotting in jail behind killing her. I can't do this!"

"Do you think he can fix it?"

"I've given him numerous chances to fix this. Then she ends up pregnant. He asked her to marry him!"

I dropped my pizza. "He did what?" I knew I didn't hear her right.

"He wasn't even sure that the baby was his." She said

"He did what!" I couldn't believe it.

"She turned him down. The other guy she's seeing is on a football scholarship. She figured the other guy is the bigger fish. He's most likely the daddy but she got an abortion so that's supposed to make everything ok I guess. Andrew doesn't get it. She doesn't care about him." She cried some more.

"He did what?" I know what she said but I couldn't believe what she said. I hugged Jennay, I felt horrible. I apologized to her; I didn't know what else to say.

We walked back to the apartment in silence. I didn't walk her up to the door I went to my car. I drove around for a long time. My pager started going off. Andrew was paging, then Derrick paged, then Malcolm paged. Then my car phone started ringing. I let it ring, and ring. I was so disappointed in Andrew. What if that girl would've said yes?

I found myself driving over the bridge even though my palms were extremely sweaty I pushed through. I needed to see Dwayne and just get away from everything else. I entered the gate and my eyes immediately went to Michelle's car. I parked next to her car in the driveway. I took a deep breath not knowing what I was about to walk in on. I used my key to open the door. Dwayne and Michelle were standing ten feet away from the front door. She jumped when I opened the door, Dwayne didn't. He smiled real big when he saw me. She looked disappointed to see me. He gave me the biggest hug and kiss. Michelle looked like it was a horrible scene out of a nightmare to watch us. I asked if I was interrupting something. Michelle didn't say anything, and Dwayne welcomed me. Michelle hurried out the door and Dwayne gave me the biggest hug. He was surprised that I drove myself.

I told him about my day, I told him I just needed to get away. He told me I came to the right place. We walked to the kitchen where he exaggerated bartending skills he didn't have to make me a drink. He was being extra cute and pulling out all the stops to make sure I laughed and smiled. Something worked because my drink was delicious and he put a smile on my face. I asked him why he and Michelle looked so serious when I walked in. He said they were having a serious conversation, and then he told me that Michelle wants to get back with him. She just stopped begging when I walked in the door. I asked him if he wanted to get back with her. He looked at me and asked me why he would go back to her when he had me. I told him she was going to end up pregnant. I told him it worked once why wouldn't she go back to her old trick. He didn't know what to say to that. Then I reminded him that we promised to tell the truth no matter what. I told him that he should go back to her; at least he could finally get his son. He had a pained look on his face. He told me to stop talking, and then he said he hadn't touched her in six months. I asked him if that was why she suddenly had the clarity to see that they needed to get back together. He took a deep breath, and then asked me, "where do you see us in a year from now?"

I felt like everything was closing in on me. "Dwayne honestly I don't hear wedding bells. I don't love you. Michelle is offering you love and the chance to be a family again. Why wouldn't you jump on that?"

"Cause it's not with you! I want all of that with you."

I wished he were Malcolm saying this to me. "Dwayne, baby you are a good man. You deserve to be with someone who loves you."

"You love me, I know you do. What's so scary about telling me the truth about how you feel?" He was searching my eyes. "I see it in your face. I feel it in your touch. It's in everything we do, but you keep lying to me."

I had to side step that. "Michelle still loves you! Could you be mistaken her feelings for mine?"

He sat me on the kitchen counter so I could be closer to eye level with him. He bent down some and put his hands in my hair. I kissed his arm. "She loves me, but she and I are nothing like you and I. I want to be with you. I want a family with you, even if it means that we make due with our almost Brady Bunch. I don't have to have a son." He kissed me.

"That's what you're saying right now but pretty soon your clock is gonna start ticking, you're forty-one, by forty-three you're gonna want one real bad. You heard my day; at thirty-five, I could've been a grandmother. Besides, I can't have any more babies, and I know you want at least one more. I care about you enough to let you go be happy."

He stood up, he was frustrated, and "Why aren't you hearing me? Are your ears stopped up that much with Malcolm that you can't hear me?" I blank stared at him. "I know you still care about him. No..." He put his hands on the top of his head. "I know you're still in love with him but I'm in love with you. I want you forever, why does he still win when he's not even playing the game?"

I felt horrible. "Maybe I should go." I said hopping off the counter.

His voice cracked. "Why would you leave?"

"Because I feel horrible, you deserve better than this. Doesn't matter how long we sit here going back and forth it won't change the fact that I don't love you."

He picked me up and kissed me deep. His kiss curled my toes; it was full of love, passion, and desperation. My body became one big tingle. "You do love me! Stop lying to yourself, because you're not fooling me." Then he put me down.

I took him by the hand, and I led him upstairs. I undressed him, while his serious eyes tried to force me to admit what was in my heart. I made love to him like my life depended on it. When he seemed completely spent, I forced him back to life. When there was no life left in him, I snuck out of the bed. He was so spent his mouth was open while he slept. I took his key off my keys and I left it on his nightstand. I snuck out the door. I cried all the way home.

142

When I pulled up to my house, there were a bunch of cars outside. Malachi came out to my car. He asked me if I was ok, I shook my head no. Malachi made me get in the passenger seat of my car; he sat in the driver's seat. I told him how disappointed I was in Andrew, and then I told him I broke up with Dwayne. He asked me why in the world I did that. I looked at him with tears pouring out of my eyes. He looked at me and said, "Malcolm!" He asked me if I was sure that was what I wanted to do.

I told him I couldn't keep him and Michelle apart when I couldn't go where he wanted to go. My pager started going off, I didn't have to look at it to know who it was. I told Malachi to tell everyone inside that I was fine, but I was going to spend the night away. Malachi asked me to at least let one person know where I ended up. I asked him to protect Dwayne from Malcolm when he showed up, Malachi agreed. I got back in the driver's seat, I put the car on the freeway, and I ended up in San Jose at a beautiful hotel. I stripped down to my underwear then I sat on the floor crying. When the phone in my room started ringing, I knew who it was. I picked up the phone but I didn't say anything. "I'm coming up, open the door!" I blew air because I didn't want to see him. It's not like I could run anywhere. I cracked the door then I got in the bed under the covers. Tears were pouring out my eyes. He walked in the room and sat on my bed. He looked at me I didn't look at him.

"He wanted to marry me Malcolm!" He didn't respond he just looked at me. "I didn't want to tell him no. He offered me my dream, and I turned him down. I hate you Malcolm! You've done this to me twice." He didn't say anything he just stared at me. I cried my heart out into the pillow.

"He came to the house." I looked at Malcolm. "He was pretty upset. He even tried to walk up on me." Malcolm smiled as if the thought of it tickled him. "He really does love you." Then he sighed, "Sometimes love isn't enough." I hit him with my pillow. He laughed, but I didn't see anything funny.

"Glad my pain provides you with amusement!"

He stopped smiling. "It doesn't."

"Yes it does! All I've ever told you was that I wanted a husband and a family. You make everything difficult and painful. Yea so maybe both guys weren't perfect, but if you aren't gonna be perfect then why stop me from trying to be happy? You're miserable so I must be miserable too. If I could go back and talk to my thirteen-year-old self, I'd tell her to never have approach you. I'd tell her you are as mean as you said you were. I'd tell her to run the other way. I wouldn't have Andrew, but maybe that wouldn't be the worse thing since he's breaking hearts just like you."

He kissed my forehead. "Are you done?"

My mouth fell open. "Why are you here?"

"I wanted to check on you. Make sure you're ok." I blank stared at him. "Oh and before I forget, Brad's been making threats. I'm having cameras installed at the school. I don't know why I didn't think of this sooner and locks on the doors that require badge access or buzzing from the inside to gain access. Security on you guys is gonna be a lot tighter. I have someone outside your door now. There'll be someone with each of the boys, literally with them."

"Why is he so angry?"

"His label isn't doing too well at the moment. He has to blame somebody. So...."

"Why us?"

"Not us, me. But he'll lash out at all of you to get to me." He said

"Why you?"

"Let's see first I tell him you can't do his videos anymore, and then I won't book him for studio time. Then a few other things, it adds up." Malcolm shrugged.

"A few other things means a female doesn't it?" Malcolm looked at me but didn't answer the question. I shook my head; of course, there's a female in here somewhere. "Like peas in a pod, you, and your son."

"When are you going to talk to Drew?" I just shook my head. "He's just a boy; don't be too hard on him."

"What do you care? You're not teaching him to be any better." I exhaled. "Malcolm please leave, looking at you is making me hurt more."

He kissed my forehead and hugged me. "I love you!"

"Yea right!" When Malcolm was gone, I took out my birth control pills and threw them away, without Dwayne in my life there was no point in being on them.

****

When I woke up, I had to hurry, shower, and get dressed. My alarm didn't go off and I was running late.

When I got to North Star, Tony told me he had everyone set up in the conference room. He ordered an impromptu breakfast when I told him I was running late.

When I walked in everyone was smiling and just sitting down to eat so I wasn't too late, but had they been sitting and waiting ten minutes, without the distraction of the food there would be no smiles. I made a mental note to do something special for Tony for thinking on his feet.

Corey had good ideas; although this video was being shot in Oakland you wouldn't know it by the photos he chose for our locations. This job wasn't going to be my most high paying job, but it was gonna be nice to work with nice people. After Corey and everyone, left I chatted with Jade and Tony for a few hours.

After all the work Malcolm had done to the building, it actually looked better if you ask me. The windows were all tinted where sunlight came in we could see out but you couldn't see in. People keep telling us that the building looks like an office building more than a dance school. As we were talking, Jade tapped me and then we watched Torrie march up to the building. She almost ran into the door when she didn't realize it was locked. She rang the bell in the most annoying fashion. Tony looked at me and I told him to let her in, she came through the door all huffy. She walked in with her hair all pulled back, no makeup or earrings on, A T-shirt that clung to her, jeans, and combat boots. I smiled at Jade and she sat there shaking her head. Torrie was making a beeline to Tony when she slowed as she saw me.

"I didn't think you were here, I didn't see your car."

"Oh you mean my everyday car; I gave that away a long time ago. My car is out there."

"Do you have an appointment?" Tony asked pretending like he was looking at the schedule.

She put her hand in the air to say she wasn't there for him. "Where's Malcolm?" She said with as much attitude as she could muster.

"My Malcolm?" I said innocently.

"Your Malcolm! Ha! He ain't been your Malcolm for some years now! He does what I tell him." She said wiggling her neck and talking as loud as she could.

"Oh you mean like that night at the Theater, when he showered my family with VIP treatment all night?"

"Where do you think he got the money to do all that?" She said

144

"Little girl please, clearly you don't know who you're dealing with. Malcolm doesn't need your little lunch money. You look so dumb; you don't ever pay a man to do anything."

"You're just jealous because you will never have it like I got it." She said

"What should I be jealous of? Your little career that may last you for a little while and that you actually may make some nice change on, but keep giving your money away like you do. You'll be working at McDonald's in ten years, talking about all the stuff you used to have. Or how pretty soon you won't be able to take a walk around the mall or lead a normal life!"

"All that and how your Malcolm will be on my arm begging me for a son!" She said

I smiled, "now why would he do that when he has the three I gave him?"

"The what?"

I shook my head, "yea! You met our oldest at the club that night. I believe you spoke to him at Shylight too." Clearly, she forgot she met Andrew. I leaned against the counter smiling. She looked like she was about to pop.

"Can you step outside?" She said walking to the door.

"Sure thing." I said to her as I took my earrings off. I wrapped my hair in a bun.

"Tony be a doll and call Malcolm and tell him I'm about to handle his whore."

"Amber! Let her be stupid by herself. We're getting too old to be fighting over guys." Jade said

"I won't swing on her first. I'm just going prepared." I said walking out the door, as I heard Tony talking to Malcolm.

Not too far behind me, Jade followed us out of the building. Two girls were waiting in her car; they smiled real big when they saw me. The guys Malcolm had watching our building started making calls from their car and the other one came close to the end of Torrie's car. Torrie came charging at me, as she swung wide. I popped her in her nose. The surprised look on her face as she realized what just happened was priceless. I stood there smiling. She was so angry and surprised that her strength was working against her. She came at me again, and I dropped and lifted her by her legs, she went flying over my shoulder. Her face hit the asphalt and her friend got mad and hopped out of the car. She squared off; I tried to stay aware of where Torrie was while this girl was closing in. Jade put her foot in Torrie's back, she told her to stay down. The girl popped me in my mouth, I could feel my lip swelling which made me mad. I charged the girl before she had a chance to steady herself I hit her with a right and when her head followed the direction of my right I followed with a left. I could feel all my anger coming out on this girl. The girl's eyes were big and I told her to stay down if she was smart. I wanted to beat Torrie. Jade let her go and she scurried to get up. The right side of her face was skinned up and red, blood was coming to the surface. She was crying and I squared off. Malcolm pulled up speeding like a bat out of hell. He was cursing before he got out the car. He walked up to Torrie and grabbed her by her neck. He kept telling her, "What did I tell you?" Juan pulled up in one car and another car pulled up. They boxed in Torrie's car. "Get rid of her! Them! The car! I'm done!" Malcolm yelled

Juan's guys each grabbed a girl, one grabbed Torrie.

"Wait a minute! Malcolm!" Juan said

Torrie's eyes were big, her friends started crying, and asking Torrie what was going on. Malcolm looked at me and he got mad all over again. He pushed Torrie up against Juan's car. The whole car shook. "Didn't I tell you not to even talk to her?" And yes, Torrie was now staring in the eyes of the beast that is Malcolm. I almost felt bad for her.

"Malcolm!" Jade yelled. She broke his attention on Torrie. "Come here!" Jade commanded him.

To everybody's surprise he went. Jade put her arm in his then she started talking calmly and they paced the walkway from the parking lot to the front door back to the parking lot. Malcolm was angry, but she was making him think about what he was saying. She kept telling him you're smarter than this. Juan had both of the girl's driver's licenses. Torrie was asking me what was going on. I just stood there cause I still wanted to beat her, but I kept telling myself that was going to be an ugly scar on her face. Just be satisfied with that. One of the guys gave her a napkin for her face. Malcolm came back, he pointed at the cameras. He told her she better forget she ever knew him or me otherwise the police and all the media were getting copies of her provoking the fight and then getting beat up. Torrie started crying and then she said she loved him. He looked at her in complete disgust. "You are the dumbest female I've ever met! How could you miss how in love I am with this woman!" He said pointing at me. "This whole situation better teach you a lesson. When a man gives you specific instructions, you listen! If you disobey me again there will be no one to save you!"

Juan's men were talking to her friends, they were crying. Neither one of them realized what they were getting their selves into by coming here with her. Malcolm hugged me and asked me if I was ok. I looked at Torrie who was in shock looking at Malcolm like she couldn't believe it. "Get them off of my property!" He said. We turned to walk towards the building then suddenly we heard a car speed up and then we heard gunshots. I fell on Jade and Malcolm jumped on top of us. The girls screamed as Juan's men threw them down to the ground. Torrie's car got completely sprayed up. Juan pulled out two guns and started shooting back. He hit the tire on the car and it spun out of control. It was going so fast that as it spun out of control it wrapped around the telephone pole across the street. Torrie was sitting on the ground screaming as she looked at us. Malcolm's hand moved real fast over me and Jade as he asked us if we were ok. Juan asked us if we were hit. Then I saw blood on Malcolm's shirt. "MALCOLM!!" I screamed!

He looked at his shoulder. He grimaced then he moved his arm. "Calm down!" He said

Juan looked at his shoulder, "it's just a graze. You'll be fine!"

"Can I please leave now?" Torrie screamed

"SHUT UP! No, you can't! You gotta give the police a statement now." Juan said

"We can't stay, we got warrants!" One of the girls yelled.

"Torrie if you don't shut them up!" Malcolm said he walked towards the slowly growing crowd.

The police, the fire department, and paramedics came. There were four guys in the car two of them died upon impact. The other two left in ambulances, but one was dead on arrival, the other was in critical condition. The police took statements from all of us. They took Torrie's friends into custody because of their warrants. Andrew pulled up and came straight to me. "Momma are you ok?" Torrie looked at us with wide eyes. Daddy and Uncle Frank came and they spoke with the officers. Sonny wanted names, we pretty much figured out it was Mister's guys. When the news van pulled up we went inside but we left Torrie outside to deal with it. Someone came to pick her up eventually. On the news, they were reporting that crazy fans were stalking Torrie and her bodyguard returned fire killing three of the four gunmen. Media was all over the hospital where Torrie was having her face bandaged. She actually came out looking like a victim and people were so sympathetic towards her. Dwayne paged me; I know he saw the school. I paged him back my code to let him know I was ok.

****

Dwayne's still having a hard time accepting that I broke up with him. Knowing that I was breaking his heart is one thing, seeing it all over him, horrifying. The couple of times he's popped up on me have been extremely emotional and draining. He doesn't wanna give up on me and I've been begging him to. A couple of times I almost broke down and told him what was on my heart, but I didn't see the point in that. It would just build false hope for him. He's sent me flowers, written me letters all which I cherish and will keep forever. I dried the flowers and put them in a vase on my dresser. Sometimes I read the letters over and over, especially when I'm missing him the most.

In his last letter, he told me I was right. Michelle gave him the news earlier that day. He said he was so disappointed in himself for allowing this to happen again. I could see the tear stains on the paper as he said he was gonna make the best of it and man up to his responsibility. He asked that if our paths should cross that I don't ignore him or act like we had nothing. He still knows that I love him, and he's still holding on until he hears me admit it. He said he refused to have a big ceremony, and that they were going to the justice of the peace. He said his heart wasn't in it like it was before. He told me he loved me and he missed me.

My insides burned with disappointment. I know I said she'd end up pregnant, but reading that my words came true was heart breaking. With no Malcolm and now no Dwayne, I was alone again, out here on my own. To massage my broken heart I threw myself into work. Over the summer, I took Derrick and Darryl to work with me. They got to meet all kinds of celebrities and having them with me gave me joy. When our travels took us to Chicago, we visited with Jennay. She told me she transferred schools and she wasn't coming back to Berkeley. We all told her how much we were going to miss her.

When we were in New York, we went to an awards ceremony. It was a black tie affair, and the boys and I had a great time. We met a rapper who went by the name Comfort, but he introduced himself as Ramell. He was a few years younger than I was but he carried himself like he was older than me. What I liked about Comfort is that he was all about building up and up lifting women. He told me that the word on the street was that I was the choreographer to get. I told him I didn't think he danced and he assured me he didn't dance, but his concept for a upcoming video was to have a beautiful woman dancing in the video. I told him I could give him a list of names of dancers that could audition for him. He stared at me and said he was thinking of me. His eyes glowed like brownish yellow pieces of amber. I thanked him for the compliment, and then I told him to have his people give me a call. Then he said this was all pending Dwayne's approval of course. I told him that Dwayne and I broke up and that he was married. Ramell smiled real big. Of course my Derrick being the man he is. When he noticed the body language between Ramell and me, he promptly came over, interrupted our conversation, and took me away. Who needs a bodyguard when you've got a Derrick by your side?

****

"Momma I'm sorry! I had no idea you would take it so hard." Andrew said he looked like he had been sick all summer. "I've been trying to find Jennay ever since classes reconvened."

"Andy she transferred schools, she's not coming back."

"WHAT? Where did she go? I gotta find her. I'll leave Toya alone. I'll do whatever she wants." Andrew was falling apart.

"If you mean all that then you gotta let her go. If she comes back to you don't blow it again. And that's a very big if." I said matter of factly.

"No! It can't be over! I gotta find her! I can't just give up! I'm really sorry!"

"Andy baby you broke her heart. She's still hurting; you can't win her back right now, no matter how hard you try. It will only make things worse for you right now. Just give her some space."

Andrew sat back on the couch; his body was fighting his mind and heart. I know he wanted to disregard me and go get her, but his mind told him to listen to me.

Then there was a knock at the door. I went to the door it was Ms. Connie. "She's here!" She said too excited as she walked back to her house. Hubby was standing outside all proud next to his girlfriend. Ms. Connie loved her and was constantly talking about her. A lot of Ms. Connie's family and friends were surrounding the poor child so I didn't expect her to remember me but she was every bit as pretty as Ms. Connie had painted her to be. "It's nice to meet you I'm Nicole," she said. Andrew sat on the porch all pale and rough looking. He nodded to Hubby, Hubby nodded back. I asked Andrew if he met Hubby's girlfriend before. He said he had of course. He said she was good for him they were growing up together. Andrew tried to hold back his jealousy, but you might as well have painted him green with jealousy. In that moment, I wondered how Betty took the news that Dwayne and Michelle were back together and that she was pregnant again. I wish I could've been a fly on the wall for that conversation.

****

The gossip reels were a buzz with Dwayne and I's breakup. Even though we broke up over a year ago, the world was just finding out about it. The question everyone wanted an answer to is whether Comfort and I were dating. We had spent sometime together, and we decided we were better off as friends.

Although, it was after this weird night, we were at a party and Torrie was there but she made sure she stayed on her side of the room and if she accidentally found herself by me, she hurried to the other side of the room. Although Terrell was guarding me, I thought I saw Juan. If that was him, he floated in and out without saying a word to me. I lost track of Ramell for a bit, that night on our way back to the hotel he gave me this whole spill about loving our friendship yadda, yadda, yadda. But that was ok, because I wasn't feeling him relationship wise. He filled the void of having a male friend in my life.

"And the winner is? ... COMFORT!" The camera panned to us. He hugged me, his hands were sweaty, and the snippet from his video with me dancing was on the screen. So imagine my surprise when he dedicated his win to our friendship. He said, "without your friendship Amber I would be so lost!"

I put hands over my mouth. I was completely surprised, when he came back to the seats. He gave me the biggest hug and whispered in my ear that he loved me. Ok now I was confused.

Chapter 45

My baby is wilding out! Instead of healing his broken heart, I keep seeing him out with different girls. I knew it was bad when he wouldn't even bother to introduce some of them. I couldn't even be mad when I saw him with Toya, I was disappointed but I couldn't be mad and I was happy for the times I saw her with her hair down. Whenever I saw her with her hair in a ponytail I pulled momma rank and I'd interrupt whatever was going on. Derrick was the one who pointed out her mood indicator hairstyle, I was so happy he shared with me that insight into her crazy world. My baby started fighting and really acting like his father. It was to the point if you said Drew anywhere in Oakland, especially in East Oakland people would shudder. He was still excelling in school, but my baby was acting out and it hurt my heart to see.

****

He put a badge in my face. "Amber Wallace, we need to ask you some questions." My heart dropped. "Ok, follow me." I led the officers to the conference room. I had no idea what they wanted; no one told me they were coming. They had to be detectives they were in plain clothes. "How may I help you?"

"I'm detective White. We're investigating a homicide. Does the name Bradley Caruthers ring any bells?"

"No I can't say that it does." I had no clue who he was talking about.

"Oh wait, let me see." The woman took out her note pad. "He was known on the streets and in the industry as Mister MC."

I gasped, "He's dead? What happened?" My mind instantly thought of Malcolm.

"He was found dead in his car on the side of the freeway." They studied my face.

"That is horrible!" I said, "But what does that have to do with me?"

"Well we know it was some years ago but we know that your then boyfriend Dwayne Reed and Bradley Caruthers got into an altercation after an awards ceremony. We were wondering if you could tell us about that."

Oh no, Malcolm please don't do this. "It was so long ago I really don't remember. It was probably a lot of testosterone in one space."

"Are you still dating Dwayne Reed?"

"No" all they had to do is brush up on their gossip. My favorite story was the one where they had a picture of Michelle pleading and the caption read that I was holding Dwayne captive as my sex toy and Michelle was begging for her family back. Dwayne was on everything commercials, magazines, TV shows, even a cameo here and there in movies. Women loved looking at him and he was being paid to be looked at.

"When was the last time you talked to him?"

"I don't remember." I said

"You don't seem to remember too much do you?" The female detective said sarcastically.

I sarcastically smiled at her. "Try asking me about something I actually devoted to memory. Besides I don't know how much I can remember without having a lawyer present."

Detective White stared at my face. "You're Franklin Wallace's grand daughter aren't you?"

"What does that mean?" I asked trying not to turn red.

He turned red. "Nothing." Then he turned to his partner. "We're done here."

She looked surprised. "What? We have more questions."

149

He stood up. "No we don't. Here's my card. Call me if you have any more problems." Then he turned to his partner. "Let's go!"

The woman was visibly irritated, when they exited the building I hurried to Jade's office. She was already looking at the monitor. She turned up the volume and the detectives were arguing in the parking lot. Detective White told the woman to leave the Wallace Family alone. He told her if she wanted to go up against us, she was on her own. Then they got in the car and drove off. I looked at Jade her eyes were wide. I reached for the phone; she grabbed my hand and asked what I was doing. I told her I was going to call Malcolm. She told me not to; she said they could be tapped. She said business as usual, and that we needed to wait to speak to each other face to face. Then she told me not to go out of my way to talk to anyone either. I asked her if we were under surveillance. She didn't know, but some how no one let us know they were coming it was for a reason.

****

"I need to refocus my energy. I'm getting tired of the quote unquote game. I don't want to be an old man chasing tail. I want a family, a wife of my own. I want what Hubby has. I had it in my grasp once and being stupid, I lost it. I just need a change of pace."

"You better not have Toya in that equation! I'll kick your butt right now." I said

"I second that!" Derrick said smiling at Andrew.

"Let me put my three cent on it!" Darryl cleared his throat. "That chicken head tell you I saw her at Durant Circle?"

"Yes, I heard all about it." Andrew said exhaling.

"We didn't hear about it. Share with the class Darryl, your audience is waiting." Derrick said putting an imaginary microphone up to Darryl's mouth.

Darryl snatched the invisible microphone and stood up. "So I'm walking around the circle, minding my own business, looking at a young tender that I might want to holler at AND THAT CHICKEN HEAD WALKS PAST ME MUGGING ME ON SOME NIGGA I DON'T KNOW ARM. I wasn't going to sweat her, wasn't going to pay her any attention but she sees me talking to the tender and she come running her mouth. I looked at her dude like check your chick. He threw his hands in the air as if he wasn't responsible for her so I had to backhand her. She didn't shut up she kept running her mouth so I followed her to her car. I broke her window pulled her out head first through the glass and told her she better never disrespect me ever again! Bet you she don't say nothing else to me no more."

"Does that make you a man, handling her like that?" I asked. All three of them looked at me with the same expression. "Ok, I know Toya is a special case. But I don't want you guys walking around here thinking it's ok to put your hands on females."

"Momma trust, there's no David's at this table. But if there is a Toya like female all bets are off." Derrick said.

"What does that mean?"

"You know Toya! You know how she is and what she does. She's not a female! Momma you know how she is." Darryl said smacking Derrick's hand. Andrew turned his head.

"Yes I know how Toya is and she'll push you to that point. I just don't want to think of my boys as guys who are ok with putting hands on females."

"Again! Toya is a special breed of female dog. She doesn't count!" Darryl said

"Females like that don't count!" Derrick said

I looked at Andrew, he blew air, and "I know the temptation is there. I'm not saying I wouldn't have pulled her out the car through her window. I just can't get with actually putting my hands on even a special breed like you guys call her. Because I don't care how justified some fool feels they are if they put their hands on my momma, Sasha, or Tanisha its lights out for them."

Derrick and Darryl both laughed. "I wanna see the fool stupid enough to step to Tanisha!" They all belly laughed.

"You know what I mean." Andrew said still laughing. "I missed you guys. I know I'm just down the street. But I've missed you guys."

"Guess that means you need to come around more often." I said running my hand through his curls.

"Where are you gonna go?" Andrew asked Derrick

"I got my eye on Stanford." He said

"Uncle Timothy wore you down?" Andrew said smiling.

"Man! He makes it sound golden!" Derrick exhaled. "Okay but you were saying before we veered off to chicken heads."

"Oh that was it; I don't wanna end up like Malcolm." Andrew said

Derrick and Darryl blew air. "What am I missing? What's wrong with Malcolm?" I asked

"He wanna be here, but he gets in his own way." Derrick said

"He loves you momma, something just goes wrong." Andrew said

"Remember how he was losing it when she was with Dwayne?" Darryl said

They all nodded. "Please fill me in cause I don't know." I said

They all made exhausted sounds and started talking all at once. "Let me speak first!" Darryl said above them. He swallowed. "First let me put this caveat out there. If you ever tell him, I told you I will LIE! I WILL LIE MY BUTT OFF! YOU AIN'T HEARD THIS FROM ME!" Derrick and Andrew asked for the same anonymity. "Ok so when he heard that we went to the game. He wasn't tripping until he asked why we went to a NINER game. He fell in his chair when I said Gwen hooked you up." They all started laughing. "He wanted play by plays every time anything involved you and him. That time he came over here throwing a tantrum slamming doors. The next day he came over accusing us of being traitors. Derrick had to calm him down. With every hour you were gone he was sweating that much more. Then when you came, he tries to act all calm and cool. That's why I was always laughing at him."

"I don't know about him being all that dramatic, but he was all ears and full of questions whenever Dwayne was involved." Derrick said

"And when you guys broke up he was too happy! When Dwayne came over looking for you, of course Malcolm had to rub his nose in it Uncle Mali had to calm Dwayne down and take him outside. They were out there for a long time then Malcolm went out there. He said something as he walked past Dwayne, Mali fell trying to hold that big ole linebacker back. Malcolm laughed at him." Andrew said smiling.

"That is horrible!" I said Andrew's smile dropped.

"You're right!" Andrew cleared his throat.

"But honestly I couldn't see you with that pretty boy forever anyways." Derrick said

"You're always team Malcolm!" I said

"Of course he got issues, but no one could love you more." Derrick said

"You're so sure. I don't know, sometimes I think Dwayne loved me more."

All of them rolled their eyes. "He may have had some feelings. They may have run deep. But he still doesn't top Malcolm." Darryl said

"I get it. Malcolm loves you, you love him. But I'm not opposed to you moving on." Andrew said matter of factly.

Derrick and Darryl paused. They looked at Andrew like he was a traitor. "Drew! What is wrong with you? You know that's not gonna happen! You saw how fast he was with Ramell!" They all laughed.

"What did he do to Ramell?"

"He shut him down!" Darryl said laughing. "You haven't heard his song? ' The unattainable Goddess' he called Malcolm the evil spirit surrounding you dimming your light. It's pretty deep. He poured out his heart in that song, I'm surprised you didn't make the connection." Darryl said matter of factly.

"Sitting with you guys I'm getting such an education. I didn't make the connection." I said

We sat in Gonzalez's for hours talking about everything. Andrew was telling us about the club he wanted to open. The three of them came to life talking about it. I asked Darryl what he knew about clubs, and they all smiled at me. Darryl said when you're tall they don't ask as many questions. I shook my head at them. When we got in Andrew's new to him car, I say new to him cause it was a used four door sedan but he said it would do. He gave Derrick Malachi's car as promised when he got his license. When we got in the car I told them about the visit I had from Detective White. I told them I had no idea Mister's name was Bradley Caruthers. They all got quiet; I asked what I was missing. Andrew asked me if I remembered Camille Caruthers. I kept saying the name because it was very familiar but I couldn't put my finger on why. Andrew reminded me that she used to work at Drew's. I wanted to spit acid; I went off calling her every name I could think of. The boys sat silently as I went on my rant then I asked him what she had to do with Mister. He said she was his ex wife aka current wife. He said they were married got divorced then got remarried. That didn't sound unfamiliar, but I put the dots together she was the old woman Torrie was talking about. Good grief! How old is she now? She had to be in her thirties or close to them when we were teenagers so she has to be in her late forties to early fifties now. Goodness time moves! The boys told me that Malcolm and Mister were at all out war after his failed drive by attempt. They were all thoughtful after that. We rode in silence the rest of the way home.

****

"You look AMAZING!" Kimmy said as I stepped out in my designer original. "Thanks girl! Do my stretch marks show?" I asked holding my arms out and moving them around so that the dress moved around my skin. This dress was very sexy and a little risky for a mother of three to be wearing but our dancer turned designer friend begged me to wear it. She said she made it with me in mind. Meaning since I was going to the awards with Ramell I would be in at least one to two pictures and her dress would be seen. I didn't mind I just didn't want to look ridiculous.

"You don't have stretch marks." Kimmy protested.

"Ha! Yes I do!" I lifted my dress to show her my hips. "See those right there; they have twins that live on this hip." I turned to show her the other side.

"You can barely see them. I've got real stretch marks, and they're not only on my hips. But I'm not crazy enough to pull up my dress to show them either." She laughed.

I looked at them, they had gotten a lot lighter than when they first came, but I knew they were there so it didn't matter. The hair and makeup people came to Kimmy's house to service us. We looked incredible. Ramell came to pick me up in his limo. He gasped out loud when he saw me. In the car, he kept staring at my legs and licking his lips. His inner struggle was clear, but the sad part is that if the boys wouldn't have pointed it out, I don't think I would've noticed Ramell's struggle. When we pulled into the procession of limos arriving on the red carpet, we both watched out the window as different stars exited their vehicles. Then I saw him two limos ahead of us, Dwayne arrived with Michelle. He had the nerve to look GOOD! I caught myself before I licked my lips. Michelle looked nice, but I knew she wasn't gonna be happy when she saw me. Someone was interviewing Dwayne when it was our turn to arrive. Ramell got out of the limo first, my hands turned sweaty as I gave him my hand to help me out. There were so many camera clicks I started to see dots before my eyes. Ramell and I walked together, and then I stepped to the side so he could be photographed. Someone called my name to ask me questions, Michelle was watching me. Dwayne hadn't seen me yet. They all wanted to know whose design I was wearing. I told them it was a Gabrielle original, it seemed like they scribbled her name down. Cameras kept clicking and the reporters kept asking me questions. This was new; normally I was just arm candy but I also knew that they were probably capturing Michelle's reaction to me, and hoping for a reaction from Dwayne when he saw me. I was happy that he didn't see me though. I was really hoping that we were not seated by each other, that somehow we could go the night without bumping into each other. When we walked into the lobby, I saw Dwayne and Michelle go to the left so I steered Ramell to the right. He saw Dwayne ahead of us so he didn't protest. We mingled with the other guests until it was ten minutes to the start of the show. One of the ushers came over to show us to our seats. We sat towards the end of the middle aisle in the middle of the auditorium. I saw Dwayne and Michelle walk in on the left side. They were seated closer to the front; I exhaled because that meant he wouldn't see me if and when I went to the bathroom. I saw Torrie come in with her man of the moment. She looked good; I guess she decided to keep the scars on her face for now. Watching her on talk shows talking about the incident, she turned it into this whole spiritual incident where she learned a lot about herself and her ability to survive. She hasn't even put out a new album yet. She's been riding the wave of the hype of her beat down. Her makeup was still on point even with the scars. Her hair was all weaved up, and her dress was really cute. She looked good but ask me if I cared. Kimmy and her man were seated next to us. Other people and some seat fillers were seated in our row. The show started and we were rocking to music. Comfort was nominated three times but he didn't win. I appreciated that they didn't get me in any of the shots of him when he was nominated. His performance was coming up; he told me he'd be back. "And now performing his latest single, 'The Unattainable Goddess' everybody give it up for Comfort!"

Ramell sat on a stool in front of a screen that ran heavenly clouds. His deep voice told the story of a beautiful Goddess who blessed him with a glimpse of her light. He described how wonderful the light was, and then the baseline got deeper along with his voice infliction as he described the evil spirit that suddenly surrounded them. The heavenly clouds turned in a violent storm. The song was beautiful, but oh my goodness he put our business out there. From what I could see, Dwayne had serious eyes as he bopped to the music. At the end of the song, the audience gave him a standing ovation. During the commercial break, he came back to his seat. He looked me in my eyes and asked me if I liked the song. I told him it was beautiful and that he had serious talent. He kept staring so I patted his hand. When they came back from commercial, the host announced that Dwayne Reed and R & B recording artist Gia would be announcing the next category. Dwayne and Gia's back and forth banter was cute. She mentioned something about his wife and of course, they had to show her on the screen. My heart sank I could feel the set up coming.

"And the nominees for the best new single are!" Gia said, "Genova Stewart for 'Parade Day'". The camera showed Genova.

"Dirty T for 'You'" Dwayne said. The camera showed Dirty T

"Tootie for 'Beautiful Mind'" Gia said. The camera showed Tootie

Dwayne's eyes were serious. "And Comfort for 'The Unattainable Goddess'" the camera showed Ramell.

"And the winner is" they said in unison. My hands started sweating because I knew he was going to win and they'd have the excuse to show Ramell hugging me. I knew they would somehow capture Dwayne's reaction. "Comfort for 'The Unattainable Goddess'!" They said in unison. Just like I said Ramell hugged me, it was on the big screen. Dwayne looked at the big screen and that vein popped out on his forehead but he didn't have any other reaction. Dwayne congratulated Ramell on his win, then he handed him his trophy. Dwayne didn't look out into the audience or at the screen, he focused on Ramell. Ramell thanked everyone for accepting and understanding the spiritual journey he took us on for four minutes. Then again, he paid tribute to our friendship. He said, "without your friendship Amber I would be so lost!" AGAIN! The camera shot was wide so that you could see Dwayne the entire time. My body was stiff and I held on to my smile, then they walked off the stage. The host came out; of course he had to make a joke about my ex and my next sharing the same space backstage. I wanted to scream that Ramell and I weren't a couple. But I told myself to be cool. He said something about the artist and the black cloud being backstage in the same space. I smiled, but I didn't move. As soon as the camera was off of me, I looked at Torrie who jumped when I looked at her. She turned around quick, fast, and in a hurry. Kimmy could tell I was irritated; she patted my arm and all she felt was heat. I was getting ready to get up to go to the bathroom or something when a seat filler with a familiar cologne sat next to me. My heart sped up when he said, "that is some song huh."

I smiled and instantly I calmed down. "It sure is." I said with a smile.

"Dwayne ain't even black; I wonder why everyone would assume he's the darkness. He's more like a..." He snapped his fingers. "A caramel or butterscotch at best."

"What are you doing here?" I smiled at him.

"I heard about all this, so I wanted to come check it out for myself." Then he looked around. "So you still liking all of this?"

"All of this?" I said

"Hanging out with all these celebs and being a minor celeb yourself?" Then Ramell came back to the seat. He looked at his occupied chair. "Oh my bad dude, this seat is taken you gonna have to go find another one." Malcolm said. An usher came up to Ramell and said something in his ear. Ramell looked angry but not stupid. As he walked away, Malcolm threw him a peace symbol followed by the middle finger. Then Malcolm leaned back and got comfortable in his chair. "I don't appreciate the way they did all that." Malcolm said with serious eyes.

"Did what?" I asked knowing he was talking about the scene on stage.

"Giving the pretty boy credit for being me. He wishes he could be me!"

"Yes he does." I said then I leaned over and kissed his cheek.

Then I looked over and saw Torrie watching us. I smiled again, Malcolm looked at her. He blew air then he flipped her off too. You could tell that hurt her feelings as she turned around. "What after party are you guys going to?" He asked

"Why are you asking me when I know you already know?" I said smiling at him. He chuckled, "I know huh."

Kimmy looked at Malcolm with a huge question mark on her face. Malcolm looked at her with a serious expression as usual. "Kimmy this is Malcolm." They nodded at each other.

She whispered to me, "who is he?"

"My baby daddy." I said.

She mouthed "whoa" to me then she looked at him again. She nudged me and gave me a thumbs up.

Malcolm stayed in the seat until the ceremony was almost over then he told me he'd see me in a bit. Ramell came back to the seat angry. "What is he doing here?"

I shrugged, "I don't know." Then I asked him, "you know who he is?"

Ramell looked at me like I just asked him the stupidest question in life. "Of course I do!"

I didn't see Dwayne return to his seat the rest of the night.

On the way to the after party, Ramell grabbed my hand. "I was hoping tonight would be our night."

"Our night for what?" I didn't have a clue as to what he meant.

"Our night together, just me and you." He said

"We are just friends remember, you told me. Besides we've had plenty of nights of just you and me."

"I know, but tonight I was hoping we could test the boundaries." He said shyly.

I squeezed his hand. "Is that why you exploited our friendship on national TV?"

"They made me do it; I didn't want to do that like that." He said

"Ramell we are best at being friends, and I say that loosely. That whole thing was embarrassing and annoying. If '*THEY*' have got you under their finger like that, it's best that we only be friends. I can't imagine the circus if we were actually dating like they think we are. There's a measure of privacy I need to keep in my life. Especially when it comes to Malcolm."

"You're still in love with him." He said like it pained him. "I saw the way you looked at him. You looked at Dwayne almost the same way. There's no room in your heart for one more?"

I kissed his cheek, and then he came in for a real kiss. I let him kiss me although it did nothing for me, his eyes glazed over. "Friends it is I guess." I smiled at him. "But if you ever have a change of heart you know how to find me."

When we arrived at the after party, like the red carpet, cameras were flashing all over the place. I was getting tired of all the cameras; I just wanted to get to the party. I was kind of excited to see Malcolm and I didn't know when he was going to pop up again. Tons of people were there, and coming and congratulating Ramell on his win and asking what Dwayne said to him back stage. He said they didn't speak back stage. When Michelle and Dwayne arrived, I tried to fade to the background. But people kept looking at us. Michelle and Dwayne came over to me.

"You look beautiful Amber." Michelle genuinely said

"Thank you; I was gonna say the same to you." I said to her.

Dwayne looked like he was about to explode. "I miss you!"

I looked at Michelle with a surprised look. She had sad eyes, "we've already discussed this." She said to me.

"Dwayne I'm not comfortable with this." I said trying to keep a measure of a smile on my face for the people who were watching us.

"She knows. She knows it all." He said then exhaling.

I looked at Michelle. "I'm sorry." I felt bad for her. She wiped the tear that escaped from her eye then she smiled. "I'm gonna go." I said. Then I walked away. I wanted to see Dwayne; I even wanted to talk to him, but not like that. That was uncomfortable and painful.

I could feel eyes on me, I looked for Torrie. I found her sitting in a corner watching me. I smiled at her and then she rolled her eyes and looked away. When someone walked up behind me and touched the small of my back, I smiled because I knew the touch. "Did I tell you how beautiful you look tonight?"

My smile was a mile wide. "No you didn't."

"Let's go dance." Malcolm said taking my hand. As we walked to the dance floor, almost all the recording artists were saying their hellos to Malcolm. He nodded and said hello back, but he stopped to talk to no one.

A slow song came on in perfect timing. Malcolm pulled me in close and kissed me deep. "I've been dying to do that all night!" I smiled because this whole very public scene is not normally his style. We danced pelvis to pelvis; I thought I was going to melt! I could see what only appeared to be gossip columnist standing around taking notes. Torrie was still at her seat, she looked like she wanted to cry from a distance, but she could've been I don't know. Ramell was standing by the bar with a drink in his hand. He didn't look happy either. "How long do we have to stay here?" He asked me.

"You wanna leave?" I asked

"I want some real food for one and two I need to be alone with you!" He said looking down into my eyes.

I got excited! It's been a long time; I hoped this FINALLY meant it's time for us to stop playing these games. "I'm ready when you are." I said. I saw Kimmy along the way out. I stopped and whispered in her ear. "Can you tell Ramell I'm leaving and I'll catch him later?"

"Ooh girl I don't blame you!" She said giving me her approval.

Malcolm took me through the service elevator, which took us to the garage. He took out keys and chirped a black Lamborghini. It was beautiful. "Did you rent this?" He smiled at me, "no." He said. "Just got it though." It didn't even have plates. He opened my door and the smell of new leather hit me in the face. The interior was the color of creamy peanut butter. When I sat in the soft leather seat, it felt like it curved to fit my body. Malcolm got in the driver's seat. "I look good huh!" He smiled at me.

"You'd look good in a bucket." I said

His smile got bigger. "That's why I love you! You always pump me up. You wanna see what else I bought?"

"Of course." I said

He drove out of the garage. I saw all the reporters looking for something to report. They looked at the car then they looked at Malcolm. No one recognized him, so they went back to what they were doing. He drove down Rodeo Dr., and then he made a right turn on a beautifully lit street in Beverly Hills. We pulled into the garage of a condominium complex. There was a water fountain in the front and a doorman at the door. "Good evening Mr. Latour!" The doorman said

"Hey how's it going? This is Ms. Wallace she'll be staying here from time to time when business brings her out this way. Can you let the staff know?"

"Sure thing Mr. Latour!" The doorman said

Malcolm handed him two one hundred dollar bills. "For your trouble."

"No sir we're not supposed to take tips." He said trying to give the money back to him.

"Are we gonna have a problem?" Malcolm said giving him serious eyes.

"No sir" he said turning a little red.

"Alright, have a good night."

We got in the elevator and went to the seventh floor. Malcolm put keys in my hand, and then he told me to go to the right. He told me to go to the unit on the end, number 707. I opened the door and a system chimed "front door open." I could smell the fresh paint. The entry way and the hallway had marble tile. The living room was huge and it had plush white carpet and a fireplace. Malcolm smiled at me as I looked around. There was a balcony that stretched the whole length of that side of the condo. The kitchen was huge and it had a huge dining room off the kitchen. There was a guest half bathroom just off the family room which was a good size and it had a wet bar and a built in bar. There were two bedrooms and both were master suites with their own bathrooms and huge walk in closets. There was a smaller room that he claimed as his office. Malcolm said I had to be tired of staying in hotels whenever I came out there, plus we needed something together. My heart fluttered when he said that. He asked me if I liked it and I told him I loved it. He said the place needed furniture. I agreed. He handed me a platinum card with my name on it, and he told me to go crazy. I smiled and jumped around. Then he told me I'd need a car for whenever I came out there because I couldn't drive his. When I asked why, he said it was his new toy and he was allowed to be selfish. I asked him what kind of car I should get, and he told me to get whatever car I wanted. Since there was no bed or blankets, we decided to stay in my hotel room and order room service. We stayed up to all hours of the night talking like we used to do and enjoying each other's company. He kept telling me how pretty I looked and I thanked him. I put Gabrielle's dress back in the garment bag she gave it to me in. As I fell asleep, it tickled me that we didn't make love but the intimacy was still there but when the morning came it was on. My legs wouldn't stop shaking, my body kept tingling and convulsing. My mouth was dry and I was in love.

Not that I wanted to talk about it right then, but I didn't know when else. I told him about Detective White coming by the school. Malcolm didn't say anything he just listened. Then he smiled and said Poppa's name still carries weight. Then I asked him if he was setting Dwayne up for that. He asked me why I cared through serious eyes. I told him that Dwayne was living in enough pain as it was. I asked him not to do it for me. Malcolm stared in my eyes, I wanted to run and hide. He told me he'd think about it. Then I asked him how old Camille was now. He said he didn't know. I asked him if she looked her age, and he said no. I asked him if she asked him to kill her husband. He frowned and said no. I asked him if she knew what he did, he said no again. I asked him if he was still sleeping with her. He just blank stared at me. I exhaled cause last night was progress, but it didn't mean what I thought it meant. We got in the shower, oh the shower! I guess he felt bad so he decided to make me feel good. SMILES! Then I called Kimmy, I told her I didn't know where to go to buy furniture out there. Malcolm needed to go to one of the studios so he dropped me to the condo and then he said he'd be back later. Kimmy came to the condo, she said she was impressed. She took me to the office of her interior decorator Shasta. I picked out color schemes for each room. The painters would be there tomorrow and done in one day. Then we went from furniture store to furniture store. I was starting to like the feeling of spending money even though I knew I wouldn't do this too often. I scheduled everything to arrive two days after the painting. I was flying home in the morning, Malcolm was not happy about buying a place he couldn't use for a few days, but what was he going to do? He asked me what kind of car I wanted. He kept rejecting the cars I said. He said when we come to Beverly Hills we can't live as we do in Oakland. So I told him to surprise me. I told him I'd bring the boys back with me in three days.

I felt a little disappointed when Malcolm dropped me off at the airport; I was hoping the condo meant more than it did. He felt bad because he didn't have time to walk me to the gate. I kissed him and told him not to worry about it. I told him I'd call him as soon as I booked our tickets. I kissed him and then I got out of the car. I checked in at the gate, I sat in a chair facing the window. I sat there watching my plane arrive wrestling with my feelings of disappointment. I guess the condo was a step in the right direction, or was he just competing with the fact that I had access to Dwayne's when we were together. Then I saw the reflection of Dwayne in the window. I searched the window for Michelle, I didn't see her. He looked at me but I could tell he wasn't sure if it was me. Then he found my eyes in the window; I saw a whole range of emotions run over his face. He came and sat next to me.

"Where's Michelle?" I asked

"She left yesterday; I had business to tend to last night. I'm going home now."

"Is this your flight?"

"Yes"

"But you're flying into Oakland." I said

"It was the only flight to the bay at this time."

"Oh" I said not knowing what else to say.

"How come you're leaving now?" He asked

"I was gonna hang out with Ramell but I had a last minute change."

"I saw you and Malcolm on the dance floor." I smiled an embarrassed smile. "That was a crazy night huh?"

"To say the least."

"Funny how I'm supposed to be the darkness. The media circus is ridiculous."

"Tell me about it. It's starting to get old. I was never into this to be a star. I just want to dance you know. I'm thinking especially after the other night I need to lay low."

"There isn't a small part of you that likes it?" He asked

"Not as much anymore, you know what I mean? The other night put a bad taste in my mouth. You didn't feel like a puppet?" I asked

"I was confused when I was labeled the darkness."

"You know Malcolm said the same thing."

"Well look at that we finally have something else we agree on."

"Something else?"

"Something besides you." He looked at me with longing eyes.

"How are the girls? And what did you have?"

"The girls are good. They're happy to have me home every night. We had a girl Chelsea." He showed me a picture.

She was cute and looked just like her big sisters. "She's beautiful! You gonna try again?"

"She's pregnant." He said then he exhaled.

"Don't sound so excited!"

"It's a nightmare!"

"Why? Babies are always a blessing. I panicked with Andrew but for a good reason, and I panicked with Darryl. But I tell you; my boys are my joy these days. I can't imagine my life without one of them. It may seem drastic right now, but it will get better just hang in there."

"It's just not the same. I didn't want this with her. I made my bed, I gotta lay in it." Then he looked at me. "Amber what did I do wrong?"

My heart sank. "What do you mean?"

"Why am I married to Michelle, when all I wanted to do was love you?" His eyes were serious and full of pain.

"Dwayne you're married, I don't think we should be talking like this." I said trying to find any excuse not to have this conversation.

"Michelle knows. When we started that whole complete honesty thing, it's kind of hard to let go of. Besides she was there, she saw us, and she knows me. We talk about you all the time." He stared at me. "Please have this conversation with me. Who knows when we'll be able to ever speak again?" I hesitated. "Amber! I'm dying over here."

I could feel emotion washing over me. I looked out the window. "What's your question?"

"What did I do wrong?"

"Nothing Dwayne, you didn't do anything wrong."

"There had to be something. Did I smother you?"

"No"

"Was I too forceful?"

"No"

"Did you think I didn't care?"

"No"

"There has to be something."

"Dwayne you were good to me. You just didn't believe me when I told you I wasn't gonna fall in love with you."

"Then why did it feel like you did? There's more than one way to tell someone you love them, and you did everything but say it." He said

"Probably because I cared about you. Cause I did."

"What is your definition of love then?"

I exhaled, "if at the end of the day I still want to be with someone else, how can I say I loved you? That's not love. Michelle wanted you back; Tiffany and Crystal deserved to have their daddy back. I couldn't be that selfish, not to those girls. They deserve to have you everyday just like they do. Besides you and Michelle were still bonded, it's not like she was just some random female."

"My girls deserve to have a father who's happy." He exhaled. "I knew you still loved him. And I wasn't forcing you to let him go. I know you guys probably hooked up from time to time, I didn't like it, but I understood. We could've taken our time."

"Baby you were getting that itch. Pretty soon you were gonna ask me to choose." He exhaled; we watched a plane pull up. "Does he know?"

"Know what?" I said truly not knowing where he was going with his question. "That you love me?"

I exhaled; I tried to think of how to answer that. "He knows how much I love him and that's all that matters to him."

"You can't even tell me now? I am over here punking out, putting everything on the line here."

"Maybe we should stop talking or change the subject. In the end you're married, I would go off if my husband was having an emotional conversation with someone else."

"Amber, this is our chance to talk. We may not have this chance again. Besides, I'm discussing switching teams. So if all goes down like it appears, I'll be leaving the bay."

"Where would you go?"

"Right now it's looking like New York. More seniority eventually I'm gonna be head coach. Tag is going to Oakland."

"The Raiders? Really?"

"Yep, they wanted me. I couldn't support Malcolm's team." We both laughed.

"Honestly, it would've been too distracting being that close to you."

"I hear you. The Bay is gonna seem empty without you."

He smiled. He asked me how the boys were. I told him that Derrick and Andrew were gonna be graduating soon. I told him how Andrew is already turning down job offers. He told me that the girls ask about them all the time. He said they miss their big brothers especially Darryl. I told him that maybe the kids could meet up at the theme park or something before they move. He said that would be good. When we boarded the plane, we both had coach seats. I don't know how much he paid the guy sitting next to me to switch seats with him, but the guy gladly accepted. I asked him if he was still hoping for a boy. He said he didn't care anymore he just wanted the baby to be healthy. Internally I was battling with myself. I wanted to tell him, but I couldn't do it. Flash backs of making love to him kept creeping into my mind. Conversations where he pumped my head up to make me feel like the most beautiful woman in the world. My whole "I look good!" attitude didn't happen until he started pumping my head up with so much positivity. Dwayne is definitely good for your self-esteem. He definitely made me feel like a beautiful swan. He was talking and I realized that I definitely missed him. Thank goodness, I was so spent from making love to Malcolm this morning or else I know I wouldn't like myself very much come nightfall. I looked out the window trying to get a grip on my emotions, this is a married man. He stopped talking and started staring; he was trying to read me.

"When I was a little girl, I felt so unworthy. There was so much going on, it made my head swirl. My escape at first was Malcolm. I've been in love with him since I was a child, I don't think it's ever going away. Do you even realize you are the third serious relationship in my life? I'm not in the know about how relationships work and all that jazz. All three of you couldn't be more different. But only David was all about me. As far as I know, my Daddy didn't cheat on my Momma. I think he was so in love with her that the thought of another woman didn't appeal to him. I guess my problem is that I want what my parents had, but at the end of the day, my reality is that men aren't built that way anymore. Malcolm loves me to death but he has to have other women and I can't accept that from him. David didn't cheat on me, but I don't know that I'll ever recover from the affects of him. Then there's you, I never gave you all of me. I was too afraid of you." He frowned. "You let me have the upper hand. You didn't try to force Malcolm out. You made me feel like I was the most beautiful woman in the world! Nobody else seemed to exist to you; you even put me before Michelle." I swallowed. "I know you want to hear me tell you that I love you. But it wouldn't be fair. Who knows what the future holds for us. Maybe we'll find each other when we're finally and truly free. But to tell you I love you now wouldn't be fair to anyone. You understand?"

He grabbed my hand and laid his head on the top of my head. "You just did!" I could hear his heart beating outside his chest. But my heart was racing too. We were quiet the rest of the flight. We were the last two to get off the plane. When I stood up he hugged me tightly, he told me I'll always be first. He gave me my bag out of the overhead compartment. He walked behind me through the airport. I got my suitcase off the turnstile and kept moving. I didn't look back for fear I might not like myself if I did. I pushed myself to keep walking.

****

When we got off of the plane, Malcolm was waiting for us. He gave me a big hug and kiss. He told me he drove my car to pick us up. I was curious to see what he picked out for me. He said furniture was arriving as he left and the interior decorator was there making sure things were being set up according to our wishes. Andrew said Sasha and Joseph were coming after Joseph's last morning class. Malcolm put his hands over my eyes but the boys whistles let me know I was gonna like what I saw. When he released me, we were standing in front of a beautiful silver jaguar. It looked like a bullet! The interior was a silvery white. I screamed and jumped around. It was beautiful! He gave me the keys. "I thought you said this car wasn't nice enough?"

He shrugged "when I thought about it, you needed a sedan. If I think of something better we'll trade up."

"No I love it!" I said then I kissed his cheek.

The boys loaded our luggage in the trunk. Delivery trucks were still out front when we pulled into the garage. I parked next to Malcolm's car. The boys almost lost it, Andrew and Derrick asked for the keys. Malcolm laughed at them and told them to go buy their own. Andrew said he just might do that. I reminded him that he'd need somewhere to park it. When Malcolm walked ahead, I told Andrew and Derrick I'd wear him down for them. They high fived over me because they knew before the weekend was over they'd be driving that car. There was a different doorman for the day; we introduced him to the boys. Then we told him we were expecting visitors shortly. Shasta was cracking her whip on those delivery guys. I heard her telling them to take their boxes with them. Malcolm asked if his office was setup and she said his desk and chairs had arrived, but the bookshelves were still on their way. Malcolm told the boys to come with him and they went in his office. My dinette set was calling me. I went in the kitchen and got to work. I lined the cabinets and ran my new dishes through the dishwasher. I opened the box with my custom-made tablecloth and the matching linen napkins. I was so in love with the purple, chocolate, and green in this fabric. The purple and green made me think of Jade and I's room at home. I had purple everywhere and Jade always wanted anything as close to the color jade as she could find. I have jade napkin holders and candlestick holders on order. What I loved about this condo is I could decorate it as nicely as I wanted to. The boys were older so I didn't have to be practical and how often would they be here honestly? I stepped back and looked at my partially done kitchen and dining room and I got very excited. The entire time I was working in the kitchen, I heard Shasta bossing the different workers around. I felt bad for them so I kept slipping them cash on their way out. Shasta was good at what she does, but the way she treated people did not impress me. She was in my room fussing with the delivery guys about the boxes from our furniture. The guy was telling her cleanup was not part of the extra fee for delivery. She was angry and threatening to call the store. She was so loud Malcolm and the boys came in just after me. Malcolm asked what was going on. She told him what the issue was, but it was the way she was talking to them. Malcolm looked at me; he could tell Shasta was on my nerves. He asked the workers to follow him. You could hear the rumble of Malcolm's voice. The boys were ear hustling of course, then the workers came back with huge smiles and they gladly gathered the boxes and packing trash. Shasta rolled her eyes and then she brought in the bags with our bedding in it. When Malcolm came back in the room, he asked Shasta if she was going to continue to be so loud and rude. She had the nerve to look surprised. He told her, "my wife and I don't appreciate the way you're treating the people that make you look good. If you're going to continue to be this rude, we will have to find someone else." Malcolm's voice was serious and unapologetic.

The workers smiles got even bigger. I looked at Andrew's face and he was stuck on Malcolm's choice of words as well. "I'm sorry if I offended you, but I'm just...."

"No! No, see as soon as you say '*but*' that '*but*' cancels out your apology. If you're sorry then that's what you are, a sorry person who doesn't know how to treat people. If you're apologizing, I think that apology needs to swing in their direction. These are nice reasonable guys who would've helped you out in the first place had you asked nicely. It's not always what you're asking for its how you ask."

Shasta looked like she wanted to cry. She turned to the workers, who now stood with their heads high with a sense of vindication. "I apologize for being rude, and thank you for taking the trash away."

Darryl started belly laughing, and then Malcolm shot him serious eyes. He straightened up but he still had a mile wide grin on his face. "Thank you..." The worker waited for Malcolm to give his name.

"Malcolm"

"Thank you Malcolm. Please let us know if we could ever be of service to you in the future. It was a pleasure doing business with you. Thank you again for EVERYTHING!" The main guy said, and then he shook Malcolm's hand. Malcolm and the boys walked the workers out.

"Is he always that scary?" Shasta whispered to me.

"That wasn't scary Malcolm. You don't want to see scary Malcolm." I assured her. Shasta swallowed hard and turned a little red then she busied herself. She did a complete 360, which was nice. The vibe in the house lightened. By the time Sasha and Joseph came to the condo it was looking pretty decent. Sasha said she loved the way the place flowed. Then Sasha started telling them about her campus. I gave Derrick my keys so they could go site seeing. Plus I wanted to know if Malcolm meant to refer to me that way. I mean it flowed from his mouth so freely, like that wasn't the first time he's said it. I didn't want to have an audience for this conversation. I was ready to jump his bones.

Last but not least to arrive were Malcolm's bookshelves. Shasta asked Malcolm if he liked the placements and he gave her serious eyes but no response. Shasta turned red and then sweat beads popped up on her forehead. She came out the office and she fell on me. "Oh my god! He hates me!" She hysterically whispered on me. Her reaction tickled me. After all the attitude she threw around here all day, the none verbal dismissal from Malcolm destroyed her day. I walked Shasta to the door, she couldn't leave fast enough. I walked back to his office he was moving his desk over a few inches. I stood there smiling at him; he eyed me and waited for me to speak. I waited for him to sit down and then I took my seat in his lap. I kissed him and then I smiled at him.

"You're welcome." He said. I looked at him with a question mark on my face. "You were saying thank you weren't you?"

"Yes amongst other things."

He smiled, "other things?"

"You didn't hear what you said?"

He looked confused, "what did I say?"

I tried to make my voice deep like his. "My wife and I don't appreciate" I smiled. "I can't recall the rest verbatim, but I'm your wife now?"

He exhaled and buried his head in my chest. "Did I say that?" He started laughing

"Yes you did. I looked at Andy to make sure I heard you right." I said with a gigantic smile.

He was completely embarrassed and acting shy. I loved every bit of it. "I've been trying it on, seeing how it fit me."

"Really like where?"

He blew air into my shirt. He groaned as he chuckled a little. "When I bought the car, I told them it was a surprise for my wife."

I smiled bigger, and then I lifted his chin. His expression was child like and completely embarrassed. "I love you!" I said then I kissed him.

"I love you!" He said

"Are you hinting at something?" I asked hoping he had a plan.

"Baby" he put his face back in my chest. "Not yet!" He kept blowing hot air into my shirt.

I kissed his head. "It's okay, progress works for me. As long as we keep moving forward." I said then he kissed me.

Then as if it was perfectly timed, his cellphone rang. He picked it up. "Hey Juan what's going on... Un huh..." His face turned serious, and then he shot me a look. "Un huh........... Why am I just hearing about this?............. I should've received a call right away! I'm not happy!......... Doesn't matter... Doesn't matter..." His body was now stiff and no longer warm and inviting. "Let me think... Right... Stand by!" Then he closed his phone. His eyes were evil and he looked at me. "So what happened at the airport?"

I didn't know what he was talking about. "I did something?" I was shocked that it was me in the hot seat.

"What happened at the airport?" He asked again.

"It was a straight shot we got here without incident." I said

He started moving his hands. "Get up! Get off of me!" I got up but I was confused. "The flight home Amber!"

Oh! Crap! I looked at Malcolm. "All we did was talk. I know you know that." His eyes were evil. "About?"

"The kids, the fact that he's leaving the bay stuff like that."

"It sounds like the conversation was more emotionally charged than that." He was pissed.

"Malcolm come on!" I said completely frustrated.

"Come on what?" He said in a wicked voice.

"You're mad at me over a conversation? We were just lying in bed when I asked you if you were still sleeping with that woman. But you're mad over a conversation!"

"It's not the same thing!"

"You're right! Sleeping with someone is worse than a conversation could ever be!"

"He's dead!" Malcolm said coldly.

My heart dropped. I snatched his phone off the desk and threw it at my freshly painted wall. It broke into pieces. Malcolm squinted at me. Then he turned the desk over. I backed up against the wall just in time. I climbed over the desk and ran to the kitchen. I took his keys off the hook on the wall in the kitchen and dropped them inside my bra on my right side. Then I yanked the phone out the wall in the kitchen. I remembered the phone in the bedroom and I took off running. As I passed the office, he remembered it too, I stopped in the doorway to the bedroom suddenly, and he ran into me. He felt like a wall slamming into me. I flew forward but I caught myself and I grabbed the phone. I yanked it out the wall right as he grabbed my leg. "You would risk my anger for him?" He said looking like he wanted to hit me.

"You're being ridiculous! I can talk to him. All we did was talk. You have no right to react this way!"

"No right? No right? You're either with him or you're with me!"

"I'm with you!"

"Then he dies, and you shut up about it!"

"No he doesn't!"

Malcolm looked like he couldn't believe what he was hearing. "If you're with me he dies. If you're with him, let me know and I'll arrange for yours too!" His face was stone.

Fire started burning in my stomach. Before I could think I lunged at him. I punched him in the face. Then I hit him again. He picked me up and threw me on the bed. I bounced up and jumped on his back as he walked away. I don't know how he reached behind himself but he grabbed me and slammed me on the bed. Then he pinned me down. There was fire in his eyes; I knew he was hurt more than he was angry. But he couldn't think I would take his threat like I was scared of him.

"Amber! Stay down!" As soon as he loosened his grip a little, I'd try to get free to come at him again. He pushed my shoulders into the bed. "Stay down!"

"I am not one of your hookers off East 14th! You don't threaten me!" I screamed. He pushed again. "I SAID STAY DOWN!!"

"AND I SAID DON'T THREATEN ME!!" I started kicking him.

My hair was all over my head. He pushed me again and then he let go. I started swinging at him and kicking at him. He turned his back on me and walked out of the room. I knew he was going to get his keys. I ran to the balcony, took the keys out of my bra, and tossed them over the rail. They fell in the grass next to our building. Then I came back inside. He was looking around looking like he didn't remember where he left his keys. Then he looked at me, the fire in his eyes was back. I had two options run, through the kitchen or run to the bedroom again. He started charging, I thought I was gonna make it to the kitchen but he caught me and slammed me on the couch. "Did you throw my keys?"

"Huh?"

"Amber! Did you throw my keys?"

"Se habla espanol?" I said

He growled and he had to back away from me, I pushed my hair out of my face. He put his hands in the air while he backed away from me. "I see how a man could beat you!" He might as well have shot me. I couldn't move, I couldn't believe he said that to me. He turned around and walked out of the door. I went out on the balcony and I watched him search the grass for his keys. When he found them, he flipped me off and walked to the garage. I went in the closet and pulled my purse out. I called Andrew; there was noise in the background like they were having a good time. I tried to make my voice sound as up beat as I could I even put a smile in it. "Hey Andy, there's been a change in plans. I'm gonna find a flight home tonight."

His voice was instantly serious. "What's wrong?"

"Oh nothing sweetheart. I'm just gonna go home. You can stay if you like. You have my car, I'm gonna..."

"No! Derrick will bring me. I'm leaving with you!" He said forcefully.

"No Andy you stay, visit with Sasha. I'll see...."

"Bye momma I'm hanging up now!" Then he hung up.

I called a couple airlines and finally found a flight out tonight to Oakland. I booked four seats in case Derrick and Darryl were coming. I only grabbed my purse. I left everything else inside, and I waited in the lobby. The kids came. Joseph and Sasha gave me hugs then Derrick parked the car. The doorman called us a cab. The boys all looked at me but none of them said anything. When Andrew put his arm around me, I cried into his arm. Derrick and Darryl's eyes turned evil, and then they looked at Andrew. He told them we're going to the airport. When we got to Oakland, everyone still sat in silence. Andrew drove my car and he kept looking at me. I kept running my hands over my hair. I felt like it was out, still wild even though I had smoothed it out into a ponytail. When we got to the house, I went straight to my room; I took off my jacket and looked at my shoulders in the mirror. The feeling of looking at the damage afterwards was all too familiar. My shoulders were red from where he pushed me. I exhaled, pulled my shirt down, and laid on my bed crying my eyes out. They gave me an hour then all three of them came knocking.

"Momma are you ok?" Darryl asked

I tried to fix my voice because my head was buried in my pillow. "I'm fine sweetheart. Sorry I ruined your fun."

"You didn't ruin anything. We can go back any time."

Then the phone rang. Derrick answered it. "It's your Daddy."

"Hi Daddy." I said exhaling

"What's going on Amber? Malcolm called me all upset about you and Dwayne."

"One minute" I put my hand over the receiver. "Can you guys give me a minute to talk to him?" They left the room and shut the door. "Daddy?"

"Yes baby girl, I'm here." He said

"He's mad because I had a 'conversation' with Dwayne on the plane the other day. He was talking about him being dead. And when I said no, he accused me of being with Dwayne. I told him I was with him, but I don't want to see anything happen to Dwayne either. He was good to me, just not good enough."

Daddy's voice got serious. "What did he do?"

"I broke his cellphone and yanked all of the phones out of the wall. I threw the keys to his new car in the yard next door."

"What did he do?"

"He turned his desk over, threw me on the bed, and threw me on the couch."

Daddy was silent for a minute. "Is that all?"

"He pinned me on the bed because I was punching and kicking him."

"Is that all?" I could tell Daddy was angry.

"Yes Daddy, he didn't do anything else."

"Amber?"

"Yes Daddy?"

"You wouldn't lie to protect him would you?"

"Daddy I don't lie to you, I know I didn't tell you about the stuff before, but I'm not that same little girl."

"Ok..." He was silent. "Why is this conversation so upsetting?"

"I guess he felt it was too emotional."

"Was it an emotional conversation?"

"Yes, but it was more closure than it was anything else. I hugged him goodbye, I went this way, and he went that way. He's moving away, he's a married man Daddy. What would that make me messing with a married man?"

"You can't even allow emotional conversations with a married man. They can lead to emotions that get you caught up."

"Yes Daddy." I said

Daddy exhaled. "This is getting old. You guys are about to be forty soon. I think it's time you guys let it go. Aren't you tired of this?"

"Yes Daddy, I am!" I said through tears.

"I know matters of the heart are never easy, I would've lost it if your mother was having any kind of conversation with an ex-boyfriend, lover, or whatever. Cause I knew her heart, and I couldn't stand for anyone to be in it but me. I know he loves you baby girl, but sometimes love isn't enough. He's had more than enough time to step up, and every time he's lacking in some kind of way. Your life is too all over the place! You got rappers writing you love songs." I cringed; I didn't know he knew about that. "Ex-boyfriends doing stuff to almost get their selves killed! Enough is enough Amber! Either you're gonna be with him and you guys find some peace or you go your separate ways. You understand me?"

"Yes Daddy."

"When is he coming home?"

"Tomorrow."

"Matters of the heart aren't easy, but it's time to put your big girl panties on."

"Eeewwllll! Daddy!"

He laughed. "You know what I mean."

I couldn't sleep all night; I tossed and turned. I would've called him but I broke his phone. Andrew brought me breakfast in bed but I couldn't really eat. The boys hung around me all day trying to cheer me up. I let the water beat me in the face as I thought about Daddy's words. When I came down the stairs, Andrew and Darryl stood up. They were in the middle of a game of chest. Derrick ended his conversation on the phone and stood too. "Where we going?" He said

"I'm going over Malcolm's house. You guys can stay here."

"Are you gonna call first?" Darryl asked

"No" I said, he never calls before he comes to my house, so I shouldn't have to announce when I pop up although I never pop up at his house.

Darryl blew air. "We're coming!"

"Seriously, you guys can stay here." I said

"No, momma we need to go with you." Derrick said in a firm voice.

I rolled my eyes. Andrew took my keys from me and we got in my car again. Everybody was silent as we drove, the further we went up skyline the more my heart pounded. Why did they have to come with me? I prepared myself for anything. I decided to take off my earrings. Andrew peeked at me out the corner of his eye. Andrew pulled in the driveway of Malcolm's house. My heart was pounding. When I got out of the car, all three of them got out too. I told them to stay at the car. Darryl gave me his key, but his eyes were serious. When I walked to the door, Andrew told me to leave it cracked when I went in. Malcolm's house smelled like fresh baked cookies. I could hear the shower running upstairs. I called out to Malcolm but he didn't answer. His house was beautiful; he had the same furniture I picked out from our first place. At the top of the stairs was a huge picture of me. I smiled when I saw it, then I called out to him again. I took a deep breath; I could feel it in my stomach this was not going to end well. I opened the bedroom door in the middle of our old bed there was a girl knocked out sleep. She was naked and the covers were barely covering her. My heart sunk but I kept walking. When I walked into his bathroom, Malcolm was in the shower with another girl. He was pounding the life out of her and she was yelling ouch. I couldn't see her face, but I opened the shower so that Malcolm could see it was me. He looked angry but when he saw me, his face dropped and he instantly went flaccid. His condom-covered penis fell out of her. I tilted my head at him. "How is this not worse?"

Malcolm was speechless. His mouth kept opening and closing, but nothing was coming out. When the girl turned around, I pushed Malcolm into the wall, and I pulled Torrie out by her hair. I kept her weave in my fist and I kept punching her in her face. The other girl staggered to the bathroom. She started screaming when she saw me beating Torrie. She rushed at me, I let Torrie go, and as soon as she stepped in my range, I hit her full force in her eye. She spun around and hit the wall.

Malcolm hopped out the shower went and got his boxers, as I proceeded to continue to beat on Torrie. "Amber! Hold on!" Malcolm said. I let go of Torrie and I started firing on him. He caught my leg as I tried to kick him between his legs. I turned towards Torrie, she was crying holding her face, and I saw blood dripping to the floor. The other girl had slid to the floor holding her eye. Just above her eye had opened up and she had blood too. "Amber! Hold on!"

"SERIOUSLY MALCOLM? THIS WHORE? HER!" Then I started punching him. "DON'T YOU EVER IN YOUR LIFE THREATEN ME AGAIN!"

Then I saw the boys walking in the door. Malcolm looked at them. "You let her in here?" He was angry.

I got in his face. "I LET MYSELF IN HERE!" Tears started pouring out of my eyes. "I was coming to..." I was crying so hard I couldn't talk. Then I looked at Torrie still bent over on the floor holding her face. I booted her in the ribs as hard as I could! "Malcolm! I'm done! I refuse to do this anymore!" I said through tears. "You are not allowed inside my house anymore! Forget you EVER KNEW ME! Stay AWAY FROM ME!" I screamed through tears. I slapped him as hard as I could.

"Amber no! No! I'm sorry! No!" He said pulling at my clothes. "I won't touch him. He lives ok?"

"Let me go Malcolm! I'm DONE!" I screamed. "I WILL NOT SPEND THE REST OF MY LIFE LIKE THIS! YOU DON'T OWN ME!"

"Amber baby please! I'm sorry! I'm sorry!" He put his hands on my face.

I pushed his hands away and slapped him as hard as I could. My hand was numb and the boys all cringed at the sound of it. "You were just touching that whore! Keep your filthy hands off of me." I tried to walk away but he kept trying to stop me. "Stop Malcolm!"

Derrick and Darryl backed away, Andrew stayed put. "Amber please!" Malcolm pleaded

I looked in the bedroom. "That was our bed!" I said through tears. "You filled this house with our stuff, and then you dirty it with whores!" I couldn't push any more sound out; it was like my heart was ripping in my chest. "I wish I never met you!" He tried to grab me again, I slapped his hand away.

I was almost to the door when he started running at me. Now I knew he was probably just gonna hug me and beg me not to leave, but my over protective son didn't see it that way. Andrew jumped in front of Malcolm and told him to back up.

Malcolm instantly changed modes and he stood up straight. "Stand down son! This is between me and your momma!" Malcolm barked

"She wants to leave, let her leave!" Andrew barked back.

Derrick and Darryl came back in the room. They didn't look like my babies anymore. All three of them looked eight feet tall each, Derrick and Darryl stood on either side of Andrew. "You got to be kidding me! I know I didn't raise any of you to be this stupid!" Malcolm barked, "you all know me! I will hang all three of your heads on my wall!"

"And you know us, I guess we all dying tonight then!" Derrick said

Malcolm squared off and they did too. I know Malcolm and I'm aware of my babies. I screamed to the top of my lungs, "STOP! WE'RE LEAVING! DARRYL, DERRICK, ANDREW GET IN THE CAR! I DON'T WANT THIS!" No one budged they were about to go at it. I jumped in the middle. "WE'RE LEAVING!" All of their eyes softened, when they looked at me. I pushed the three of them out the door.

When we came down stairs Juan and three men were standing in the doorway. Juan gave me sad eyes when he saw how hard I was crying. He patted each of the boys on the shoulder as we walked past. "I'm sorry Amber." He said real low when I walked past him.

"No he's sorry!" I said through tears.

Chapter 46

My period was late! I told myself it was the stress. It had to be the stress right? When it finally came it came with the worse cramps I ever had, I was bent over in pain. When Ibuprofen wasn't strong enough to help with the pain, I became concerned, and then when I noticed blood clots. I made an emergency appointment with my gynecologist. I told the boys I had a woman's troubles appointment, which made them all cringe and put their hands in the air. Jade took me to the doctor. The doctor told me I miscarried; I felt like I couldn't breathe, joy and pain crashed into me all at once. The joy of knowing I could conceive, and the pain of losing yet another baby. I asked him how that was possible. He told me I still had a perfectly healthy and functioning Fallopian tube even if the other was scarred. He said it may be a little more challenging but it was possible. Those nights in the hotel, Malcolm and I were flesh to flesh. Thinking about that reminded me of the image I saw of him and Torrie only days later. My heart broke all over again. The last thing I wanted to do was tell him about this. I didn't want to talk to him, and this just made my broken heart heavier. The doctor said since I was less than ten weeks, everything should pass on its own. He scheduled a follow up appointment for me. With eyes full of tears I told Jade what the doctor told me. She asked if I needed a D&C, and I told her no and what the doctor said. Just when I thought my heart couldn't break anymore, here I am! I didn't know this kind of pain existed!

I had to seriously convince Andrew to go home. After two months of him sleeping on the couch or the floor in my room, you would think he would be happy to go home to his bed. But no, he said he was worried about me and he couldn't leave until he knew I was ok. But I know he mostly wanted to keep Malcolm away from me. Darryl took Skylar and Samara away. He said their loyalty was compromised and they couldn't be trusted. He said he gave them to a friend and they were in a good home. I told Darryl that I wished he would've at least let me say goodbye. He told me I would've made him keep them and that couldn't happen. I had the doggie door taken out, and I had a door and a security gate installed instead. Darryl changed all the locks; he even changed out the system on the garage door opener. The boys wouldn't allow me to answer my house phone or cell. Even though I changed both numbers, they told me it didn't matter. They were being so protective; one of them came with me whenever I went anywhere. It was cute at first, but after a couple of months, it got old. I knew they meant well. But to me it felt like my boys were bossing me around. I finally told them I had enough! I was grown and they needed to handle their business, and I had business of my own to tend to. Derrick's graduation was coming up and Jade and I were planning away. Then we had to prepare for Sasha's, Tanisha's, and Andrew's college graduations. Like Jeff and Joseph, Sasha and Andrew were going to continue to get their Masters. Since Jeff was graduating from his Master's program, we decided to use the Sophia's in Walnut Creek for all the college graduates since they'd already had their high school parties in their honor. But I needed space to plan, so I sent Andrew packing. He was reluctant to go, but he went eventually. One by one, they went back to their usual routines, which also gave me space to truly grieve. Every time I felt consumed by my depression, I would go for a run. So needless to say, I was running a lot. I didn't have much of an appetite so weight kept leaving me.

There were a few labels requesting my services, but I turned them all down. I told them I wouldn't be available until October and most of them couldn't wait that long. When Kimmy told me Torrie was back in the studio and that the label was going to be coming to me soon, it took everything in me to keep my composure and calmly tell her there was no way in hell I would do it! When she mentioned the money, which had more than doubled from my last deal, based on the video request and rotations could maybe triple I still laughed at it. I told her I was sitting on close to eight figures in the bank and I didn't need the money. She thought I was kidding but I didn't laugh. I told her I lived simply enough to never have to work again if I didn't want to. "I said all that to say that I will not EVER work with Torrie AGAIN!" Kimmy asked me if I was ok because I had been real short lately. I told her I was ok, and we'd talk next time I saw her.

Daddy asked me if I was going to have Malcolm at Derrick's graduation. I told him I hadn't planned on it. Daddy said I couldn't do that to Derrick, Malcolm was his father. And if Malcolm wasn't gonna be at the graduation then that had to be between them. I didn't wanna listen to Daddy, I frowned at him. When his eyes softened and he called me Annette, I forgot I was mad. Daddy could've told me to go do anything at that point. Daddy addressed the envelope to Malcolm. He told me he would deliver it personally. I tried not to let the idea of it put me in knots. But for the next few days, I don't know how many nights I couldn't sleep. I was exhausted, I would fall asleep for a few minutes, and then I would wake up because my mind would be racing. A couple of times, I was so spent and I couldn't stop crying, that I couldn't help it, it was like I didn't have a choice in the matter. I would call Daddy at all hours of the night crying so hard I couldn't speak. Daddy would come over no matter the hour and hold me. He said every tear was making me stronger but it didn't feel that way. I eventually told Daddy about the surprise miscarriage. Daddy said I needed more help than anyone in the family could give. He said he'd been seeing a therapist off and on ever since losing Momma. He said some periods of time were harder than others and he needed the help. He said Nana set him up with this specific doctor and she was really good. He made an appointment for me to see her. I didn't want to go, but when he said she knew Nana, I took that as a sign that she had to be at least a little ok.

Her name was Joanne and she sounded fine enough over the phone. When I pulled up to the building it didn't look like it was anything special. When I got to her lobby, there were three wooden chairs, and a small bookshelf with magazines and books. I flipped the switch like she told me to with her name on it so she would know I was there. I kept feeling like my hair was wild and all over my head even though I knew I had slicked it down into a flat ponytail and the ends were smoothed into a tight bun. Darryl said I looked like a schoolteacher before I left the house. Andrew asked me if I wanted him to drive, especially since her office was in Berkeley and I told him no. Her door opened slowly and out stepped this middle aged, brown-skinned woman. She invited me into her office; she didn't try to put phony softness in her voice or anything like that. Her office was simple, lots of cabinets, a desk, three comfy chairs, no couch, pillows, and footstools if you needed them to make you comfortable. She said it was nice to meet me, and then she asked what brought me today. I started unloading, I didn't hold back anything. There was a small clock facing me and I kept glancing at it so I would know when my hour was up. There was a small end table next to my chair; it had a box of tissue on it. I kept blowing my nose because I was crying so hard. Then she noticed that I kept touching my hair. She asked me why I kept doing that, and I explained to her how I felt wild. I felt like it reflected in my hair. She didn't take notes like the doctors did on TV, it was like we were kicking back and talking. When my hour was up, she told me I could keep going if I needed to. And I did feel like I needed to keep going so I did. We went all the way back to Uncle and the things he did to Jade and me.

She told me my parents did the right thing by going to the police and pressing charges. We spent the rest of the hour talking about how I felt my mother hated me the most. I told her that as an adult I understand that we were so much alike, that we probably clashed or that she saw me in herself and probably freaked out a lot. She assured me that Momma never hated me. I told her how I would go in my room and cry when I felt like beating those knucklehead boys for being little boys. I told her I would feel out of control sometimes, but I didn't want to hurt them as Momma hurt me so I would pull back. She commended me on not continuing the cycle, and consciously making the choice to give my boys better. She explained that the emotions that I feel and go through were more than likely the same way Momma felt. She said the hard part is that Momma's not here to answer my questions. She asked me if Momma had been molested as a child, and I told her I had no idea. But I wouldn't doubt it with seeing how trifling her family is. We talked about my childhood in detail; all of my feelings of being ugly and believing everything those kids on the playground told me about myself. I told her it was such a self-esteem booster when Malcolm noticed me. I told her how it killed me every time he rejected me. I told her about Tag, and how in the end he never made sense to me. Through talking it out, I realized that Tag saw me at my worst and it made me feel wrong that he still wanted me. She wasn't assigning anything honorable to his interest in me, and saying that maybe it was my defenses going up as a protection. When the next hour came, she told me to keep going but only if I wanted to. Just saying David's name made me sob for like two minutes without any words. I told her how I always thought of him as a good guy, too good to be with me. I told her how good it felt to love him and to be with him at first. When he proposed to me, how loved I felt. How happy it made Momma to know I was getting married. I told her he was my prince saving me from all this. I told her it took awhile before it registered with me that his lashing out at me wasn't ok. But I still felt responsible for his demise. I told her I should've broken up with him when I knew I couldn't marry him, but I wanted a piece of him that I could keep forever. I told her it wasn't until Malcolm was out that I realized I still wanted Malcolm and that I made a mistake. When Malcolm rejected me, I went back to David, and I accepted him treating me like garbage, I felt like that was the best I deserved. I told her when Momma died I started remembering who I was. I told her how it broke my heart when I saw my boys turn on Malcolm to protect me. After three hours, I was drained, but I felt a little better. That night I slept so hard that I didn't realize I was sleep. In the morning, I felt rested and a lot better. I understood why people went to therapy; I just couldn't see doing it every week.

****

Derrick walked in the conference room as the staff was leaving. I had to make sure I looked at him good; his presence was very young Malcolm like. My eyes were playing tricks on me. I gave him a hug and a kiss; he asked how my day was going. I told him it was going good. Then he asked me to sit down. "I went to see Malcolm." He said

My whole body stiffened and I turned red. "Why?"

"He's my father; I couldn't leave him out there by his self."

"What does any of this have to do with me?"

"I need him to come to my graduation and I need you to be okay with it."

"I don't want to see him Derrick!"

"Momma no disrespect but my graduation is not about you."

"Daddy has his invitation already. But I can't tell you I'll be ok with it. Maybe I shouldn't go." I said pouting in my chair.

Derrick sat there staring at me. "This isn't you."

"What's not me?"

"You're not this insecure ball of emotion." He said

I rolled my eyes. "Clearly you're just looking at me for the first time. Insecure is all I've ever been, and emotional! Ask your butt how many whooping's you got that weren't emotional!"

"I get it; you're going through a tough time right now. Malcolm's pretty bad too." I rolled my eyes. "I know you don't wanna hear about him!" He put his hands up to calm me. "I'm just saying, we're all going through it right now, but we're still family, and we're all the family the man's got." Then he sat up and gave me serious eyes. "Now let me be clear, I don't want, and I am not promoting that you guys get back together! That ship has sailed but you got to learn to get a long or just be cordial with the man; you have three kids."

"Whatever Derrick!" I said re-crossing my arms. "You think you know, but you have no idea! He betrayed me, he betrayed everything always for some females, and he always claimed he didn't care about them. Well what was it? Did he not care about me? Cause the way he's always hurt me didn't feel like love. Or was I dumb like the rest of them thinking he cared when he really didn't? I've wasted my life loving and waiting on him! Now when I'm finally done with him you're telling me to suck it up! Wait until it's your turn! People who've been through nothing surely do have ideas about the way things should go! I hope you never know!"

Derrick sat there watching me go through my whole speech. "Are you done? Do you feel better?"

I caught myself; I almost lunged on him as if he was his father. "Derrick you need to leave! I almost forgot you were my baby."

Derrick looked surprised. "I'm sorry momma. I know this whole thing is painful, but I'm trying to tell you as unemotionally as I possibly can what I need. Momma I need him to be there, and I need to see how proud both of you are of me! I need approval from both of you!" He put his hands on mine. "Please momma!"

He was pulling at the strings of my heart. "Ok baby, I'll be good." Then I thought of Malcolm. "AS LONG AS HE DON'T TRY NOTHING! I'm raw over here!"

"Thank you!" Derrick smiled like he was relieved.

"What about your brothers?"

"I'll have to drag Darryl there kicking and screaming but he'll come around. I don't know about Drew. That's gonna take some work, but I'm on it!"

****

"So who gets the condo?" Sophia asked

"Are you kidding?" I said sitting at the table coloring with Sabrina in Sophia's office. "That's his place, I barely stepped my foot in there."

"The car everything? It's all his?" She asked like she couldn't believe it. I shook my head. "I would ask him about it. Sasha said it was beautiful!"

I blew air. "I'm not talking to him! It's bad enough he's coming to Derrick's graduation! I don't know how I'm gonna get through this."

"So I've heard." I gave her a question mark expression. "You know Jeff and Andrew escape here on a regular basis. They say this is their honeycomb hideout. Amber I don't understand something about your boy, if he's trying to escape the craziness of the east bay why would he bring Toya here? That girl is nothing but trouble. Jeff kicked her out, made her walk to the Bart station." She faked sympathy, "and her shoes were cute too. But he brings her back and so I told her at the door that I didn't want any of her drama. She said she agreed and understood, and then I found myself picking her up by her neck and literally throwing her out. I told Andrew and Jeff don't bring no ignorant hood rats around my place. She better hope she listens. I don't know what she was thinking, but she better not let this creamy tanned complexion fool her, I ain't the one!" Sophia said putting her finger up and wiggling her neck

"Did he tell you he tried to reach out to Jennay?" Sophia dramatically paused and waited for me to finish. "He said they talked for a little bit, but she has a boyfriend and he was broken hearted all over again."

Sophia shook her head. "Can't you do something?" Her eyes pleading with me to say yes.

"Oh yes right! I'm gonna call and say 'This is Andy's mother please give him another chance. I promise he'll be good.'" Sophia looked at me as if to say yes. "I did that already it didn't work!"

We both fell out laughing. "When was this?"

"When I took Darryl and Derrick with me for the summer. Some how we ended up in Chicago, and of course she came to see us after I assured her that Andrew was not with us." I tapped the wall, that made Sabrina laugh and she started doing it too.

"I tap out; I can't get my own life together. What I look like interfering in his?"

"If Sasha would tell me, I'd be all over it!" Sophia said

"That's why she doesn't tell you anything. Who wants their momma in the middle of their love life?" I said

"Like yours wasn't in the middle of yours?"

"She wasn't." I said

"Please! Auntie Annette was always talking to Malcolm, Uncle Tim too. "

She had a point. "But we were so young, they took him in."

"Yea, but wouldn't you want to have that kind of bond with your daughter in-laws?"

"Yea, but there's only Toya. I'd beat Andrew myself if he married that girl."

"You! You'd need to get in line. I haven't put hands on anyone in years and she took me there."

"She keeps making her way through the family. Pretty soon it'll be like you don't fit in if you haven't put hands on her." I said

"Anyways back to the condo. If it's too much to ask..." She thought about it. "Never mind! Do you ever forget you can afford to pay for stuff?"

"All the time! But I think that's why we haven't burned through our money like some." I said, even though in my mind it seemed impossible some of our cousins were out of money. They blew through their inheritance, and now it seemed like they were always trying to plot on those who were more responsible.

"Yea, I can afford to stay in a hotel for Sasha's graduation. I guess I just wanted to see the condo." She said, and then she had a worried look on her face.

I smiled at her. "Are you nervous about seeing Richard?"

"Yes! I keep saying please don't look good! Please don't look good! Aren't you nervous about seeing Malcolm?" She asked

"I'm more annoyed than nervous. He still has people watching me, but at least they stay back. They've gotten more stealth like, if I didn't know better; I wouldn't even know they're there. Mister is dead so it makes no sense but whatever!"

"Maybe because this is his only way of connecting with you." Sophia said

My blood started boiling. "I guess he'll be watching me forever because I will NEVER connect with him again!" Then a worker knocked on the door. She brought in meatball sandwiches and a grilled cheese for Sabrina. I looked at the sandwich and normally I would be too excited to eat it. But now it just looked like bread and nastiness on a plate. I sat at the side table with Sabrina while she ate her sandwich. But I couldn't even bring myself to touch the sandwich.

"Amber please eat." Sophia pleaded

"I'm not really hungry right now, I'll take it home." I said

"I'm worried about you. You're losing too much weight." She said with sad eyes.

"No I haven't, I've been exercising harder, working hard for those endorphins." I cracked a fake smile.

"If you say so, but I'd feel better if I saw you eat something." Sophia said

I rolled my eyes at Sophia. I picked up the sandwich and took a bite. I know I normally love this sandwich, I know that normally my mouth salutes me when I eat it, but today it felt like a burden to have it in my mouth. "Happy now?"

****

First thing I did was make sure I went to Bob's and got a tub of ice cream. There would be NO evening strolls tonight! I couldn't figure out what to do with my hair and that frustrated me! I left it down, I put on my dress, and then I went to check on my graduate. Derrick and Darryl were clowning around in the mirror when I walked in the room. When he smiled at me, I saw David for a moment, which made tears fall from my eyes. I had a flashback of how happy he was when I told him I was pregnant. He smiled at me the same way Derrick just did. Maybe he knows he looks like David when he smiles so that's why he doesn't do it often. I congratulated Derrick and I told him how proud I was of him. We took Derrick to the school and he disappeared through the doors. Darryl and I blocked off seats in a section. Darryl was unusually quiet, when I asked him what was wrong he shrugged and kept moving. So I made him sit down and talk to me before family arrived. He was worried about me and how I would react to Malcolm. I told him everything would be fine. Bernadette and her large family arrived first as usual. She put her hands on my arms and she rubbed them. She asked me if I was ok. I pretended I didn't know what she was talking about and started talking about Derrick's achievements. Everyone started arriving, and then Daddy walked in with Malcolm. When I looked at them, Malcolm was already looking at me. His face was a lot thinner too, and he had sad eyes. But I guess mine weren't all that happy either. I was irritated that Daddy was sitting with him; I needed my Daddy but Andrew walked in tall and poised, I was happy to be sandwiched between him and Darryl. When Derrick approached the podium to address his class Renee leaned forward and whispered "two for two." Andrew liked the sound of that so he gave her a pound. Derrick had everyone on their feet exploding in thunderous applause once he finished his valedictorian speech. Even though my baby was only seventeen because we skipped him up a grade, he had the speaking abilities of someone Daddy's age. Andrew waited with Darryl and I for Derrick, while everyone else went back to the house. I watched a few girls hug my baby as they congratulated him. He was so different from Andrew. I think most girls were scared of him. Otherwise, they'd be all over him just like Andrew. Derrick gave me the biggest hug and he told me he loved me. They all laughed as Andrew told them how emotional he got after his ceremony. We laughed harder when Derrick pointed at his serious face and said he was emotional too. Jade had everything set up beautifully. We saw Auntie Lorraine and Dionne first when we walked into Daddy's back yard. Dionne was having a good day. She kept hugging Derrick and telling him that he was reminding her so much of David. Normally saying stuff like that to Derrick would upset him, but he always seems to accept comments like that only from Dionne. Malcolm was in the corner with Daddy, Uncle Frank, and Uncle Jeff. Malcolm kept looking at me, so I decided not to look at him anymore. Tanisha brought Rosalind, which was a rare treat. Rosalind was quiet and reserved, she didn't look happy but I didn't want to make her talk about it if she didn't want to. Auntie Lauren brought out decks of cards and the games began. Focusing on making my books had me so distracted from everything else, Sophia thinks she's slick putting a plate of food in front of me. Then Jade asked if I tried different things on my plate because they were SO good. Wanting them to shut up so I could focus on my game, I ate out of frustration. It still made them happy but I just wanted to win. Renee asked what it was like being around all those celebrities. I told her that sometimes it was really fun. Lately I didn't like being in front of the cameras and having my business in the streets and then told inaccurately. I told them Comfort and I were NEVER a couple but the media wanted to paint it that way. Thinking about it frustrated me. It kept making me think of that night, I kept having flashbacks of the next morning and how I would probably be sitting here pregnant right now if things didn't go traumatically wrong days later. I couldn't focus on a thought, and everything was spinning. I threw out my last card and told the table I'd be back. I went in the house and I went in Momma and Daddy's room. I shut the door and I laid on Momma's side of the bed. After awhile Jade came and rubbed my back, she didn't say anything, which I appreciated. I didn't have any more tears to give, so I laid there silent. Andrew knocked on the door and peeked his head in. He asked what was wrong and Jade told him I needed a breather, and that we'd be out soon. Emerald came and said that Sonny needed Jade for something. I told them I'd come out in a minute. Darryl and Malcolm were talking in the kitchen when I walked in. Malcolm nodded hello, and I rolled my eyes at him. It seemed like Darryl stopped breathing. Malcolm stared at me but didn't say anything. I walked out of the door and back out into the yard. Derrick was dancing with a girl I didn't recognize. I asked Sophia who she was, she shrugged. The way Derrick looked at this girl held my attention for a while. Then someone entered the gate, when I saw him my eyes filled with tears, and it surprised me how excited I was to see him. I took off running; he caught me with opened stretched arms. I squeezed him tight and kissed his cheek. "I'm so happy to see you!"

Above a chuckle he said, "I see! How you been? Besides what I've seen on TV?"

I smiled at him. "It's so good to see you Fuzzy! Where have you been?"

"I moved to Vegas, I've been out there laying low."

"Oh yes, cause Vegas is definitely where you go to slow down." I said sarcastically "I've been out here a bunch of times, but little miss celebrity has always been busy."

"Hey Fuzzy!" Darryl said, they hugged.

I guess that had to be true otherwise how would Darryl know who he is. Fuzzy left long before he was born, and as far as I knew he only came back out here for Troy's funeral. "Where's Malcolm?" Fuzzy asked

Darryl pointed to Malcolm who was watching us from across the yard. Malcolm waved him over. Fuzzy said we'd chat later, as he made his way through the party; others had the same reaction to him that I did. Malcolm looked annoyed cause he was waiting. When he saw me looking at him he stared back. Very clever Mr. Latour, very clever. I looked at Darryl, "how come you never told me you knew Fuzzy?"

Darryl looked at me funny and shrugged. "Didn't know it was a big deal. He's just a cousin."

"Family is never just family." I said

Watching Malcolm talk to Fuzzy was my excuse to look over. Malcolm was almost smiling while talking to him. Daddy came over and chatted with them for a while, and then Malcolm started staring again. I found my way to the domino table, Andrew and I were partners talking smack and kicking butt. Penny started cutting the cake and Timothy brought out the ice cream. Malcolm looked hurt when he saw it. He stood up and walked out of the yard. I felt a little bad, but he couldn't think I would walk with him now. Bernadette took pictures of Derrick and Malcolm then she told Darryl and Andrew to get in the picture. Andrew made it a point to stand as far away from Malcolm as he could. Then she told me to get in the picture. I didn't want to put everyone in our business, as I walked over Andrew grabbed my arm and put me between him and Darryl. Malcolm shot Andrew serious eyes and Andrew shot them back. Bernadette told us to smile, I knew that picture was gonna look awkward. Malcolm left not too long after that, he didn't say anything to me or even look in my direction. Not that I wanted him to, I just didn't expect him to leave so suddenly and he didn't make a scene all day. Maybe he was just as done with me as I was with him.

****

Jade pulled up to my house as I was talking to Mrs. Hall and Ms. Connie. Ms. Connie was excited because Hubby had a heart to heart with her. He wants to propose to Nicole, but he was really nervous about it because they had been through so much. He was still dragging his feet, but Ms. Connie was really trying to encourage him to take the plunge.

"Hey Jade! How are you doing?" Mrs. Hall said

"I'm good Mrs. Hall, how are you?" She said

"Oh I'm kicking!" She said with a smile.

Jade smiled at her then she turned to me. "I need to tell you something real quick." I excused myself, and then we went inside. "What's wrong?"

"I don't know if you could consider it technically wrong, we had a visitor at the school." I put my hands out cause I didn't feel like guessing. "Tag."

I frowned, "Tag?"

"Yes, he was hoping he caught you at the school."

I squinted at her. "What did he want?"

"He didn't say exactly, but something about a charity event and that he needed a performance. But he wanted to talk to you directly. He left his number, do you want it?" Jade was doing her best to keep any expression off her face.

"No, let's keep it professional. Did he leave his info? I really don't want to work on anything until October."

"I know I can call him when I get back to the school. I can offer one of the teachers for choreography if he absolutely needs something before October. Honestly I feel like this is a guise to talk to you."

"Why now?" I asked

"That's a question only he can answer if you want him to. I think you should lay low. I'll handle Tag, but I didn't want to take over in case you lost your mind and actually considered him. What did he do watch your breast bounce while you ran? Why is he so persistent?"

"What do you mean?"

"You guys never hooked up right?" Jade said

"Are you asking me?" I said trying to keep my face straight.

Jade's mouth dropped open. "What happened?" She sat on the couch.

I swallowed hard. "Um, you know maybe we should talk later." Suddenly I felt like my house could be bugged. I didn't trust talking on the phone anymore either. It seemed like Malcolm was everywhere.

She squinted at me. "WHAT??? You gotta tell me!"

"Did you come here just to tell me about Tag?"

Now Jade had a busted look on her face. Then she gave me sad eyes. "I'm on my way to the doctors."

I felt like the room spun. I ran and sat next to her on the couch. "Are you ok?" I couldn't handle it if she wasn't; my heart was pounding out of my chest.

She patted my hands. "I'm fine sweetheart. I'm just pregnant again." She said with a squeamish smile.

"Oh" I said feeling completely numb.

"You've had a lot going on lately. We thought it would be best to wait before telling you."

"Oh," I said again.

"I'm sorry," she said giving me sad eyes.

My eyes filled up with tears. "Don't be sorry. Every child is a blessing and should be celebrated right?" Tears fell out of my eyes.

"Oh sweetheart! I feel horrible!" Jade said releasing her own tears.

"No! No! Don't cry for my stupid messed up life. Celebrate yours! I'm so happy for you."

"It wasn't planned my body seems to have a mind of its own these days." She said sadly

"Yea right! Sonny hit that down stroke on you." I smiled

She looked surprised. "More like I hit one on him." She gave me an evil grin.

"I want to come with you." I said trying to push my emotions to the side.

"Are you sure you can handle it?" Her question brought me to tears again. "How about you come next time?"

"Ok, I'll be ready."

She stood up. "I'll let you know how it goes with Tag."

"Ok" I said

****

"Yep, this place will work just fine. It's almost exactly like mine." Andrew said as we stood in Derrick's one bedroom apartment.

Derrick nodded, "that was half the appeal." Derrick put his arm around me.

"Momma I'm gonna be home so much it won't seem like I'm gone." He said squeezing me.

"Yea right! That's what that one said." I said pointing at Andrew.

"Hey I come home regularly now. I just got lost in the crowd for a minute."

"True! But I'm still there!" Darryl said frowning.

"Yep, it's your turn to be head of the house." Derrick said

"Right! So momma this rule about no girls, we need to talk." I looked at him like he was crazy. "Never mind! It was just a joke." He said putting his hands up.

Then there was a knock at the door. Two girls were standing at the door smiling. All the boys straightened up and Derrick put his hands down. "Hello ladies" he said.

"Hello, do you own the red car blocking the carport?" One girl said

"No we don't, are you in a hurry?" Andrew asked

"We were gonna go to the grocery store to get our groceries for the week." She said

"And we've been waiting for some time for that car to move." The other girl said

"We could give you a ride to the store. I need to get some stuff for my place as well." Derrick said

"That would be great! I'm Marisa." The first girl said

"And I'm Chloe."

The boys introduced their selves. I stood there feeling like the old lady in the room. Until! "Are you their sister? You guys all favor." Marisa said

"No I'm their mother." Both of the girls gasped. "I'm Amber."

"Oh my goodness, I had no idea. You look so young!" Marisa said

"Thank you," I said feeling redeemed. Chloe stared at me like she was looking for a sign that I was kidding.

"Momma we'll be back, make yourself comfortable." Derrick said focusing on the girls.

"Ok, I guess I'm watching TV then." I said looking around for the remote. Derrick mumbled something while picking up my keys. "My car?"

Derrick winked at me, and just like that, they were gone. I found some reruns of the old but goody all black cast sitcoms. About an hour later, there was a knock at the door. I opened the door and there was a kid looking to "borrow" an egg. I told him the actual resident would be home shortly. Ten minutes later, there was another knock. This building was busy. I opened the door and my heart stopped when I looked into Malcolm's face. He looked surprised to see me as well. "Where's your car?" He said

"The boys took it to the store. Is Derrick expecting you?" I said with as much attitude as I could spit.

"Yes, we're supposed to go eat."

"You can leave or wait for him out there; I don't know when they'll be back." I said closing the door

Malcolm caught the door. "Yea right! You know I'm coming in." He said

I folded my arms and sat on the couch. He turned the chair at the table around to face the TV. He sat in the chair and stared at me. I squinted my eyes at him and then I rolled my eyes. "Why haven't you been eating?" I pretended like I didn't hear him. "You look better fat!"

My mouth fell open. He chuckled at my reaction. "Who are you to talk? Sitting over there looking like starving kids in Ethiopia. What's wrong, your hooker crew doesn't know how to cook? Just lay on their backs?" I said with an attitude.

He gave me evil eyes, I rolled mine. "What they do, they do well!" Then he went back to staring at me. I kept looking at my watch. Another hour and a half later I was dying to get out of there, Malcolm kept staring at me. When I looked at him, he didn't look away or anything. When I went to the bathroom, his stare followed me. And when I came out, he seemed like he was staring at the door waiting for me to come out. He got up and stepped into my path. "You miss me?" I backed up, walked over to the table, and grabbed my purse. I rolled my eyes at him and I walked out of the door. I called Andrew's cell phone but he didn't answer. None of those good for nothing boys answered their phones. Enough was enough! I wanted out of there. Derrick had to have forgotten about Malcolm. I walked back inside; I was looking for something with Derrick's address so I could call a cab. I didn't care how expensive the cab ride was going to be, I needed a ride to the city, to the Bart station, either that or if I found a spare key to Derrick's car I was out. Malcolm sat there watching me. My cellphone finally rang, it was Andrew. I heard cursing in the background; Andrew said they were in a car accident. He said the other car was at fault, but the police were harassing them. I asked where they were; Malcolm was standing at the door. He pulled out his phone and made a phone call. Something in the background distracted Andrew and he told me he would call me back. Malcolm told me to come on; whoever was on the phone was directing him. I couldn't tell if it was a man or a woman. We pulled up on the wreck; my car was in the intersection sitting behind the line, the other car and my car looked like they were kissing. The girls were standing on the sidewalk both of them with their arms folded. Andrew and Derrick were standing with their hands in their pockets and Darryl was in one of the officer's faces. The other officer was talking to two other guys. Andrew's eyes turned evil looking at Malcolm's car approach. We got out of the car at the same time; Andrew's face did not soften. Another police car arrived, Malcolm looked at the second car, and then he matched my pace even though his walk still seemed more casual than mine did. He put his hands in his pockets.

"Evening officers what seems to be the problem?" Malcolm said as Darryl plastered a huge smile on his face.

"You are?" The officer Darryl was just yelling at said.

"I'm the father of the boys." Malcolm said. Andrew mumbled that he wasn't a boy.

"Get over there! We'll address you when we're ready." The officer said dismissing him.

Malcolm's eyes turned evil. "Give me your badge number!" He took out his phone and dialed someone. The officer sarcastically read off the numbers, he didn't even bother to look at Malcolm or ask himself why. Malcolm gave the numbers over the phone, and then he told the person over the phone to "handle it!"

All four officers got a chirp on their shoulder things; all four of them looked at Malcolm. The rude guy swallowed hard when he looked back at Malcolm.

"Mr. Latour I'm...."

"Fired! Your pink slip is waiting for you. Get out of my face!" The rude guy looked angry.

Darryl jumped in the rude guy's face and started laughing. "Who's the nigga now?" The rude officer walked over to the other original officer. Malcolm waved him over; this guy had a respectful tone. "Yes sir?"

"What's the hold up here? You have witnesses and anyone can see that those kids hit my boys. Have you checked their blood alcohol levels?"

"We had to send for backup, so we couldn't get to the other things yet."

"When were you called here?" Malcolm barked

The officer swallowed. "Well..."

"Have you called tow trucks yet? What have you done besides harass my sons?" The officer turned beet red. "You've got thirty minutes! Otherwise, you'll be fired like your partner! Check them for alcohol! Handle this!" Then Malcolm looked at his watch.

Darryl started laughing again and Malcolm looked at him, and he straightened up. The other officers stayed in the street writing down the information. When one of the officers from the street approached Malcolm, I realized it was a woman. She was saying something to him about the wreck. Then I could see the change in her when she looked at him. I turned my back; I didn't want to see anything else. I didn't know if Malcolm was going to go for it or not, but I was not about to stand there and watch. Andrew and Darryl were watching Malcolm, while Derrick talked to his new neighbors. The guys were drunk and taken into custody. My babies took their groceries out of my car and put them in Malcolm's trunk. I made sure I took anything out my car I didn't want to lose. Mostly my CDs. A cab came and Derrick hopped in with the girls. On the way back to the apartment, Darryl rode in the front and Andrew and I sat silent in the back. Darryl told Malcolm how the officers were acting before we got there. Malcolm told Darryl that he needed to calm down, and to stop letting people push his buttons. After Derrick and the girls got their groceries out of the car, Malcolm drove us to my house. Malcolm and Darryl talked the entire way home. When I got out the back of the car, Malcolm got out. "I'll get you a new car in the morning."

Andrew shot me a look, and I shot one back. Then I looked at Malcolm. "No need I can get my own car!"

"That car was a gift, I want to replace it."

Darryl and Andrew walked on the porch. "Why don't you buy Torrie a car?" He blank stared at me. "I'm not gonna accept anything from you! It was time that car died with everything else."

"What does that mean?"

I closed my door and then I walked into Malcolm's space. He looked down at me. "Funny how you automatically assume that my lack of appetite has to do with you!" I couldn't believe I was telling him. "That day when I walked into your house you not only killed me, and our relationship." My eyes watered up. "You set the stage to kill the child you've been begging for all these years!"

Malcolm grabbed the car door; his body slumped like I just shot him. His eyes watered up, his voice cracked. He swallowed then he opened his mouth again. "Why didn't you say anything?"

"I didn't know until it was gone! I don't want your car! I don't want your money! And I don't want you!" I said as evilly as I could.

Malcolm stared at me wide eyed while tears fell from his eyes. "I'm..."

"Yes you are sorry!" I said as I walked away.

Malcolm stood there wounded by my words. Andrew and Darryl had question marks on their faces but they didn't say anything. Andrew followed me inside, and Darryl went to Malcolm. Once the front door closed, I cried into Andrew's chest.

Chapter 47

"I'll be at your hotel around 4pm, will you be ready?" Tag said

"I will be, I'll meet you in the lobby." I said

"You don't want me to come up to your room? You know, like a gentleman would." I laughed. "No, I think I'm ok. I'll see you in a bit." I hung up the phone, and then I continued my conversation with the salesgirl. I was telling her about my event tonight. Seems like history repeats it's self huh. I'm completely down in the dumps and Tag comes a long to help me rebuild. We had Shelby choreograph his performance for his event; however, I did actually go to the event. The event was nice, but Tag was concerned from the moment he laid eyes on me. He immediately switched gears and turned into the sweetest friend. First, he asked me if I was sick. And when I told him no, he didn't ask me any more questions because that obviously meant it was Malcolm. He kept inviting me to Raider games, and I kept declining on account of Malcolm. I didn't want to run into him. But eventually, I agreed to go, and I had a good time. I was in the skybox with the player's wives and girlfriends, they were so animated and colorful, and I had no choice but to enjoy myself. Tag kept taking Darryl and me out to dinner. I started feeling bad about ordering stuff and not eating. Joanne told me that my appetite would return eventually and to not try to force myself just to make others happy which helped. Going out with Tag was the push I needed in the right direction. Plus going back to work in October really helped me refocus my thoughts. I tried to do as much as I could at home so that I wouldn't have to leave Darryl and I took him with me as much as I could. Whenever we went to LA like we are now, Darryl would spend time with Sasha and Joseph while I worked. A lot of the time the three of them would join me on the set. Tag has been a good friend and he hasn't tried to push up on me or anything. He's become a really good friend. I said that already, but it's the truth.

The salesgirl brought eight different looks for me to pick the four I liked best to try them on and then make a final decision. Sasha was in love with everything the girl brought out. She was no help finalizing the four. So it came down to functionality of the outfits. Although the shoes were SICK! I easily ex'd out five just because I knew the shoes would kill me. So then, I tried on all three looks. Sasha took pictures of me in each one on her digital camera. The hard part was that I loved all three, but I didn't need all three. After a long discussion over all three, the black dress won. The salesgirl happily rang everything up; she gave me her card for future events. Then Sasha and I went to "The Salon" off of Rodeo drive. I made appointments for both of us to get our hair, facials, manicures, and pedicures done. It was a complete pamper me session with my little cousin. I got my hair straightened for the first time in years. My hair was super long, curls deceive you so much. Sasha's excitement about everything was so much fun; I really missed having her in the bay. She told me how well things were going with her and Richard. She said at first, it was hard because she had to have it out with him about lying to her for so long. She said she couldn't understand how he could do that to her. Then she thought about it and he was always there, and even though no one had said anything, in her heart she already knew. It was still a complete shock when they finally told her. She said once they got past that, things got one hundred percent better between them, and she and her father were so close now. She said she felt like sometimes they were growing up together. I wondered if Andrew felt that way, I couldn't blame him if he did. I was a baby when I had him. I asked Sasha if she was going to come home after she got her masters. She said it depended on where

she landed a job, but her heart was leaning more towards Southern California. I asked her if she discussed this with her mother. She swallowed hard and told me she didn't know how. I promised I wouldn't say anything and I took in the time I spent with my honorary daughter. Being with her, I didn't feel daughterless.
Kimmy's makeup person came to my hotel room and did our makeup. Sasha said I looked amazing and I felt beautiful for the first time in a long time. My cheeks finally filled in some and I looked healthy again. I thanked Sasha for spending the day with me. She walked with me to the lobby at 3:45. Tag arrived at 3:55 while we're sitting at the bar. Sasha whispered that he has aged well as he approached us. He couldn't get over how grown Sasha was. Then he stood silently taking me in with the biggest smile on his face. Sasha got her car out of valet, and then Tag and I got in his limo. He kept looking at me and smiling. "How do you feel?"
I smiled. "I feel good. Tonight should be fun." I said
And it was a lot of fun for the most part. The only thing was, I guess with me being on the arm of Tag and my hair straightened you couldn't get a good read on my background. And you know how people are when they think no one's watching. One guy made a reference to urban areas that rubbed me the wrong way. I rolled my eyes and walked away. Tag walked away from the guy just after me and we went out on the dance floor. Later this lady said I had a very exotic look. That was her way of inquiring about my background. I thanked her and changed the subject. It had been awhile since I had received the "what are you question" but I guess when I normally had my boys or someone with me; people assumed I was black by association, which I had no problem with. Tag came to check-in and he could see that I was not amused with this woman. He held my hand, which was sweating as I tried to keep my composure. He chatted with the lady and then moved me away from her. Other than those two idiots, I had a good time. At one point, I needed to cool down so I stood by the door; I was dancing with a guy who knew how to move. He had us dancing all over the floor it was a lot of fun, but I was trying to preserve my hair for at least another day. Tag walked over from behind and he kissed my shoulder, which made me jump. He smiled at me. "I feel like we finally have our moment."
There was a lump in my throat. "Tag!"
"I want to be with you. I haven't seen Malcolm around since we've been hanging out. So I can safely assume you guys are on the outs right now. Dwayne's gone; it's just me and you."
"Yea but..."
"I was young and I was hurting. I dated Gwen, but she's married with a family now. Can't we move past that?"
"Tag that's really gross to me. I can't even imagine a physical relationship with you. It's like you're off limits."
"But I was with you first." He smiled.
"We didn't have sex."
"If you say so. I'll do whatever it takes to wear you down."
"All you've ever wanted from me was sex, don't you understand how much of a turn off that is." I said still dealing with the lump in my throat.
"I've never said that."
"No, but your actions. You want me, I say no; then you go on and on about sex."
"As a last resort, I've always wanted you, but if I couldn't have your mind or your heart. I'd settle for your body. "He said with a smile.
"You should want all of me or nothing at all." I said

"Are you offering all of you?"

"I'm offering my friendship. You have been a great friend at this point in my life, just what the doctor ordered. But I don't want to sleep with you. So how could we ever be more than friends?"

"I don't want to be just your friend! I want to be with you."

"That ex girlfriend that you mentioned, did you ever try to get back with her?"

"What ex girlfriend?"

"Who ever the girl was before me."

"We've spoken, but we've both moved on with our lives. I want you. I want you to be my wife. I want to come home to you everyday. I want to share my joy and my pain with you."

"Have you ever dated a black woman?"

He looked confused, "No, but I don't see what that has to do with anything."

"I was just wondering. Cause all this begging makes you seems soft."

"Soft?" He frowned

"You're not even like my Daddy or my Uncles. Gorgeous you are, but you miss the mark by one smidgen. If you can't handle only being my friend, I understand but Tag you had sex, more than once I might add, with my cousin. You guys were in a relationship, even if that relationship was purely physical. I can't ever in good conscience be anything more than friends with you. My resolve will not change."

He huffed. "You are so stubborn!"

"And so are you!"

"But what if..." He reached into his pocket and pulled out a ring box. He sat it on the rail and pushed the box towards me. "What if I told you that I love you? What if I said I want to spend the rest of my life with you? What if I said I know I crossed a line by dating your cousin, but I strongly begged and pleaded with you to forgive me? What if I said, even if you rejected me tonight, I wouldn't give up on you as long as I have breath in my body? What if..."

"Tag!" I said with my finger stroking the box. "If I could forgive you for sleeping with my cousin, then I could forgive Malcolm for everything he's done and we know who my choice would be. I'm not in a forgiving place in my life right now. I really hope this is just a dramatically romantic gesture and this box is empty." I said "Open it!" His eyes were pleading with me.

I gasped loudly when I saw the huge rock waiting for me. His ring made David's ring look like a Cracker Jack prize but I still valued David's more. "Tag!" I frowned at him. "This is beautiful! Why would you do this? We aren't even a couple."

"I was hoping that you finally understood how much I love you. I wouldn't make you jump through hoops to experience my love. I'm offering it to you freely. I'm gonna love you until the day I die, I was just hoping one day you could love me back." I smiled at him. "Is this because I'm white?" He asked with a smile.

"Um, my Daddy is white and I couldn't love him more. No Tag, it's not because you're white."

"Have you ever dated a white guy?"

"No"

"You don't know what you're missing."

I smiled, "I'm sure I don't."

****

"Momma, you know I love you right?"

"Yes Andy I know you do."

"So I'm gonna say this, but I need you to know how much I love you when I say it." He paused to read my face. "I don't want to look up and see you and Sophia like permanent fixtures in my spot."

I put my hands on my hips. "Are you saying we," I pointed at Sophia and I, "aren't welcome in your little club?"

Sophia and I walked up in Andrew's face. Jeff and Joseph laughed cause they knew he was in trouble. "No, you're welcome, just not all the time. It gets kind of old bumping into your momma at the club all the time."

I looked at Sophia, "can you believe him?"

"These kids have no idea!" She said

"What if you looked up and saw momma as you and Travis were breaking it down on the dance floor?" Jeff asked Sophia

"That's different, our momma is old." Sophia said

"And what do you guys think you are to us?" Joseph said

Sophia and I looked at each other. "We're not even old enough to be your Momma's we ain't old!"

"But yet you are!" Andrew said looking at me.

"You are one more sentence away from hurting my feelings. So we can't come to your club, fine!"

"I'm not saying ever, I just don't want to see you there all the time."

"Fine! I'll ask first, am I supposed to dress like an old woman at the Grand Opening tonight? Cause that will mean I have to go shopping for a new moo-moo."

"Getting a little dramatic in your old age?" Andrew said with a smile.

"You got one more time to call me old! I'm not too old to kick your butt!" I said then I smacked him upside his head. Jeff and Joseph laughed at him.

"Wear whatever you like." He frowned while rubbing his head.

"Is your father gonna be there?" I asked

"Yes momma, and I'm gonna tell you like I told him. You guys don't have to see each other. With all the promotion Gwen has been doing, it's guaranteed to be packed in there. You guys will specifically be on opposite sides of the VIP section. You could bring Tag if you want to." Then all the boys fell out laughing.

I looked at Sophia because I didn't get the joke, she shrugged. "What's so funny about Tag?"

"It's more like Malcolm's reaction to Tag that I'm picturing. You don't want a fight in your spot opening night." Jeff said

"He doesn't care any more." I said waving them off. Andrew stopped laughing and put his head down. "Andy?"

"Momma you know that man still loves you. I don't know what you said to him that night, but he hasn't been the same since."

Sophia and I sat down fast at the table. Even Joseph and Jeff leaned in. "What do you mean?"

Andrew looked around at all of us. "He's slowed down a lot. I'm not gonna say he's straight, but he's not as wild as he used to be. What did you say to him?"

Everybody looked at me. "Whatever! Not going into that." I said leaning back in my chair.

"Oh come on, everything said in this room stays in this room. That's our rule." Joseph said, we were in the private room at Sophia's in her Walnut Creek restaurant.

"It's personal!" I said

"Will it help if I go first?" Joseph asked

"Everybody would have to go before me!" I said

"Ok! Ok! No judgment and everything said in here stays in here!" Joseph said

"Sophia I feel like they're letting us in the boy's club." I said

"I know, what could my little brothers possibly have to share?" Sophia asked. Joseph looked at me. "You know your friend Kimmy?" I shook my head not knowing where he was going with it. "I hit that!" He smiled big.

"WHAT????" My mouth fell open.

"I met her at a club. She got into it with her man, came home with me. Didn't know you knew her until she was on the set one-day. She begged me not to tell you, oh and she still calls me. Every time she comes out this way she calls me to hook up."

"But you met her man before." I said in disbelief.

"So! I don't call her, she calls me. If he was handling business she would never call." Andrew and Jeff slapped his hand.

"Ok, ok me next." Jeff said with a big smile. "Me and Penny!" He said with an evil grin and shaking his head.

"WHAT??? My baby???? What? Why? How?" I said

"That's a grown woman!" Jeff said

"Now, but she's my baby. She was a little girl when I met her."

"Not when we hooked up!" Jeff said laughing.

I looked at Andrew, "you're ok with this?"

He put his hands up. "I didn't have a choice in the matter. They don't hook up anymore so it's kind of in the past."

"That could've been my baby she had. " Jeff said

"Is it? The baby is fair skinned." I said

"No, that's not my baby." He said

Andrew took a deep breath, and he prepared himself to run. "Me and Toya had sex in the house." I gasped! "More than once!"

He took off running; I chased him slapping him upside the head. "I would've felt better if you said Jennay."

"We did too!" Andrew was cracking up laughing.

"You nasty little boys! I guess I should assume that Derrick and Raquel did too?" I said

"Hhhhmmmm, this is my confession. I can't speak for him."

Sophia blew air. "Since everyone is sharing their whore escapades." She blew air again. "You know how Travis went with me to Sasha's graduation?" We all nodded, because we were all there. "Remember how drunk Travis got at the club? So we went back to the hotel. Richard brought my purse cause I left it in his car. Richard and I did it in the bathroom!"

"In the same room as your man?" I couldn't believe it.

"When Travis is sleep he's dead to the world. Plus he was drunk, so yea."

"You's a bad girl!" Jeff said high fiving his sister.

"What kind of brother are you?" I asked in disbelief.

"Amber, in this room we tell it all. We're not brother and sister right now. Because had I known something like that was possible, the brother in me wouldn't have let that happen. I would've at least told them to get a car or something." They started laughing. "It's your turn."

"Mine isn't like that."

"Doesn't matter, it broke the wall we know as Malcolm down, we wanna know what it was." Joseph said

"I have to give you the background for you to understand." They all leaned in. "When Andy was two, Malcolm decided he wanted a little girl. Through some plotting and scheming, he knocked me up. The day the doctor confirmed my pregnancy I got in a car accident and lost the baby."

"I was two?" Andrew asked like he was getting in line with the timeline.

"Yes, now he wanted to try again but I didn't like him all that much, so I wasn't going for it. Then he got locked up."

"For killing that guy." Joseph said

"Right! Then I had Derrick and Darryl. He didn't like it, but what could he do, they were here. I don't know how but his clock started ticking. I didn't want any more babies, but he did. Through some, I'll say powerful manipulation, he convinced me to give it one more college try. I was pregnant and I lost that baby due to a tubal pregnancy. The doctor explained the situation, we tried after that, but nothing was happening. So fast-forward to a year and a half ago. Things are going well with he and I, I broke up with Dwayne, and I'm checking for him. He pops up in LA, we enjoyed each other. We broke up, since I'm convinced I can't have any more babies, I don't even go get checked when I notice my period is late. Remember my women's troubles appointment when you guys had me on lock down?" Andrew nodded. "The doctor told me I miscarried again."

"WHAT????? YOU DIDN'T TELL ME!" Sophia screamed

"I know, I didn't want to talk about it or think about it but I told him he killed the child he had been begging for."

Jeff whistled, "yea that'll do it! Man! Your dad has been through a lot."

Andrew sat there quiet for a minute. "I hate the back and forth with you guys. That's rough on a kid."

"I'm sorry Andy; I never meant to hurt you."

"I know it was never intentional but it was still painful. All of your up and downs, I was right there going through them too. Guess I kind of mimic that behavior with Toya huh?"

"Just a little bit, but just so that we're clear. I don't care if that girl did a total 360 today, DON'T EVER MARRY HER!"

****

The limo was coming at nine. Sophia and I twirled in the mirror checking out our reflections. Travis had to stay home with Sabrina when their sitter fell through at the last minute. Sophia said she was kind of glad he was staying home; he had been getting on her nerves lately. I asked her if that was because she was catching feelings for Richard again. She blushed but she didn't answer. When we came, downstairs Hubby and Nicole were waiting in the living room. Nicole really is beautiful, and it's clear to see that Hubby was sprung stupid off of her; they make a really cute couple. Hubby told me he got another letter from Dude the other day. He said he's studying to be a lawyer, and hopefully he would be able to be his own representation for his case. I told him to send a hello for me when he wrote back. I was disappointed when I didn't see the ring on Nicole's finger yet but I guess everything in its due time. Darryl came down in slacks, nice shoes, button up, and a leather jacket. Fresh hair cut at Drew's earlier in the day, he was ready to go. When we pulled up to Elegant Affairs there were searchlights, and the line to get in wrapped around the building. When we got out of the limo, someone screamed my name. That was weird cause I had been staying out of the spotlight. It was very rare that someone recognized me anymore. The bouncers smiled at us and we glided in. Andrew said the third booth in VIP was ours. I asked why we couldn't have the first

one, which was closest to the dance floor. He said that one was Malcolm's, I threw my hands up and happily walked to the third booth. The people who were inside were all taking in the scenery. It was really nice in this club. Better than any club, I had been to in Oakland, ever. Sophia and I sat in our booth and a waiter came over with drinks. "Two house specials," she said with a smile. I tasted it and told her to keep them coming. In a party environment, the guys who are paid to watch you tend to standout when they're not partying. One guy looked really familiar and I couldn't figure out why. Derrick came in with Marisa and Chloe. Then not too far behind him was Malcolm. Sophia looked at me with big eyes because Malcolm looked good. He had that stupid fedora that I only like on him, just about all black with a pop of crisp white. He didn't look at me, that doesn't mean he didn't see me. Fuzzy and a couple guys I didn't recognize were with him. Darryl went over to Derrick and the next thing you know he's on the dance floor with Chloe. Hubby and Nicole basically stayed on the dance floor. I watched them and remembered what it was like to be that young. Then we saw Joseph and Jeff making their way through the crowd with Sasha and Richard. It sounded like Sophia had an orgasm right next to me; I shot her a look like she needed to check herself. She gave me an embarrassed smile. Malcolm and Richard hugged, and then Malcolm introduced Richard around the booth. Sasha hugged Malcolm, waved hello to everyone then she came running to us. Sophia was happy and surprised to see her. Sasha asked where Tanisha was and we told her she was in the middle of her academy training so she couldn't make it. Richard sat next to Sophia and immediately they were flirting and acting like the same ole Sophia and Richard I've always known. I had to go say hi and get my hug. I put my second drink down and Sasha and I walked to the dance floor. I felt sexy, I felt confident, and in that moment I was so happy I picked the dress that hugged my butt ever so nicely. My eyes were locked on Malcolm as we walked. He stared back; I didn't smile or give him any indication that I was happy or mad to see him. I just looked at him, and I knew by how quiet that booth was when we walked past that all eyes were on me. I hugged Derrick on the dance floor, and I waved hi to Marisa. Minutes after Sasha and I stepped on the dance floor a couple of guys came from nowhere and we were dancing. When I felt my buzz wearing off, I started back to our booth. VIP was pretty empty; everyone was on the dance floor. Andrew was dancing with Toya who had her hair down looking fabulous. Malcolm was dancing with some girl I didn't recognize. My fresh drink was waiting for me. I downed it, and waited for my next drink. Malcolm was returning to his booth when he saw me sitting alone. He took a deep breath then came over to my booth. He sat down on the end and said something. The music was loud and bumping, so I couldn't hear him. He moved close enough where he could lean in to speak but wasn't invading my personal space. "How are you tonight?" He asked
"I'm good and you?" I said being polite.
I could tell he was relieved that I didn't bite his head off. "I'm as good as could be expected." Then he looked around. "Where's Tag?"
I couldn't even act surprised. "I didn't invite him. This is Andy's night." Then I looked at the girl on the dance floor who was trying to get his attention. "Your friend is trying to get your attention." I said pointing at her.
Malcolm looked at her, "I don't know her. I was just dancing with her."
"Un huh" I said
He scooted in a little closer. "So you know Darryl's gonna be sixteen soon."
"I know, can you believe it?" Then the waitress gave me a fresh drink and took my old glass away. She asked Malcolm if he wanted his drink here or at the booth. He

told her he'd take it here for now. She brought him his drink. He downed it and asked for another.

I looked at him waiting for him to talk and I wondered what he was drinking that he could throw it back like that. "Tell me what you think? Darryl gets Mali's car. Derrick gets Drew's car. Drew gets whatever you're driving now. And I have your car shipped to you from LA."

"You still have that car?"

"It's just sitting there collecting dust, and it's still new."

"Or you could give that car to Sasha as a happy belated graduation gift, and I can give Andrew one of my cars."

He looked disappointed. "I bought that car for you."

"I know and at the time I really appreciated it. But we're in different places now."

"Has enough time passed where we can sit down and talk?" He asked

"Isn't that what we're doing now?"

He moved his hands around, "it's too much noise in here."

I made my face look uninterested. "What did you have in mind?"

"There's a restaurant in the city that I'd like to take you to." My body jerked. He looked me in my eyes. "You don't ever have to be afraid when you're with me." I looked at him for a minute. "Trust me, you'll like it." Then he smiled.

I finished my drink. "When did you have in mind?" I said as I exhaled.

"How's next week Friday? I'll pick you up around seven?"

"Fine," I rolled my eyes. I crossed my legs cause out of nowhere I felt the tingles I hadn't felt since the last time we slept together. I cursed my body for reacting to him.

Andrew came, stepped in the middle of us, and sat down. "Hey Malcolm, I think Fuzzy's looking for you."

Malcolm frowned at Andrew. "Why you always act like you gotta protect your momma from me?"

Andrew and I both looked at Malcolm. He was a few minutes away from slurring his words. "Come on Malcolm." Andrew said helping his father back to his booth. Then he came back, "are you ok?" He said searching my face.

"I'm fine sweetheart." I said, Toya was watching us from the dance floor. She looked like she had a problem with Andrew talking to me.

"Good then let's go dance." Andrew said pulling me to the dance floor.

****

I put on a simple nice short dress, bare legged, and heels. I didn't want to look like I was trying to look sexy even though sexy is what I am. I thought about Dwayne and I said a silent thank you to him for pumping my head up. I told Darryl I was going out, but it didn't matter, he was going back to the club with Andrew and the boys. He was gonna spend the night with Andrew so I didn't have to make sure he didn't break curfew. I was ready at six o'clock, but my nerves were all over the place. I told Joanne about tonight, and her advice was all over the place or maybe it felt that way cause I couldn't grab it. Basically, she was saying to be careful, and to not let Malcolm suck me back in. She told me I had control and nothing that I didn't want didn't have to happen. Six-forty-five my doorbell rang. I jumped really hard. My heart was pounding. I stepped out of the door, I didn't invite him in. He didn't seem to mind. He told me I looked beautiful, he looked nice himself. Like me, he wasn't trying to be over dressed but he did hire a car service to drive us.

He pointed at my car. "Honda?"

"Very good Malcolm!" I said clapping my hands together. He flashed me a look. "That's my every day car. My other car is just a little nicer. But it doesn't feel practical to drive around Oakland in much more."

He shrugged, "I don't agree but ok." The driver opened the door for us, and we were off. As soon as we hit the bridge, I got butterflies. I started breathing to calm myself. "You're with me!" He said calmly. He was reading my eyes. We got off on the first San Francisco exit on the right, after a couple right turns we were near Embarcadero. The driver opened the door and Malcolm held my hand as I got out of the car. It was the first time we've touched in over a year. His hand was warm while the air was crisp. He led me inside the restaurant; he gave his name stating he had a reservation. The hostess took us to our table. The entire restaurant was dimly lit, but there was enough light to see everything we needed to see. Our waiter asked if we'd like to start with a cocktail. I ordered a grey goose White Russian. Malcolm ordered three fingers Martell Cordon Bleu XO neat. Our waiter returned shortly with our drinks. I studied the menu for a minute trying to decide what I wanted. Once we gave our orders. Malcolm asked the waiter to pair our meals with the best wines available. Our waiter smiled and went away.

"So" Malcolm said taking a drink.

"So" I said taking a drink of my drink.

"I think we need to clear the air." Malcolm said

"Ok, shoot." I said

Malcolm took a big swig of his drink. "I apologize for everything I've done to you. I know such a vague apology doesn't cover anything, but let's face it. I've done so much it would take the whole weekend to apologize for everything individually. Off the top of my head, I need to apologize for forcing two pregnancies on you that both ended traumatically. They rob me of my sleep. I'm still in shock about that last one. I should've talked to you. I shouldn't have left."

"Where did you go?" I asked

"I went to the studio to use the phone. I said he was dead and I meant it." That made me sad. "I called it off before anything happened."

"Obviously, he's still a live." I said

"I felt like you were playing with me. I keep thinking about how vulnerable I felt right before that phone rang. Everything was too perfect."

"I came to your house to talk to you. Instead of waiting on you to say it, I was going to pour my heart out to you in hopes that we could keep moving forward." I took a deep breath. "Sometimes I get flashbacks of the whole thing. That was the final straw for me."

"At the time, I was hurt to see how my sons turned on me but that is the way we raised them to be. Once Derrick and I talked, things started getting better for me."

"That's good." I said looking around.

"I still love you, you know."

I gave him evil eyes. "Still?"

"Don't clam up on me. What?" He said trying to hold back his reaction to my glare.

"How can you..." The waiter brought our salads. "How can you say you ever loved me? I feel so dumb forever believing that you ever loved me! Money is not an issue for you. The fact that you spent it on me, I thought meant something, but maybe spending money doesn't mean that your heart belonged to me. Maybe it was a seniority thing or something. I saw you lose it when that girl confronted me. She took us all off our game, had us outside knowing it wasn't safe and everything. You threatened to end her life because she made you that angry. Then I watched your dick fall out of her! Was she there because she thought you loved her too?"

"I don't know what she thought."

"How did you get her to come over?" I asked

"When I called her, I asked her to come over. She said she was with her friend, and I told her to bring her."

I took another drink. "That hurt!"

"I know, I wish I could take it back. All of it!" He smiled, "we'd have a little butter ball person with us right now."

"I still could've miscarried." I said

"I know" then he exhaled.

"What did you do with the condo?" I asked

"Nothing"

"I didn't know you kept it."

"You still have your keys don't you?" I nodded yes. "It's there if you need to use it. Should we leave your car there?"

"You don't want to give it to Sasha?"

He tried to control his irritation. "I bought that car for you; I don't want to give it to someone else. I'd rather it sit and wait for you than it be driven by someone else."

"Malcolm, now we both know that car isn't gonna sit there for me forever. Eventually you'll give it away."

"I may start it up from time to time, and I test drive it, but it's your car. It's waiting for you whenever you're ready for it."

I rolled my eyes. "Yea right! I don't want a community car. I can't do it."

He looked at me, "I'm not asking you to share."

"I guess I'd have to still want the car to even care to know if that was true." I said

"You don't want me?" He asked

I blew air. Our waiter brought our entrees, and side dishes. He showed Malcolm the bottle; I looked around while he tasted the little bit the waiter poured. The waiter was explaining the wine choice to Malcolm while I was distracted with looking around the restaurant. When the waiter left, Malcolm's stare made my body temp go up. Suddenly I felt nervous and hot. He asked me the question again. "I'm in no hurry to go back to living my life like I had been. I've spent my entire life waiting on you. What's funny to me is that when Momma told me a long time ago that I was doing everything you told me to, I was so hurt by what she said, that I didn't think about what she said. I've been so hurt by you that I bleed before I can form an actual thought in regards to you. As I get over you, I calm down and have the ability to sit here and look at you."

Malcolm shifted in his chair. Then he squinted his eyes at me. "Amber, I know I hurt you. You hurt me! The love we have for each other doesn't just go away." He exhaled, and then he shook his head. "How could you live without me?" I swallowed. "I know you still love me. Now what you do about it, I can't dictate, but let's not sit here and act like there's no love between us." He wasn't begging me; he was speaking matter of factly. The unintentional bass in his voice mixed with my wine.

I wondered if they drugged my wine. "Let me quote Tina, what's love got to do with it? I've spent almost all of my life waiting for you to do right by me. I don't have it in me to wait for you one more day." I rubbed my legs together under the table.

"I guess it's my turn to wait on you." Malcolm said trying to read me.

"Like you ever wait for anything!" I said, getting irritated with myself cause this wine was delicious. It complimented my meal so well, it almost bubbled on my tongue. The flavor danced with my meal in the most exquisite and sexual dance. My body temp went up, and the tingles!!!!

Malcolm was watching me. "I'm waiting for you."

"Did you drug me?" I asked accusingly, as I fanned myself.

He frowned at me. "No, what's wrong?"

I shook my head. I don't care what he said; yes, he's looking good but for my body to turn on me so rapidly!!! Every swallow of that delicious wine sent my body into a tizzy. I took a big chug of my water. Then I excused myself and went to the bathroom. I put a cool towel on my face and I looked in the mirror. My ears were red and I was a little red in the face. Yes I was hot, is there really a drug that suddenly makes you horny? Malcolm was drinking from the same bottle so maybe it wasn't the wine. Maybe it was in my food. I have been dead to the world for the past, I don't know how long and now suddenly I'm on fire? I don't appreciate this! When I returned to the table, Malcolm looked concerned. He asked me if I was ok, I smiled a half smile and shook my head yes. Then I looked at him, I was trying to gauge what his intent was. Whenever he did something to me on purpose, I could see his deliberate actions on his face. His face was sincere and genuine. I cursed in my brain. "You were saying?"

Malcolm looked a little confused. He composed himself. "I'm as tired of the dumb stuff as you are. There is no excuse for how I've hurt you and kept hurting you over all these years. Tell me what to do to fix this, and then consider it done."

I crossed and uncrossed my legs under the table. "I don't think our relationship is fixable. I think we can be cordial for the kid's sake. I can't get that last scene out of my head. I am so angry and hurt. My emotional conversation with Dwayne was about why I couldn't marry him." Malcolm swallowed and shifted in his chair. "I told him I couldn't marry him because the whole time I was with him, I really wanted to be with you. Why didn't your man tell you that? You know I cared for him, but I was in love with you! Look at the thanks I got for that huh." I smiled at him. He didn't say anything he just looked defeated. "I figure now I need to start figuring out what I want, and start living for me. Put me first, for the first time in my life." I sighed. "You know what Andy told me the other day? That our back and forth affected him. I can't even imagine what that feels like. As crazy as my Momma was, she was crazy for and about her man and vice versa. That's what I grew up knowing and thinking I would have in my life. Were you ever crazy for me or just crazy? Everyone can agree on the crazy part, but for me? I raise my hand to argue."

"I've been crazy about you from the first time I saw you. Anyone who knows me could tell you if my word isn't good enough. I put down my momma and my grand momma because they came at you! No one has ever come before you, you are my Queen!"

"No one but you, you mean."

The waiter came and asked us if we'd like dessert. Malcolm looked to me, I said yes. He gave us menus; I ordered chocolate cake that came with ice cream. I was hoping the ice cream would cool me down. Malcolm couldn't decide, so I told him he could share with me. Our waiter asked if we'd like a dessert wine as well. I told him to bring what he thought would pair best. "I know I'm selfish, I'm working on it."

"Prove it!"

He looked at me. "I can tell you're turned on right now. I don't know why, but I can see it. It's taking everything in me not to react to that. I'm not here about sex; I want to be with you."

"I'm an open book?" I asked

"Sometimes, I've known you since before you knew yourself."

I rolled my eyes. The waiter brought out the dessert wine; it was a raspberry wine and deliciously sweet. Then he brought the cake and ice cream. Malcolm started cracking up laughing when he saw my reaction to the thimble-sized scoop of ice cream. "Uh, what is this?"

"We can swing by Bob's on the way back."

"They're playing with my emotions." I took a bite of the cake; it was chocolaty and moist. I put some on the spoon and fed it to Malcolm.

His eyes were serious. "Why are you messing with me?"

"You don't want some cake?" I said feeding him another spoonful.

"I want the whole cake!"

"Un huh, tonight Momma's only offering a piece. I got an itch that needs to be scratched."

Chapter 48

"How come every time I see you, you got those girls on your arms?" I asked

"It's just easier this way." Derrick said nonchalantly.

"How are two girls easy?" I asked

Derrick sat up and leaned forward, like he was about to enlighten me. "First off, there's no commitment between me and them. They leave me alone when I need to study, shoot sometimes we study together. There's no drama about me belonging to one person over the other. We all get what we want."

"Until you make one feel more special than the other or one gets pregnant! Or...."

"Nobody's getting pregnant! Momma! I got this!" Derrick said sniffing himself.

"What about that girl at the club last night, I saw the way you guys were talking?" I said

Derrick looked around the room, "she's different, that's for later." He said as nonchalantly as he could.

I looked at Malcolm, "and this is ok with you? You probably encourage this!" Malcolm attempted to open his mouth. "No he doesn't. He's said the same things you just said.

My blood boiled. "I WANNA BEAT YOU IN YOUR FACE RIGHT NOW! YOU NEVER SOUNDED AS DUMB TO ME AS YOU DO RIGHT NOW! I DIDN'T RAISE YOU TO ACT LIKE THIS! IT'S DISRESPECTFUL!" Derrick looked surprised by my reaction. He sat there quiet. Then I turned to Darryl. "AND DON'T YOU EVER...."

"Little Annette, what are you over here going off about?" Daddy said sitting down. We were having breakfast at this little cafe in West Oakland; Darryl brought us claiming this place had the best French toast.

Hearing Daddy tell me anything about me was like Momma always seemed to soothe and calm me down. "That fool's head is so far up his butt he can't hear what I'm saying to him. He thinks he knows it all!"

Daddy looked at Derrick. "This must be about those girls?" Daddy frowned and moved his left arm like it was sore.

"You ok?" Malcolm asked Daddy

"Yea, I'm ok. Derrick?" He said

"Yea"

Daddy adjusted in his seat. "You're spinning your wheels for no reason son. I know it may seem exciting to you right now, but there's a price to pay for acting like that. Look at your parents. You wanna be as old as them and sitting here confused about life?"

"Hey Daddy!" I said

"Am I lying?" He asked

"No, but that was mean. I'm sitting right here." I said feeling embarrassed.

"Treat your woman the way you'd want someone to treat your mother or even your daughter." Then Daddy grabbed his arm.

My heart dropped. "DADDY!"

Malcolm was frozen; it looked like he stopped breathing.

"Somebody call 911!!!!" Darryl yelled

"DADDY! WHAT'S WRONG?" Daddy was gasping for air.

The hostess guy came running over. "Sir! Sir are you ok? Can you respond?"

Daddy sounded winded, "My chest!" Daddy said still holding his arm.

"Sir, the paramedics are on their way!"

"Ok! Ok!" Daddy said like he was trying to calm himself. Daddy looked at me with tears in his hazel eyes. "I love you!"

I couldn't stop crying. Daddy slumped into Malcolm. "DON'T JUST SIT THERE DO SOMETHING!! HELP ME!!!!" I screamed at Malcolm

Malcolm tried to snap out of his trance. We could hear the ambulance approaching. Malcolm picked Daddy up and carried him out to the paramedics. I grabbed my purse, I threw my keys to Darryl, then I got in the ambulance with Daddy. They were checking his vitals, and they gave him a shot of something. Daddy's eyes opened, and they asked him what medicines he was taking. I grabbed Daddy's hand. "Daddy don't leave me! Please Daddy!"

"I'm right here baby girl." Daddy could barely say.

When we got to the hospital, they rushed Daddy to the back. They shoved a bunch of papers at me. Malcolm and the boys walked in a few minutes later. Derrick told me he called Timothy, Jade, and Malachi. I pulled my cellphone out and I called Uncle Jeff in tears. He said he was on his way. I called Uncle Frank, I could hear him yelling as he hung up the phone. Jade hurried in the door with the baby in her arms and little Sonny and Emerald in tow. She gave the baby to Darryl, and then she started drilling me with questions. They think it's a heart attack I don't know yet, I told her as she kept hammering me with questions. I wondered if she was the lawyer or Sonny. Grace came running in the door, LT was still in his baseball uniform and cleats, and Tina was there. Grace started in on her questions just like Jade. I told her the same things I told Jade, I don't know. Every person who came through the doors asked me the same questions. When we could finally go to the back, they told us there were too many people and that only two people could go to the back with Daddy and the doctor. Uncle Frank told them everybody was going and he told them to put Daddy in a Private room so we could go. The hospital staff jumped to Uncle Frank's command and lightning fast, Daddy was in a huge private room. The doctor explained to our crowd that Daddy had clogged arteries and he was going to need surgery immediately, they had a surgeon in route to Daddy but he wouldn't arrive until the morning. There were so many questions we had to raise our hands like we were in school. In the end, just about everybody was camping out. The four of us and Malcolm stayed in the room. When Malcolm tried to go in the waiting room with everybody else, Daddy frowned and then Malachi and Timothy made him come back. "I know you guys want to spend time with your father." Malcolm said

"He's just as much your father as he is mine!" Malachi said and both of them cried and hugged each other.

Daddy told the girls to "cut it out," which made them laugh.

Jade and I sat on Daddy's bed telling him how much we loved him, and how when he came home we were changing his diet. Jade showed him the list of things that were changing and she said she had just started the list. Daddy rolled his eyes and said she was trying to make his life as boring as possible. Then he said it should be Uncle Frank in that bed, instead of him. He said Uncle Frank got that big ole belly. Then Andrew came in the room, he had a ton of questions since he wasn't there earlier when the doctor was talking to us. His hand was swollen a little, I looked at his face. He had that same beastly look his father would have sometimes when things had to be taken care of. Malcolm jumped to his feet; he asked Andrew if he was ok. Andrew nodded then he hugged Daddy and went out in the waiting room with the rest of the family. Daddy asked for a moment alone with each of us. We left Timothy in the room with him. They were talking for a long time. Then Malachi went in and they were in there equally as long. Jade went in, and I told Malcolm he had to go next. His face looked panicked and he asked me why, I told him I wasn't ready. Malcolm took a deep breath and went in when Jade came out, we hugged for a long time crying. When Malcolm finally came out, his eyes were red, and he grabbed me and put me in a bear hug. He kissed my cheek, and then I went in the room. I asked Daddy why all the dramatics when he was gonna be ok. He said the scene earlier in the day was scary and all he could think about was all the things he wanted to say to us. He said he was getting tired, but he needed to talk to his baby girl. He told me to remember to give my boys credit for being good kids. Then he told me to stop acting like I was unworthy of anyone. He said he wasn't telling me to be with Malcolm, but he was entrusting my safety to him. Daddy told me not to get back with him unless it was because he met my terms. He said Jade and I act so much like Momma that it was like she never left. He apologized for being so busy when I was growing up. I kissed his hand and I told him he didn't need to apologize for anything. I told him he was coming home because we needed him. I told him no one could put me in my place like he did. He smiled and said that was because I was just like Momma. That made me so happy. He told me to make sure Malachi married Denise and stopped stringing her a long. Then he told me he wouldn't be mad if I married Malcolm, but if? And I repeated what he said earlier. He said I had to put my foot down with him; he would respect me more that way. I asked Daddy if it made me weak if I chose to still want Malcolm. He said it didn't but I needed to make sure of it. I said that it was on my terms. I told Daddy I wasn't ready to forgive him yet. Daddy told me to take my time. Then he got sleepy. I told everyone they could come back into the room. Then I climbed on the bed and laid my head on his chest. Daddy put his arms around me. I kissed him goodnight, I told him to have sweet dreams. He smiled and thanked me. Everyone found their spots and one by one, we all fell asleep to the sound of Daddy's heart monitor. I woke up to Daddy calling for Momma. He kept saying, "Annette! Annette!" Then his heart stopped. Jade started screaming, nurses and doctors rushed in trying to revive Daddy. They pushed us out of the room, Jade was hysterical. Malcolm caught her as her body went limp. Sonny came rushing down the hallway. Family came out the waiting room. They would get a heartbeat on Daddy and then it would stop. They tried for a long time, a nurse convinced us to go back in the waiting room. When the doctor walked in the room, we already knew. I buried my head in Malachi's chest, this could not be happening. All you could hear in that waiting room was crying and sobbing. Looking at Jade I could tell she clocked out. My skin felt like it was on fire, I felt like a wild animal. Then I went to my boys who were all crying and we sat there hugging. Some family members went back in the room to say goodbye. But my thing was he was already gone. But I guess in moments like that it was about whatever gave you closure.

At the funeral, Malcolm and the boys wore shades. I sat between Malcolm and Andrew. Jade was a mess, but so was Malachi. Timothy was hurting and I know I was hurting as well. But I had to push my pain to the side to take care of the baby while Sonny tended to his wife. I looked down at his little sweet face; he had no idea what was going on. He held on to me for dear life. I zoned everybody out and I played with and cared for my nephew. Aunties, Uncles, and cousins came and shed tears with me. They offered their condolences, as Daddy's passing was so unexpected. I felt so empty when Jade came to get the baby. She thanked me for keeping him, but she was going home. Timothy and Grace went home, Malachi and Denise came over. The boys and Malcolm came over too. I leaned on one side of

Malachi and Denise leaned on the other. We were all quiet then Malachi said, "Denise?"

She sat up wiping tears from her eyes. "Yes baby, what do you need?" she said holding his hand.

"I need a family of my own." He said while tears dropped from his eyes.

"Ok baby" she said like she thought the pain was talking.

Six months later, they were married in Hawaii, in a beautiful ceremony on the beach. Malachi had all of his siblings including Malcolm in his wedding. The whole thing was beautiful. Malcolm kept shooting me longing looks, but I couldn't focus on him right now I was running from the pain.

****

"Why do you want to live in Albany?" I asked walking around the condo styled apartment.

"It's closer to work, and I'm done with Toya! I want a fresh start!"

"Should I ask?"

Andrew ignored my question out of irritation. "Things have been going really well at work. I wanted to stay close to you, but get closer than Oakland to work."

"That's good, I'm happy for you." Then I swallowed. "What's this that I hear about you declining to be Hubby's best man?"

Andrew sat on the couch and exhaled. "I already apologized to him for flipping out. I'm just jealous!"

"Why?"

"He has love, I want love. Toya broke up with me and I didn't see it coming. I understood Uncle Mali, in moments like that you need to have the person you love and who loves you at your side. I know Toya doesn't know how to be there for anyone like that but I didn't expect her to break up with me when she did."

"Probably because she thought she had a bigger fish on the line." I said

Andrew nodded, "I got money, and you know I got money. I just never felt comfortable letting her know I had it. As soon as someone comes around who she thinks has more, she's gone. I'm tired of playing this game."

"What happens when she finds out where you work?"

"I'll play it down as much as I can, but I'm cool off her right now."

"So you will be at the Engagement party tonight?"

Andrew huffed. "I'm going, but I'm not promising a good time."

"You better be on your best behavior or I will take you over my knee!" I said.

That night I saw my baby perk up, he was talking to a girl. I asked Ms. Connie who this girl was, she didn't know her. Because of the conversation Andy and I had earlier, I didn't want to see my baby get hurt. The way he was hovering around this girl was making me nervous. She didn't look like trouble, you can't always tell by looking at a person. Sonya called herself liking my baby before and Andrew wasn't having it. I found Nicole coming from the bathroom. She was all giggly and beaming with happiness.

"Congratulations again sweetheart!" I said giving her a hug.

"Thank you Ms. Amber."

"It's just Amber to you." She smiled. "Tell me something," I turned her to face Andrew. "Who's the girl my baby seems to be taken with?"

Nicole got excited, she started jumping around and clapping her hands. "That's my friend Tracy. Don't worry she's nothing like Toya. I wish I would've thought of them before. THIS COULD BE PERFECT!" She said too excited. I looked back at my baby's smile; I hope she's right.

Chapter 49

I didn't want to get up this morning, Last night I dreamed that I was updating Momma and Daddy on everything that was going on. When I realized I was dreaming, I fought to stay asleep, I didn't want to wake up. Waking up meant that the reality of life as the orphan Amber was real. I sat up and looked around my room. Dried flowers from a dead relationship, a bed that sometimes smelled like Malcolm to me. I loved the house that Nana bought for me, but I needed a change. I stripped my bed down to nothing. I put the comforter and sheets in the washer and dryer then I put them in garbage bags. Darryl was spending the weekend with Derrick so I left his room untouched. I bagged up all my comforters, and just about everything that could be moved. I called Timothy and asked if he and LT could come and help me take some stuff to the Goodwill. Timothy asked me if I was ok, I was pretty much taking everything out of the house. I told Timothy I needed a fresh canvas. When we took everything to the Goodwill I said goodbye to the table that I sat at with David; the couch I had sex with Malcolm on; the bed I had sex with Malcolm and Dwayne in; Darryl's old bedroom furniture, rugs, curtains, lamps, end tables, etc., it all went in the truck. The house was empty like I moved out. I thanked Timothy and LT by taking them to Bob's.

I sat in the middle of the floor with the yellow pages. I flipped and flipped through the pages. I exhaled because I didn't know what I was looking for. I touched the carpet. It had to go; flashbacks of everything kept running through my mind. David knocking me down on this carpet, Malcolm laying me down on this carpet, the boys wrestling and fighting each other on this carpet, Momma and Daddy sitting on the couch while I vacuumed this carpet. Darryl came in the door he was about to run up the stairs when he stopped in his tracks, cursed, and then looked at me sitting on the floor. He reached to the back of his waistline, "momma we've been robbed!" He said in disbelief, I laughed and assured him that was not the case. I told him to stop reaching for his gun and to calm down. I gave everything to Goodwill. He sat on the floor in front of me. He asked me if I was ok, I said yes, as my eyes danced around the room. Darryl made me look at him as he inspected me to make sure. "Why did you get rid of everything?" He asked

"I need a fresh canvas. I need to change everything. I don't know where to go first." I said

"Are you upset because Auntie Jade moved to San Ramon? I thought you might have a reaction to that."

"She had to do what she had to do." I said although as soon as they packed up I missed them. I was at their house every weekend and at the school with Jade as much as I could be. Even though Hubby bought their house in preparation for his new life, it doesn't even seem the same when I drive by it.

"What's going on then?"

I exhaled slowly and deeply. "I feel like everything is closing in on me. I need to change this house. There's too many memories attached to everything. I wanna get the house remodeled; your room is the only room I didn't touch."

Darryl's eyes looked worried. "Ok momma whatever you need. I can pay for something if you need me to."

I smiled, "money I got, thank you for offering baby. Daddy left you that money for you. But we might need to move out for a minute until the house is ready. I'm sitting here trying to figure out where to start."

"Why are you in the phone book?" Then he exhaled. "Did you get rid of the computer too?"

I laughed. "No, but I got rid of the desk. Guess I went a little crazy huh."
Darryl exhaled like he didn't get it. "You? Crazy? Never!" He said sarcastically as he went up stairs. "MOMMA! YOUR BED THOUGH? WHERE YOU SUPPOSED TO SLEEP?" Darryl yelled down the stairs.
"Floor or hotel doesn't matter." I said exhaling. I picked up my phone to call Kimmy. Then Andrew walked in the door, he paused as he saw me sitting in the middle of the floor. "Don't worry I took everything out!"
Andrew relaxed some, but he was visibly upset. He leaned against the wall looking defeated; I waited for him to spill it. "You ever feel like no matter how hard you try to do right it doesn't work?"
"All the time." I said
"She's a good girl, she don't know anything about life like we know it. I feel like I would be making her dirty by continuing."
"Like she's too good for you?" I asked
"Yea." He exhaled
"Who's too good for you Andy? Don't forget, you're a prince! You deserve someone worthy of being a queen. Did she say or do something to make you feel unworthy?"
"No" he exhaled. "I try to tell myself that. Last week we ran into Toya at the movies."
"Please tell me Toya didn't cause a scene!" I said as my blood started to boil.
"No, but she's been on my phone ever since."
"Andy! Toya's evil! Anyone is better than her." I whined
"I know momma but I don't want to hurt Tracy. She doesn't deserve to hang on while I get what I thought was out of my system out. I can't do this to her momma."
I exhaled. "It's your life sweetheart, but I was hoping you found some peace in your life. Toya doesn't bring peace."
"I know, but I find myself waiting for the other shoe to drop with Tracy. She's real chill, and laid back, no stress; she's got a cool job. She doesn't ask for much but it feels too good to be true." He smiled, "can I tell you something personal?"
"I'm scared, don't gross me out!" I said looking at him wide eyed.
Andrew laughed. "We haven't slept together yet." I looked at him surprised. "I KNOW! I'm like this has never happened to me before." Then he smiled through a frown. "It feels good though."
"How do you know she's not a man, that could be your other shoe!" I said
He evil grinned. "We've done other stuff; she's not letting me in yet." He stood up straight. "Makes me all warm and giddy, I don't like it!" He said with a smile.
"So why are we talking about Toya? She had her chance, she lost. Step into the light."
Andrew exhaled. "I know you're right, but I'm not ready."
"Is this gonna affect the wedding? I don't think Hubby would appreciate drama at his wedding."
"I think I can talk to her. I just don't want her to hate me."
"I understand." I said feeling defeated myself.
"So why is everything gone?"
"I want to remodel I decided just a few minutes ago." I said
Then Darryl came downstairs. "Drew, man your momma is tripping! She got rid of her bed." Darryl said
Andrew frowned at me. "You didn't think that through did you?"
"I started moving and stuff started happening."
"Where are you gonna sleep?"

"Blow up bed or hotel. Depends on what I feel like tonight."

"Or you could come stay with me." He said

"Naw you got your own life over there. Besides if Toya happens to show up there's no telling what I might do."

"You coming home tonight?" He asked Darryl

"Naw, I'm hanging with D-Rick tonight. I'll be back on...." Then he looked at me.

"Momma! How are we supposed to have dinner on Sunday without a table? Chairs?" He threw his hands in the air.

"Calm down! We can just go to Sophia's. It's not a big deal! Why are you over reacting?" I asked Darryl

"Everything is changing, you acting like you want me to leave!"

"How am I acting like that?"

"You're changing the house. Fixing it up to be your bachelorette pad! Can I graduate before you make me leave?"

"Whoa! Whoa! I never said all of that. You haven't even shared where you're going to school yet." I said, "and I didn't touch your room! If I was gonna make this a bachelorette pad why would that matter to you? What am I missing?"

Andrew put his hands in his pockets, "Slow down and use your words. She's about to snap," He warned him.

Darryl sat on the bottom stair. "I want to go to Berkeley, I don't want to move out and leave you all by yourself. Then I come home and everything is gone. Are you trying to leave? You wanna move away to get away from Malcolm or something? You and Tag gonna sneak off and get married?"

Andrew looked at me like Darryl asked good questions. "Please don't choose Berkeley because you wanna settle for me. I want you to go where you wanna go. I'm gonna be ok. If you decide to go to Berkeley, or wherever you don't have to move out. You're my baby baby; you're always welcomed no matter where I am. There were too many memories attached to all that stuff I had to get rid of it."

"Even the computer desk?" He asked, Andrew started laughing.

"I may have gone a little over board with that but too much has happened, I keep seeing people who aren't here anymore. I need a clean slate." Then I frowned, "running away to marry Tag? Seriously?"

"You and Tag do look cozy sometimes, I wonder myself." Andrew said

I frowned. "Daddy would turn over in his grave! He's never liked him."

"But you like him." Darryl said

"We're just friends! And I don't mean friends like those friends you be running around with."

"Yea right! But I'm not ready to leave yet. I hope that's ok." Darryl said

"Of course it's ok." I said

"So you bunking with me tonight?" Andrew said rubbing his hands together.

"Not tonight, but how about tomorrow night?" I said

"Why not tonight?"

"Because I'm going out." I said

"With who? Where?" Andrew asked

"Boy! I'm grown!" I said putting my hands on my hips.

Andrew cut his eyes at me. "You going on a date?"

"Get out of my business!" I said

"Un huh! Don't make me put my eye on you." He said pointing and squinting his eyes at me.

"You must wanna get hit! As long as you still messing with Toya, you can't say anything to me!"
Andrew opened his mouth to pretend like I offended him, "Toya is a respectable..." We all started cracking up. "Let me fix that."
"Toya is a freak! You a got a thing for freaks that's all!" Darryl said like he understood.
"Whatever! You do realize I'm standing here." I said
"Ok that's my queue. I'm out!" Darryl said. He hugged me, gave Andrew a pound then he left.
I called Kimmy and asked for Shasta's number. I asked Shasta if she had any partners in Northern California near me. She asked for details about the project. She said business had been slow and she wouldn't mind flying out to get a good feel for the project. We made a date for her to come out Monday. I called Kimmy back and we chatted for a while. She said she'd come out as well; Andrew smiled real big at me in the background when he heard it. When she and I got off of the phone, Andrew said she was coming for Joseph. I frowned at him.
****
I liked this restaurant, it had live music, the drippy candles, and dim lighting made the place very romantic. I was bopping to the music, enjoying my Irish dessert coffee. "Do you want to go dancing or are you done for the evening?" He asked "There's a place in the city..."
I cut him off. "Nope! Not going to the city!"
He frowned. "What's wrong with the city?"
"I don't go to the city as much as I can avoid it but you know we can just call it a night, this was fun." I said taking another swig of my coffee.
Gary seemed like a nice enough guy. Nothing fancy about him; average working Joe. We had been on a few dates, each time was nice enough to accept his next invitation, but I didn't see this going anywhere.
"It's kind of early to be knocking off, you want to come back to my place?"
I kind of frowned at him. "I don't know about that."
He smiled, "I'm a good puppy I don't bite unless you want me to." He raised his eyebrows. I looked at the man behind him to the left. He looked down at his dessert before my eyes met his.
If I didn't know that Malcolm still had men on me, I would've told him no. I don't know him like that but this guy definitely worked for Malcolm no matter how calm and relaxed he tried to appear to be. "I don't want to give you the wrong idea, by accepting your invitation."
"What would that be?"
"You're not getting any booty just because I come to your house."
He smiled a sneaky smile. "That's fine, we can watch a movie or something."
I rolled my eyes. He's going to try something, I can feel it, I'm trying to give him the benefit of a doubt. He paid the check and then we left. In the car, he couldn't stop smiling, everything he said, he said with a smile. He was too excited about me coming back to his place, "Can you take me to get my car?" I had him meet me at the grocery store a couple blocks from the hospital. Since I had nothing to go off, I didn't want him knowing where I lived in case he was a stalker.
"My apartment is right here. I promise I'll take you to your car as soon as the movie is over." He said turning into a drive way and pulling behind a four unit apartment building.

I huffed cause I didn't like being without my car. He opened my door still cheesing from ear to ear. We walked over loose gravel under his umbrella to the front. He was in the unit downstairs on the right. He opened the door to his place all proud. He had a big screen TV with bookshelves on either side full of movies and video games. His couches were too big for his space. It was too much crammed into a small place. But I gave a courtesy smile because he seemed so proud. He told me to have a seat while he put the wet umbrella in the tub. When he opened his bedroom door, I heard little feet, then I saw a fluffy white cat. That explained all the white hairs all over the black couch. A man with a cat? First one on me, he came out of the room in sweats and no shirt. I looked at him as if he had to be kidding. He said he wanted to get comfortable to watch the movie. Putting a few muscles on a bird chest does not make you sexy! Darryl had a better body than Gary when he was five, but Gary was proud. And honestly who am I to judge maybe someone pumped him up making him believe it was ok to stand before me like this. Then he went down his list of movies, I wanted to see a comedy, then he looked at me and said he had the perfect movie for me. I was curious to see what he thought was perfect for me, he puts on a movie, but he wouldn't let me see the cover. He sat on the couch kind of close but not too close. He reached under his coffee table after the movie started. "Do you smoke?" He said opening his box

"No" I said looking at his blunt. "And you're gonna have to drive me to my car in the rain, please don't smoke that until I've gotten my car."

He looked disappointed. "What if you spend the night, I'll let you have the bed?" He said lighting up.

"I don't want to spend the night." I said

He took two drags. "For real, my bad! You might as well hit this and get on my level."

I was getting angry. "No thank you."

"You've never smoked before?" He said blowing rings at me.

"I have, but if I was going to, there's only one person I would do that with. I don't know where you buy from and I didn't see you roll that, anything could be in there." I huffed, "guess I'm calling a cab."

"Or I can take you to your car in the morning." He said taking another puff.

"I'm NOT spending the night over here." I said irritated

"Ok! Ok!" He said turning his attention back to the movie. You remind me of her. "He said pointing to Nia Long.

I rolled my eyes and looked at him. "I know you're not talking about appearance wise cause we look nothing a like."

"She's sexy; you don't see yourself as sexy?"

"I don't have a question about who or what I am. I'm just trying to understand you." His face was all droopy because he was high. He looked semi mentally challenged. "I'm just saying you so sexy!" Then he licked his lips. "Can I have a kiss?"

My stomach turned. "You know what Gary, I'm gonna go!" I stood up. "Thank you for dinner, have a good life."

"What? Why? What's wrong?" He said standing up

"I'm gonna go." I said

Then he smiled. "You need me to drive you, and I'm not ready to go yet."

"No, I got a ride." I said walking to the door.

"Oh come on!" He said following me.

"Gary, I'm gonna walk out of this door. It's not safe for you to follow me." I warned He twisted his face. "What? Why?"

"Just don't or it's your funeral."

He grabbed my wrist, I HATE WHEN GUYS DO THAT! "Hold on, come back and finish the movie. I'll take you home."

I tried to control my temper, "Gary if you don't let me go!" I said jerking my hand back.

I opened the door and it was pouring outside. Gary smiled, "come on back." I stepped out on the porch. Gary ran and got his umbrella, while I went down the three steps in front of his door. My hair was getting wet but I didn't care, I was looking for the car, I didn't see it. Gary came out barefoot with the umbrella.

"Amber! You're messing with my high, stop playing and come back inside!" He demanded. Then he grabbed my jacket, "I can't believe you got me out here in the rain!"

"Let go of me!" I said hitting his hand away. Then I saw it, the bull's-eye on his chest. I pointed at it, "I told you to stay in the house." I said with a smile.

Gary's eyes got big as we saw the red dot on his chest. "Oh shoot! What is that?" He said trying to flick the light off his chest.

"Go inside Gary!" I said

"What are you CIA? You trying to get a nigga killed out here!"

"And you're still talking! Go on! Get! Unless you wanna die." I bucked my eyes at him.

He ran up the stairs, "You are CRAZY! I hope you melt out here!" Then he ran inside.

Headlights came on and a black car pulled up slowly. It slowed down by the curb and I got in the back. I didn't recognize the guy driving, but it didn't matter. I sat in silence as he called in, "we're in route." The driver blasted the heater and I was grateful because I was wet and freezing. We drove up the skyline hill, and he pulled into Malcolm's driveway. Malcolm came out with an umbrella; he looked like he was relaxing at home. When we got in the door he gave me a towel for my hair, I tied it around my head. The fireplace was going; it looked like it had been on a while. There was a book and a drink next to a chair, and soft music playing on his system. "Were you expecting someone?"

"No, I was just reading." Then he looked me in my eyes. "Are you ok?"

"Yea, I'm fine. Just another loser." I said as I shivered.

"You wanna put your clothes in the dryer?" He asked

"It's just my shirt; this jacket will dry as it hangs." I said putting my jacket on the coat rack.

"Ok, come on." He said signaling me to follow him. I took off my shoes and left them by the door.

As we walked up the stairs, he still had the big picture of me up there. "Why do you still have this up?"

"Is there a reason why I should take it down?" He asked not looking back at me. "Whatever it's your house." I said

He changed his bedroom furniture; I liked it a lot better this way any ways. He opened the double doors to his closet and turned on the light. We walked in and he pointed to the side where his T-shirts were. "Take whatever you need." Then he walked out. I grabbed a navy blue shirt that came to my mid-thigh and took off my soaking wet bra and blouse. I folded them rewrapped the towel around my hair, and then I looked around his closet. Everything was organized according to color and type. Suits up top a variety of colors. Slacks below a variety of colors. Dress shirts top and bottom on the next rack according to color. The other side of the closet was more casual clothes but the same organization. Everything had its place, "this man has issues," I whispered to myself. Nothing in his room was the way I remembered it from that night, which was nice to see. On either nightstand, there were pictures of me they were old pictures from when I was a teenager. Although they were framed, they looked old and a little worn. Since he wasn't in the room, I looked around upstairs. I went in the room next to his, which was obviously his office. Wall to wall bookshelves that held all kinds of books. His desk was in the middle of the floor; it held his computer and pictures of he and I, and a picture of the boys. I touched the biggest picture, which was of he and I. He had his arms around me, we were kissing, both of our eyes closed. The only time mark I could put on the picture was that my hair was straight, so it was taken at some point when I had a perm. The next room had our old bed, but it had no covers on it or anything. It looked like he put it in there because he didn't want to throw it away, but it was cold and non-inviting. The next room was his TV room, average sized TV, a couple of recliners and a couch. There were framed pictures all over the wall. Most of them starring yours truly but he had pictures of Momma, Daddy, Leonard, Tiffany, Penny, the boys, Troy, Poppa & Nana, etc. Oh no! The tingles were washing over me; I went back in his room and took off my pants. I grabbed my clothes and I went down the stairs. The laundry room was to the left of the bottom of the stairs just before the garage. "Is it ok if I put my stuff in the washer too?" I called out.

"That's fine," he said

I put the towel in with my clothes and started the washer. I took a deep breath then I walked around the corner. Malcolm was back in his chair sipping on his drink and reading his book. "You want something to drink?" He asked without looking at me.

"Sure, I was drinking dark earlier." I said walking towards his bar.

"I meant...." He watched me walk, "juice, or something."

I picked up the prettiest bottle of brown liquor; he had simple round glasses. I poured a good amount of liquor in the glass. Then I put the bottle back. As I walked towards him, his eyes danced all over me. I could see the question in his eyes, but he was debating with himself whether to ask. "That's some shrine you got up there." I said smiling at him, he put his eyes back in his book but his breathing changed; he was trying to control it. "This is what you do on a Saturday night?"

"Lately" he said not taking his eyes off the book.

"Why?" I said taking a taste of my drink; it was velvety smooth, and delicious. "This is really good!" I said taking another taste.

"Be careful! It'll bite you in the end." His eyes still stuck to the book.

I looked around, I didn't want to sit there and watch him read. "Is it ok if I watch TV?"

"You don't have to ask. You're not a guest here."

"I'm not?"

"What's mine is yours." He said as if I should know.

"Ok!" I said standing up. His eyes danced all over me again then he turned around in his chair to watch me walk upstairs. I debated whether to go in his room or the TV room. I decided to go in his room. I grabbed the remotes off his nightstand; I got cozy under his covers with my drink in hand. I flipped through the channels; nothing was on so I settled on the cooking channel, after a while Malcolm came in the room.

"What are you watching?"

"Cooking channel." He didn't exactly seem his normal self, "What's wrong?"

He sat on the edge of the bed by my feet; he took a deep breath. "I know I'm partly to blame, but this" he gestured towards the bed and me. "Isn't cool."
I sat up, "you want me to leave?"
He shook his head and put his hand out towards me. "That's not what I'm saying." I relaxed, "what are you doing? Why are you dating? I'm right here!"
"You still date too." I said defensively.
"Only to pass the time, I'm waiting on you."
"Yea right!" I said rolling my eyes. Then I looked at the pictures on his nightstand. "Why aren't these as crisp as all the others."
"They're the ones I had while I was in jail." He said
"You still have them? Wow!" Then I looked at him sitting there. "I'm not ready Malcolm, I'm still mad at you!"
"How many years later?" He said
"Doesn't matter! It still hurts like it was seconds ago."
"So then why are you in my bed?"
"Seeing your reaction to me always turns me on, all of this," I said pointing at the pictures.
"It would break my heart to touch you right now." He said sounding defeated. "You were just out with some idiot, you come in smelling like many clouds of smoke. You're ready to go, we haven't spoken or anything. I get what you're saying, but it's not clicking for me tonight."
"Why did you bring me here then?"
"Every time I see you we gotta have sex?"
"No"
"Okay then, I wanted to finish my chapter and then spend time with you but you come down stairs just about naked, and so I had to read a few more chapters."
"Fine Malcolm!" I said frustrated.
He got up and went to his closet. He stripped down to silk boxers, and then came back in the room. "Oh no! Who's messing with who right now? Go put on some long johns or something! You can't come to bed like that and expect me to be controlled!"
He stood in the doorway. "How about a compromise? I'll take off the boxers if you take off the shirt. Deal?"
"DEAL!" I said real happy.

Chapter 50

"I have an announcement to make!" Sophia said, everyone stopped talking and looked at her. "It's with a heavy heart that I'm going to close this location."

"Why?" Auntie Lauren asked

"It's getting to be a bit much to manage both locations. I want to have more time for Sabrina; Walnut Creek is closer to home, etc. etc."

"That's what you hire people for." Joseph said.

"We can do Sunday dinners there, if that will make it easier on everybody else. Jade I know that's closer for you."

"But further for us." Malachi said

"Malachi you know it's fine, don't do that." Denise said while rubbing her pregnant belly.

"Or we could go somewhere else. I'm just saying that Sophia's in Piedmont is closing." Sophia said getting fed up.

I personally didn't think it was a good idea but I think this is her way of dealing with her breakup. Although Travis couldn't prove anything, he knew something was up with her. He kept trying to work it out with her, but her attention was so focused on Richard that she couldn't get it together. It was better that Travis thought they grew apart than he found out about Richard. It would've broken his heart, and regardless of anything else, Travis was a good man and he didn't deserve this. Sophia felt horrible, but she couldn't get Richard out of her system. Then Sasha finding a job out there didn't help. Richard asked Sophia to move out there to be with him, but she declined. When he asked her I held my breath, it was right after Daddy died and I think I would've lost it. I needed her close by at the time. Not that I'm much better today, but I think I could handle it a little more now rather than then.

Everyone was conversing when Andrew walked in with Toya. It was like the whole room stopped and looked at him like, "no he didn't!" First of all, he was LATE and second, her hair was pulled into a ponytail, I was on guard. "I'm sorry I'm late, some people take forever to get ready." Andrew said putting her on blast. She gave him an irritated glare. Andrew didn't care; he brought her to my table and sat her across from me. Now why did he do that, is all I could think? He came around the table and gave me a kiss on the cheek, "hi momma, I'm sorry I'm late."

I didn't say anything I just looked at Toya. "Ms. Amber I apologize for making Drew late. I just couldn't decide on what to wear." She said taking off her jacket and revealing a short form fitting dress.

"And that's what you chose?" I said disapprovingly.

Caught off guard by my response she looked at Andrew. "We're going to EA later; I didn't wanna do another wardrobe change later." Andrew said

"You should've left her at home." I said

Malcolm came back to our table. He sat down next to me. "Drew."

"Malcolm" Andrew said rolling his eyes and looking towards Sophia.

"Hello Malcolm" Toya said

Malcolm looked at her for a minute. "Toya".

She swallowed hard. "I hear you got new equipment at the studio, congrats." She said with a fake smile.

"Oh yea? Who told you that?" Malcolm asked giving her serious eyes.

"Just a friend." She said getting nervous.

"Who?" Malcolm said

She swallowed real hard. "My friend Desmond. He's been working on his demo in your studio."

"Ok, well you tell your friend to find another studio. Any friend of yours is not welcomed." Malcolm said nonchalantly.

Toya's mouth fell open. Darryl started laughing. Malcolm looked at him and he straightened up. "Malcolm please! Don't take away his opportunity on account of me." Toya said

"He should be more selective about the company he keeps. I keep telling my son the same thing, hopefully Desmond will understand through this lesson." Malcolm took a swallow of his water. "It's a shame too. Desmond has real talent."

Toya was mad; she looked at Andrew hoping he would say something but he didn't seem to care, sitting her in front of me was definitely a set up, and she just caught on. "You mean like Torrie!" Toya said

Andrew looked at her like she was crazy.

Darryl jumped out of his seat like he was coming for her but Malcolm grabbed his arm and had to seriously convince him to sit down. "What do you know about Torrie?" Malcolm asked

"I remember when she was hanging around. Then one day she was gone. Now she looks all rough and tired. Did you do that to her face? She gotta wear a ton of makeup just to look as rough as she does these days." Toya said proud of herself.

"Actually I didn't do that to her face, but I can make arrangements for yours." Malcolm said glaring at her. "Son you need to cut that one loose!"

"The last person I'll take relationship advice from is you. What would you know?" Andrew said glaring at Malcolm

Toya looked at me. "I'm sorry if you didn't know about him and Torrie." She said almost smiling.

I looked at my son. "Andrew! You must want me to hurt her!"

"Sorry momma," Andrew said standing up and signaling Toya to stand up.

She looked at me. "Aren't you too old to be fighting?" She said with a smirk.

I don't even remember getting out of my seat. I just felt the pleasure of my fist connecting with her chin. I was trying to break it I hit her so hard. Toya went down like a sack of potatoes. "You tell me!" I was about to get on her but Andrew put his arm around me. My baby's touch pulled me out of my rage. Everybody else looked at my table, but no one had a real reaction to Toya trying to get up.

"Why you guys always picking on me? I'm not gonna fight my man's mother." She said sounding like she was slurring her words.

"Toya just leave! You didn't want to be here anyways. No matter how hard you try, we will not turn our backs on Drew because of you. You just come out looking dumb!" Darryl said,

I looked at Andrew and he grabbed me again. "Is that what this is about? You want my baby out there vulnerable and alone while you cause drama and mess!" I tried my best to get to her, but Andrew's hold on my waist was strong. "Andrew get her out of here before I kill her! She hasn't changed one bit!"

Toya got up and walked out of the restaurant holding her face. I looked at Malcolm and rolled my eyes. Just hearing that chick's name made me mad at him all over again. Malcolm looked angry too but I didn't care. Darryl looked at the change in our body language and he was out the door. Joseph looked out the window and took off. Darryl had his gun pulled on Toya. I ran outside. Andrew was standing by the driver's side of his new car with his hands in his pockets. Toya was standing by the passenger side door; she was trembling with fear. "D! I know you're upset, but think about the mess. Do you really wanna have to clean it up?" Joseph said

"Drew! I'm sick of her! She's a waste of air and space! Why would you let her upset our parents like that?" Darryl was livid

"I know man! I messed up!" Andrew said calmly. "I was trying to see if she really changed. I was wrong. Please forgive me." Andrew said calmly

"Darryl your mother and I are fine! What are you doing?" Malcolm said calmly

"I HATE HER!" Darryl yelled

"But you know I taught you better. Only pull your gun out when you're gonna use it. You're not gonna shoot her now, as stupid as she is, there will be a next time. Don't worry you can shoot her then." Malcolm said nonchalantly.

"You promise?" Darryl asked

"I promise that I will let you shoot her when the time is right. Let's go back inside, we're about to eat dessert and everything." Malcolm said

"Oh yea? What kind?" Darryl said still pointing the gun at Toya.

"There's a bunch of different cakes. I think I even saw Red Velvet!"

Darryl lowered his hand. "Did Sharon make it? I love her red velvet cake!" He put the safety back on, and put his gun back in his waist of the back of his pants.

"Alright Drew! I'm going to go eat some cake. See you later on tonight." Darryl tossed Andrew the peace sign and he went back inside with Joseph.

"Alright man!" Andrew said nonchalantly to Darryl

Toya stood there shaking and crying her eyes out. Malcolm and Andrew stood there staring each other down. Toya had pissed herself, so Sophia brought Andrew a bunch of paper towels for his car. No one said anything to or paid Toya any attention. She was here barely fifteen minutes and she caused a bunch of drama. When Andrew got in his car, Toya slowly got in, but she was still crying, as she should've been. It doesn't make any sense for her to be so troublesome. Out of my boys, Darryl is the only one who can turn off and on like that. I asked him if he was ok, and he gave me sad eyes. He hugged me and told me nobody could disrespect his momma and think he wouldn't do anything. I told him I did something about it, but he said it wasn't good enough. I told him I understood he was upset but he couldn't whip out his gun whenever he's angry. I told him that detective White told me that the family is under surveillance; all it would've taken was for someone to see him with his gun out. Then he said shooting Toya would've been worth it. I told him no idiot is worth losing my baby over.

****

The boys said they liked my remodeled house. Everything was brand new; Darryl even let me remodel his room. The entire house has hardwood floors, and marble tile in the entryway, kitchen, and all three bathrooms, except for the bathrooms, which had already been done, they pretty much gutted the house. I had crown molding, and I loved the new lighting. Track lighting made my house seem glamorous. I even had the outside of the house redone. I had my front and backyards redone, I even paid to have Mrs. Hall's and Connie's houses painted. Since the house looked so great, Shasta and I went with an antique look to make the house more classic looking. I loved it, and I smiled every time I came home. I felt more mature when I walked in my front door. My bedroom was trendier, but that was fine with me. Shasta did such a good job I had no problem paying her. Her attitude was one hundred percent better too. Uncle Frank loved my house, so I gave him her info. I asked him not to sleep with this one. He said he couldn't make any guarantees.

Love Is Just Enough

Darryl was all smiles; his day was finally here. The night before, Derrick and Andrew came over. We were having a good time laughing and carrying on then Derrick started crying in the middle of a belly laugh, and the next thing you know we're all crying. Andrew said something funny about Daddy; it's funny how laughter could turn into pain in the blink of an eye. Seeing Derrick cry was jarring because I wasn't expecting it. I was trying to chew back my pain, but it was contagious. Andrew and Derrick told Darryl stories about Momma, which made us all, cry more. Then we went down the list, Derrick stopped crying when Andrew brought up David. Derrick asked Andrew how he could still have love for that man knowing the truth about him. Andrew tried to explain it, but the best he could do was say that David was to him what Malcolm is to them. They didn't understand how, he told them they had to be there when he was there. Darryl said he just remembers him being mean and grabbing me all the time, Derrick remembered that too. Andrew was quiet, and then he said Malcolm got a chance to apologize for what he's done wrong, David wasn't given that chance. Derrick was getting angry; he told Andrew Malcolm's never hit me or seriously threatened their lives. Andrew said David said that because he was drunk. Derrick looked at Andrew in disbelief. Derrick told Andrew David is like Toya. He said Andrew knows they're toxic, and they mean him no good but he couldn't shake them for whatever reason. Andrew got angry to match Derrick's anger. Derrick told Andrew that the sooner he realized that Malcolm saved all of our lives the sooner he'd be able to let go of a lot of his ambiguity about life and start making good choices. He said Toya was going to get him killed or locked up. Darryl was the peacemaker; he got them to laugh in the middle of their anger. I couldn't say anything; it was too painful to speak on. Darryl was his goofy self until everyone was laughing and having a good time again. I think it made Darryl happy being able to defuse his brothers like that. He woke up bright and early making breakfast for everyone. It was weird going to Timothy's and Daddy wasn't there. I think it hit all four of us at the same time we were quiet for a minute. Darryl disappeared like his two brothers before him as we sectioned off seats. That girl from Andrew's club came over to Derrick all happy and excited to see him. At first, I didn't know why she looked familiar outside of singing at EA, until I remembered that she was the girl at his graduation party that he danced with. Derrick didn't bring her over to say hi both times so I figured that meant not to be concerned with her. Andrew was in the corner on his cellphone, most likely talking to Toya. Bernadette was on crutches so Andrew helped her up to her seat. Family filled up the section as my baby stood with complete pride in his stance. I was sitting next to Auntie Lorraine and Dionne, when Darryl walked past. Dionne stood up and she called out to David. Everybody looked at her; she stared at Darryl and wondered why he didn't respond to his name. Derrick came down to calm her, and she jumped when she saw him. "David! Honey how did you get here so fast? You were just down there!"

Derrick swallowed hard. "I'm super quick! Let's go talk about it in the hallway."

"Oh no honey let me take her." Auntie Lorraine said standing.

"No Auntie you go ahead and stay, I'll still see him cross the stage." Derrick said strongly.

Auntie Lorraine sat down, then she looked at me like "did he just tell me what to do?" I smiled at her and she had the biggest smile on her face. Then she told me I did a good job with my boys. That made me explode in tears but I just put my head down trying to pull myself together. Malcolm was watching from across the room, he winked at me and went back to the ceremony. Darryl wasn't the class valedictorian, but he was the runner up. He was so disappointed that he didn't get the title, but we all assured him it was just a title and it didn't matter. When they called Darryl Mason, the entire class stood up and cheered with us. Darryl danced across the stage blowing kisses to everybody. My baby was born a clown; we loved every minute of it. When the ceremony was over, Derrick and his friend rode with Auntie Lorraine and Dionne to Timothy's. Andrew and I waited for Darryl. Darryl emerged with a girl on his arm. "Momma this is Nellie, Nellie this is my momma." He said proudly.

Nellie's mouth fell open when she saw me. "You look like you could be his sister." She said in amazement. She looked like she was looking for scars from surgery or something. "It's nice to finally meet you."

"Finally?" I asked shaking her hand.

She looked at Darryl, "I see you've spent so much time talking about me."

Darryl looked at Andrew. Andrew jumped in, "it's nice to finally meet you, and I'm his big brother Drew." He said shaking her hand with both hands.

I looked at Darryl to say who she was; all of a sudden, this boy is shy? I looked at him in disbelief. He told her he would come to her graduation party tomorrow but he had to leave with me. Andrew could tell I was getting ready to invite her to the house. He distracted me by asking what was in my hair. Darryl said bye to the girl and sent her on her way. Both of them gave me a look, I told them not to pretend like they've been telling me about someone and think I'm gonna play along like it's true. The party was a lot of fun; whenever Andrew was distracted, Malcolm and I would sneak on the dance floor. Andrew accused us of acting like kids, that made it even more fun. Then Darryl came with a different girl. He introduced me to Kendra without any pretenses. She was a nice girl, and naturally, I liked her a lot better than Nellie. When it was time to walk to Bob's I didn't see Malcolm in the yard. When I went out front, Malcolm was talking to one of his workers. His demeanor was a little different with this guy than it normally is with his workers. It was like he was talking to one of the boys. When he saw me he waved me over, he wanted me to meet one of his most promising new hires. The guy was brown, cute, with dreads. "This is Yussef, Yussef this is Amber. Got her?" Malcolm said with a smile. "Hello." Yussef said with a serious tone as he took me in. "Got her." He said, Malcolm patted his shoulders and then he asked me if it was time for Bob's. I nodded then I excused us. Yussef watched us walk away. I told Malcolm he looked familiar, Malcolm shrugged, and said black kids with dreads will look familiar. Malcolm was in a good mood; he picked me up above his head. "Our baby graduated!" I laughed and told him to put me down. Bob was happy to see us. He told us he was going to retire next year. Malcolm thanked him for everything he's done for our family just in case we didn't see him before then. Bob told Malcolm to lock the door in the back after we left. Malcolm kept kissing me, he said it was like we were empty nesters and the world was our oyster. I smiled at him, but I didn't say anything. Yes, for the first time since I was fourteen I was free again, and young enough to enjoy being free. I just didn't know where Malcolm fit into that yet.

****

"I can't go." Malcolm said sounding disappointed.

"Why?" I said making sure; I had all my toiletries in my bag.

"Mitigated is expanding to the East Coast. I gotta go to LA to work on some of the forecasting." He said

"But tomorrow is Saturday; it has to be done this weekend?" I said moving around my room.

"I know, I thought I had everything together but the forecasting I have is a little sketchy, I want it all together before Monday. Juan has to come as well. Do you mind if Gloria joins you? Apparently they had plans this weekend as well and she is not happy about this sudden change."

"This is what I get for actually being excited about spending time with you! What am I supposed to do with Gloria in Monterey?" Malcolm exhaled. "Beautiful beach, romantic setting, open bar, Andrew distracted with the wedding. It was a win! Win! Win! Now I gotta explain to Ms. Connie why you're not there."

"Amber! I feel horrible I got to go. This is important for us; you'll thank me later." He said

"I bet you I won't! Whatever Malcolm, you disappointed me AGAIN!"

"A! Don't give me that, this is business! Stop acting like you don't understand! I feel bad enough!"

"Yes sir Mr. Latour sir! Anything you say sir!" I said like I was saluting him.

"We'll plan something when I get back." He said

"No thanks, I don't want to go anywhere with you." I said rolling my eyes.

"This is getting old Amber!"

"And so are you! Bye Malcolm! I gotta go!" Then I hung up on him.

I made sure I had everything I needed then I hurried to my car. I knew I only had so long before he showed up. Malcolm hates when I hang up on him, but so do I. I started to pull out of my driveway and a car blocked me in. Yea it was pretty dumb to think I'd get away that easy. The car slowly pulled away as Malcolm pulled in its place. Malcolm started to get out of his car when I decided to drive over my beautiful grass and off the curb. I didn't care if my yard got messed up, I'd fix it later. When I pulled in the street Malcolm looked mad, I blew him a kiss and stopped at the stop sign. He tapped my car with his. I looked in my rear view mirror at him like he lost his mind. I put my car in reversed and tapped his car back. I made a right and then as he was almost on my bumpers I hit a U-turn. My car screeched as I did it, stinking Malcolm was still right behind me as if he anticipated that move. I was going in the wrong direction I needed to get on the freeway. There was no way my car was going to out run his, and I knew he'd risk missing his flight just to follow me. I pulled over, threw the car in park, and hopped out the car.

"What's wrong with you?" I said getting out of the car.

Malcolm walked up to me and picked me up. "Don't hang up in my face!"

"You tapped my car because I hung up on you; what sense does that make?" I said kicking my legs.

"No I tapped your car because you need to calm your little happy go lucky butt down!"

"You calm down! I'm mad!"

"You think I'm not?" He said

"Put me down! All you need is for Andrew to drive past and see this!"

"Now you're threatening me with my own son!" He held me up higher. Then he started jerking me up and down.

"Stop! You're gonna make me sick!" When he put me down, I started slapping his hands. "You know I bruise easily!"

"Now give me a kiss and wish me well on my trip!" Malcolm said

I rolled my eyes. "I'm not kissing you! I'm hooking up with one of the groomsmen. See how the little boys do it!"

Malcolm squinted at me, "you play too much!"
"Whatever Malcolm! I ain't playing!" I said walking back to my car. He spun me around; pulled my hair to pull my head back and he kissed me long, deep, and hard. My knees buckled. I felt like he drugged me. I held on to him to keep from falling. "Now go have fun!" He said walking away from me and getting back in his car. I leaned against the car getting my bearings about myself. I looked at him sitting in his car satisfied with himself. I rolled my eyes and flipped him off as I got back in my car. Before I could put my car in drive, he tapped my car again, I screamed at him in my rear view mirror. Then he pulled next to me. "The house looks nice." He smiled then he drove off just before I crashed him like I was trying to.
When I got to the hotel the rehearsal, dinner was over and the groomsmen were at the bar. I hugged and kissed Hubby and Andrew and waved hello to the rest. I checked into my room, and then I went looking for Ms. Connie. She was giddy with excitement, her baby was getting married, and most importantly, she loved her daughter in-law. We chatted for a while, and then I went back to my room. As I was on my way, I see Andrew and Toya fussing downstairs. I shook my head; I don't know why he even brought her. I ordered room service in my room then I went to bed. In the morning, I had breakfast with Ms. Connie. Gloria showed up, and she and I exchanged irritation with those idiots. Gloria checked into her room and then the three of us went and got massages and facials. I felt so relaxed and calm; I definitely needed to keep that up. I put on my dress then I checked myself in the mirror. I took a picture of myself in the mirror showing off my curves, I sent it to Malcolm and I told him to check what he was missing. He texted me a sad face back right away. I met Gloria and Ms. Connie in the lobby then we rode to the ceremony site in Gloria's car. When we got there, Andrew looked relieved to see me with Gloria. I didn't tell him his dad stood me up. Gloria found seats in the front just behind the family. Toya came in with her hair half up and half down, I had no idea what that meant, but she looked very pretty. Pretty soon, the auditorium was packed and the people who couldn't find seats crowded around the back. I was happy somebody was getting their happily ever after. Hubby and Ms. Connie started the procession, they were both grinning from ear to ear. The flower girls were adorable. There goes that Sonya girl, she looked very pretty; the doors opened my mouth fell open, my baby looked very handsome in his tux, I couldn't be prouder but Tracy was stunning, did anyone tell her you're not supposed to up stage the bride? Andy looked so proud escorting her too. I saw Tracy's eye dart over to Toya who I'm sure should've just turned green with jealousy right there on the spot. Then Tracy's eyes darted to someone else, but I couldn't tell who. I was so busy staring at Tracy and Andrew that I missed the all rise part and I had to hurry to stand. Nicole looked beautiful; no, she was an exquisite bride. Hubby stood there with his chest all puffed out and proud. I know I should've been watching the bride and groom but I couldn't take my eyes off of Tracy. She seemed like she was trying not to be affected by my baby, and my baby didn't care who saw him digging her. I frowned because even though I didn't like Toya I didn't want him to put a bad taste in Tracy's mouth. I had to tell myself to stay out of it, which was hard. When Andy and Tracy walked out I looked at the both of them and I imagined the beautiful grand babies, that pulled me out of it. I had a lot more living to do before I was a Nana. Toya made a beeline over to some guy who you could tell thought he was too cool for school. When Toya saw me looking, she ended her conversation and hurried to her car. The guy looked me up and down as I walked past with Gloria. Gloria said these

little boys are bold. I told her he probably thinks I'm one of these little girls who would be impressed by something like that.

The reception was in a huge banquet hall back at the hotel. Everything was laid out beautifully. Gloria and I found our seats, and I watched Toya follow that guy around like a lovesick puppy. It made me mad and if we weren't at this wedding I would've beat her down on the spot. Gloria told me to breathe and to hold onto the peace we found with our prior massages.

When the wedding party arrived, Toya didn't seem to care but the guy she was talking to stopped showing any interest in anything she was saying; his eyes were glued to Tracy. I sighed; she kept looking at him too. I could tell by the look on Andy's face he was realizing how much of a mistake he made. I couldn't watch them anymore; they had my stomach in knots. Gloria brought a drink for me, she said it was the house special and we both laughed. It was good and it definitely took the edge off. At one point I saw Andrew dancing with Toya and Tracy and that guy dancing, the outcome of the evening was a little disappointing. Poor Andy, I knew this probably felt like Jennay all over again. Gloria was pouting as well, I told her to turn her back to the whole thing like I did. One of the groomsmen came and asked me to dance. This little cutie had the nerve to know how to dance. When I went back to the table, I asked Gloria what happened to everybody. She said most people left. Gloria and I went out on the dance floor. My groomsmen and another little tender came to dance with us. This little boy and I were grooving, I started thinking I've never had a one-night stand, I wondered if they were any good like people made them seem. I told myself to keep dancing and just see what happens. I felt eyes on me, I looked at Gloria, and she was having fun dancing not paying me any attention. Then I saw Juan sitting in the far corner watching. He didn't look mad, but that didn't mean he wasn't. I danced over to Gloria, "girl your man is watching!" She frowned, "huh?" I made her follow my eyes, instantly her body became stiff. Her partner not getting it tried to encourage her to keep dancing. "Stop! Stop!" Then she straightened her dress and hurried over to Juan.

"Boyfriend?" The cutie asked me

"Husband."

"Whoa!" Then he looked at me. "Are you married?"

I shook my head no, "But she is spoken for." Malcolm came out of nowhere. The cutie released me and put his hands up. "No, I'm not!" I said with a ton of attitude.

Malcolm leaned in, "she's trying to get you killed! Don't listen to her!" The cutie turned on his heels and walked away. "What is wrong with you this weekend?" He said eyeing me.

I put my hands on my hips. "Ain't nothing wrong with me! What's wrong with you?" That's when I realized I might be a little drunk. "Why are you here?"

"I broke my neck to get here and you ask me why? Isn't it obvious?"

"I guess," I said turning on my heels. I could hear Malcolm exhale hard. I walked over to Juan and Gloria. "Don't worry Juan, Gloria is a good girl, I didn't rub off on her." Gloria gave me sad eyes. Juan looked at Malcolm; I couldn't put my finger on the look on Malcolm's face. He picked up my shoes and purse. I waved bye to the cutie, he turned his back on me and continued talking to his friend. Malcolm grabbed my arm and pulled me out of the banquet hall. I looked back, there were probably twenty people left from the two hundred guests earlier. Malcolm kept pulling me to the room every time I looked like I was gonna stop he pulled me again. Once we were in the room he stood by the door like he was trying to calm himself. He would take a calm breath and then he would look at me and get angry all over again. I sat on the bed laughing at him silently to myself. Sweat beads popped up on his forehead. He took off his jacket and threw it on the floor. I was trying to calm down but the affects of my drinks kept getting stronger and stronger. "Amber! This isn't working! It seems like the more I try, the more ungrateful you become! I CANNOT KEEP PUNKING OUT FOR YOU! Especially when you don't respect it!"

"Did I ask you to punk out for me? All I'm asking you to be is the dick when I need some but if that's too much for you! Hey!" I heard myself say.

Malcolm's face turns to stone. "You're drunk!"

I stood on the bed. "Nana says your truth comes out when you're drunk! You don't like just being my dick? Does that bother you? Does that make you feel like less than a man?"

"Amber! What is wrong with you?"

"You are what's wrong with me! All of my life I was your quote unquote good girl, believing that you just needed more time you would come around. YOU BROKE MY HEART! I CAN'T MARRY NOBODY ELSE FOR FEAR OF WHAT YOU WOULD DO TO THEM! Now that I'm finally with the program, it makes you mad now! You only change the game long enough for me to fall for you again, and then you go back to being selfish Malcolm. The man who has to screw EVERYBODY! You say you've changed, I don't believe you! You just want me to open my heart back up to you so you can hurt me even worse than before! I don't believe you, I don't trust you!"

"So then what are we doing?" He said looking at me.

"Amber is waiting for the next good guy to come along. I can't tell you what you're doing." I heard myself say.

"I am a good guy Amber!"

"You're selfish! You have to have whomever you please whenever you want them. Even if they almost get us all killed! You don't care! If you have to have her, it doesn't matter!" Then I started crying, "Amber deserves a man of her own! One who won't make her Momma stop talking to her or make her Daddy stop hiding his under handed ways! Amber could've been anything, instead she had to get knocked up by someone who didn't even want her baby or her! I couldn't breathe! "You've broken my heart for the last time! This is not my fault! THIS IS NOT MY FAULT!"

Malcolm snatched me off the bed and put me in a bear hug. He didn't say anything else. I don't remember falling asleep, but when I woke up my head was pounding. We were both fully dressed except for our shoes. Malcolm gave me medicine and water. Malcolm looked like he was in pain but he didn't say anything. I started to ask him what was wrong, but last night came washing back over me. "That was a lot of truth serum huh?" I said trying to make a joke. Malcolm agreed but didn't say anything. "Are you not talking to me now?"

"One lie spoils a thousand truths!" He exhaled and rubbed his eyes.

"Meaning?"

"I can't name one thing I haven't done for you. I've killed for you, provided for you, even raise your sons as my own. Your family has been my family; even though we differ on the interpretation, I've always put you first but yet and still it doesn't matter. My one shortcoming messes up everything doesn't it?" I laid there looking at him. He wasn't yelling he was speaking matter of factly, which in my mind was scarier. "You know what you do that hurts?" He looked at me to see if I wanted to know. He scooted back so that he could rest his back against the headboard. He started using his hands to gesture. "See it was like this. I'm with you, I love you, and you are my heart, nothing between us, just you and me; there's no other feeling like it. Those dumb tramps will get sprung off anything. I need to blow off some steam; I'd pound it out on them. Let them walk funny for a while claiming that I just got carried away. I never brought that to you. No matter who it was, it was just sex even if it happened more than once, for me it was sex. For you, you're so mad at me that you're willing to give them everything and even lock it down forever with them. I could never give someone else what I've given you nobody else is worthy. You get with David behind my back, and when I'm away, you promise him forever and you have his child, not once but twice. I bet you he didn't ask for either one of those boys. He wanted you; he didn't care about having kids other than the control it gave him over you. But I deserved it, knowing you were with him hurt but ok moving on. Even though you didn't understand it and I couldn't vocalize it, there are no words to describe what losing Troy was like. I thought I was losing it over Leonard; Troy took the cake. Imagine losing Sophia over some nonsense. I wanted to clock out from everything and everyone. I knew the boys would never understand, but I thought at least you would. We lost the baby and couldn't replace it and then I lose my closest relationship besides you. I thought we were so in sync that you would get it but then there's Dwayne!" He held his hands out and shrugged. "Ok maybe you need to blow off some steam fine but I'm looking at this pretty boy, and he's doing the same things I do and again you want to give him everything! You wanna promise forever to a man who doesn't even know you. So here we are, I don't wanna let you go but it looks like trying to hold on to you is pushing you further and further outside of yourself. Were you really gonna sleep with that kid last night?" He looked at me but he didn't wait for me to answer. "There were a lot of promises I made to your father on his death bed, that are becoming impossible to keep. You'll always be safe as long as there's breath in my body. Financially, what's mine is yours. Although I ache for you, I won't keep putting you through this. My heart can't take no more Amber!" Then he got emotional. "You lost our child because of my failure to communicate!" He started waving his hands. "I'm done! I throw in the towel!"

I sat up; my headache was just about gone. I hugged him, and he squeezed me tightly. I kissed him and he kissed me back, morning breath after a night drinking and all. Three hours later we got a late checkout, I drove him home. We kissed goodbye and I went home.

Chapter 51

I couldn't breathe! Joanne has been watching me cry for the past five minutes. Every time I start to open my mouth tears start pouring out. Joanne's eyes watered up watching me cry and cry. "It feels like he broke up with me, but we weren't together." I said through tears

"How does he respond to you when he sees you?"

"Fine I guess. He's kind of normal, but it's not the same. I feel powerless."

"Honey he's always been the man in your life. It's very easy to take that for granted."

I stopped crying. "You think I was taking him for granted too?"

"Yes" she said, and I started crying again. "Honey you need to pull it together. You need to decide where you want him in your life. You may decide you don't want him in the forefront of your life anymore, then you have to decide where you go from there or you may decide that you want him to still be the star of your show and if that's the case, you have to sort out all of your feelings." She touched my shoulder, "that means you would have to forgive him and if you can't forgive him, he can't hold that spot. You can't glaze over forgiveness, that's how you end up here."

"Do I want him back?" I asked her

"That's something you have to answer for yourself. No one can answer that for you."

"I don't know. He's always been a factor in my life. Life doesn't feel right without him wanting me."

"But do you want him?"

"I love Malcolm! But he broke my heart. Every time I try to think about that love I get angry, and I wanna bash his face in! I want to hurt him really bad. I want him to experience everything I've gone through. You can say you understand, but until you experience it, it's not the same." I said

"You feel like he doesn't understand?"

"NO! I DON'T! How could he? He was the one doing it to me. He was mad at me when I got pregnant like I did it on purpose."

"But he came around." She said

"He treated me like I was a fat blob unworthy of being loved just before and right after I gave birth to his child. He even had one of his tramps in the car when he came to my house."

"So he abandoned you? Left you alone completely?"

"I see what you're doing. He would come, bring money for the baby, buy anything I said he needed. He'd play with him a little bit then he'd leave. He forgot about me needing him so I spent the entire summer at my Nana's. She had me on a strict diet and tons of exercise. I got my body back, but he made me feel horrible about it. Anytime I choose something for me, he makes me feel like I put it before him."

"Do you?"

"I guess so, but I guess I don't get it. For instance, when I was fat, he ignored me; he didn't even look at me. Everybody was telling me he was running around with that girl so I didn't come home. Momma said he was looking for us after a while, but I figured that meant the baby cause he didn't pay me any attention. Then when he did see me he made me feel bad about losing my weight."

"How was he supposed to respond?" She asked

"Happy for me I guess."

"How much of your interpretation of him is based on emotion? Did you try to talk to him?"

"Joanne I was fifteen, I didn't have communication skills."

"Ok so when did you start sitting him down and talking to him?"

"Our communication vastly improved after David died. I'd ask him questions we'd sit and talk about anything for hours. I always feel like he's teaching me something, whether I wanna learn or not. Is this supposed to be a lesson?"

"Honestly, I don't think so. From what you've said I think he's hurting."

My stomach tightened. "Like I could hurt him." I said in disbelief.

"Apparently you have." She said, "the question is what are you gonna do about it? Something or nothing?"

****

He looked angry as he asked me to sit. He took a deep breath, "momma she's pregnant, and she's keeping it!"

"Toya?"

"Yes"

I exhaled, "are you sure it's yours this time?" I asked hoping he said no.

"I'm pretty sure, I know the exact moment when it happened but I can always get a DNA test later if doubt starts to rise." He said disappointedly.

"Of all people Toya? You know she's really going to act ugly now. Have you told your father?" I asked

"No! And I'm not going to! He'll give me some cold-blooded answer that will probably kill Toya and my baby. I never wanted her to get rid of the other two." He sat down on the couch. "But I don't want to be with her either. Too much emotion happened at that wedding. Did you see Tracy?"

"She was beautiful son." I remembered.

"She's with some guy that's all wrong for her but she wouldn't give me the time of day. It hurt because I really thought we had something. I guess it's for the best with this whole Toya thing." Andrew said

"I think she did the right thing. If she were yours, would you want someone from her past coming and changing her mind? Wouldn't you want the same loyalty?" I sighed. "So we're stuck with Toya? How far a long is she? She could miscarry."

"She's almost four months."

"You waited to tell me?"

"Yea, I wanted to be sure there was a reason to tell you." Andy exhaled and leaned back. "As soon as I did it I knew what I did! Now I don't want to be with her but here we are. Should I propose? I don't want to though."

"Are you CRAZY! Just because she's pregnant doesn't mean you marry her. We're talking about Toya!"

"I get the feeling she expects it." He said in a defeated tone.

I thought about it. "Call your Uncle Sonny and ask him for a referral for a family law attorney. Find out what you need to do to protect yourself. You better believe she's already plotting against you."

"You're right!" He got up and went to the phone.

I sat there pouting! I'm not ready to be a Nana! I'm still young Dag Nabit! I could still have my own child right now but that won't be happening. I threw an internal tantrum, why? Why? Me? I bet the baby comes out half normal and half a manipulating crazy person. When Andrew got off the phone, he said Auntie Jade invited us to go skating. I needed to do something to clear my head.

****

Carey Anderson

"Momma, she's in labor." Andrew said he sounds tired.
"Are you ok Andy?"
"It's been a long day, I just need my momma."
"I'm coming baby!" I said hopping out the bed. I ran to Darryl's room. I opened the door he was spread out on his bed all the covers kicked off like he's always done.
"Psst! Darryl!"
He jumped. "Huh?"
"Toya's in labor!"
"I hope it hurts!" He said rolling over.
"Darryl!"
"Huh?" He said sounding irritated
"It's your nephew! Get up! Don't make me tell you again!" I closed his door.
I could hear him fussing in his room as he got up. I called Derrick and he had the same reaction, I told him the same thing I told Darryl. As long as immediate family was there, the rest could come afterwards. Darryl drove like he was pissy the whole way to the hospital. When we got to the L&D floor, Darryl went straight to the waiting room, slouched in the chair, and closed his eyes. Andrew met me in the hallway, I asked him if she was in a lot of pain, he said yes and things have been moving slow. He thanked me for coming because Toya's mother was driving him crazy. When I walked in the room, her mother was yelling and telling her to hurry up because they had been at the hospital all day, all while Toya was in the middle of a contraction. I don't know what I expected to see when I saw her mother but her mother was a more petite version of Toya. Her mother was a little shorter than her. Almost light skin, but Toya looked just like her. She had long hair like Toya, but her hair was brown and Toya's was black. When you first saw her, you would say, wow, she's pretty but then she spoke. "Drew! I thought you said your mother was here?" She said looking me up and down.
"This is my mother Regina."
She laughed. "You never told me your mother is white."
"Regina, I've had about enough of you. Get out!" Andrew said
She looked at him like she was surprised. "What?"
"You heard me! You're bringing all kinds of negativity in here. How you talk to your daughter is your business, but you will not disrespect my mother or me. Now go wait in the waiting room or I'll have you removed."
You could tell Regina didn't believe or respect him. "Yea right Drew! This heifer just needs to HURRY UP! We been up here all day!" She said kicking at the bed.
Andrew took out his phone. He told the person on the phone he needed them to come handle something for him. Not even a minute later, Derrick walked in the room. His face was stone. Andrew pointed at Regina, "she's got to go."
Regina looked Derrick up and down. "What's he supposed to do? I'll leave when I'm ready." She plopped down on the sofa.
"You can walk or I'll carry you, it doesn't matter to me." Derrick said real calm and scary as he walked towards her.
"Touch me and I'll...." Derrick's hand looked like it was two times the size of her face. He slapped a tight seal on her face so fast with his hand it made me jump and scared the crap out of Regina. In her defense, it didn't seem like he was that close to her.
"Scream, and I will take you outside and put a bullet in your head! Like I said you can walk out of here or I can carry you but I promise if I have to carry you, it will not end well for you." Then he let go of her mouth. "Now let's go in the waiting

room!" Regina hurried and got her stuff without making a peep. "Toya!" Derrick called out. She was lying on her side going through a contraction. "I hope it hurts! I'm outside Drew!" Derrick didn't look to see if Regina was following him, he knew she knew better.

Toya labored for another hour. Andrew was there and he was concerned, but he wasn't concerned about Toya like a father should be about the mother of his child. I didn't know what happened, but I could tell my baby clocked out. On the third push, Toya screamed that it burned. The doctor told her she was tearing and with the next push the baby was out; all seven pounds and five ounces of him. There are no words to describe my son when he looked at and held his son for the first time. Looking at them moved me to tears. When they offered the baby to Toya, she didn't want to hold him right away. She said her body was in so much pain. Her leg was shaking and they had to give her something for the pain. The baby looked exactly like Andy. In the back of my mind, I was prepared to insist on a DNA test, but looking at this Xerox copy of my baby I knew it was pointless. I knew it not only with my eyes but I could feel it in my heart. When Andrew handed me the baby I felt fifteen again. I found myself looking for Momma to calm me from my disappointment that my baby was a boy and suggesting that I name him Andrew. I felt like Malcolm should've been here, but I knew better than to bring it up. I didn't know anyone so precious could come from Toya. Once they had Toya all stitched up and cleaned up, they moved us to the postpartum room. When Andy left to get everyone, I walked over to Toya who was in tears. She was looking at the baby, "sorry! Sorry!"

"Toya why are you sorry?"

"I'm not prepared for this. I don't know how to be a good mother. He's gonna hate me." Then she cried harder.

"Nonsense! Your baby loves you."

She listened but she didn't say anything. Andy brought the boys and Regina in the room. I thought Regina would check on her daughter first. "Does he look like Drew?" She said, and then she looked at him. She clapped her hands together and said, "perfect."

Toya kept her eyes down, and Andy had to hold Darryl back. "The baby is healthy by the way!" I was irritated with the source of Toya's malfunctions.

"Of course he is!" She said, and then she looked at my baby. "Take out that checkbook, it's time to pay!"

Andrew looked at Regina in disgust. "Not that it's any of your business, but we've already signed paperwork."

She looked at Toya, "why didn't you tell me? How much do we get?" She was too excited.

"An apartment, a car, all expenses paid, and two thousand a month for me." Toya said proudly.

"That's it? I thought you said he went to college?" Regina barked.

"He did."

"Sounds like you're being low balled to me." Regina looked at us, then Toya. "We'll discuss how to fix this later."

Now Regina was right, Toya was being low-balled but if she wasn't paying for anything two thousand a month was a good amount, more than a lot of people get but it tickled me that little miss ghetto actually thought they were going to be able to find a loophole she could play. Regina didn't even hold the baby. She told Toya she was going to need some money, and then she left. Toya laid there quiet while we all admired the baby. Sophia and Sabrina came to the hospital early. Slowly but

Carey Anderson

surely, family trickled in to meet the baby. He wasn't much of a crier either which was good. I was tired but I didn't want to leave the hospital. At some point, I expected to see Malcolm, but Andrew was against it. Sophia was holding the baby and she asked if he was a junior. Andrew shook his head no, "Andre." I love it!

****

"Ms. Amber, can you please keep the baby for me until Andrew gets home?" Toya sounded like she was at the end of her rope.

"Of course! I'm on my way." I said not asking any questions. Of course, Toya had the most expensive apartment she could find. She pitched a complete fit when Andrew gave her my everyday Honda. I guess she thought if she wrecked it, he would come back with something better. When he kept coming with the same exact car, she had a fit each time. She told the judge on their fifth trip to court that she wanted a better car. The judge reviewed the finances and told her since her apartment was so expensive Andrew wasn't required to provide a car for her, she lost it. Then she kept petitioning the court for more money claiming that the amount that they agreed upon was hardly enough. The courts denied her again; I was so relieved. Andrew was getting tired of fighting over his son like he was a cash cow. So he started showing the cost associated with each court visit, etc. so her monthly support started going down every time they went to court. That's when Toya couldn't take it anymore. She started calling me or dropping the baby off to Andrew, which was fine by my baby, he wanted his son with him as much as possible. I was so proud of him for stepping up to his responsibility. I would look at my grand baby in amazement; it was like looking at Andy all over again. When I got to Toya's door, she was on the phone making plans to go out. Andre was so happy to see me, if he could've he would've leaped out of her arms. He was dressed in a jumper type outfit with no socks, his diaper was full, and he was sour smelling like she hadn't bathed him. No diaper bag or anything. She closed the door continuing her conversation. I took deep breaths then I banged the mess out of her door. She opened the door looking irritated. "Get off the phone!" I said through clinched teeth.

Toya's eyes got big, and she hung up the phone without even saying bye. "You gotta do better than this! His diaper needs to be changed! He's dirty! And WHERE IS HIS COAT!" I asked having a flashback of Momma Shuga. Toya started stammering and backing up. Ok so clearly I put the fear in her already, but this was out of line and unacceptable! "MOVE OUT THE WAY!" I said through clinched teeth again. I went in Andre's room; the crib had a naked mattress with milk stains on it. The diaper pail was over loaded with dirty diapers; his room was chaos. The rest of the house was neat as a pin. I looked at Toya like you got to be kidding me! "Seriously?" Toya started stammering again. I grabbed André's jacket off the floor. I used the last diaper, and then I looked for socks. I couldn't find a matching pair, I know I gave this girl at least ten pair at her stupid shower. I gave her a huge basket full of everything she needed socks, t-shirts, bibs, burping cloths, etc., irritated I pushed Toya into the wall. "Where's his stuff!" Her eyes were wide.

"I don't know." She said lowly.

I put the baby's coat on him. He gripped my neck as I carried him out of there. I called Andrew going completely off about the conditions that girl was subjecting my grandson to. I took Andre home; I bathed him, and fed him. We were sitting on the couch when Andrew walked in the door. He had on a suit and tie. He got a huge smile on his face when he saw Andre, and vice versa. Andre started bouncing on the couch and stretching his arms to his daddy, Andrew picked up his son he hugged

220

and kissed him. We went over the things I saw. Andrew had a defeated tone when he said he didn't know how he was gonna bounce back from this. He said he knew Toya didn't want Andre, but she wanted the money. He said he talked to his lawyer and they could try to build something around the living conditions, but it wasn't a crime to be dirty. Andrew sighed, he said he was thankful for Andre, but everything else surrounding his life was depressing. I told him to hang in there because it would get better. Darryl came home and completely ignored us. He took Andre with him, Andrew and I made dinner together, and I spent that time encouraging him to hang in there because things would get better. My baby looked like he didn't believe me. I knew that look, it's the look I've always had when dealing with relationships.

****

"Stop staring!" I said

"I'm trying to imagine you as a grandmother." Tag said

"I know right! I can't see it either." I shook my head.

"I have a grand child."

I looked at him in disbelief. "Why am I just hearing that you have a child?"

"I've got two kids, I'm sure I've told you."

I pointed to my face. "Does this look like the face of a person in the know?"

"I'm sure I told you." Then he put his glass down. "Wanna dance?"

"No! I wanna know more about these kids. How old are they?"

I could tell he regretted saying anything. "My daughter Wendy is a little older than Derrick. My son Neil was born right after her."

"Why haven't we met them?"

"My breakup with their mom was pretty ugly. She wouldn't let me see them for a long time. Now I have a grand daughter." He shrugged

"Do you have pictures, I want to see?"

"I haven't met her."

I frowned at him. "These kids are in their twenties, you have a grandchild you've never met? What am I missing?"

He exhaled, "the kids have sided with their mother. They won't give me a chance, so what am I supposed to do?"

"Were you a deadbeat dad or something?" Tag looked at me. I gasped, "you were a dead beat dad!"

He turned red, "no I wasn't, what does that mean any ways?"

I frowned at him. "That you weren't involved in your children's lives that you didn't provide for them." My eyes were big.

He turned his head while shaking his leg. "She wouldn't let me see them, what was I supposed to do?"

"Pay your child support!" His leg started shaking faster. "Look Tag, all I'm saying is that you couldn't talk to them. The only way you could show you cared was by paying for them."

"That's not the kind of mother she was. She would've spent my money on her and not them."

"Even still, you could've paid, and if she didn't do what she was supposed to that was on her."

"I couldn't afford to pay her knowing she was wasting it. I had to live too."

"Um I recall you pulling out a credit card and paying whatever the price was to sit next to me in first class. Even if you were hurting at first you weren't hurting in the end."

Tag was mad now! He sat there shaking his leg. "That was different, it was for you!"

"So you put me before your kids?" He blank stared at me. "You should know I wouldn't have ever approved of something like that."

"Let's go dance or something I don't like how this evening is turning out." He said reaching for my hand.

I didn't give it to him. Maybe Daddy didn't know about this, but maybe he saw this selfishness in him, and that's why he never liked him. "No, I think I'm gonna go home. I don't feel like dancing anymore."

"Oh come on, my kids don't have anything to do with you." He said not getting why I was upset.

I think if Malcolm would've turned out like that, forget about Daddy, Momma would've skinned him alive. It hit me like an epiphany, "I don't think I can be your friend any more Tag." I said feeling like I was hit by this revelation.

"WHAT???" He turned beet red. "BECAUSE OF MARGARET! Amber this is crazy! My kids don't have anything to do with you! This isn't fair!"

"What's not fair is those kids going without so you could chase your dreams! They didn't ask to be here! I can't be friends with someone who would do that to their kids!"

"Who are you to judge me? At least my kids have the same mother! You got one too many 'baby daddies'!" He yelled.

I didn't get mad I took a deep breath. "Thanks for letting me know how you truly feel. Doesn't matter how many there are. My children never went without because their fathers were too selfish to care whether they ate or starved." I stood up and put my jacket on.

"Wait a minute! Wait!" He said standing as well. "I'm sorry, I'll fix this. Don't go." He pleaded with his eyes.

"No, I wanna go home. Please take me home." I said matter of factly. "If you can't I understand, I'll just catch a cab."

"Yea right! You'll have one of Malcolm's guys take you home."

I smiled, "well at least you know. That actually sounds a whole lot better than riding with you. Have a good life Tag." I started to walk away and Tag was trying to stop me.

Then he came out of nowhere. "Amber I'm here to take you home." If it weren't for the dreads, I wouldn't have recognized him.

"Thank you?" I waited for him to say his name.

"Yussef" he said straight faced no smile or anything.

Tag kicked the air and swung at it. "I don't believe this!" He put his hands out. "Really Amber? You don't think you owe me more than this!"

"I already paid you, don't you remember!" Then I looked at Yussef to guide the way.

He put his cellphone to his ear, "we're leaving."

Then he handed the phone to me. He guided me out of the ballroom to the parking lot. "Hello?" My heart was pounding hoping Malcolm didn't hear me say that.

"How did you pay him?" Malcolm asked

I exhaled, "I'm not talking about this right now!"

"Let me know when you're ready."

"Um! Let's make that never! I don't want to discuss it Malcolm!"

"But I do, especially now!"

"I don't have to report to you. Were you eavesdropping on my whole conversation?"

"Only when it got heated but you handled it. Do you need anything?"

"Like what?" I asked hoping it was an invitation.

"Yussef can take you to the store or something before he takes you home if you need something."

I was disappointed. "No I'm fine. I'm giving him back his phone now." Then I gave Yussef back his phone as he held the door open for me.

Yussef got in the car, turned off the radio, and drove in silence to my house. Derrick was coming down the porch when we pulled around the corner. Derrick walked up to the driver's side window before Yussef could get out. "Who are you?"

"Yussef"

"When did you get hired?" Derrick asked

"It's been a while now." Yussef said

Derrick opened my door without looking at me. "Malcolm normally informs me of new hires in this division, who brought you on?"

"Malcolm" Yussef said matter of factly.

Derrick took out his phone, kissed me on my cheek and walked towards his truck while talking to Malcolm. Yussef parked in front of the house, he got out of the car and walked around the house while I went inside. I felt irritated and dirty. I took a shower and washed my hair. I put on sweats and then I paced my floor. I picked up my phone and I called Malcolm, he answered on the first ring. I asked him if he was busy or expecting company. He said no and no. I asked him if he knew about Tag's kids. He said he didn't, but he didn't care either. I told him I wanted to find them. He asked me why, and I told him what Tag did wasn't right and I needed to see for myself if everything was like he said. Malcolm said he'd find her. "Malcolm I just want to say I do appreciate that you stepped up with not only Andrew but all of the boys. I do recognize that you never had to do all that you've done." His breathing sounded like a smile but he didn't say anything. "And even though you still put money in my account, you never let me pay for anything. Everyone isn't built like you, and I just wanted you to know I see it and I appreciate it."

I could hear his smile. "I could never turn my back on you. Our boys are an extension of you."

"I love that you said that!" I sat on the bed. "Would it confuse things if I came over?"

Malcolm was quiet for a long time. "You're always welcome here but in the morning I'll still be longing and you'll be gone."

"Oh" I said sounding disappointed

"I wanna see you! I don't know!" That fast the firm commanding tone was gone from his voice. "It's up to you!"

"Then that just makes me responsible for hurting you in the morning." I screamed into the pillow.

"Come on, it's ok. I'll call Yussef. See you in a minute." Then he hung up.

I screamed into the pillow again. I told myself to man up. I pulled my hair back in a slick ponytail, and then I tucked the ends under. Then I put on my jet-black bob wig with the china bangs. I put on a black silk gown, red lipstick, and the baddest red heels. I put my long trench coat and shades on, I grabbed my purse and walked out of the door. Yussef opened my car door. I admit it was kind of dumb to wear shades at night, but I needed this and I didn't wanna feel bad about it in the morning. Malcolm was standing in the doorway when we pulled up. When I stood up, Malcolm was shocked to see me. His mouth was open as he took me in walking to his door. Once he closed the door, I gave him my coat. I went up to his room, he quietly followed me. I went in his bathroom and grabbed his lotion. "Lay down!" I commanded him. He stood there frozen. I kissed him then I took his clothes off. I stepped back and looked at him. "Malcolm you are beautiful!" He blushed while holding his frown. "Please lay down!" I said nicer this time. He laid on his stomach and I put lotion on his back and shoulders, then I straddled him. I massaged him as deeply as I could. "I just want to say thank you for everything you've done for our family. We wouldn't be who we are if it wasn't for you. You are the glue that holds us together!"

Malcolm turned over. He pulled my face to his then he kissed me. "It's only because you love me that makes me who I am."

Round two, he made me take the wig off and let my hair down, but he was ok with me keeping the heels on.

Chapter 52

"Margaret Harper 1801 Leland, Pittsburg California. It looks like both the kids still live with her." Malcolm said

"What can you tell me about her? Is she a Toya or not?" I asked

"I'm assuming things went crazy with them three years in. She got on welfare then and stayed on until her son turned eighteen."

"Shouldn't the state be after him?"

"There's a technical difficulty. They can't exactly go after him if they can't prove he's the father."

"HE DENIES HIS KIDS??" I couldn't believe it.

"Pretty much. Now they all live together to support each other."

"What is she like?" I asked Yussef

"What do you mean?" He said

"He knows Toya?" I asked Malcolm. Malcolm nodded yes. "Is she more like Toya or me?"

"Reading people is a very important part of your job. She wants to know your read on Margaret." Malcolm said

Yussef looked at me. "She's more like you than she could be Toya."

Malcolm sat there confident in Yussef's assessment, but the curiosity in me wouldn't let me drop it. "I know I'm gonna regret this, but what's your read on me?" Both of them relaxed in their chairs, Malcolm cracked a little smile. "She's like you because she will do anything for her kids, you are confused."

"WHAT?" He insulted me.

Yussef held back most of his smile. "You struggle with hatred and love daily. You fall in love with people for various reasons daily. You're always looking for the good in people. You look so hard sometimes that you miss the bad. Because of that, you've been in some bad situations. Now you struggle with yourself, you automatically fall in love with people, but the moment they step outside of that love, you find it difficult to forgive, although your true nature wants to forgive and move on." I frowned at Malcolm who was too tickled, and then I shifted in my chair. "Should I continue?" Yussef asked me.

"How do I know he didn't tell you to say this? How do you read him?" I pointed to Malcolm.

He looked at Malcolm, Malcolm sat up straight, and then he nodded at Yussef to give him permission to speak, although it didn't seem like he wanted to. "Malcolm is constantly reading and rereading people. A lot of his moves are always strategically motivated. He's the master game player, but he has an obvious weakness." Yussef gestured towards me. "Your family, his children mean the world to him. He loves you more than he's ever loved anyone, and it causes him conflict. Life has taught him not to trust anyone, except for a select few. He trusts you right now even though we all know he shouldn't."

"Why shouldn't he trust me?" I was still frowning

"You don't trust him. When you trust someone who doesn't trust you it's a recipe for disaster!"

I looked at Malcolm and he was looking at me. "Meaning I'm gonna do something to hurt you?"

"That or get me killed, one or the other; I personally choose death." He said matter of factly.

I swallowed, "ok I'm over this. Please tell me more about Margaret."

Yussef had doctor's records for Margaret and the kids, school records for the kids, financial records for Margaret's mom for all the things she did to help her child and grandchildren. Margaret's mother had done everything she could for them until she got sick herself. I imagined being in her shoes. I wondered if she knew about Tag's job, or if she knew about me. Malcolm asked me what I was going to do. I gave him a "Duh!" expression. I told him I wanted to give her some money. Malcolm asked me why, and I told him because I felt bad for her. Malcolm told Yussef to leave us. Then he asked me why was it any of my business, I didn't have anything to do with what happened between Tag and Margaret. So I told Malcolm about the plane ride, and how Tag didn't flinch at the price to upgrade his ticket to sit next to me.

Malcolm said that still wasn't my business what happened between him and her. "Did you sleep with him knowing there was someone in his life, and now you feel guilty knowing the details?"

"No! I told you I never had sex with Tag. I just feel bad for her that could've easily been me."

"How?"

"What if I would've run away with David and Andy while you were locked up? My life would be totally different."

Malcolm stared at me for a minute. "You never told me you thought about running."

"On the drive home before Derrick was conceived I thought about it all. Running was one thought."

"That would've been ugly." He said picking up his water glass.

I exhaled, "I know and it wouldn't have worked."

"Here's my point, as unfortunate as it is, this whole thing is between Margaret and Tag. If you wanna help her, I'll point the state in the right direction to make him pay but there's no reason why you should dig into your pockets to help her. You don't owe her anything." I didn't want him to be right, I don't know why I wanted to fight him on this, but I knew he was right. Tag created this situation so he should pay. Malcolm stared at me. "So how did you," he searched my eyes.

My heart rate sped up. I turned my eyes from him. "Malcolm please stop asking." He looked irritated, but I knew better than to discuss it. I felt eyes on me, I sat up and looked at Malcolm, and then I started looking around. "They've been taking our picture for the past five minutes, just act natural." Malcolm kept his eyes on me. "Ok"

"So, how is my grandson?"

"Minus the crazy mother, he's exactly like Andy was at his age. When you talk to him, I swear he's soaking it up like he understands." I said with a smile.

"So you have him quite regularly?"

I pursed my lips at Malcolm. "I love how you ask me questions like you don't already know. You know I help out as much as I can but Andy has a new girlfriend who happens to be pretty ok so far, so I don't see either of them as much as I did." Then I sat back. "Now you tell me about her."

"So far she checks out ok. She seems like your run of the mill girl next door." He shrugged.

"But?"

"Drew's using Mitigated, and he has for awhile. He seems to really like this girl."

"You don't?"

"Haven't met her. I think he needs to focus on his son and business. I don't see the value in introducing the baby to this girl who may not be around."

"I think he's thinking long term with this one. Besides, Andre was kind of thrown in the mix by Toya."

"Andre's not gonna know she was here today and gone tomorrow. I just don't see the point in getting your kids attached to someone who really doesn't matter." His voice got deeper on the "doesn't matter" part.

I exhaled. "So... You've been mad at me for how long for introducing Andy to David?"

"Since it happened. You let him weasel his way into my son's heart! 'Til this day we haven't been right because David left his mark." Malcolm was trying to control his anger.

I was quiet for a minute. A part of me wanted to accept what he was saying as truth, but then I remembered. "No! The disconnect between you two is your fault. David showed him something different, but take responsibility for your actions."

"How you figure?"

"He's always responded to affection from you but your focus has always been to make him hard. You pushed him away by your actions. All David had to do was show him affection and happiness to have him around."

"That's because you were always babying him. What kind of man is he supposed to be?"

"The kind of man who cares about how he affects his family. Andy is how he should be with his son. He shows him that he's happy to see him; he hugs and kisses his son. He's concerned when his son cries."

"And watch your grandson is gonna be a little crybaby whimp! Drew is a softer version of me. He has his chicks on the side. This girl is gonna drop him just like the one before. Then he's gonna have to deal with his son being attached for the rest of his life to a female who never mattered." Malcolm said angrily and full of resentment.

"Because your ideas of hardness have worked out so well! You have no idea of how affection works, all you know about it is what you've seen being around my family. Your first hug probably came from me."

"All I know is you let some twisted fool work on my son and turn him against me! His loyalty is still to that fool! What kind of mother does that?" His eyes were angry.

I'm not gonna cry! I'm not gonna cry! I kept telling myself. "To be so smart you are the dumbest person I know!" I said standing up. "Caring about how you affect your family is a wonderful quality to have. My Daddy always showed us love and affection, my brothers are fine."

Malcolm stood up. "Yea Tim was so good that you were well rounded and didn't get knocked up at fourteen years old by an unaffectionate thug!" I swung to slap him, but he moved his face. "Stop hitting me Amber! Civilized well rounded affectionate people don't hit!"

"Thank you for reminding me of why I hate you!" I said through clinched teeth.

"All I'm saying is history is repeating its self. David checked out on paper too, and you see how he ended up. Your son is acting dumb just like you." Then he walked away.

My blood was boiling as I walked out of the restaurant. When I looked back at Malcolm, he had the nerve to smile at me.

When I got in my car to go home, I noticed the car following me. It wasn't one of Malcolm's guys though. I was too irritated to be nervous about it; I wanted to be left alone. I called Darryl and I told him I was going to LA. He asked me why and for how long. I told him I needed to get away for a few days, but I didn't want him to worry. He still sounded worried but I did my best to assure him that everything was ok. The car was still following me. I tossed my keys to the valet, I told him I wouldn't be back for a couple days. I used Malcolm's card to purchase my last minute first class ticket. When I went through the security checkpoint, the guy looked at me big eyed. At first, I looked at him like what was his problem. Then I realized he probably worked for Malcolm. I went to my gate and sat down. Then I saw a woman and a man approaching me. I braced myself for whatever.

"Hello Amber" the woman said.

"Hello?" I said, recognizing the woman as the woman who came with Detective White.

"Detective Dartnell, you remember me don't you?" She said sarcastically

"I guess."

"This is detective Turan." She said pointing to the guy with her

"Ok?" I looked at them.

"That looked like a pretty heated conversation between you and your man." She said with a smile. I blank stared at her. "So where you off to?" I pointed to the board, and then she asked, "Why?"

"Not that it's any of your business but I have friends and family out there." I was irritated.

"All of a sudden? You aren't bringing any luggage. Are you coming back tonight?"

"Why is that any of your business?" I pressed the number one on my cellphone in my pocket to call Malcolm on my speed dial.

She tried to soften her tone. "We got off on the wrong foot. Can we start over?"

"I think we're fine exactly where we are. What do you want?"

"I have some questions about your man."

"I don't have a man." I said defensively.

"That would explain why you only go to his house." Then she leaned in, "aren't you a bit grown to still respond to booty calls?"

I turned red; I wanted to punch her in her mouth! I could see myself beating her down and feeling SO GOOD ABOUT IT! "You can leave me alone!"

"Has he ever hit you?" She asked trying to read my response.

I looked at the guy. "Why are you here?"

"We were hoping you would cooperate with some questions."

"As long as you guys keep sending her, you will need my lawyer present for anything other than a hello. She's rude and trying to provoke me. I don't appreciate it. I know I don't pay taxes to be treated like this."

He looked at Detective Dartnell and nodded his head telling her to take a walk. She rolled her eyes; Detective Turan came and sat next to me. He had a pretty smile like Dwayne and dimples like Andy. He even had the nerve to smell good. "I apologize for her rudeness." He said. I braced myself for whatever he was going to say. "You remember when Bradley Caruthers died?"

"Yes."

"Detective Dartnell has been fascinated with your family ever since then. I have to admit your family is very interesting. I've never seen a family full of so many masterminds that actually work so well together. Normally when you have so many intelligent people together like that, someone's ego gets in the way. There's normally a slip up that brings the whole family down but you guys are rather remarkable." He said while looking me up and down. The sad part is, if I didn't know who he was I would've dated him in a heartbeat. He seemed like he could be my speed. I had to check myself because I knew Malcolm was listening. "Do you love Malcolm Latour?"

"Yes, the father of my children."

"But he's only fathered one of your kids right?"

"He is the biological father of one, but the natural father of all three."

He flashed that pretty smile again. "I like that the natural father of all three." His breath deepened when his eyes danced on my shirt. He looked to the left and Detective Dartnell was way across the floor looking irritated. "I've been watching you."

"Have you now?" I said crossing my legs. I had on pants, but he still looked at my thighs.

"Yes, I wish we could've met some other way."

I gestured with my hands. "Unfortunately we didn't so..." I gestured again. My plane pulled up, "It's something about you that draws me in. I like watching you like some people like watching TV."

I leaned a little closer so he could get a good look down my cleavage. I knew it would piss Dartnell off, plus I was digging this interchange with him. "What do you need?" I asked in a regular voice.

His eyes were down the shirt I wore for Malcolm, but his biscuit head didn't even respond to it. He almost forgot himself. He straightened up, and cleared his throat. I smiled at him. "Don't be a tease Amber." He said with a smile.

I tried to look innocent. "Who me?" Then we both laughed. Dartnell didn't like that at all. "Seriously, flattery will get you everywhere. What do you need?"

"I need to be able to touch base with you. Ask you some questions from time to time."

"Well that would be betraying my family and we both know that's not gonna happen."

"But I thought Malcolm wasn't your man?"

"He's not, but you also asked me if I loved him." I reminded him.

"You have a beautiful mouth!" He stared at my lips.

I smiled. "Thank you!"

He bit his lip. "So here's my card." He reached into his jacket and pulled out a card. "Call me when you get back."

I took the card. "Thank you, but I won't be calling you."

"Why not?" He said smiling.

"We don't need to talk about anything or anyone. You're a cop against me."

"I just wanna make sure you don't have any questions."

"Thanks, but I don't."

He looked me in my eyes. "You don't?"

I returned his stare. "What's to know, you wanna do me so bad you'd risk your job. I don't think that's a very wise course for anyone. Thank you for the pick me up though. You have definitely put a smile on my face today."

"It's something about you, this has never happened to me before. I know you're probably used to guys drooling over you, but I can't believe this!"

"Guys don't drool over me."

"Yes they do, you must be blind."

"I must be, because that's not what happens."

"But I know Malcolm blows your head up on a regular basis." I smiled a polite smile, but I had nothing to say to that. Dartnell started coming back. "I'll try to get her to calm down."

She gave Turan the evilest look, and then she looked at me. "Your flight will be boarding soon, so we're gonna go. When you come back I'll see about getting that warrant to bring you in for questioning."

"Whatever!" I said rolling my eyes. The flight attendant announced that the first class customers and those flying with children and handicapped were now boarding. I didn't look at either of them; I stood up and walked. Just as I entered the walkway, I looked back and Turan was still watching me. As soon as I rounded the corner, I took my phone out of my pocket. "Hello?"

"Where are you going?" Malcolm sounded irritated.

"I decided to take my dumb behind to a random place for a quick getaway. I'll be back in a few days." Then I hung up.

When I opened the door, the smell of the fresh paint still hit my nose. Shasta asked me what I thought about her placement of things in the condo when we were shopping for things for my house. I lied and told her I loved it, and I thanked her. It's taken some years, but I wanted to see my finished product at least once. I fell in love with my finished dining room. The jade napkin and candlestick holders were beautiful! My gold and cream china set with gold chargers complimented my purple, chocolate, and green tablecloth. The credenza matched my table perfectly and it held the rest of my china like a display case. The kitchen matched the dining room perfectly. None of my pots and pans have ever been used. The rest of my furniture arrived and the living room invited you to come in and relax. I started crying as I walked from room to room. I decorated that place with my heart. Even his office looked amazing. It was also the only sign that he's been here at all. I could tell he worked in there whenever he came out here. The bed was huge and beautiful in our room. This was supposed to be our love nest. My suitcases were still in the closet, but he took my clothes out and hung them on my side of the walk-in closet. It looked like he was trying to show that I had been there. I pulled myself together then I called Sasha. I told her I was at the condo. She got excited and asked if Malcolm and I were back together. I told her we weren't but I was curious to see the final product. I asked her if she wanted to have dinner after work. She screamed of course!! I told her I'd invite Kimmy too if she could make it. Then I treated myself to a little shopping spree on Malcolm of course. I drove my beautiful bullet, and I hit a bunch of the shops on Rodeo Dr. They were beautiful pieces. I hung them up on my side of the closet and set my shoes on my side. When Sasha came, she oohed and awed with me over the place. Then she eyeballed my clothes. She drooled over a black dress and shoes I just bought. So I put them in a bag and gave them to her. Who knows when I would be back and able to wear them? She got so excited she jumped on me, kissing my face all over. I told her she was too grown to be jumping on me like that, but I loved every minute of it. We picked Kimmy up then went to the Vine for dinner. I showed them pictures of Andre. I felt eyes on me and I looked around. There was Torrie looking at me trying to act like she wasn't. I hadn't seen her since that night, and Toya was right. She did look rough; I still wanted to sock her up as soon as I saw her but as long as she stayed out my way, we'd be fine. Kimmy told me that the label wants to drop her and wish her well on her future projects. She's still selling records, but she hasn't had a hit since she moved to LA. Kimmy asked if I was looking to get back in the game, shooting videos. I told her I liked spending time at home and not flying all over the world for gigs. She told me Ramell asked about me. I forgot to give him my new number. I didn't want to be pulled into any more media circus acts, so I wasn't in any hurry to call. I told her, just that fast the world had forgotten about me, and I liked it. I said I wanted to keep my hands dirty and stay in the game, but I didn't want to go hard like I was before. I wanted to spend time with my grandson. Kimmy asked me to stay on top of my craft because she may need me in the near future for a few gigs. She said Corey has been on her back about getting me back together with him. Torrie walked the long way around the restaurant to leave. I smiled to myself saying, "she better had!" On our way to taking Kimmy home, she mentioned a meeting that she was gonna have in the city. She asked if we could do dinner, when she came out. I asked if her man was coming with her, and she said she never brought him to the bay. Laughing to myself, I told her to let me know when she was coming.

Sasha and I said goodbye in the garage, she had to get home for work in the morning. I told her I would probably go home Friday but I'd let her know if I changed my mind. I took a wonderful bubble bath, and since I was alone and didn't have any pj's I decided to sleep commando.

I was knocked out when I heard the alarm chime that the front door opened. Then I heard it close. I sat up and listened. I felt around for my robe in the dark. I could hear the wheels on the suitcase coming towards my room. The footsteps stopped in front of the closed door. "Amber?" Malcolm's voice cracked as he opened the door. I couldn't find my robe in the dark. I put the covers up to my neck as the light from the hallway came in the room. "Yea, it's me." He reached for the light switch.

"Bright light!" I said before he turned it on.

"What are you doing here?"

I spotted my robe on the floor next to the bed. I rolled my eyes at it. "Are you expecting someone?"

"No one comes here." He said still standing in the doorway.

"You want me to leave?"

He exhaled and went to the closet. "Just figured you might've wanted to hang out with your detective friend." He had an attitude.

I grabbed my robe off the floor and put it on. "Whatever, since when you care about someone flirting with me?" I said somewhat laughing as I walked to the closet doorway.

He was standing there looking at my clothes. "No ones ever been crazy enough to do that in front of me."

"I called you when the chick was harassing me. I had no idea it was gonna change like that. Has she ever approached you?"

"Or else you wouldn't have called?" The look on his face said answer right.

"Of course!"

He pointed to my clothes. "You moving in?"

"I just figured there should be more appropriate representation for me than what you had hanging." I smiled

He shook his head. "Whatever!" He was still irritated with me. "I have a meeting in the morning and a date in the evening. How long you staying?"

"I don't know."

"I'll sleep in the other room."

"Why would you tell me you have a date?" I asked annoyed.

"I'm just being honest. Since I'm such a liar, or I guess I don't tell you nothing." He said taking off his clothes like he was irritated.

"Meaning?" I said crossing my arms.

"Whatever you were telling that punk over the phone. I have half a mind to get him fired!"

"Why? Because he was acknowledging he liked what he saw? I got dressed this morning with you in mind. Can you even tell me what I was wearing?"

His eyes swept around the closet trying to cheat. "Whatever, you can't tell me what I was wearing?"

"You had a grey sweater that hung off your body like it was made with you in it. Black slacks that had been pressed with a perfect crease. Grey socks, black Stacy Adams, and a black leather jacket." Then I smiled again.

He tried not to smile. "You be checking for me like that?"

"Why are you jealous about someone else flirting with me?"

He stiffened again. "You were going for it. Probably would've said more if I wasn't on the phone."

"So what's your point?"

"I don't wanna hear all that. How he know I'm not your man?"

"Cause that chick implied it at the beginning of our convo and I told her we aren't together."

"Well that's only because of you!" He barked

"Here we go!" I said throwing my hands up and walking away. I climbed back in the middle of the bed and pulled the covers up to my neck.

"You don't wanna talk about that though!" He barked from the closet.

"You have a date tomorrow, goodnight!" I turned my back to the closet.

"How you gonna be here and act like that?" He sounded more frustrated.

"Act like what?"

"First you call me, and have me sit through your whole flirting episode. Then you hung up in my face, YOU KNOW I HATE THAT! Then you gonna be here, knowing what this place means, not even caring."

"Not caring about what?"

"ME!"

"I'm confused, how am I not caring about you?"

"You know what Amber! If you don't get it, I don't have time to explain it to you!" He stormed out the room slammed my door, went in the other room and slammed the door.

What in the world is his problem? I sat there for a minute making sure in my brain that I was looking at Malcolm. I got out of the bed and I knocked on his door. He told me to go away so I opened the door. He was sitting on the edge of the bed pissed off. I sat next to him and I waited for him to come back to earth. "So now you want me to visibly trip all over myself over you? Nothing I do is enough for you."

"I know the feeling."

He looked at me. "Is that how you took it? Like I cheated cause you weren't enough?"

"I told you that all the time."

"I don't remember that." He said sounding deflated.

"And you know why, because you were just too busy asking me 'why you let them bother you?' Like I was crazy for feeling some kind of way about it." I said bumping him.

He smiled, "I do remember saying that."

"I'm not trying to confuse you or make you feel badly. I really wanted to see what this place looked like all put together, even though I vowed I wouldn't come back here." I said, "I saw Torrie tonight."

"Where?"

"At the Vine. I had dinner with Sasha and Kimmy, she was there. I still wanna beat on her when I see her. Thinking about her makes me angry with you all over again."

"Are you gonna hold that over my head forever?"

"I'm not over it yet, but it doesn't hurt as much today as it did yesterday. It might stop hurting just in time for you to meet somebody else."

"That's not even funny."

I stood up. "Goodnight Malcolm."

"We really gonna sleep like room mates?"

"You got a date tomorrow, and I came out to get my dumb behind away from you." He exhaled. "The cold piece about what you said is that our boys know first hand ALL about you and your tramps. They wouldn't say anything to me but the way they insisted on coming with me that night; they knew what they'd find at your house. I was the only one stupid enough to think I was gonna find you there alone so we could talk. Maybe they didn't have proper introductions to your tramps, but you're no better than me. I thought I was in love and if Andy is giving this relationship his all, who are you to judge him? Stop being so prepared to not like her. I haven't been properly introduced yet either but he has a poster child for how not to be. Andre is still young enough that if it doesn't workout at this point, he wouldn't remember her anyways. Be nice Malcolm."

"Fine! I apologize for what I said." He barked.

Then I walked to the door. "Doesn't count if you don't mean it." Then I shut his door.

Chapter 53

"MOMMA! DREW ALMOST KILLED HIM!"

I was leaving the school when Darryl called me. "Almost killed who?"

"THE GUY! SHOOT I DON'T EVEN REMEMBER HIS NAME, YOU REMEMBER?" He asked in the background. "TRACY'S EX! TOYA BROUGHT HIM TO SOPHIA'S. HE FOLLOWED HER IN THE BATHROOM SLAPPING HER AROUND AND STUFF! IT EXPLODED FROM THERE!"

"Baby please stop screaming in my ear." My stomach was in knots

"Sorry momma, I'm just a little pumped up right now." Darryl said

"Where's Andy right now?"

"We left them at Sophia's."

"Ok so now tell me what happened, calmly!"

Darryl told me how he and Derrick went to court this morning to see what was happening. Andrew and Tracy were having restraining orders enforced by the courts against Toya and Tracy's ex boyfriend. Apparently, they had a fight not too long ago. Darryl said Toya was looking very pregnant. I asked him why she was fighting if she's pregnant and he said he didn't know. Derrick said he told her she better be happy that Andrew didn't kill the guy she was with cause that would've meant lights out for her. I asked if the baby was with them, Darryl said Andre was at daycare. I got off the phone with Darryl and I called Andrew. Although he was trying to be calm, I could tell he was still very upset. I asked if they were ok, he said they were. I told him I would get the baby from daycare and they could take all the time they needed. When I called Malcolm, he answered the phone saying he was already aware. I asked him what he was gonna do about it, and he said nothing. I asked him why and he said he had talked to Andrew already and Andrew didn't want his help dealing with the guy or Toya. Malcolm said that he knows that Toya's been talking to Detective Dartnell, which explains why she would be so bold to go to Sophia's. She feels somewhat protected. Malcolm was quiet for a minute, and then he told me he met Tracy. I smiled real big, and then I asked him what he thought of her. He was quiet again for a minute. He said until proven otherwise, he thought she was ok. This was his way of saying that maybe just maybe he liked her, which meant he really did like her. I asked him if he talked to her and real fast, he said NO but he could see why we all liked her and wanted to bring her in. Then he said he hoped Andrew didn't mess it up. I told him I hoped so as well.

****

"That is my pre whipped Shea butter. It's an excellent moisturizer for your skin, hair, and nails." The woman said trying to get me to buy from her.

It was a nice day in Berkeley at the Ashby Bart station. Andrew and Andre were on their way to meet me here. I was strolling through all the vendor booths. "Um, let me think about it. I'll be back." I said

Then I heard, "NANA!" Andre yelled as he ran towards me.

I held out my arms and scooped my baby up as he landed in my arms. "My goodness! You are getting big! Have you been eating your fruits and vegetables?"

"Yes! Just like you told me to." He said with a big smile.

I gave him hugs and kisses, and then I hugged and kissed Andy. His face looked really bothered. I asked him what was wrong, he grabbed my hand. My heart dropped; please don't tell me that he and Tracy broke up after all this. "What is it baby?" I said searching his face for a clue.

He blew air. He opened his mouth and then closed it. "Can we go somewhere we can sit?" He asked.

"I wanted to go to Rockridge after this to get some more soaps and lotions, we could go there?" I said

Still holding my hand he said, "let's go." We got in his car, he strapped Andre in, and then we drove up Ashby. Andrew showed me where Tracy lived, and then he found a parking space on the street next to a meter. When he turned off the engine he sat there gripping the steering wheel. "I'm scared momma! I am really scared!" He had a look of disbelief on his face.

"Is something wrong?" I asked even though I didn't want to.

"No," then he exhaled. "For the first time ever, everything feels right and it's terrifying to me. She loves me momma, I know it. I can see it, and I feel it." He took a deep breath. "All this time I thought Jennay was the one, but it's Tracy. She loves my son like he's her own. She has a little temper on her, which I think is so cute. She can be a little dramatic but it's not bad or anything like that. She doesn't look at me and see Malcolm's son or that cute guy with money. She sees me, and she loves what she sees." He said trying to hold back tears.

But I was already crying, his little speech moved me. "Does she know who you are?"

He exhaled, "at this point it doesn't matter. She can't leave me! I won't let her!"

"What do you mean?"

"I'm showing her things here and there. My goal is to not overwhelm her where she runs from me. I don't want her to be afraid of me." Then he exhaled again. "Do you like her momma? I need to know the truth, make sure I'm not being too idealistic."

"Andy you like her, I love her! You've calmed down so much since you two have gotten together but why all the sudden angst about your relationship?"

"I wanna propose, but I'm scared."

I got butterflies. "Why?"

"I don't know, I wanna do it right! I don't want anyone feeling left out but I don't want a whole crowd there either. This is a personal moment you know what I mean?"

"How about a small dinner?"

"She's nosey, she might catch on if we do anything outside of the norm." He said

We got out of the car bouncing ideas off of each other. I was so excited you would think it was my proposal we were pondering. I took them to all my fancy body stuff spots. We decided that they should have a dinner at her house under the guise that our families should meet, in which we should. I told him to plant the ideas, but let her believe she came up with it. He liked that idea; we started the stage for his proposal. Then I asked him if he had the ring yet. When he said no, I told him we had to go to Tiffany's pronto! Andy was acting so cute the whole way there. He was giggly and nervous. I loved seeing my baby like this. I looked at what we were wearing, neither one of us were dressed the part for the damage we were about to do in this store. When we walked in the store a few sales people looked at us but only a young girl named Katie, she was probably new, offered to help us. The rest of the staff kind of turned their noses up at us. Andy was nervous at first, I saw him give his self a pep talk, and then his presence changed. He told the sales girl that he needed an engagement ring that could easily be upgraded with a wedding band. She looked at both of us and asked if we had a style in mind. Andy gave her specific details, he wanted a platinum setting, heart shaped center diamond with very few as close to none as he could get inclusions, he told her Tracy's favorite color was blue so he wanted sapphires in the ring as well. Katie asked him what size diamond did he have in mind for the center stone. He told her nothing smaller than a carat to start. Another salesperson overheard Andrew's list of demands and told Katie that they didn't have anything like that in the store. Katie asked if they could get it, and the salesperson said she'd have to speak to the manager. They said it like it was a waste of time. Katie was as irritated as I was; she excused herself and went to the back. She came out with an older woman who looked a little surprised when she saw us. I was holding Andre on my hip trying my hardest not to go off.

The manager shook our hands, and then Andrew explained what he wanted in the ring. "As your other salesperson rudely pointed out, what I'm looking for you may not have in the store. My question is when can you get it?" Andrew had his business voice on and suddenly they were all paying attention.

Katie took out a sketchpad and she drew what she thought Andrew was looking for. She had the center stone heart shaped, with a sapphire on each side. Andrew told her to add another diamond next to the sapphires and she had his ring. They went over size, color, cuts, and clarity. Listening to my baby talk, he had done his homework, he knew exactly what he wanted. The manager wrote down the final price according to his request. Andrew looked at the price, he didn't flinch. He pulled out his wallet, looked Katie in her eyes, and told her to charge it. Katie and the manager stared at Andrew's Black card. The manager looked at me, "you're a very lucky woman."

"Thank you, but this is my son." I said with the biggest smile. "But thank you all the same. I'm very proud of him and his soon to be fiancée is a very special lady."

Katie had the biggest smile as Andrew signed the order. Katie went to the back to get everything in order. Andrew told the manager that he was very pleased with the service he received today from Katie. He told her that in the future he only wanted to deal with her for future purchases. He said the rest of her staff needed to learn not to judge a book by its cover. The manager agreed with him. I wandered over to the side and wondered if someone was picking a ring for me what would they choose? I looked in display case after display case, but nothing said Amber to me. Then Andre called me over, he pointed to a pair of amethyst earrings that begged me to try them on. I asked Katie to take them out for me. They were the cutest studs. I asked Andre if he liked them. He shook his head yes; I put on the matching pendant and ring. The ring was a little big, but Katie said they would resize it for me. I looked at myself in the mirror and I fell in love with my reflection. Katie took out boxes for my jewelry and started wrapping them. When I looked at her with a question mark, Andrew and Andre stood there with huge smiles. "They look beautiful on you momma, you deserve them." I got excited and thanked Andrew. "Why don't you buy more jewelry?"

"I don't know." I said sounding deflated. Dwayne bought me diamond chips and I love them to pieces. I guess I kind of felt like it was no fun having jewelry unless it came from someone's heart. I hadn't thought about Dwayne in years, I literally shook my head to shake him out.

I thanked Katie again for everything then we left the store. We could hear applauds for Katie sounding off as we left.

****

"AND THAT'S A WRAP!" Corey yelled through his bullhorn. "GREAT JOB EVERYBODY! This is gonna be EPIC!"

Krissy and Asia came over hugging me so tight and jumping up and down. They cried when I picked them out of the line up for this video. During one of our many lunch breaks they shared their stories. Girls from out of the area, they come to one of the big cities to try and make it, they put it all on the line in hopes that someone would see in them what they feel is real within their selves. Sasha came to the set a few times and she hit it off with quite a few of the dancers. I don't know where those girls found the energy to dance all day and sometimes all night and still go out and party. Aw! To be young, but tonight Sasha's having dinner with Corey and I. Kimmy couldn't make it. Sasha and Corey were helping their selves to cocktails while I got ready. I took a shower, lotioned up, put my black bra and matching panties on and then I went in the closet. Even though most of the items in this closet were so many seasons ago, I took the price tag off one of my dresses and pulled out the never worn shoes. This look had a hat, which is why I choose it. I pulled all my hair back in a low bun. Then I sat at the vanity and lightly made up my face. I heard the front door chime; I assumed it was Sasha or Corey stepping out for a minute. Then Malcolm walked in the door. I hadn't laid eyes on him in what felt like forever but more like almost two years. "Whoa!"

"What?" He said closing the door behind him.

"Didn't know you were coming, that's all." I watched his eyes in the mirror.

"You shy all of a sudden?" He scanned my body in the chair.

"Maybe." I did not want to get up.

"I've seen you naked." He said with a smile like he was reminiscing.

"That was a long time ago. Can you hand me that robe?" I pointed to my black silk robe laying on the bed.

He picked it up then he held it out like he was inspecting it. "I remember this!" He handed it to me.

I grinned trying to act like I didn't know what he was talking about. "You do?"

"Un huh! You made me massage you, but you weren't giving it up! I know you remember." He smiled at me.

"You're in a good mood." I said putting my arms in the robe even though I was still sitting down.

"Even though I talk to you all the time, I realized I haven't laid eyes on you in sometime. It's good to see you."

"It's good to see you." I stood up, my robe was open. I didn't think about it until I saw Malcolm staring. "Stop staring, look away, or something." I blushed.

Malcolm sat on the bed. "I take it the video finished early?"

"Yes, thank goodness! We're going out to eat, if you don't have plans you can come." I smiled.

Malcolm was quiet for a minute. "Where are we going?" He said, going to the closet as he changed his shirt.

I peeked in; yep he's still got it! I said to myself. "Corey made reservations somewhere I'll tell him to increase them." I opened the bedroom door, "Corey" I sang...

"Already done!" He said to me. Then I heard Sasha laugh as he told her he was right.

"It's done!" I dropped my robe to the floor and picking up my dress.

"Ok, cool!" He said as he walked out the closet. He pursed his lips as he looked at me.

I stepped into my dress and pulled it up. I admired the fit in the mirror and then I smiled at him. "I still feel like that little fifteen year old fat girl most of the time. I say thank you Nana every time I look in the mirror."

Malcolm looked down then he went back in the closet. My dress, shoes, newsboy styled hat, and purse were black and white. Then I put on my cocktail length red coat. I felt spiffy, and I could care less about seasons. Sasha eyeballed my outfit as I walked out of the room. "You can have it tomorrow." I said, she smiled and clapped her hands.

Corey's limo took us to the restaurant. Malcolm and Corey were talking about some old school movie, while Sasha told me about her new love. I smiled while she talked about how new everything was. I pretended not to notice Malcolm staring at my legs on the car ride to the restaurant. He was acting weird, or maybe he's always acted like this and I don't remember. When we got to the restaurant he held my hand as I climbed out. "There's Corey Alexander!" Someone said, and then a camera was on him. "Oh snap! Is that Amber Wallace???" The guy said. "You look AMAZING! You haven't changed one bit!" The camera guy said. Embarrassed, I said thank you. Then the guy asked if we hung out on a regular basis. Corey said, "we work hard we play hard!" Then we went inside the restaurant.

"Do people still recognize you a lot?" Sasha asked

"They haven't in a long time, that was weird." I frowned.

"Why are you frowning?" Malcolm asked

"Because tomorrow they'll probably say I'm really a man or that I'm dating Corey. The media circus was a definite a turn off to being in the lime light."

Dinner was nice; there was never an awkward silence at any point. Corey was telling Malcolm about our last video project. It was for this guy group and very futuristic. Corey told Malcolm he thought I would shy away from the project because of all the wires and the direction of the choreography. He told Malcolm they let me loose on those wires for three days and what I came back with was amazing on film. I blushed and thanked Corey for the compliment. "Amber can be pretty fearless." Malcolm said smiling at me. "Did she ever tell you how we met?"

"I thought you guys went to school together?" Sasha said

"That's where, but not how." Malcolm said

Corey smiled, "please tell us."

"Some back ground first. Back then most people was scared of me."

"Only then?" Sasha said, "I'm still nervous around you."

"I don't see why, I've been around all of your life. You're like a daughter to me." Malcolm said matter of factly. Then he returned to his story. "Anyways, most people were afraid of me. I noticed her one day walking with your mom," he said pointing to Sasha. "And her sister Jade, Jade and I had almost every class together. Jade never showed me any fear either so I would talk to her from time to time. I asked her who she was walking with and she said her sister and her cousin. Then I realized we had the same PE period, so I kind of watched her being a little girl not concerned with anything. Just when I was gonna write her off as too prissy, I see her jump in a girl's face like she was gonna handle her. My curiosity was peaked, that's when you noticed me watching huh?" I smiled at the memory and nodded my head yes. "Since she was in a grade lower than me she had lunch a period before mine. So I went to the cafeteria and sat down at the end of her table and I kept looking at her. I wanted to see if she was gonna be scared of me like everybody else. This little girl walks right over to me and starts talking. No one had ever done that before. It made me nervous kind of, like I was losing my edge or something."

"You didn't seem nervous, just mysterious, and creepy." We all laughed

"Then she made my heart skip a beat when she made mincemeat out of this girl almost twice her size. Her mother was the only person I saw her run from, and that was for a good reason. She's always been kind of fearless. Guess that's why she's made it so far." He was looking at me, I was blushing. Sasha and Corey were looking back and forth between us.

"So why aren't you guys together?" Corey asked

"I've got a lot of issues. She put up with me for as long as she could, but everyone has a limit of how much they can take and being young and dumb, I pushed her there. Tonight is the first time I've laid eyes on her in, how long did we say?"

"Almost two years." I said

"Right! Almost two years, and look at you. You're even better than I remembered!" Then he took another swallow of his drink.

"How many of those have you had? I think you need to slow down." I blushed harder than I ever had.

"This is only my first drink and I miss you! I know you miss me, but I'm gonna ask you anyways. Do you miss me?" He said staring me in my eyes.

I shifted in my seat. Then I sat up, leaned forward, and touched his hand. I looked him straight in his eyes. "No!" We all started laughing. "I have been enjoying the peace and quiet." We laughed some more. "We talk on the phone at least two to three times a week. I could only miss your face."

"And she always has jokes and then she wonders where our youngest got it from." He said with a smile. I smiled back.

Corey shared pictures of his wife and kids. He said his wife hates the circus too. He said she was the reason he tries his best to stay out of the limelight. Sasha told Malcolm about the guy she's seeing even though I nudged her under the table to stop talking but she kept going. Malcolm was soaking it in, when we were walking out of the restaurant I told her she could kiss her relationship goodbye, because Malcolm was gonna hunt him down. When she asked me why, I asked her what part of like a daughter to him didn't she understand? Sasha swallowed hard as the reality of what she did settled in. She said oh well and shrugged it off. We made sure Sasha was in her car safe and sound then we went upstairs. Malcolm kept staring at me like he used to way back in the day. I smiled at him but I didn't have anything to say. I took out one of my shopping bags and I put my shoes in it, with my coat and hat. Malcolm asked what I was doing; I told him I was giving Sasha my clothes. I told him she was always eyeballing all of my clothes, I give her the stuff she likes. I told him it wasn't like I was going to miss them. He asked if we wore the same size shoe, my feet were a size bigger than hers, she never cared. I let my hair fall out of the bun. Malcolm rushed me and kissed me. He made my knees buckle! "What was that?"

"I've been dying to do that all night." He said with a smile, and then he walked into the closet.

"Ok!" I said trying to get my bearings. "How long are you here?"

"Just the night, you?"

"I leave in the morning too. I was asking because I asked the housekeeper to come tomorrow. If you were still gonna be here I would've told her to wait but since you're not, I'll leave it alone." I pulled out a nightgown from my drawer. It wasn't fancy, or seductive but it was soft and comfortable. Of course Malcolm walks out the closet as I'm pulling my dress over my head.

"Nice underwear."

I hurried to get the dress over my head. "Thanks, you weren't supposed to come out so fast." I said feeling embarrassed and hurried to put my gown on. I took my bra off under the gown.

"You know what they remind me of?" He said with a, *you know* smile.

"No."

"What you wore the first time we did it."

I smiled remembering my underwear. He said he liked it then too. "Oh yea. It felt like you were trying to kill me!"

He smiled, "sorry."

"What's up with all the reminiscing tonight?"

"I've just been thinking about us. I could've flown back home earlier, but I figured I wanted to see you since we were both out here."

"Oh" I said folding my dress and putting it in the bag. "So you changed your flight?"

"Yep" he said watching me.

"What?" He kept staring at me.

"I think I got it."

"You got what?" I said

He sat on the bed and patted the seat next to him. I sat down; he put my hand in his. "Did I tell you I've been going to Joanne?" I shook my head no. "Yea, I see why you go when you do. It helps to purge sometimes." Then he cleared his throat. "I know I hurt you!" My body stiffened. "I can't tell you how sorry I am about that. My nightmares came back worse after you told me." He swallowed and then shook off the bad feeling. "I keep a lot of stuff bottled up, and it comes out angry every time. I think I've told you all about this. I had you in my life bending over backwards to please me, because I thought I needed stuff that it turns I didn't have to have. At the time, I honestly thought I needed it though. I left the door open for Dwayne, and as much as I try to blame anyone else for David, I couldn't blame anyone but myself for Dwayne. To this day and probably forever, I will always be jealous about that one. So this is your warning, I'm gonna lose it whenever he's involved because he should've never been." He took a breath. "Whenever I pissed you off in the past, did I ever let you lay in it?" I shook my head no. "But I never messed up that bad before either. It's not helping either one of us for me to be so scared to face you. Besides, I'm Malcolm Latour, besides Momma who am I really scared of?"

"Me!" I smiled.

"You and Momma." He smiled. "So just know, I'm back in the game. Where should we start?"

"Game? I'm not a game Malcolm."

"Not game, you know what I mean. What I need you to do is tell me how to make this right? I'll do... Almost anything."

"Almost?"

"You know you, I have to say almost." He smiled.

"You're serious?"

"As a heart attack!" My body jerked when he said it. "Wrong choice of words. You know what I mean."

"You've made peace with Derrick and Darryl, what about Andy?"

His body slumped. "How did I know you'd pick the most difficult thing!"

"Because it's the truth. I need you to try harder. Our son is going to get married; he has a family of his own. He's gonna need you just like you needed Daddy."

He put his leg around me so that I could lean back in to him. "Has he ever liked me?" He asked as he put his arms around me.

"Of course he has, he's your son. I think he's always been a little apprehensive when it comes to you but he loves you, not more than he loves his momma though." I said with a smile.

"Look at us." Malcolm said looking in the mirror across from the bed. "We never got the chance to break this place in." I blew air, he squeezed me tighter. "I know what you like!" He said pulling my gown up to show my black panties. He tried to pull them down but I wouldn't cooperate by raising up so he could pull them off, so he put his hand under them and started rubbing me. I didn't want to give in to the feeling, I kept trying to think about clouds, bubbles, the sun anything other than how good this felt. My body betrayed me and started jerking. He licked his fingers. "Delicious!"

"I hate you!" I said breathless.

"I love you too!" He kissed my cheek.

****

"Hey girl, what you got going on tonight?" Sophia asked

"Nothing, I may go get my grand baby and just hang out here. You?"

"Don't you wanna let your hair down tonight?" I could hear her snapping her fingers over the phone. "You can play grandma another night."

I smiled, "what did you have in mind?"

"I don't know, let's get dressed up and go out. I know Malcolm's got your head all twisted up right now. Let's just leave that on the floor for tonight. We need to blow off steam!"

"You mean you need to stop thinking about Richard!"

"I mean we need to let our hair down, and whatever happens tonight, happens. Here we are in our forties, worried about fools who met us when we were thirteen and fourteen! Are you in? You know I can keep going."

I laughed, "I know you can. Is there anywhere out there?"

"A karaoke bar, you feel like singing?"

"No, but I feel like dancing!"

"Ok! So that exes out this area."

"What about EA? We haven't been in a minute. They all went the other night. Everybody was there but us!" I said like we were left out.

"Now they know the party doesn't start until we walk in!"

"Ok!" We both started laughing. "Ok, so talking like that can be exhausting." Sophia blew air. "Tell me about it."

"Andy will have a fit if we just show up. So let me invite him and see what he says."

"He's gonna say no. Invite Tracy and tell her Sabrina will watch the baby."

"Ooh good thinking! I'll hire a limo after we have the green light. Let me call Tracy and I'll call you back."

I talked to Tracy and sure enough they were in. As we were leaving the house something told me don't leave, that my original plan to stay in was best. But Sophia was excited to leave. I told Sabrina to call us if she needed ANYTHING! I kissed Andre, then we were off to pick up his parents. In the limo Sophia told me that we gotta whip our hair back and forth showing that we were letting our hair down. After awhile, I had to stop cause I was getting dizzy but when we went in the house we did it a couple more times for the fun of it. Andy seemed happy but tired. Tracy kept looking at us and smiling, this was her first time with Sophia and I unprofessionally attached. Talk about letting your hair down. When we got to EA it was like I remembered, I hadn't been here in quite some time, they made a few upgrades, everything was still nice, and this was still the place to be. Darryl came over all excited cause we were there. He said he was calling Derrick to tell him we were there. When our drinks came we all downed them. I gave Tracy a thumbs up

for this one. Sophia and I took Tracy out on the floor to do what we came to do, which is dance and let our hair down. We were dancing for a minute when Nicole joined us. She was talking to Tracy and pointing at Hubby back with Andrew. We kept dancing then this wanna be cool looking kid called himself dancing up on Tracy. He was trying to be all over her, and you don't do that to just anybody. Sophia grabbed my arm cause I was about to go off on him, but Tracy handled it like a lady and simply walked away as she shook her head no at him. I stepped on his foot with my heel, and said "oops." Andrew was already looking when we got back to the seats. He seemed ok, but was definitely paying attention. Then I saw him coming, I nudged Sophia and she nudged me back. Malcolm's eyes were locked on me and my body temp went up. I could see Tracy out the corner of my eye watching us like we were a screenplay. Malcolm said his hellos then he sat next to me. "So what brings you out tonight?" He asked me.
"Sophia and I wanted to let our hair down. How about you?"
"I came to see you!"
"Un huh" I smiled. "You look good Malcolm!"
He blushed, "thank you."
We were chatting for quite a few minutes when I realized everyone was gone and we were the only ones in the booth; everybody else was on the dance floor. I convinced Malcolm to dance with me, which wasn't hard. As we were walking to the dance floor, I asked him if he remembered the first time we danced at a club together and I didn't think he could dance. He stood in the middle of the floor just like he did then and I danced around him like I did then. We started cracking up laughing. He told me I still had it, I told him and I always will. We were dancing and the music changed, they put on step music. Oh yea! The dance floor kind of cleared out which was good cause we needed space to move. We got lost in the music and good time. When the music changed again the crowd kind of came back. Then that same stupid kid bumped into Malcolm so hard he almost lost it. The stupid kid started yelling and carrying on when Malcolm ordered to have him taken out. So much for our dancing fun. I was irritated especially when I thought Malcolm was gonna be irritated for the rest of the night. Malcolm, to my surprise returned to his normal self. We returned to our seats and seemed to pick up right where we left off. Malcolm was saying how happy he was that he came. Then I heard Sophia say that she was getting tired too. True we had been there for a few hours but it was still early.
"Tired? Who's tired?" I asked. Our group raised their hands. "Wimps!" I said disappointed "I guess I gotta go."
"What?" Malcolm said sounding disappointed.
"We came together, we gotta leave together." I shrugged.
"But I can take you home." He said holding my hand
"Some other time."
"We might as well go too." Malcolm said to Derrick
We all walked out of the door together. The air was crisp and cool, we were waiting for the limo. Malcolm was trying to control his disappointment. Then we heard the footsteps hurrying towards us, I turned around and I saw some girl running up. Derrick pulled his gun out and pointed it in her face, "female you must feel like dying today!" She stopped dead in her tracks.
"Seriously Karen? You wanna fight outside a club? How old are you?" Tracy yelled.
Sophia laughed, "she's a stupid somebody!"

Derrick put his gun down. "This is what you're gonna do! Take you're little busted self and go tend to your man! Next time you think about running up on somebody, just say no. If I ever hear about my sister having problems with you, well, I'll just have to pay you a little visit at 2121 Arlington Ave!" She gasped! She didn't move right away she was stuck out of fear. "If you stay, well that's gonna irritate me. You won't like me when I'm angry but the choice is yours." She started backing away slowly. "I thought so!" Then he looked across the street at Toya. "If you don't stop instigating!" He put a fist up, "you know what's up!" She walked away annoyed. Malcolm looked at Andrew, "I keep telling you about that one." He said in an authoritative tone.

"Malcolm not right now!" Andrew barked.

"Mark my words! You gonna have to do something about that one." Malcolm said matter of factly.

Andrew was completely pissed off; I squeezed Malcolm's hand in hopes that he would tone it down some. Andrew was about to come apart.

"She just needs a visit." Derrick said matter of factly.

"She needs more than a visit." Malcolm said.

"Come on you guys," I said trying to calm everyone down. "Let's not talk about this tonight. Let's just go get something to eat. I need something to soak up this liquor."

"We could go back to my restaurant. It's almost closing so we can have the place to ourselves." Sophia suggested.

Everyone liked the idea, so Hubby told Nicole to ride with us, and Andrew went with him.

"You ok?" Nicole asked Tracy

She said "Yea," but she didn't look like it.

When we got to the restaurant Sophia called all of her staff out. She asked who would be willing to stay for double and a half overtime pay. Only one lady couldn't stay. She had to get home to her kids. I knew Sophia would pay her anyways. They made a long table for us in the middle of the main floor. We had wine and delicious food. Sophia told her staff to bring out all the specials and to keep the wine coming. Tracy and Nicole got up and went to the bathroom. Andrew watched Tracy walk away then he told Malcolm to stop talking about paying people visits in front of Tracy. She didn't know what he meant and he didn't want to explain it either. Malcolm asked him when were they supposed to discuss it because Andrew kept avoiding the subject. Andrew was trying to keep his voice down; he told Malcolm that he was talking about Andre's mother! Malcolm asked Andrew if Toya cared that she was Andre's mother especially now that she wasn't getting any kind of money for him. He said she's been talking to the police about all of them; meanwhile she keeps trying to provoke them. Malcolm said she was a waste of a person, set on causing other people pain. Malcolm told Andrew that if he didn't do anything she was going to end up getting to Tracy and then what? Andrew was quiet for a minute, and then Malcolm told him he needed to make the call. Andrew got angry and asked how Malcolm could be so cold blooded. Malcolm told Andrew to stop acting like he's never made the call before. Andrew yelled, "THAT'S ANDRE'S MOTHER!"

"Son get mad at me if you want to. I'm just telling you what needs to be done!" Malcolm's voice was booming as he talked to Andrew.

Andrew was livid pacing back and forth on the opposite side of the table. "You're always so quick to make those calls! These are people's lives!"

"You think she cares about your life, how she affects you or your son? The way I see it, it's either you or her. I can't let it be you!"

"Like you care!"

"Andy!"

"Oh I don't care? Who paid the way so that you could have something different?"

"You paid the bill, but I got myself there despite you!" Andrew was so angry, Tracy and Nicole stood at the hallway. Tracy had sad eyes, as she looked at Andrew.

"Son we can go round and round, but I am your father!" Malcolm's voice boomed. Andrew yelled, "I KNOW! I KNOW!" In that moment it seemed like he was wishing he wasn't.

I looked at Tracy and Nicole. "Come sit down ladies."

Tracy hesitated. "NO! WE'RE LEAVING!" Andrew said.

"Andy come on, let's not let this ruin the evening."

"YOU DON'T EVEN CARE!"

My eyes filled up with tears. "Of course I care, but people have to make their own beds."

"That's how you felt about dad? He made his bed, so he had to lye in it?"

"Andy that's not fair!" I couldn't believe he said that, especially when it felt like he was saying David was the victim, I started crying. Sophia came over and hugged me

"I'm just saying..." Andrew said

"You always move slow when a female's involved. All of this could be resolved!" Malcolm said

Andrew turned to Tracy, "let's go!" His fists were flexing. Hubby stood up, and took Nicole by the hand.

"Andy! Don't leave!" I pleaded; I wanted to try to calm things down before he left. Andrew looked at me sitting next to Malcolm. He rolled his eyes and his face was like stone. He grabbed Tracy's hand and walked out of the door. No one said anything right away; all you could hear was me crying. Darryl rushed over and put his arms around me. Malcolm got up and walked away from the table. He started pacing the floor just like Andrew just did. Malcolm asked Derrick if he was saying something wrong. Derrick told him that Andrew was still attached to Toya. He told him to give him some time and he would come around, he said if she keeps up like she has, Andrew wouldn't have a choice.

The next day I tried calling Andrew, but he wouldn't answer. I called Tracy and she answered, but I heard movement then the phone hung up. I kept calling but I was only getting voicemail. I wanted to hear that Andrew was ok. I could tell he was on the verge of cracking last night. Sabrina said he still seemed upset when he came to get Andre. I sat by my phone all day waiting for it to ring. Finally, I left Tracy a voicemail asking her to tell Andrew that I loved him once he gave her her phone back, then I waited. It was after ten thirty when he finally called me back. At first he was giving me one-word answers, I could hear him breathing so I knew he was crying. I told him how much I loved him, and how much I loved his gigantic heart. I told him it took someone with a huge heart to have any kind of love for a female like Toya. Andrew said he knew what Malcolm was saying, but Toya could change one day or maybe one day Andre would want to talk to her, ask her some questions, he felt Andre should have that right. I told him I understood what he was saying, but I also asked him to consider how she keeps lashing out at him. I told him she's not above hurting Andre just to hurt him. Andrew started crying again. We got off of the phone after one in the morning. I laid down and fell asleep, but my eyes popped open at five and they would not close. All I could think about was how much my baby was in pain. I got up, showered, and then I went over Tracy's house. I parked in the driveway next to Andrew's car. I texted Tracy hoping she'd respond right away and she did. I apologized for the hour; she hugged me and thanked me for coming. I followed her to their bedroom, Andrew was sleep, but it wasn't peaceful sleep. I rubbed his back, Andy's eye popped open. Then he sat up. I rubbed his back and sang him a song. Tracy smiled at us, and then she took her workout clothes into the room next door. I told Andy I couldn't sleep because he was on my mind. He hugged me and thanked me for coming. He asked me if I thought it was crazy that he held on to the good things about David. He said he remembered the bad, he remembered it all. I told him that's what he felt he had to do. I told him that the part that didn't make sense to me was that he blamed Malcolm for David. I asked if he understood everything that happened the last time we saw David. He was quiet for a minute. I told him that David said we needed to get rid of him. My heart started burning at the memory. I told him that Daddy tried to explain that to him, and Malcolm wasn't having it. I told him that Malcolm has saved us so many times that we all owe him an extreme amount of gratitude. Andrew listened but he didn't say anything. "I remember that night he was having a nightmare. I came to your room and he hugged me. I can't remember him hugging me before or after that. Kids need hugs from their fathers too. I needed to know he cared about me. He was always telling me how to be better, but... I don't get how Derrick and Darryl can be so attached to him."

"Think about it baby, you know he loves you. He's always been there for you. The only father figure they know is Malcolm; your memories of David aren't theirs. They don't understand how you can be attached to David. It goes both ways."

"Don't you miss him?"

"The David you remember died just after Derrick was born. I miss that guy terribly but I also remember the next almost five years with a monster, and I don't miss him."

"I wanna be better than Malcolm!" Andrew said frustrated

"Baby!" I lifted his face to me. "You already are!"

Andrew smiled as a tear fell. "I am?"

"Yes! You are a man about everything! Even when it comes to sharing your heart. Where Malcolm has proven to be lacking you have that and then some." Andrew smiled and hugged me. "But baby you can't keep comparing yourself to Malcolm. You two are almost exactly the same sometimes, but you are totally different. Malcolm didn't have love in his life until he met us. There's gonna be things that he's lacking. You can show him better, you already have."

"You mean with Tracy?"

"Yes! Most importantly, he's not as bad as you think he is." I said, and then I kissed his forehead.

We heard Tracy and Andre talking. Really it was Andre going at fifty miles a minute, and Tracy laughing. "That's how I remember me and David being." He said with a smile.

We talked about him and David like it was yesterday. We talked about how attached he was to David, and when it changed. He had so many questions for David. Then his stomach rumbled. He mentioned donuts and my mouth watered. He asked me where I parked my car. I told him it was in the driveway, I gave him the keys. Then I went downstairs so he could dress. I asked Andre to show his daddy which donut I liked. I spent the day with them. Andrew told me he put my car in the garage. His eyes were still sad, and I didn't feel comfortable leaving him like that. Besides any time I looked like I was leaving, his eyes pleaded with me to stay. We were upstairs watching Andrew run his heart out on the treadmill when the doorbell rang. We thought it was the pizza delivery guy so Tracy and Andre went downstairs. I stayed in the doorway, Andrew slowed down to hear. We looked at each other when we heard Malcolm's voice. When Malcolm spoke to Andre I wondered if they had ever met. It didn't sound like it from their dialog. Andrew went downstairs and I felt stuck, I didn't know whether to go down or stay up. Tracy came up with Andre and her eyes were wide. Like two kids we pushed each other in her room then she turned on music so we wouldn't invade their privacy. I couldn't believe he was actually here and trying to make amends with Andrew. I thought for sure the other night was the nail in the coffin. When the doorbell rang again, we raced to the door. I offered to pay for the pizza just so I could go down, but she said they already charged her card. Then she stuck her tongue at me right before she snuck out. Andre and I cracked up laughing. The dog looked at us like we were crazy. Tracy came back in the room all excited for me. She said Andrew invited him to stay for pizza. I got butterflies in my stomach. Tracy was acting like it was her, she was so excited. We grabbed our composure and then we calmly walked down the stairs. Malcolm's face completely lit up when he saw me. Malcolm's eyes were on me the rest of the evening. When Andre gave us his version of a tour of the house Malcolm's breathing was heavy and he kept grabbing me whenever Andre wasn't looking. I smiled at him, but I didn't tell him to stop which probably made him crazier. When we were in Andre's room he was telling us about one of his toys, Malcolm asked Andre if he could tell me a secret real fast. Andre agreed, Malcolm pulled me into the bathroom and gave me the most passionate kiss. If my feet would've been touching the floor they would've buckled. He said he needed encouragement to keep pushing forward. The way Andre smiled at us when we came out it was almost like he knew what happened in there but he went back to showing us his toys. Then we went downstairs, Andrew was reading both of our faces when we came down. Malcolm looked normal but I know I looked guilty. After a bit, Andre announced he was going to take a bath, so I went with him. I drew the bath water for him and once he was in and covered by bubbles, he said I could come in. That tickled me so much.

"Nana, who is Malcolm?"

"Who is he?" I asked to make sure I heard the question right. Andre shook his head yes. "You gotta ask your daddy baby." I said getting his hair wet. "Do you like him?"

Andre thought about it for a minute. "I don't know."

"I guess that's fair."

"But you do!" Andre said pointing and laughing.

"What?" I tickled him. "How do you know that?"

"Cause you look at him like this." Then Andre made his face all goofy and crossed his eyes. "That's how mommy and daddy look at each other."

"What?" I tickled him again. "How does Malcolm look at me?" Andre made his face more serious but goofy and cross-eyed. I tickled him again.

When I went downstairs, Andrew and Malcolm were playing dominos. I volunteered Tracy to play with Andrew against Malcolm and I. We had so much fun, Tracy was actually good and I liked that but they were no match for Malcolm and I. When it was time to go, Andrew was not having us walking out together alone, always my protector. He asked me dumb questions to keep me engaged in conversation until Malcolm left. Ten minutes later, I rounded the corner and Malcolm was standing outside his car waiting. I pulled over, got out of the car, and threw my legs around Malcolm. I thanked him for trying today; I didn't expect him to do that. He told me he'd do anything for me. We talked for a minute, then I kissed him goodnight.

Chapter 54

"Weddings are so exciting!" Cassondra said, it still amazes me how the wedding planner Carina and Tracy randomly picked Cassondra's bridal store.

I exhaled, "I know! Everyone has had one but me! My own child is getting married before me."

"Doesn't mean you won't have one." She said

"Right! I'll be coming down the aisle with my walker. I'll have to turn up my hearing aide to repeat my vowels! Yea, that's the fantasy."

"That other guy never proposed?"

"Dwayne?"

"I think so, the one you were always on TV with."

"Yea, that's Dwayne. He wanted to, but I never gave him the impression it was ok to ask me. Why waste your breath asking a question you know the answer is going to be no to."

"I couldn't see you married to a rapper anyways."

"Eeewwllll! You mean Comfort! HE WAS NEVER MY MAN!! We were just friends. We kissed once maybe twice, but there was nothing between us other than friendship."

"That's not the way they made it look on TV."

"I KNOW! And then Amber exits stage left. That whole thing was crazy. I guess every person I escorted to one of those ceremonies was my man right? I had been around for years, but when I started dating Dwayne the world seemed to take notice."

"Rightfully so though, that man is gorgeous!" She said with emphasis.

"Says the happily married woman."

"I may be married but I'm not blind. Xavier knows I love him."

"I guess." I sighed.

"Amber please! You and Malcolm have been married since the seventh grade."

"I guess. This would be the sorriest excuse for a marriage ever!"

"Hey! Different marriages are made of different things."

My call waiting clicked. "Hold on Cassondra I have another call." I looked at my phone. "It's Andy hold on." Then I clicked over. "Hello?"

His voice was stressed and very deep. "Momma have you heard from Tracy?"

My eyes looked at the clock. It was eight thirty four. My alarm went off. "No, did you check with Nicole, or her other friend Joy?"

He growled. "Of course!"

"Hold on baby" I clicked back to Cassondra. "Cassondra let me call you back."

"Ok sweetheart, I'll call Carina when your dresses arrive."

"Ok" then I clicked back to Andrew, "baby where are you?"

"I'M OUT LOOKING FOR HER!" He sounds frustrated.

"What happened?"

He sighed, "We ran into Jennay the other day."

"Jennay is out here?"

"Yes momma. She's out here for work. She called me at work today, we chatted for a little bit. Then she invited me out to lunch, I figured lunch was harmless. When we came back we were wrapping up when Tracy walks in my office, goes off, and leaves. I told Jennay she had to go. I walk out to the parking lot, to find Jennay beat up and Tracy speeding off."

"Just call Yussef, that's who you have on her right now right?"

He exhaled, "no, he's suspended right now."

"Why would he be suspended? He was hand picked by Malcolm."
"I know! I know! He came highly recommended blah blah blah! He's suspended!" Andrew barked.
"Does Malcolm know?"
"Momma! Can we please focus! I need to find her!"
I looked at the phone like he has completely lost his mind. Then I hung up; I didn't know where Tracy was. I called her phone and it immediately went to voicemail. I left her a message asking her to call me. Then Andrew called me back, he apologized for snapping on me. I told him I didn't know where she was. I asked if he talked to her parents or her brother. He said they were all at service and she wasn't there. Then he walked in my front door, he looked at me on the couch then he scanned the room. "Who are you looking for? I told you she's not here!"
He took his phone off his ear. He looked defeated. He growled, "WHERE IS SHE?"
"So she's mad because you went out to lunch?" I stood up.
"Yes"
"And?" I said gesturing with my hands. I couldn't see the whole picture. "Where's Andre?"
"In the car sleep." He said
I smacked him on the back of his head. "Go get my baby out of the car!"
"I'm going home." He said rubbing the back of his head.
"Andrew, you're not making any sense to me. Why would Tracy disappear just because you had lunch with Jennay? Why is Yussef suspended? What's going on?" I was frustrated.
"Yussef is in love with Tracy!" I gasped. "And when we ran into Jennay at the store, I kind of forgot myself. I didn't introduce her, didn't mention the wedding, and then she wasn't happy with me this morning."
I smacked him harder upside the head. "Why every time a female is involved you turn dumb!" I started smacking him rapid fire. "I'm disappointed in you!"
Andrew didn't even duck. He just hung his head. "I know momma, I know!"
"How are you supposed to be a husband making her feel like this? She should never feel second best to anyone! ANYONE! Jennay had her chance to come back and she didn't. Let that go!"
"I know momma." He kept his head down. "Will you call me if she shows up here?" He said sounding deflated.
"Of course."
Darryl and Derrick walked in the door. Darryl was smiling until he saw Andrew's face. "What did Toya do?"
Andrew shook his head, "it was all me." Then he walked out the door.
Darryl and Derrick followed him; they stood next to the car talking. I watched for a while, I thought about calling Malcolm but I didn't. I know Yussef is special to Malcolm, but I'm sure that Malcolm is aware of the whole situation. I decided to wait for Tracy to call me back. They stood out there for a few minutes. Then all three of them went their separate ways. I'm glad to know they stick together when it comes down to it.
The later it got the more anxious I got. Finally I couldn't take it any more, and I put myself in the bed. I knew Tracy was ok, wherever she was but I know Andrew is going crazy. My eyes popped open just after six. I got up showered and kept sticking my head out of the shower because I thought I heard my phone. Then I paced the floor, my heart fluttered when my phone rang. It was Tracy! She was crying when I answered. I told her to come over. I called the school. I asked Jade to

run the staff meeting for me. She was excited because that meant she got to announce who some of our invitees were going to be for our upcoming charity event for the community. All the staff really cared about was which celebrities were gonna be there but it promised to be a really fun meeting. I hated that I was going to have to miss it. I opened my garage door and then I sat on the porch. I waved at some of the kids making their way to school. Without getting too close to the car, I could see Tracy's wild hair all over her head. I pointed to the garage and then I walked behind her car. I closed the door then she got out of her car. Her eyes and nose were red, from crying. She was swimming in her clothes, and when I hugged her I smelled a man. My heart sunk, it wasn't my baby's smell. If Andrew sees her like this he will completely lose it. I told her to come inside, and I had her follow me up the stairs. I took her in my room. I went into my new clothes stash and pulled out options for her. The only thing I couldn't give her was a bra; she had me out gunned there.

I looked at this poor girl who had no idea how crazy her life could be just by being a part of this family. She was in love with Andy; I know she didn't expect all these twist and turns. Maybe she didn't understand that she still had a choice. As much as I hated to say it, she didn't have to marry my son. She could just pick up and walk away but I didn't want her to. I really like Tracy, and it's important to like your daughter in-law. I told myself not to take sides, to treat her the way I would want to be treated, and to let them work it out. I gave her towels, pointed out my soaps and lotions. I told her to help herself to whatever she needed.

Then I called Andrew; I could tell he was depressed. "Baby I wanna let you know that I have Tracy." I could hear the excitement in his breath. "BUT!!!!! You gotta stay away for now!"

"WHAT???? MOMMA COME ON!!! I'M DYING OVER HERE!" He pleaded

"I know baby, but everything in its due time. She's not ready to see you yet."

"I don't care what she's ready for! I need to see her!" He pleaded.

"You do care! Don't say stuff like that cause you might actually believe it and I'm gonna tell you, thinking like that will get you nowhere fast."

Andrew growled in the background. "Fine! Fine! Fine! Please call me the moment it's ok." He pleaded again.

"Of course baby. I love you, and I'll see you soon."

"Love you, and I hope so." He said sounding defeated.

I paced in the hallway; I could hear her still crying in the shower. I felt horrible; I didn't know what to say. I felt like throwing myself on her feet and begging her to forgive my son. I was hoping that wherever she was last night wouldn't result in another hurdle for them to get over.

After she had been out of the shower a minute, I went in the room. Her eyes were still sad, but she looked more like herself. We sat on my bed talking for a while; she calmed down enough to go downstairs. I kept looking at the clock; I knew it was only a matter of time before Andrew showed up. When the door opened, I looked at Tracy and then I saw Darryl walk in. He was looking for Tracy. He smiled then he walked back out the door, got in his car and left. Tracy sighed; she stopped breathing when she thought it was Andrew.

Andrew did better than I thought he would. He made it to mid afternoon before coming over. She didn't look surprised when she saw him either. I let Andre say his very excited hello, and then I took him out to the back yard. We played my unskilled version of basketball. Andre kept telling me I was doing it wrong and then he'd try to show me how to do it right. I asked him who showed him, and he said his daddy and Uncle Anthony. He would stop in his tracks when he heard his daddy yell. He would start to look sad, and I told him not to worry. Sometimes when you love someone you yell at them. I told him it wasn't a very nice thing to do, but it happens. I told him mommy and daddy were gonna be fine. I was happy Andre believed me cause I couldn't really say if I believed me. After a while, it was quiet and I forgot all about them. Then Andrew opened the door his eyes were red and puffy. My baby was calming down, but I could tell it was gonna take a minute. He said they were going to get something to eat and they wanted me to go. In that invitation he didn't really give me an option, so I just shrugged and went along with it. Andre chose Mexican so we went to Gonzalez's. Andrew was trying to calm down, but the lack of sleep and all of the emotion of the day had him pretty wound up. We were talking about the wedding and I was hoping that the topic would help him relax. It did a little but he had one more time to snap at me before I went off. Tracy was trying to calm him as well. This boy! He took Andre to the bathroom and Tracy and I exhaled. As we were talking, in walks Toya. She was with a guy, little man on her hip, and a very pregnant belly. Nobody told me she was pregnant again! Without saying a word to each other Tracy and I slid into our booth as far as we could hoping she wouldn't notice us. When Andrew came out the bathroom he saw her, and her eyes immediately went to Andre who didn't see her. I started shaking my leg because the tension in the room was driving me crazy. Andrew came to the table, took out his phone and texted someone. He walked over to the table and introduced himself. Her husband was fine with meeting Andrew. He didn't seem bothered at all. Toya looked nervous all the same. Andre looked over, and his face changed as he recognized Toya.

"Did you want to say hi to Andre?" Andrew asked since Toya was staring at him.
"Andre come here." Andre walked over slowly, he had the saddest face. He grabbed his daddy's hand. "Do you remember her?" Andre shook his head yes.
Tears flew out of Toya's eyes. "It's been a long time." She said looking at Andre.
"How you doing little man, I'm Will." He said sticking his hand out for a shake.
Then he looked at Toya, then back at Andrew. "These pregnancy hormones got her acting so crazy." Will attempted to explain.
"Is that right?" Andrew smiled a knowing smile.
Then Darryl walked in. "Look who's here!" He announced to the restaurant. Toya hissed!
Then she looked at Will, "we need to go!"
"Why you wanna leave so soon? Do I offend?" Darryl said sniffing himself. Toya attempted to stand up, and Darryl shoved her back down.
"A! Man! That's my wife." Will said in an authoritive tone.
"Andre go sit with your Mommy and Nana." Andrew said.
Toya sucked her teeth. "You have him calling her Mommy?"
"Yea, she takes care of him loves him like a mother should love her son; you have a problem with that?" Andrew said
"Why would you have a problem with that?" Will asked Toya. She shook her head and put her eyes on the floor.
"Ask her again!" Darryl said with a smile.
She turned her voice really sweet. "Baby can we discuss this later? Let's go!"
"Un huh! Naw! It's about to get interesting in 5, 4, 3, 2," Darryl said right as Derrick walked in.
Toya started crying. I didn't like seeing my boys like this, I didn't know how ugly this was going to get. Tracy looked at me with questioning eyes.

Derrick's tone was no nonsense and cold, Toya kept flipping back and forth. When she was talking to her husband she had this sugary sweet tone, a tone for when she was talking to my boys, and a tone for when she was scared. The boys put truths out on the table that I didn't completely understand. Something about a guy who her husband Will thought was her cousin. Will was trying to take everything in but he was blinded by his love for her.

"Oh and the police is looking for her. She got two counts of attempted murder hanging over her head." Darryl said

"What?"

"Get this, she flew into a jealous rage over my brother and some girl he used to toss. She tried to run them off the road over in Orinda."

"The hit and run you told me about?" Will asked putting it altogether. "This is why we're moving? You're running from the police?"

"Ok so check it, meanwhile, she keeps trying to put people up to hurting my sister-in-law. Why, because if she can't have Drew nobody can. Now I know you don't know who Malcolm is, but he don't play. She knows this, but ask me why she messing with him? I guess she's hoping to plea bargain her way out of a possible life sentence because she knows she messed up. The question is, does she walk out of here?"

Will's face was so hurt while he held the baby. He just kept staring at Toya. "This is all true, isn't it?" Toya kept her head to the ground. The front of her shirt was wet from all the tears.

The owner of the restaurant came out; he shook Andrew's hand. "I just wanted to let you know, we did call the police. This is Oakland, but they should be here soon."

"Alright man, thanks." Andrew said.

Derrick pulled Toya in to him. "You better pray the police get here before Malcolm does."

"LaToya what did I do to deserve this? I love you!" Poor Will believed everything she told him, I felt sorry for him. He probably thought she was this beautiful angel.

"Where's Steve?" Darryl asked.

"I don't know!" She said.

"Why do you like that fool? He's an idiot who thinks he knows so much."

Toya started breathing. "I think my water just broke!" Derrick released her arm and she stood up. Water gushed on the floor, her pants were wet.

"Did you just throw your water on your pants?" Darryl said

"Naw man, there's no ice. I think it did, Eeewwllll!" Derrick said backing up.

"Please let me take her to the hospital." Will pleaded.

Andrew stepped back. "Go!"

Andre was eating his quesadilla not really paying attention. Will and Toya hurried out of the door. Will was calling someone as they got in the car. He strapped the baby in, and then he got in the driver's seat. You could tell he was yelling at Toya. Of course the police showed up five minutes later. Darryl told them to check the hospitals. Andrew, Derrick, and Darryl came back to our table and proceeded to eat like nothing happened. Derrick's phone rang; he told us it was Malcolm. He told Malcolm they let her go because she started leaking. I could hear Malcolm's voice booming through the phone, he wasn't happy but I couldn't imagine what he expected them to do. Then his voice calmed, Derrick's eyes bounced to Tracy and then Andrew. Andrew sat up; he said, "she's here, I haven't heard from him." Then Derrick handed Andrew the phone. Andrew's face was serious, he said hello. His eyes turned evil, Andrew walked out of the door with the phone on his ear. Darryl started playing with Andre to distract him from Andrew. All I know is he wasn't happy.

****

"So the meeting with the Director of The Center is this morning. We're offering them an hour within the showcase." Jade said.

"Why only an hour? How long is the showcase?" I asked.

Jade smiled, "it's four hours including intermission."

"Why wouldn't we offer them at least half if not more? I owe them everything."

Jade smiled at Tony, "see! I told you!" Then she spoke through clinched teeth. "Fix it!"

Tony huffed and switched the proposal papers. "What was that?"

"Mister know it all over there is trying to push for more stage time for North Star."

"Why?" I asked him.

He rolled his eyes, and then he exhaled. "I was just trying to make sure my little niece's class made it in the ensemble."

"Why is this performance any more important than any others?"

"There's gonna be important people there." Tony said.

"No more important than any other performance. Shame on you Tony!" I tisked .

When the meeting was over I called Tracy and asked her if I could take her out to lunch. When I picked her up she was all smiles. Her smile lowered a little when she saw the car following us. I told her to get in, I put my hand on hers, and I told her that after awhile it's not so bad. Then we drove to The Bakery by Merritt for lunch. We had a good time talking, and then I told her about my charity event I had coming up. I asked her what she thought of, "Tracy's Tasty Treats"? Tracy smiled a curious smile. I asked her if she would be willing to donate some desserts to sell at intermission. Her face completely lit up, I was relieved. "Do you really think people would pay for my desserts?"

"The cakes we've had at your house have been just as good as any of these other bakeries. Have you ever thought about opening a bakery?"

Tracy blushed, "no way! I couldn't see making a living that way."

"Just like I couldn't see making a living dancing." I smiled at her. "I know it's not the easiest thing to believe in yourself but I know you'll get there. Meanwhile, for my event will you do it?"

Of course she agreed. We went over the types of cakes she could mass-produce. Uncle Frank rented and donated The SR Center since the guest list and media quickly exceeded the capacity of my theater. Initially, we had control of who was coming, after talking with Kimmy I quickly realized that she was bringing almost every contact she had, and they were bringing friends as well. She told me that Comfort said he was coming and he was bringing people as well. I guess Kimmy thought I would be excited about that, but I couldn't help but wonder if there was something else motivating his appearance. I talked to Malcolm about bringing Mitigated staff in for security, and ushers. Since Toya didn't turn up at any of the immediate hospitals it was an all out search for her. I had Tracy's table front and center in the lobby. She had a few items out as displays to spike interest before the intermission. I got to the venue in the morning; Juan was there with his staff. Malcolm didn't hold back, it seemed as though he had all of his special services division in the Bay Area there. Making mistakes were not an option. We didn't want to deal with the paparazzi invading the theater and making our guests uncomfortable. The kids came to do their sound checks and run through. Andrew had just gotten off of the phone and I asked him to walk me out. He looked stressed and angry. "Baby what's wrong?"

Andrew tried to control his tone. "I find it real interesting how..." He took a deep breath. "Who is Yussef? Is that his son?"

"Whose son, Malcolm's?" I asked as my stomach turned into knots.

"Yes!" Andrew looked confused and hurt. "He brings this guy in differently than anyone else. Malcolm personally vouches for him, outside of us he doesn't do that."

"What has Yussef done that was so terrible?"

"I told you, he's in love with Tracy!" He barked.

"Did he try to sleep with her?"

"She says no"

"Was he bad mouthing you?"

"No"

"Did he do anything other than recognize in her the same things you did?"

"She was with him that night she disappeared."

"She told you that?"

He looked at me like I was crazy. "No, but I know it."

I needed to steer clear of that. "What does Malcolm say about it?"

"He says what Tracy says, Yussef wouldn't go against me like that. I feel like he's protecting him."

I felt sad, "you want him gone?"

Andrew looked at my sad face, and he started huffing. "Why does everyone react like that about him?"

"He and I never had any life changing conversations, but he's a good kid. I would hate for something to happen to him." Andrew rolled his eyes. "Tell me something, because I'm a little confused. Yussef, you want him gone for having the same taste in a good woman that you do?" Andrew blank stared. "But Toya has done ten million times worse, and you're constantly pleading for her life."

"That's Andre's mother!" He barked.

"That's your excuse now, but even before Andre you had some other excuse for her. She's done nothing but hurt you and deliberately cause you pain and yet you still plead for her life but because he likes your woman he has to die? It doesn't sound too balanced to me baby."

Andrew's chest went up and down. "You don't understand!"

"I don't understand what baby? Please help me get it."

"You are my mother!" He barked frustrated. "You're supposed to be on my side!"

"Andy I am on your side. However, it's also my job to tell you when you're wrong. And baby you got the rolls reversed. Toya needs to go, let her go! She's not David, she's not" I swallowed hard. "She's not Tanisha." Andrew had the most surprised look on his face. "She's not Jennay, she's just evil! If you don't let her go now. She's only gonna end up hurting everyone you love."

"She told you?" He asked with sad eyes.

"No, but I know. " I touched his cheek.

He exhaled, "what if Tracy decides she doesn't love me any more and she wants him? I can't handle that."

"If you honestly feel something like that could happen, then she isn't the one. Otherwise, that's the risk you take with love. You love someone, give them your heart. You hope they don't lose it, destroy it, or abuse it. You hope that they cherish it and hold on to your heart as the true gift it is but it's up to each person what they do with it. Either way you're gonna be fine. I really believe my young prince has found his princess." I hugged him.

We walked out together, and then I went home. I showered and got dressed, and then I waited for Malcolm, I was so anxious to see him. Darryl flew through the house. He ran up, showered, got dressed, and was out all in a half an hour. I stepped out onto the porch, then I saw Malcolm's car coming down the street. His eyes were serious when he got out of the car. He asked me if everything was ok, I guess it showed on my face. I sat in the car, but I put my hand on his when he attempted to start the car. He looked confused. "I can trust you to tell me the truth right? Even when it hurts my feelings?"

He exhaled, "what did I do?"

"I don't know, answer the question please."

"I'm not a liar Amber. Go ahead, ask your question."

He sat back bracing himself for whatever I was going to ask. "Is Yussef your son?"

"Uh!" His mouth fell open and he looked at me. "Seriously? For real? Really?"

I searched his eyes but all I saw was the shock of the question. "Is he Yvette's son? Or Camille's?"

"Yvette! Camille!" I could see him getting angry.

"Why wouldn't you tell me? What could I say about it honestly? I just need to hear you say it."

Malcolm rubbed his hand over his face. He was beyond upset. He turned his body to face me. "Amber! How in the world could you ask me that?"

"I wasn't gonna assume, so I'm asking you."

"But you sound like you've already made up your mind about it." He said, and then he looked me in the eyes. "Don't you know me at all by now?"

"Whose son is he? Yvette's?"

"Ugh!" He yelled! "I can't believe this!"

"Who's Malcolm."

"He's Shonda's son." Malcolm watched my face for a reaction.

I blew air slowly. "Ok, and where is she?"

"I honestly don't know and I don't care." He said matter of factly and still watching my face.

"You have a child with this woman and you don't care where she is?"

"Shonda is not my concern. Yussef is!"

"How could you go after Tag like that? Yussef needs to know his brothers. He shouldn't have grown up isolated like that."

"Go after Tag like what? He got what he deserved and it's not like he's hurting from it. He paid all that money back to the state, reimbursed Margaret's mother for every penny and Margaret and her kids got a nice little piece of pocket change. All that and he's still in tack. He's not destitute!"

"Andrew is against his brother maybe if they knew, this never would've happened! How could you not tell me? Are you still seeing her? Is that what it is?" I could feel jealousy turning in my stomach.

"Amber! Who am I?" I gave him an evil look. "Shonda is not my concern."

"How could that be? You still have to talk to her."

He interrupted me. "Think about it, you've met her. Think about Yussef. Think about it before you say something you can't take back."

"I met her?" I shook my head. "No I would remember beating her down."

Malcolm smiled. "You met her, and there was no reason to fight her. Close your eyes and think of Yussef's face." I did. "Now" I heard his voice crack and I looked at him. "Now, think of Troy."

I screamed! How did I not see it! Malcolm's eyes watered up but he didn't cry. "Oh my goodness! The little boy."

"Shonda used Yussef to hurt Troy. She used that little boy to hurt him and have control. When he dies, then she wants to feel bad about it! About everything she did! Yussef is like a son to me, but he's not my son."

"I'm sorry!" Tears were falling down my face.

"I expect you to know me better than anyone. I didn't have a father. Pam was too twisted and evil to even point me in the right direction. My children know me. I thought you did too." He reached to start the car.

I unfastened my seat belt. "DON'T BE MAD AT ME!" I threw my bosom at his head, and wrapped my arms around him. "I'M SORRY! I GOT CONFUSED! I'M SORRY! I'M SORRY!"

He started laughing. "You're blinding me with your breast."

"I KNOW BUT I'M SORRY! PLEASE TELL ME YOU FORGIVE ME! Don't be mad at me Malcolm, please!"

He pushed me away and then he kissed me deeply! The kiss was so powerful that I started tapping on the window, cause I was about to lose it. "I'm not mad at you, this time! You should know better." Then he started the car.

"You should tell the boys."

"Derrick knows, I can't trust Darryl not to tell Drew, and I need Drew to calm down first. The only reason you know is because you were trying to pin the kid on me. You better not say anything."

"I won't."

When we got to the center vendors were arriving and setting up. Tracy and her friend Joy were setting up her table. She had boxes and boxes of cakes and pies. Tracy had her family helping her putting everything up according to the sketch she came up with for placement and display. "Psst! Tracy!" Darryl was signaling her over by me. Then he whispered, "did you make any red velvet?" She smiled and nodded yes. "Hook your brother up with a piece before my cousin Sharon gets here." He said looking around like he was on a covert mission.

"Un huh! If you can't love my cake in public, you ain't getting none in private." Darryl looked shocked and offended. He put his hands up to quiet her down while he looked around to see who could hear. Then he whispered again, "don't be like that! You see, what had happened was..." he swallowed. "I thought Sharon's was the best until I had yours that one time. I don't wanna hurt anybody. Hers is still good, but it don't compare to yours. Can you hook your brother up?"

I was cracking up. "I'll think about it." She said with a smile.

"Think about it!" He loudly whispered. "She gonna be here soon. You don't even know which one she is. You gonna give it to me right in front of her, and then I'm gonna have to pretend like its not as good as it is and I don't wanna hold back." He pleaded in his whisper.

"I couldn't give it to you right now anyways. We gotta set up first." She was still smiling.

Darryl looked at me like he was heartbroken. "Momma you see how she do me! This ain't right! It ain't fair! Where's Drew? I need to take this to a higher power!" Darryl said hurrying off.

"That boy has always been a clown!" I said laughing. "So what do you need me to help with?"

"Nothing! You've done enough! My family is here, and Nicole & Hubby are on the way. Between Joy and Amy, my display will be perfect and ready by the time guests start arriving." Andrew winked at Tracy as he hurried by with Darryl on his heels explaining why he needed to check his woman so he could get some cake.

I made my rounds and everyone and everything was in place. Some guests started to arrive and just beyond security, Tony's niece Natalie and Teresa passed out programs to the guest as they arrived. I was standing by Tracy admiring her beautiful display when I heard. "Hello Amber"

I turned around to see Ramell, I smiled real big. "Hello!" I gave him a hug and then I introduced him to Tracy. Her eyes were big, as she was a little star struck.

"Man! When you disappear, you disappear. I have been looking for you." He said with a smile

"Oh really, why?"

He took two steps back and two steps forward. "We were friends! What you mean why?"

"You left a bad taste in my mouth Ramell. I didn't like being played with like that. I told you that." I said

"I know, I thought we talked all that out. A brotha try to call you and the number's changed."

Oh yea, I was running from Malcolm then. "A lot was going on, I didn't mean to leave you hanging like that, but the number to the school is on the program, call whenever you like."

His smile dropped. "The school? Like that? I flew all the way from the east coast to see you and you tell me to call the school?"

"You know why don't you?" I don't even know where Malcolm came from, Tracy and I both jumped. Malcolm shook Ramell's hand. "She ain't married, but she ain't single either."

Ramell deflated a little bit. "Hey how you doing?"

"I'm good!" Malcolm said almost smiling.

Tracy looked like she wanted to stop breathing. I nudged her and smiled, she kept her eyes on Malcolm. "Did you come alone?" I asked

"No I brought friends, they're up at the seats. I guess I'll talk to you after the show." Ramell said then he walked away.

Tracy still had her eyes on Malcolm. "Why you do that to him?" I asked smiling

"I was doing you a favor." Malcolm said kissing my cheek and walking away.

"I still don't get it!" Tracy said

"Get what sweetheart."

"How you were ever with him? Malcolm is scary."

I laughed. "Andrew acts just like him, he just smiles more."

She laughed and then she started thinking about it. Then I saw a tall guy walk in with a side profile like Dwayne. I grabbed Tracy's hand and told her we should find our seats.

Jade looked beautiful as she greeted everybody. I had to do a double take when I saw her, because I thought I was looking at a lighter version of Momma at first. I think Timothy and Malachi saw it too, we were all leaning in looking at her on the stage. She kept the show running on time and the audience was thoroughly entertained.

At the intermission, guests went to the banquet hall to purchase food and drinks. Then we sent them to Tracy's booth for desserts. People started coming back for seconds, thirds, etc. until everything was gone. After she sold her last pieces we brought out store bought stuff that we gave away for free but that didn't stop people from showing their disappointment. Sophia asked Tracy if she could make something for Uncle and Aunties' anniversary party in a couple weeks, Andrew said they had a work event for him that same day so she couldn't. Darryl looked like he was going to cry as he saw them packing up. I couldn't hear what he was saying but he was pouring it on real thick. Then Tracy pulled out a cake box and handed it to him. His entire face lit up and he started jumping around. He took off with his box; I was so busy looking at Darryl I didn't see Tag walk up on me.

"Hello Amber" I gave him evil eyes. "Before you start acting all mad I just want you to know I got all that taken care of. I even put a little change in their pockets." I turned red! The lights started flickering to signal the second half. I turned on my heels and walked away. Malcolm came and sat next to me during the second half. He put his arm around me and I was in heaven. Knowing it wasn't originally in Malcolm's nature to show public displays of affection melted my heart that much more with every expression. I know he was doing it because I loved it. Seven on the nose our show ended. Jade was so good. After donations, tickets sales, etc., we raised almost three hundred thousand dollars towards scholarship funds to be split between The Center and North Star. That was almost double the amount we were hoping for. We thanked everyone for all of their support. Then I stayed glued to Malcolm's side. I was over all the possibilities for the evening and if that really was Dwayne, I didn't want to see him. People came over to say goodbye, to congratulate, and to take pictures with me. I noticed Malcolm standing to the side and he got a phone call. He looked irritated, I wanted to ask him what was wrong, and then I saw Detective Turan coming. He almost had a smile on his face, I blank stared at him. When I finished talking to the person I was talking to Malcolm walked back over. He put his hand out as if that would stop Malcolm. "Detective Turan!" He said flashing his badge.

"So!" Malcolm said standing next to me.

"I need to speak to Ms. Wallace alone!" He said, "maybe you didn't see the badge."

"I don't care who you are! What is that Cracker Jack badge supposed to mean to me?"

Detective Turan stood there glaring at Malcolm and Malcolm who was a good two inches taller returned his glare. Uncle Frank caught Malcolm's demeanor and walked over. As he approached, Detective Dartnell came over. "Oh my goodness look at all the Wallace's under one roof! I wish I had a wagon to load you all up tonight!" She said

"What do you want Sheila?" Uncle Frank said.

"We're looking for Latoya Spencer have you seen her?" She asked me. "No!"

She looked at Malcolm and Turan. "Come on guys! Have you settled it yet? Whoever has the bigger dick gets to bone Amber tonight." Dartnell said nonchalantly.

Turan cracked a sideways smile. "Sorry! I guess that means you get to watch." I grabbed Malcolm's hand because I knew that was more than enough to make him lose it.

"Amber, when was the last time you saw her?" Dartnell asked. I did a my lips are sealed gesture. She rolled her eyes. "Everybody wants a lawyer!"

"Sheila why are you here?" Uncle Frank said.

"I'm looking for Latoya. She's the only person who can testify against your whole family and suddenly she vanishes into thin air." Dartnell said

"Testify for what? We're clean!" Uncle Frank said with a smile.

"Right! And I look just like Georgette Paris!" Even Detective Turan looked at her with a question mark. "Whatever! As soon as we find her your family is going down!"

Malcolm's hand was sweating; I kept squeezing and releasing, squeezing and releasing his hand so he wouldn't forget I was touching him. "If you think so, but she's not here. If you don't have a ticket you can't be in here. You can walk out or we can have security escort you out." Uncle Frank said.

Dartnell put her hands up. "Rules are rules right." Then she looked at Turan, "let's go!"

Turan looked at me, I knew he was gonna do something and I knew Malcolm wouldn't care who he's supposed to be, he'd react. So I buried my head in Malcolm's chest, I couldn't watch. "I guess I'll talk to you another time Amber." I didn't respond I kept my head buried.

Malcolm and Uncle Frank were talking and I don't even know what they were saying. I just wanted this nonsense over. Malcolm put his arms around me and rubbed my back. He asked me if I was ready to go. I shook my head yes. I hugged Uncle Frank goodbye, and I told him I would see him in a couple of weeks at the anniversary party. On our way out of the building, Mitigated staff were already on the job cleaning up. "So, your options. We could go to Shylight and invite our sons, OR!!!! We could go to my house and I'll cook you dinner." He said with a smile, as he opened my car door for me to get in.

I thought about it as he got in the car. Although I wanted to spend time with the boys I didn't feel up to being around a bunch of people. I was still nerved up from what just happened but if I went to Malcolm's I didn't want him to think I was relaxing on my request. I needed him to fix his relationship with Andrew, and Andrew was not making it easy on him. "If I go back to your house..."

"I know! I know!" He said rolling his eyes.

Then I smiled, "what are you going to make me?"

He smiled, "you'll see." Then he put his hand between my thighs. I gave him a evil smile.

He turned on music as soon as we walked in and he lit his already prepared fireplace. He had steaks and vegetables marinating. He poured a glass of wine for me and told me to sit on the stool at his counter. "Oh so you just knew I was coming back here?" I said, He shrugged while smiling.

He grilled the steaks on his stovetop, while he sautéed the vegetables. When dinner was ready we sat at the table. He lit candles then he turned off the lights. He smiled at me real big. He pointed at my earrings and necklace. "That's nice where did it come from?"

I touched them to remember what I was wearing. "Andy and Andre, isn't it nice." I said with a smile. I put a piece of my steak in my mouth. Oh my goodness! I moaned to show my appreciation for how good it was.

"It's that good?"

"Yes! You've out done yourself Malcolm." I dug into my plate.

"I'm glad you like it." He said with a smile.

For dessert, he grilled peaches that he paired with lavender ice cream. It was sinful enough, but he fed it to me on the carpet by the fireplace. On my last bite he put ice cream on my lip that he had to wipe off with his tongue. We were kissing for a while when my phone rang. He put the dishes in the sink and I answered without looking to see who it was.

"Why are you acting so stuck up?" Tag said

"Seriously? Why are you on my phone?"

"I told you I got everything cleared up."

Malcolm took my phone and hung it up. "We don't need that negativity in here right now." My phone started ringing. He picked it up, "she's busy!"

Then he hung up the phone. "What is his fascination with you?"

"I guess he feels like I'm the one that got away."

"It doesn't add up to me. I don't understand why he continues to try so hard to get your attention. You met almost thirty years ago."

I just smiled and felt guilty for not admitting that one little thing that happened but with the more time that passes the worse it gets that I didn't say anything. At this point, I can't say anything, I gotta take it to my grave. I helped Malcolm wash dishes then we spent a long time kissing. Then he took me home.

****

"So Sasha told me that you and Malcolm had sparks flying last time she saw you two." Sophia said with a knowing smile. "Are you guys on again?"

"Not exactly."

Her smile dropped. "Not exactly? What does that mean?"

"He showed up out of the blue! I was finally content with doing my own thing. No man, and no worrying about a man. Finally ok with being alone you know?"

"No." Sophia looked at me like I was crazy. "Weren't you complaining about being backed up?"

I snapped my towel at her. "Doesn't mean I wasn't ok." I laughed. "But he was being all soft and cuddly. I realized how much I missed him. He told me he wanted to get back together. He asked me what he needed to do to make amends with me once and for all."

Sophia grabbed my shoulders and started shaking me. "PLEASE TELL ME YOU ASKED FOR SOMETHING GOOD! Please!"

I laughed. "You're gonna give me a headache shaking me like that." I packed more dishes in a box. "I asked for the most complicated and most needed thing I could think of. I asked him to fix his relationship with Andrew." She put her hand on her chest and gasped. "When all of that happened before Andrew was the only one who stood by me. Derrick caved first."

"Or maybe Andrew has always had issues with his father. The thing with you two was just more fuel for him. What did Malcolm say?"

"Ok" I shrugged.

"So how's that going?"

I clinched my jaw. "Toya!" I shook my head. "I swear there's a reason why I don't carry a gun. BUT, after that night here, that Sunday, I went to Andy's early and spent the day there. Malcolm showed up, he's trying. It's hard because they don't agree on the method of resolution." I blew air.

"What?"

"What if he gives up and walks away? We've been trying to get rid of Toya since forever. She keeps coming back like a bad rash."

"You think she could be the deal breaker?"

"I'm sure of it. You saw how worked up he got. Meanwhile though, I've been enjoying the attention. What about you and Richard?"

"Nothing." She said flatly. "Oh and Travis is getting married."

"Whoa! Are you ok?" She shook her hand from side to side. "Sabrina met her?"

"Yep, she doesn't like her. I really hoped for her sake that she did, but she doesn't. Travis is going to be a good husband. I just wish Sabrina's opinion mattered."

We finished packing the food and equipment for the party at Uncle Jeff and Auntie Lauren's tonight. Then we loaded up Sabrina and Andre and headed to Sacramento. We changed into our nice clothes once we had everything set up. As family arrived they would say hello and then immediately talk about Andy's upcoming wedding. Everyone was so excited about the wedding. As if he heard us talking Andrew called me. He sounded stressed; he confirmed that he was coming to the party as soon as his work event was over. I told him we'd keep an eye out for them. Everyone got excited about seeing them before the wedding. Darryl arrived with Chantel in tow, I gave her a hug and asked her how she was doing. I asked Darryl where Derrick was and he said he was coming later with Malcolm. Chantel stayed with Tina helping her with whatever we needed done. Darryl and Tim set up the lanterns in the back yard so that we'd have lighting once the sun went down. I watched my baby and my nephew in the backyard as they talked. The difference is like night and day. Tim is a very nice and respectable young man, educated, nicely dressed, he reminded me a lot of the cousins because he had no clue about the life that Darryl lives. Darryl is respectful as well, nicely dressed, educated, but he definitely has a rough side that could flare up. Timothy and Grace raised their kids in Daddy's home like Momma and Daddy tried to raise us. I wonder if Timothy ever showed Tim the things Daddy showed him just in case one day he needed to handle business. Tina was a lovely young lady, in some ways she reminded me of Sasha, but Sasha still knew what time it was. I doubt Tina could tell time, they had simple lives. I was talking to Gwen when I saw Joseph walk in the house with bags. He signaled me to the door. He told me that Andrew and Tracy were outside, and Andrew was pretty upset. I stood there debating what to do. I put my drink down and I walked out slowly. I kept bracing myself for them to tell me they called off the wedding or something crazy like that. Derrick walked past me and kissed my cheek, he was in a hurry to get to Chantel. I couldn't make out the noise I was hearing, it sounded like crying but I assumed it was Tracy. Andrew, Tracy, and Malcolm were standing very close as I approached. "What are you guys..."I stopped in my tracks, then I hurried over. " Oh my goodness! Malcolm are you crying?" I asked in disbelief, until now, Malcolm only cried in front of me. It was a little scary.

"Yes woman! Come here!" He said reaching for me, and when I did he pulled me into their hug circle.

Then he let go. Andrew grabbed Tracy's hand. "Malcolm will you come to our wedding?"

Malcolm stood up tall and proud. "I would love to!"

My heart started pounding, did Andy just say what I think he said? "What's going on?" I asked. I couldn't imagine the wedding without Malcolm there but Andrew was completely against it before.

Tracy gave me the long version of the story. How her ex showed up at Andrew's work party. How they used him to get to Toya and how they turned Toya and the guy in to the police. "You could've just said they got arrested."

"Now, where's the fun in that?" Tracy said.

While we were talking, Malcolm and Andrew had a private conversation. I heard Yussef's name but Tracy was busy giving me the long version of her story, I doubt she heard it. I looked at Malcolm his eyes were puffy, but I could see how much he was enjoying this emotional scene with his son. Andrew had the same look in his eyes, they both seemed relieved. Malcolm grabbed my face and gave me the biggest kiss covered in tears. I knew the table had turned when Andrew didn't have an automatic reaction other than a smile. I stayed on cloud nine the rest of the night. I introduced Tracy to Uncle Jeff and Auntie Lauren, I explained that they were Sophia's parents, and that it was their anniversary party. I introduced her to the family. I put emphasis on my brothers and Jade. They all kept telling her how excited they were about the wedding. When Andre saw her, he jumped into her arms. He whispered something to her, no doubt sharing with her the highlights of his day with her brother. Whatever he said tickled her, and she whispered something back that made them both laugh. The rest of the night, I wasn't the only one who noticed how Andrew and Malcolm kind of stayed around each other. Andrew looked like my little Andy talking to his father about who knows what, but they both looked happy. Tracy changed out of her beautiful gown, and then she chatted with us. One by one I could see it on everyone's faces, they loved her. But knowing Tracy she was sitting over there hoping she wasn't offending anyone, not understanding she had the nod. Uncle Frank interrupted our conversation to tell Tracy she needed to open a bakery. He told her that her desserts at my event were delicious! He told her he would finance everything, all she had to do was say when. I could tell the thought of being her own boss was a little scary, but I told her he's given all of us the same opportunity that he just offered her. She thanked him, and she promised she would discuss it with Andrew after the wedding.

Chapter 55

"So how did it go?" I asked the men.

"GREAT!" Andre yelled, "Nana did you know this is my Poppa?"

"Yes baby, who told you?" I asked

"My daddy, I asked him and he said yes." Andre was so excited

I looked at Andrew who was all smiles. "How about you? You have a good time?" I asked him.

Andrew tried to pull back his smile. "It was alright. The old man won't look horrible in our tux." Andy said

Malcolm sat on the couch behind me and put his arms around me. "What's with all this old man stuff? I'm only sixteen years older than you." He said kissing my cheek.

Tracy came downstairs, she was all smiles. Her dog was right on her heels. Andre took both of the dogs out back to play. "So how did it go?" She asked still smiling

"I'd say it went well." Malcolm said

"Are you staying for dinner? I got a roast in the oven."

"It smells good, but can you cook?" Malcolm said jokingly

"My baby can burn!" Andrew said putting his arms around Tracy.

"Ok, if it's not too much trouble." Malcolm said

"Honestly, I already counted you in, I was just making sure you understood." Tracy said

"How much time we got?" Andrew asked

Tracy looked at the timer in the kitchen. "We got about thirty." She said

Andrew pulled bones out the closet. "Rematch!"

"Wash 'em!" Malcolm said

We sat at the table playing a game on lightning speed pace. We were talking trash and having fun. Finally! Andrew and Tracy finally beat us, what they missed is that as a wedding present we let them win, that or they didn't care. Tracy's roast was delicious. Andrew brought up a few bottles of wine from the wine cellar that went perfectly with our meal. Malcolm kept staring at me the whole night. When it was time to go, Andrew and Andre walked us out. When I turned the corner Malcolm called me. "So your son told me I better have a plan, and I can't keep stringing his momma a long." Then he laughed.

"What's funny about that?" I asked

"You think we need a plan?"

"Yes! If not what are we doing?" I said

"The same thing we've always done. I love you, you love me. Do we need anything more?" He didn't sound like he was playing any more.

"Seriously Malcolm? Please tell me you're kidding! This is some kind of a joke." I said getting off the freeway.

"I am serious, we've been together so long, why would we need anything different than what we've always had.

My foot started getting heavy on the gas. "I refuse to believe you're serious! If you don't have a plan why are we even doing this song and dance?"

"What song and dance? I asked what I needed to do to make things right. You said to make things right between Drew and I. I did that! Now you're telling me that isn't good enough? Amber I don't understand the game you're playing."

I could tell by his tone he was serious. I pulled into my garage. I sat there for a minute just reminding myself to breathe. "Malcolm, there's no game to be played here. I guess I assumed that you had a plan beyond the preliminary steps but if this

existence is all you want from me." I blew air. "I guess it will be fine for now but just be aware that I'm already over this, and if this is all you're offering..."
Malcolm was quiet for a minute. "What if this is all I have to offer?"
I took a deep breath, and exhaled. I laid on my bed. "Then that would make you a liar, and me a fool for all the times I believed you when you offered more. If this is all you have, then it's all you have but it's not good enough. Maybe for someone else but not me."
"How did I become a liar?"
"Every time you dangled something more in front of my face, that means you were lying to me just to get what you wanted and if this is truly all you have to offer, I can't go back to that condo either."
"Why?" I could hear irritation in his voice
"I was under the impression that that condo was on the road to something real. Now it feels like it was all a rouse."
"What's not real about me and you? It doesn't get more real than us!" He was angry.
"You're too smart not to get it Malcolm and it's beneath me to have to explain all of this to you. If this living is fine for you, who am I to make you change it. I just find it funny that everyone else ALWAYS wanted to give me more but you, you're the only one who wouldn't." I was about to explode into tears. I didn't want to give up my nonchalant tone. So I had to end the conversation. "It hurts but at least you've stayed consistent. You'll give me what I want to a point. I gotta go, I have a flight in the morning."
"So you're telling me this was all for nothing?"
"It was if your only aspiration was to be a boyfriend." Then I thought about it. "And no it wasn't for nothing. You finally have a good relationship with all three of your sons." Tears started pouring out of my eyes. "I gotta go!" I hung up my phone. I laid there crying my eyes out. I cried so hard that I cried myself to sleep. I almost didn't hear my alarm. I was moving slow, but I was moving. I pulled my hair back into a low ponytail and I braided the ends. I put on my comfortable travel clothes then I went to the airport. The ticket counter guy tried to cheer me up as I checked my bags but I couldn't pull myself out of my funk. I called Sophia when I got to my gate. First, I apologized for calling her so early, then I unloaded everything from the night before. She said she couldn't believe it, and I told her I couldn't either. I couldn't stop saying how disappointed I was. She asked me if there was any way he could've been messing with me to throw me off of his scent. I told her he was mad last night, and he doesn't fake getting mad. I told her that a proposal from him at this point would feel fake and forced so I was just through with the whole idea. I told her the next person to propose to me outside of Tag, I was accepting. At least that way I could say I was married at least once in my life. She told me I didn't mean that, and I promised her I did. They were announcing boarding for my flight. I had a brief layover in Phoenix and then I was on my way to Atlanta. Fortunately, we had rehearsals at North Star, so filming on location should wrap up hopefully in three days. I told Sophia I loved her and that I'd call her as soon as I made it to Atlanta. As soon as I sat in my First Class seat I put on my seat belt, put my pillow behind my head, pulled out my blanket and went back to sleep. I woke up as we were pulling up to the Phoenix Gate. I went to a restaurant and ordered bacon and eggs. I heard female screams and women running. I looked up to see Shameless, an East Coast Rapper surrounded by women requesting autographs. When he looked up, he saw me and smiled. I waved then I made my way to my gate. I ate my

breakfast as Shameless made his way towards me. His bodyguard stopped people from approaching us. "Hey shorty! How you doing? Long time no see!" He said coming in for a hug.

"How you doing? It's been a long time. Do you remember my name?" I asked

"Of course I do Amber." He said sitting down. "Why wouldn't I?"

"It's not like we talked much when I worked on your stuff. Where you heading to?"

"I'm going to ATL to do this little cameo in my boy's video. How about you?"

"Choreography for Tamara Ruiz's video." I said

"Studio or location?"

"My portion is studio." I said

"Ooh! Ooh! Which one? You gotta stop by." He said getting excited.

"News Worthy Studios." I said

"Yea! Yea! You gotta swing by." Then he took a pen and paper out and wrote down his number. I didn't know where the excitement was coming from; Shame and I never had any kind of a real connection. If anything, I figured Ramell was involved in here somewhere. I put the number in my wallet. We chatted until we boarded the plane, he was on one side of first class, and I was on the other. As we were boarding, he was texting somebody and he was all smiles. I tried not to think about Malcolm and relax. I watched the inflight movie the best I could without my mind drifting to all the times Malcolm mentioned marriage. Every time he mentioned or even implied that we would get married it had a baby attached to the idea. I never understood that. especially when we already had one and then three. That last time, when he referred to me as his wife. I don't know if there was a baby attached to that idea or not but up until then, we thought I couldn't have anymore and I'm sorry, now that I'm a Nana; I don't want to have any more babies. He better not come at me with no lame request for a baby or some junk like that. Malcolm wouldn't play the game like he wasn't interested in marriage to try to surprise me with a proposal; he's never been that cheesy, That's what makes this hurt; I've waited all my life for him to put it on paper, and still this is where we sit almost three decades later. Shame asked me what hotel I was staying at, it turns out we were staying at the same one, so I shared a car service with him. I was gonna catch a cab, but he had a car so it worked out. He asked if I wanted to catch a bite to eat, but I declined. I wanted to unwind and get some rest. The time difference was gonna kick my butt if I didn't. I called Sophia and I told her about Shameless. She asked me if I thought he was trying to hook up. I told her that I thought he was friends with Ramell, and probably trying to arrange for us to meet up somewhere. She asked me if I felt up to seeing him. I told her that seeing Ramell wasn't a problem, we were never a couple and he knew that. She told me to be careful and to call her if I needed her.

The studio called and said they were sending a car at six am to pick me up. I cursed in my mind at the thought of being ready for work at three am on my internal clock. I grabbed a quick bite to eat and then I went to bed. It wasn't hard to sleep because I was depressed anyways.

When I got to the studio, Corey greeted me with a big sleepy hug. Once I got the dancers warmed up, I wasn't so sleepy anymore. Day One was good, Day Two was even better, Day Three was best! At the close of day three I asked Corey what lot Shame was on since he told me he talked to him earlier. We hopped in a golf cart and he took me over to lot 63. The bass was pumping and the set was designed to look like a club. Everyone had on suits and hats like they were at an OG event. The director came over to Corey and asked him for his opinion. They started speaking director jargon. Shame came over and he was very excited to see me. He said I was supposed to call him before I came. I told him I wanted to pop my head in real quick and that I wasn't gonna stay. He told everyone in the booth to wave at me. I didn't focus on anyone specifically, I waved and said hello. He begged me to go out with them tonight. I kept trying to think of a reason to get out of it but he was persistent. I asked Corey if he would come with me. He frowned at me, I told him I was gonna tell Shame he was the reason I couldn't go. Corey said he knew who my man was and he didn't want any problems. I told him as long as we stuck together there wouldn't be any. Corey said he had to get up in the morning, I told him that would be my excuse to leave. I told Shame I would come, but I had to leave when Corey left. Shame frowned, but he agreed. I had a nice massage and facial back at the hotel. Since it was really warm out there and I didn't know where we were going I put on pants, sandals, and a halter-top. No makeup just gloss and big hoop earrings. Corey gave me a quick up and down, he was on guard but so was I. Shame came to the lobby and greeted us, his bodyguard stayed to the side. He said the rest of the group was gonna meet us at the restaurant. In the limo, Corey asked me if I heard from Malcolm today. I smirked and said no. Shame looked at Corey then he asked me who Malcolm was. I told him he was my boyfriend. He didn't seem bothered or anything by that, and I shot Corey a "See!" look because I kept trying to explain to him that Shameless wasn't trying to push up on me. When we got to the restaurant, we went to the private room in the back, which was huge and full of people. I could see Corey relax when Shame greeted a girl, and we saw the director from their video. Stacy was like a sponge soaking up anything Corey would share with her. I followed Shame and his girl to a booth in the corner. His bodyguard sat on the end, his girl scooted next to him, then Shame, and I sat on the end. Someone came in and Shame waved them over. I looked across the room and Corey's eyes were big. I didn't wanna turn around; I knew it was Ramell I'd just say hi, enjoy the evening and leave when Corey was ready. Then I heard, "hello Amber" I got Goosebumps as soon as I heard the voice. Shame smiled at me real big while his girl looked like she wished she was me, and I wished I was anybody else other than me.

"Hi" is all I could muster to say in that moment.

"Amber scoot over so my man can sit." Shame said scooting in to give me space. I scooted over. "So how have you been?"

"Ok" I said sipping my water.

He gave me that award-winning smile. "Since when are you shy?" He asked

"Since I started feeling setup. Since when you start hanging out with rappers?" I asked

"You know what, we should give them some privacy." Shame said scooting towards his girl who didn't want to leave. "We'll be back."

"They've come to a few games. Lewis and I have become good friends. What does Malcolm think about you being here?"

"He won't like it once he finds out you're here." I knew I should've gotten up, but that would've been doing the right thing, not that it was what I wanted to do.

"He has a problem with me?" He asked innocently.

I blank stared at him. "Come on Dwayne, what would Michelle think?" Corey looked like he was on the edge of his seat.

"Michelle and I are throwing in the towel again, for good this time." He said with his eyes locked on me.

"Why? After four kids you can't make it work even for them?"

He swallowed, "five we had twins."

"Whoa!" I said feeling horrible for them. "Why?"
He told me how once they moved they both tried really hard to put their best foot forward. Then they had the boys, it was ok for a while but eventually it turned back into everything it was when they split the first time and like last time she had him served. He said he doesn't want to put his kids through this especially when she pushed the issue about having them and now this. He showed me pictures of his beautiful clan. His boys Ian and Ethan looked just like him. I guess Michelle felt like she hit the jackpot getting twins in her last go around. Then I shared how my last conversation with him destroyed my life, and almost ended his. He didn't look phased by the thought. "Honestly, I feel like I've just been existing anyways." He said staring at me.
I looked at Corey whose eyes were still glued to me. I scooted the long way out of the booth. "Dwayne I can't do this."
He gave me sad eyes, "do what?"
"I haven't recovered from our last conversation. Somehow, some way Malcolm's gonna find out about this, I don't want to have to explain or go through this." I looked at Corey, "you ready?" He nodded at me. I mouthed I was gonna run to the bathroom and then I'd be ready. Corey nodded again.
In the bathroom, there were some groupies having their loud conversation not paying attention to who was in the bathroom.
"Girl! Dwayne Reed! Did you see him?" Tramp one said
"Yea, but he came looking for somebody, otherwise he wouldn't be here." Tramp two said
"How you know?" Tramp one said
"He run with Shame sometimes. He spends most of the time whining about his ending marriage. The only time he hooks up with a female is if she reminds him of this chick he dated back in the day." Tramp two said
"Did she look like me?" Tramp one said
They laughed. "Heck if I know! I'm assuming she's light skinned though cause they always caramel colored." Tramp two said
"So why he here tonight?" Tramp one asked
"Well you saw where he was. That girl is the cookie cutter type. They all be like that. He'll probably leave here with her; don't spin your wheels on him. There are so many other choices here tonight." Tramp two said
"Who's the girl with Shame tonight?" Tramp one asked
"Ask me if I care! We all know whose name he's gonna be calling tonight! And who's going on a shopping spree in the morning!"
I heard clapping and laughter, they continued their conversation as they left the bathroom. I washed my hands telling myself not to cry or get emotionally caught up. I couldn't even think about how good it felt to see Dwayne after all of these years and to see him look at me with that same love in his eyes was amazing. No! No! I couldn't think about him, cause no matter how good he was I still wanted Malcolm. No, I'm going back to my hotel and staying there until its time to go to the airport. I took a deep breath and I walked out of the bathroom. Dwayne was standing there, he looked desperate. He grabbed me by the hand and pulled me down the hallway through the kitchen and to this area just off the kitchen. When I started to ask him what was going on, he kissed me. Oh my bleeding heart it was a good kiss too. My arms wrapped around his neck like they used to and I leaned in to the kiss. All of the wonderful memories of how much this man loved me and how he wanted to marry me, if I even gave him the look like I wanted to marry him, I bet

he'd be all over it. But for now it didn't matter, my heart still belonged to Malcolm. I pushed away from him and both our eyes filled with tears. I walked back through the kitchen, down the hallway by the bathroom and back into the private room. Dwayne silently walked behind me; I walked in the room and held the door open for him. Then I found Corey's eyes, he excused himself and walked out with me. The host called a cab for us. I knew I looked sad when Corey put his arm around me and told me to cheer up. Dwayne came over still glassy eyed but no tears dropping. He put a paper in my hand and told me if anything ever changed to contact him. Then he walked out and got in a rental car. Corey asked me if I was ok, and I inhaled deeply and exhaled. I couldn't wait to get to my room and cry my eyes out again. I shook my leg the whole car ride like that was the only thing holding in my tears. In the lobby, I hugged Corey and thanked him for going with me. Corey asked me if I wanted to get something to eat at the restaurant, but I told him I wanted to go lay down. When really I just wanted to wallow in my even bigger depression now. I barely made it in the door before I started balling. I went in the bathroom and blew my nose. As I washed my hands I looked in the mirror, that fast my eyes and nose were red. When I walked out the bathroom I reached for my suitcase that's when the big white box on the dresser caught my attention, it wasn't there before I left. I immediately stopped crying and my alarm went up. I had the feeling someone was in my room. Dwayne did leave before us, what if he somehow got in my room? But if he came in here it was all bad because he already knows it can't happen, so was he here to hurt me? I moved forward enough to look in the mirror to see the reflection of whoever was in the room. I saw blackness with piercing eyes. Even though I knew that was Malcolm my first reaction was to scream. "What are you doing here?" I said walking around the corner.

His face was very serious. "Why are you crying?"

"What do you mean? You know why."

"Do I?" He said reading my face. I rolled my eyes at him. "Why are you crying? Act like I don't know, explain it to me." He sat back in his chair.

"No!"

"No?"

"Right. No! I'm tired of explaining stuff to you. I'm tired of going round and round with you. You should know me by now. You know why I'm crying."

He stood up and walked into my face. He inhaled deeply. "You smell like a few different colognes so you hugged a few guys tonight. Let me see if I can tell you how your evening went." He straightened up and walked over to the box on the dresser. "Lewis is out here, a long with quite a few others that he runs tight with. He invited you out to dinner with them. I saw that you took Corey with you. Very wise choice. Judging by how early you came home, the pretty boy showed up right away. He told you how he's getting a divorce, and wishes there was some way you could get back together. Seeing that your back so soon you left like my good girl would, but why are you upset about it?" He looked at me in my eyes. "Could it be because you were torn about what you wanted to do and you did the right thing by default?" Then he bent down in my face. "Doing right by me upsets you that much?" He peck kissed my lips. "So I've spent the last few days thinking about our last conversation. I'm gonna tell you, spending my night perplexed is not the way I saw that evening ending. I saw us laughing, joking around, me finally getting some. You know the way it should've went but instead you're mad at me, and I can't sleep. It bothers me that you still love him. You know how I'd like to handle it; I'm trying this new thing where I try and act like an adult and not a savage but don't test me!" He looked me in my eyes. "So here's your chance. Choose where you wanna be, who do you want to be with me or him?"

I frowned, "what?"

"You can go be with the pretty boy. I promise to only pistol-whip him. He'll live and you guys can live happily ever after or you can choose me?" He stood up straight and crossed his arms.

I looked at him and smiled, "why do you let him bother you?" I asked

He exhaled, tackled me on the bed kissing me all over. "You are gonna be the death of me I can feel it!"

"What's in the box?" I asked through a smile

"Go see" he said moving so I could see inside.

I opened the box it was a dozen long stem roses. I smiled, "just like the ones you used to give me after my performances." I smiled even bigger. "Thank you they're beautiful!"

"Why were you crying?"

"You don't want to marry me. How do you think that makes me feel? Then to make matters worse, seeing someone who desperately wants to, but they aren't you is depressing. I could runaway and marry him."

"And die the very next day!" There was no joke to his tone.

I rolled my eyes, "I wouldn't be satisfied because he still wouldn't be you. I'm frustrated for now but like I told you the other day, I'm not gonna play this game indefinitely with you."

"I'm not asking you to. Now you know you're slipping right!" I looked confused. "It took you too long to see that box on the dresser. If I were here to hurt you, you'd be hurt. I gotta put somebody back on you, you were wide open."

"I'm not one of your soldiers."

"I can see that."

I kicked my sandals off, took my hair down. He stood in front of me and put his hands in my hair. "No one will ever love you like I do, no matter what they offer you. There isn't anything I wouldn't do for you." Then he kissed me.

Anything but marry me, I said to myself. I was happy he was there, and I was happy he didn't propose because it wouldn't seem genuine. I want him to want to marry me. Not like he feels forced into it. I wish Momma were here, she'd tell me what to do.

Malcolm and I went down to the restaurant. Corey's eyes got big when he saw Malcolm. We joined him at his table. "Corey you've been married for a long time. Our oldest is getting married really soon. I don't doubt that they're in love, I just don't know if love is enough sometimes." Malcolm said

Corey peeked at me while Malcolm was talking then he smiled. "Here's the thing. Your son loves this girl right? Either way he's gonna have her in his life, so that means they're gonna be going through the motions. Why wouldn't he marry her? If he loves her above anyone or anything else, why wouldn't he?"

"Marriage is just paper though." Malcolm said

"Yes, it's documented on paper but the commitment is better than anything you'll ever know. I know marriage isn't for everybody, but if you've promised forever to someone why not see it through, what could be so scary?"

"Failing!" Malcolm said

"Your son has put himself out there for so many business endeavors all with the possibility to fail, but failure didn't stop him from doing it. I know that's business, but when it comes to his heart, why would he wait until then to half step? Your son is wise, and a good guy. I applaud his bravery, putting yourself out there is never easy, but when you're in love, your heart should move you to say I DON'T CARE! And you do it anyways. Do you agree Amber?"

I swallowed. "Speaking as a woman who wants to be married because I know there are some women who don't, for me, it signifies everything that he's said. If he says he loves me, if he says he wants to be with me forever, if he's offering me all of that but we don't marry it's like he's lying. What's wrong with me that he wouldn't see it all the way through?"

"Maybe it's not you, maybe it's him."

"Could be, but if he can't take us there, that one minor step in the whole scheme of the relationship, I can't stay with him and I wouldn't try to influence anyone to stay with someone who doesn't value them enough to go there. That would be too painful for anyone to endure."

Malcolm didn't say anything he kept running his finger up and down his butter knife while he was taking it in. "What did you say when your son said he wanted to get married?" Corey asked

Malcolm smiled. "I think his wife is sweet, she reminds me a lot of his mother. I see why he wants to marry her, but my initial reaction was not positive. I've been watching them, I'm just nervous for him."

"Why?" I said

"Loving a woman can take you off your game. She's his weakness." He said

"She would be his weakness regardless, so what's your point?" I said trying not to spit venom.

He leaned back in his chair. "I guess I don't have one." His mind was wandering after that.

Corey smiled at me as he changed the subject. Malcolm was thoughtful the rest of the evening.

When we got back to the room I wasn't in the mood for anything more than sleeping. I guess the feeling was mutual because he didn't even try. He didn't sleep well until I put my arms around him in the middle of the night. His breathing smoothed out and he fell asleep hard after that. He was still weird in the morning or I should say thoughtful, but I didn't mind. He needed to make some hard decisions. I zipped the paper Dwayne gave me with his email address in the inside of my purse. We checked our bags in at the airport, and then we slowly wandered around. Malcolm was constantly thinking. We sat down in a restaurant and Malcolm kept staring at me. "So what do you want to do?" He asked

"You're joking right?" I said trying not to sound irritated.

He watched my face, and then he blew air. "You'd really leave me?"

I exhaled; I couldn't back down even if backing down was the nice thing to do. "If we just exist like this forever, I will not be satisfied. I'll resent you more than I ever have and we've already seen how I act in that space." I smiled, "this is what I need and if you can't happily and adamantly be as excited as I would be in that space we wouldn't get a long either. I need marriage but I need it with someone who needs it too. I hope you don't think I'm twisting your arm, or I'm trying to force you into a round hole. If it's not you, then it's not you but we gotta stop beating around the bush."

He exhaled in disbelief. "I can't believe you'd leave me! And over a piece of paper." He shook his head.

"It's not just a piece of paper to me." I exhaled getting frustrated. "Tell me something, if that pregnancy wouldn't have been a tubal and everything was everything, would we really be married right now? Or you if you never went to jail and you were talking about marriage like it was nothing. Would you have done it then?"

"Yes, but that was different."

"How?"

His eyes turned evil. "It just was."

"Why cause there was new life on the line? What am I too old for you?"

He blew air, I mocked him and blew air too. "Back then you weren't so rigid. I had more leeway to mess up and bounce back. Now there's no room for error and you want it on paper. It just feels like pressure." He said rubbing his neck.

"Are you planning to mess up?" I asked him

"No"

"Are you plotting on me?"

"Just your booty." He said with a smile

"Just promise to do your best! Anything less and I'll kill you regardless anyways." He belly laughed. "You're threatening me now?" He said still laughing

"It's not a threat Malcolm, it's a promise! You've got some decisions to make, but take too long and you know what happens. I'm a hot commodity, you better get it while it's hot!"

****

My suite was beautiful! The hotel itself was fabulous, but my suite!!!! It was a one bedroom with a huge living room, mini fridge, and pull out couch. Everything in my room was top of the line quality, and my big huge and wonderful bed had satin sheets! Yes! I was in heaven. Carina had my mother of the groom dress hanging in my room. Then there was a knock at the door. I was very happy to see Tanisha. I hugged her and invited her in. "Where's Carina?" I asked

"She's making sure everything is running smoothly." She exhaled, "how's everything in here? Everything to your taste?" She asked

"Yes! I even got satin sheets!" I smiled. Tanisha half smiled then she sat down. "Everything ok sweetheart?"

"Can I have a private moment with you? My mom is so lost, I can't really talk to her much these days."

"Of course. She's coming tomorrow isn't she?" I asked

"Yes, she should be here in a little bit." Then she exhaled, "can you believe he's actually getting married?" She looked at me, I smiled. Then I sat down next to her on the couch. "I guess I figured he'd always be like Malcolm. I don't know why it's affecting me one way or another. I'm happy where I am, and I really like Tracy."

"Oh me too! Have you spent time with her?" I asked

"No, at first I wasn't concerned but then it felt weird you know?" I nodded. Then she started crying. "I'm happy for him, I really am. I hate that I even feel like this. I can't even explain what this feels like."

I rubbed her back, "I understand."

"I've loved him since we were kids. I never thought he'd grow up. Besides, what other man was ever gonna love me?" She said slumping down into the couch.

"I know you don't believe that." I said

She shook her head, "it doesn't matter." Then she looked at me, "should I tell him?" Oh my goodness! These kids are gonna drive me to drinking! I tried to keep my tone as unbiased as I could. "Tell me something, when you say that to him, what are you hoping for?"

"I don't understand?" She said sitting up.

"Why would you tell him unless you're looking for a reaction? What reaction are you looking for?" I asked

"No! I'm not looking to change anything. I just thought he should know." She looked at me, "not a good idea?"

I shook my head, "no sweetheart, he knows you love him, and trust me, he loves you too, but he's happy with Tracy. Telling him right now will only confuse him and we all know how well he handles confusion. Besides it wouldn't be fair to say that now."

"Does she know about us?" Tanisha asked opening and closing her hands. I shrugged because I really didn't know. "Did he tell you?" I shook my head no. She rolled her eyes. "That woman can't keep her mouth shut to save her life." Tanisha said through clinched teeth.

"Don't be mad at her. I would've figured it out anyways. You guys aren't that slick you know. There were clues." I smiled at her.

She exhaled, "Tracy's here so you can go to her room and get ready or whatever. Just don't be late to the rehearsal or Carina will have a cow."

"Right, five o'clock. When am I ever late?" I smiled at her.

We hugged and then Tanisha left. I hoped she didn't do anything stupid and she listened to me, but who am I? I took my dress out for tonight. It was beautiful but nicely understated. I was sure Tracy would look great tonight, but just in case I didn't want to be accused of doing too much.

Then there was another knock at the door. It was Sophia, "where's Sabrina?"

"In Tracy's room getting ready. Sasha's with the boys." Sophia said looking stressed.

"Not you too!" I said sitting on the couch.

"Me too what?" She said standing in the middle of the floor.

"Nothing. Nothing. What's wrong?" I said sitting on the couch.

"I slept with Travis!"

"YOU DID WHAT???" I shouted standing up.

"It was an accident!" She said

"How do you accidentally open your legs to somebody?" I said smugly

"The same way you accidentally let someone eat you out!" She shot back.

I threw my body backwards. She wounded me with that one. "I HATE THAT YOU KNOW ME! Go on with your stupid story." We both laughed.

"I was in a mood thinking about Richard yesterday. Travis brought Sabrina home from her practice. He asked me what was wrong. I told him, about Richard. Then I don't know what happened, one minute I'm telling him how in love with Richard I am and then the next thing I know we're going at it." She said pacing and waving her hands the entire time.

"Was it good?" I asked

Sophia closed her eyes and shook her head yes like it pained her to admit it. "YES! It was like he put everything he had into it."

"That good?" I smiled

"So good I was almost like Richard who?"

"Whoa! That's never happened." I said

"No! I feel very conflicted. Richard is almost here and I got the nerve to still be in the middle of an orgasm with Travis."

"Who do you love?" I asked

"I've always been in love with Richard you know that but Travis has always been good to me. He's never left me except for when I made him."

"Do you love Travis? He's gonna marry that woman, you better speak now or forever hold your peace." I said

"I do, I love him. But..." She threw herself on the couch next to me.

"But what? You're making this more complicated than it has to be. Richard had his chance, he left. Travis put his everything into a last attempt to get your attention. It's just my opinion, but I think Travis deserves a fair chance."

She was spacing out, shaking her head. "What he did last night!" She started shivering and not the exaggerated kind. "It's was like.... And then it was like... I had to remember my baby was sleeping in the other room otherwise, I wouldn't have a voice right now!"

I sat there listening and smiling. "Go call him!"

That pulled her out of her trance. "I can't! I need to see how I feel when I see Richard tonight."

"I guess that's fair, but don't sleep with him!"

"WHAT????" She looked like I was evil for saying it.

"Yes! It helps you keep the clarity to ask for what you need." I said

"Un huh, how's that working out for you?" She said sarcastically

"Ok, so I'm not gonna lie. I'm frustrated! BUT! I told you what I told Malcolm in Atlanta."

"Right, but how is that working out for you?"

"Every time I do like this..." I raised my right arm and looked at my wrist as if there was a watch on it. "He knows exactly what I'm saying. I figure I'll leave it alone until the wedding is over but he's got thirty days from tomorrow before all hell breaks loose. I'm not playing with him, and he knows it. I'm just not telling him when but he keeps trying to put everything into his kisses. Talk about knees buckling, eyes rolling, everything! If we continue I hope the kisses stay like this." Sophia was shaking her leg smiling while she stared at the floor. "Eeewwllll! Are you having flashbacks while I'm sitting up here pouring out my heart?"

Sophia turned red. "I'm sorry but if you had a night like I did..."

I rolled my eyes. "Whatever, I gotta get dressed and do my hair. You can go now!" I said shooing her away. As she walked out, Andrew walked in. I smiled, but my insides screamed! "Hey baby, how's it going?" I said giving him a hug.

He was all smiles. "I'm good! Just making sure everything is good in your room."

"It's perfect! I even have satin sheets!" I said clapping my hands and jumping up and down.

He laughed, "you know I got you. I won't stay long, but I wanted to talk to you." He took me to the couch, and then he held my hands and looked me in my eyes.

"Momma, who loves you more than me?"

"Derrick and Darryl!" I said in a of course voice

He started cracking up. "Always with the jokes! I've known you longer, so I out rank them." He said then he kissed my cheek. "I just wanted to say thank you for everything. Even though I know it was less than ideal when you found out about me, I can say I am so happy to be here. You had options, thank you for choosing me and knowing that my life was worth saving. We grew up together and now that I have Andre I get it a lot more. I owe everything I am to you; because of you I get to marry an amazing woman. Momma thank you! I love you so much!"

We cried, we hugged, "I'm so happy for you baby. She's lovely!"

"Thank you! Thank you!" He said standing up. "I can't believe this day is finally here. Tomorrow I'm gonna be not only a father but also a husband. I get to make love with the thought of forever in mind."

I grimaced, "haven't you done that already?"

"It'll be official! I'll be a baby making machine!" We both laughed. We hugged and then he left.

I got in the shower, I put on simple makeup, and I let my curls fly free. I looked at myself in the mirror. My purple dress was a one-shoulder knee length dress. The shoulder on the dress was a gold chain, and the dress swished in the same direction of the strap. It was a wonderfully confusing dress, which loved my body. I went down to Tracy's room; everyone was busy, and looking good. Tracy was in her bedroom talking with her mother. When she came out she was beautiful! Her cream and gold complimented her glowing complexion. We hugged and I told her how beautiful she looked. When we went down to the ceremony site, everyone was happy that we finally arrived. Malcolm's eyes stayed glued to me, he was smiling. Andrew and Tracy were all over each other, it was cute but sickening. I could see her dad wasn't as appreciative about their open displays of affection. Carina gave us the marching orders. I looked at Tanisha who was sitting on the sideline watching everything. I could see guys from Mitigated all around. Something was up because Darryl wasn't being his normal silly self. Both he and Derrick were looking around and completely focused. Malcolm hugged me tight and told me how beautiful I looked in my ear. I kissed his cheek. Malcolm was full of charm, completely gentle all warm and cuddly. Rehearsals went great! I was ready to eat, Malcolm made sure I sat next to him on the limo bus. I could see Tracy's mom watching us out of the corner of my eye. She had that same look Tracy gets when she watches Malcolm and I. Malcolm kept smiling at me with eyes full of love. Malcolm kept telling everyone how thankful he was to be there, and even more thankful that he was sitting next to me. It was like it was the Malcolm show and everyone was tuning in, sitting on the edge of their seat. "I can't believe our son is getting married tomorrow, " he said reaching for my hand. Then he looked me in my eyes. "You raised a man!" Everyone got choked up, but I lost it. I went into the ugly face cry and everything. Then I laid my head on his shoulder and said, "Thank You!" He's been telling me since Andy was a baby that I was gonna make him soft, I felt so vindicated. When we got to the restaurant everyone was so excited. Sophia's staff took excellent care of us. The food was delicious and I pointed everyone in Tracy and Andrew's direction, to say hello to the happy couple. I met a lot of Tracy's family, they were nice people. I asked the staff to make sure that the guys outside had full meals. When it got late we loaded back on the bus. Malcolm had been staying by my side pretty much all evening. When we got on the bus, he sat next to me. He stared at me. "You really want all of this? It's a bunch of fuss!" He said squinting his eyes.

"Yea but it's beautiful fuss!" I said

When we got back to the hotel, Malcolm asked if he could see my room. I agreed but I told him to not even think of anything. "Oh I see how it is. I got a standard room, but you're up here in a suite living FAT!"

"You know how much Andy loves his Momma." I said taking off my shoes. Malcolm watched me take off my shoes. "Yes he does." He inhaled, then he exhaled. "You know tomorrow is gonna be so crazy, we probably won't get a chance to talk much."

"That's pretty much the idea, it's their day." I said walking into the room taking off my earrings, necklace, and ring that my babies bought for me and put them on the dresser. I put my shoes next to the dresser.

Malcolm stood in the doorway with his hands in his pockets. "You gonna be ok with everything?" I looked at him with a question mark. "You know the wedding, plotting our breakup." He smiled. I shook my finger at him as I made my way towards the mini fridge to grab a soda. He grabbed my arm, "slow down for a minute." I blew air and stood there not wanting to think about the picture he was painting. I didn't want to think about breaking up or anything that would make me sad. I wanted him to leave so I could sleep. "I know you're tired. But I can..." He scratched his head. "Dance with me? One song and then I'll leave."
I exhaled, "right now Malcolm, really?" Sadness was coming over me full force. "One song," he put his hands up to plead. "Please!"
"Fine!" I said in defeat.
He went over to the stereo alarm clock. He selected a song, on his iPod. Then he hit play. The music started and I smiled. "There'll be no darkness tonight..." Malcolm sang along with Michael as he swept me up into his arms and danced with me. I melted in his arms as I cried while he sang the song to me. When the song was over the next song came on. "Guess what I did today, those were the words I said to you..." Case sang to us. "Amber, I have been in love with you since I was in the eighth grade. I don't wanna live without you. I couldn't handle life without you in it. I bet you thought I wasn't gonna ask." He reached into his pocket and pulled out a ring box. "I had to wait for it to get here." I reached for the box. "Un un! You can't see it until you give me an answer."
"You haven't asked me anything yet." I said with a smile, and tears falling down my face.
"Amber will you marry me?" He asked breathing heavily.
"YES!" I screamed! I threw my arms around his neck.
We kissed, "you wanna see?" I shook my head yes. "The boys and Andre helped me pick it out." I opened the box slowly and the biggest and most beautiful ring I've ever seen in my life smiled at me. I started crying hysterically when I saw it. "You better cry! You are not easy to shop for!" He said with a smile. "Andre picked this one while we were arguing about other rings. We all agreed that this was the one."
"When was this?" I asked
"After we came back from Atlanta." He said
"I can't believe you got Andre to keep a secret. That boy is always running his mouth." I kissed him again.
"Tomorrow is Drew's day, you can shout it from the rooftop Sunday if you want to."
I kissed him. "Believe me I will!"
"Okay well, I'll see you tomorrow at four."
I looked at him in disbelief, "you're leaving?"
"YES! I need to look sexy and refreshed for my son's big day tomorrow. If I stay here with you I will be tired and drained." Then he kissed me again long and deep. "We got the rest of our lives, I can wait."
Then he put the ring on my finger; of course it was already sized perfectly. He kissed me again then he walked to the door. "What about your iPod?" I said
"I'll get it tomorrow." Then he left.
I called Sophia's room. I started screaming into the phone. I know she was probably busy talking to Richard but I didn't care. She said I was speaking gibberish and she'd be right up. She had on her robe. I stuck my hand out the door. "WHOA!" She screamed. Then she came in the room and we both started speaking gibberish together.

In the morning, Jade and Emerald came to my room, Jade had the same reaction Sophia had. Emerald told me she loved my ring. Then we all had breakfast and massages in Tracy's room. They sent estheticians up to do our facials, manicures, and pedicures.

The rest of the day seemed to drag but move at fast pace if that makes any sense. I kept looking at my hand to make sure it was real and I didn't dream it up. Professionals from the Mack store came to do our makeup. The photographer captured wonderful shots of us all day and as we got ready. Then we got dressed in the room, everyone got a little misty when we saw Tracy in her dress. Tracy's father came to get us. He got teary eyed when he saw her too. We walked through the lobby in the order of our procession. Carina had Tracy and her father stand in a room over to the side. Malcolm met me by the doors as I walked out. I had the biggest smile because he looked so handsome. Andy winked at me as we walked down the aisle. When Tracy and her father stepped into the doorway a lot of people cried. A few people laughed at Andy's reaction to seeing his beautiful bride. His reaction was priceless. The ceremony was short but sweet. I didn't know what to expect since I know Tracy's people are very religious. I was hoping it wasn't overly dramatic and drawn out. To my delight it was tasteful and to the point, I was very relieved. After the ceremony, the guests were asked to go to the appetizer room while we took pictures. Malcolm kept telling me how beautiful I looked. Malachi caught a glimpse of the ring from a far. He told Malcolm it was about time and they hugged real loud pounding each other's backs. It was then that I realized they were both emotional trying to push the other over the edge first. We took lots of pictures, then the guests were shown to their assigned seating, and then the wedding party was announced. It sounded like thunder when the applause erupted when the newlyweds entered. Malcolm held my hand as we watched them dance their first dance. Jade kept watching us and smiling. I blew her a kiss, and then I looked at Malcolm. FINALLY! Finally that little thirteen-year-old girl was getting what she deserved. I smiled at Malcolm. "I love you!" He said

"I love you!" I said

MORE FROM THE AUTHOR

Thank you for allowing me to entertain you. I hope you have enjoyed reading my current release. If you have not read Volumes I – VIII of the Wallace Family Affairs series, please do so. Click here for a list of all the background stories. Once you have read the background stories, please checkout the current date series Together We Are Strong. Stay tune for more to come shortly.

Wallace Family Affairs

At Last (Click here)
Tracy's Complications (Click here)
Distorted Mirrors (Click here)
Sometimes Love Isn't Enough (Click here)
Love Is Just Enough
Just A Friend (Click here)
Invisible (Click here)
Look Beyond Your Eyes (Click here)
No Regrets (Click here)
First You Laugh Then You Cry (Click here)
A Heart That's Taken (Click here)
Abandoned (Click here)
Last Words (Click here)

Together We Are Strong

Season 1 Present (Click here)
Beyond The Wallace's ~ I Knew You When (**TBD**)
Season 2 What Comes Next (Release **TBD**)

Standalones

Secrets & Lies ~ (**TBD late 2016 release**)
Anthology **Short** Story (Where Love May Find You Collection) ~ (Click here)
Waiting (**TBD**)

Hopefully you've enjoyed all of the background stories for our lovely Wallace's and Latour's. Please tune in for more from the "Together We Are Strong" Wallace & Latour Family Episodes on Amazon